THE ROSE OF
OLD ST. LOUIS

" 'Very well, I shall expect to hear from you' "

THE ROSE OF OLD ST. LOUIS

BY

MARY DILLON

WITH ILLUSTRATIONS BY
ANDRÉ CASTAIGNE AND C. M. RELYEA

NEW YORK
THE CENTURY CO.
1904

THE DE VINNE PRESS

CONTENTS

vii

LIST OF ILLUSTRATIONS

FOREWORD

My story does not claim to be history, but in every important historical detail it is absolutely faithful to the records of the times as I have found them. Every word of the debate in Congress, every word of Marbois, Livingston, Decrés, Napoleon, and his two brothers on the subject of the Louisiana Cession is verbatim from the most authentic accounts. I am indebted for the historical part of my story to Gayarré's "History of Louisiana," to Martin's "History of Louisiana," to James K. Hosmer's "History of the Louisiana Purchase," to Lucien Bonaparte's "Memoirs," to numerous lives of Napoleon, Jefferson, Talleyrand, and others, and particularly to Marbois himself, whose account of the negotiations on the subject of the cession is preserved in his own handwriting in the St. Louis Mercantile Library.

As to the local color of old St. Louis, both in its topographical setting and in its customs, I have also tried to be exact. And here I am very largely indebted to that simple and charming old writer, H. M.

Brackenridge, in his "Recollections of the West" and in his "Views of Louisiana"; and also to Timothy Flint in his "Recollections"; to J. Thomas Scharf's interesting "History of St. Louis," and especially to Mr. Frederic L. Billon, St. Louis's historian *par eminence*. I make also the same claim for exactness as to the local color of Washington at that early day; for which I have made so many gleanings in many fields—a little here, a little there—that it seems hardly worth while to give special credit to each.

In non-essential points I have occasionally taken the liberty belonging to a writer of fiction, having condensed into one several debates in Congress, as well as several interviews between Talleyrand and Livingston, and two interviews between Bonaparte and Marbois.

Nor have I hesitated to use the names of the early St. Louis settlers, because they are names still well known and honored in the city which they helped to found. I have touched upon them but lightly, and have tried to make those touches true to the characters of those estimable gentlemen and gentlewomen of the old French régime.

MARY DILLON.

THE ROSE OF OLD ST. LOUIS

THE
ROSE OF OLD ST. LOUIS

CHAPTER I

I MAKE MY BOW IN CAHOKIA

"The best-laid schemes o' mice an' men
Gang aft a-gley."

"AND this is the village of St. Louis, sir?"
I bowed respectfully to my captain standing in
the prow of the boat and looking across an expanse of
swirling muddy water to the village on the bluffs beyond. I spoke more after the manner of making
polite conversation than because I was desirous of information, for I knew without asking that it could be
none other.

My captain answered me: "Yes, my lad, yonder is
St. Louis, and this is De Soto's river; what dost think
of it?"

"I think, sir, 't is a great river, though not so clear
a stream as the Delaware, and muddier even than the
Ohio."

I spoke calmly, but my heart was beating fast, and
I could feel the blood rushing through my veins. I
had been ill with what the boatmen call river fever,

and had lain in the bottom of the boat wrapped in my blanket, alternately shivering with chills and burning with fever, oblivious to all about me, so that I had not known when we swept out of the Ohio into the Mississippi, past Fort Massac, nor when we had tied up at Kaskaskia for a long rest.

We had landed late the evening before at Cahokia, and been most hospitably entertained by Mr. Gratiot. There had been a great banquet in honor of Captain Clarke, with dancing far into the night, and many guests from St. Louis. I, being still an invalid, had been put to bed in Mr. Gratiot's beautiful guest-chamber, and given a hot posset that put me to sleep at once, though not so soundly but that I could dream-ily catch occasional strains of the fiddles and the rhythmic sound of feet on the waxed walnut, and many voices and much laughter.

Had I been well, it would have vexed me sore not to have been able to lead in the minuet one of the beauties of Cahokia, whose fame had reached even my distant home in Philadelphia, for I had been carefully trained in the steps and the figures, and was young enough to be proud of my skill in the dance. But feeling ill as I did, the sounds of revelry combined with the posset only to soothe me into a heavy slumber.

I woke in the early dawn to find Yorke, Captain Clarke's big black, standing beside my bed, with a bowl of smoking gruel. He showed a formidable array of white ivory as he grinned amiably in response to my questioning look:

"Mars' Gratiot send you de gruel wid his compli-
men's, sah, and he and de capen bofe say you 's not to
git up dis mohnen, sah."

Yorke always considered that to state a request of
"de capen" was sufficient to insure compliance. He
could not dream of any one setting his authority at
naught. With me, too, Captain Clarke's authority
was paramount. It had only been by a promise of absolute submission to that authority that I had persuaded my kinsman in Kentucky to allow me to accompany the captain on his mission to the governor
of Illinois at St. Louis.

So, when Yorke said the captain had ordered me to
remain in bed, I thought for a moment I would have
to obey; but having swallowed the hot gruel, into
which Yorke had put a modicum of good Orleans
ratafia, I was straightway infused with new spirit (I
meant not that for wit), and such strength flowed
through my limbs as I had not felt for days.

"Yorke," I said, springing out of bed with a haste
that made me light-headed for a moment, "help me
into my clothes, and be quick about it; I think I hear
sounds below that betoken getting ready for departure."

Even as I spoke I ran to a stand on which stood a
basin and a small ewer of water. I filled the basin,
and plunged my head into the icy water. I drew it
out, sputtering and shivering, and, seizing a towel,
gave my head and neck and hair so vigorous a rubbing that I did not see Yorke slip out of the room.
When I turned to speak to him I found him gone,

afraid either of being a partner in my disobedience
to the captain, or of being left behind if he delayed
longer.

Left to myself, I did my best to hurry with my
clothing. I had not much experience in dressing myself, but I had been compelled to leave behind me in
Philadelphia the black boy who had never before,
since I could remember, been absent from me a day.
I had been eager enough to part with him, thinking it
ill befitted a soldier of fortune, as I intended to be, to
be coddled by a valet, and I had not missed him much,
for Yorke had been always ready to lend a helping
hand when I needed it. Now I was of a mind to curse
the vanity that had led me to fit myself out with doeskins that were of so snug a cut they needed much
tugging to get into them, and with endless lacings
with which my awkward fingers, clumsier than ever
from the icy water and the trembling the fever had
left me in, fumbled desperately.

But I was ready at last, and seizing my sword-belt
in one hand and my hat in the other, I started with
hot haste for the door, fearing I might be, after all,
too late. As I opened it, a sound smote my ears that
struck terror to my heart: the voices and the laughter
of young maidens. I stepped back involuntarily. I
had not thought of the possibility of meeting any one
at that early hour but my host and my captain, and
I had not given a thought to my appearance. Now I
took an anxious survey of myself in the small French
mirror that hung above the stand. I was vexed beyond measure at what I saw.

"They will take me for a girl," I muttered between my teeth, "and flout me accordingly."

It had ever been a source of extreme mortification to me that I should have rosy cheeks like any maiden's, but now, owing to the hard scrubbing I had given them, they were all aflame, and their color was heightened by the pallor my recent illness had given to brow and temples. My hair, from its wetting, was curling in ringlets all around my head. I seized a brush and tried desperately to reduce them to straightness, but the brushing served only to bring out in stronger relief the glint of gold that I despised, and certainly my eyes had never looked more blue and shining.

"They will think me a girl or a baby!" I muttered once more, and was in such disgust with myself I was ready to go back to bed. But bethinking me that would only leave me the longer in this House of Dames, I seized my belt once more, buckled it on with a vicious twitch, and strode boldly to the door.

There I stopped a moment to collect all my courage, soothing myself with the reflection that I stood a good six feet in my moccasins, and though I carried no superfluous flesh, my shoulders were as broad as my captain's and my muscles like whip-cords. Fortified by these considerations, I strode on boldly to the landing at the head of the wide staircase leading down to the great hall.

There I stopped again; for while the landing was in gloom, the hall was brilliantly illuminated by a roaring, blazing lightwood fire, looking cheery enough in the gray light of the frosty morning, and throw-

ing into strong relief two groups on either side of
the fireplace. On one side stood my captain, evidently ready for a start, and making his adieus to his
host. I glanced eagerly at Mr. Gratiot and at the el-
derly man who stood beside him, who, I thought, was
likely to be none other than Mr. Francis Vigo. I had
heard much of these two men from General George
Rogers Clarke, whose lonely retreat on the Ohio I had
often visited during my stay in Kentucky. They had
been General Clarke's best friends and helpers in the
early days of the war, when he had made that daring
attack on Vincennes, and I knew Captain Clarke's
mission to St. Louis had something to do with dis-
charging his brother's obligation to them. They were
smaller men than my captain, of a slender, graceful
build, and the hair of both was quite white, but from
my post of observation I could see that they were men
of courtly manners, well used tó the ways of the world,
and talking now quite eagerly with all the wealth of
gesture and expression natural to Frenchmen.

The firelight played strongly on the face of my captain, whom I had already begun to adore, as did every
one who came into close companionship with him. I
gazed admiringly at his broad, white brow, clear-cut
features, and firmly knit figure, a little square of
build, but looking every inch the frontier soldier in
his leathern doublet and leggings and high-laced moccasins. Over one shoulder he had thrown his blue
military cloak, for the trip across the river promised
to be a cold one, and he carried in his hand a hat with
a drooping plume. I wondered if the merry group of

girls on the other side of the fireplace was not impressed by such a handsome and soldierly stranger, and a bachelor to boot. I thought I could detect an occasional conscious glance in his direction and a furtive preening of skirts and fluttering of fans, that betokened they were not insensible to the presence of the brave captain.

There were six of the young maidens, and all but two of them were in ball costume; flowered silks, and arms and shoulders gleaming white through fine lace, powdered hair, and patches and paint, they might have stepped out of a Philadelphia ball-room, I thought, and was astonished at the thought. I had not expected to find court beauties on the frontier, yet the Chouteaus, the Gratiots, and the Papins were names I had often heard in my own home as men of wealth and vast emprise.

The six girls were chatting gaily in French, and I was so absorbed in my contemplation of them that I did not at first consider the strangeness of their appearance in that costume so early in the morning. When it did occur to me, I concluded the four must have come over from St. Louis to attend the ball and had no other dress to return in, and the other two were doubtless Mr. Gratiot's daughters, which I learned afterward was the true explanation.

But now bethinking me it was high time to make my descent, and running quickly over in my mind the way to make it most effective,—for I wished to bear myself bravely before the young maidens,—I determined to place my left hand on the hilt of my sword, to hold my hat, which also bore a sweeping plume, in my right hand pressed close to my heart, and with head held high and borne a little backward, to descend with the stately minuet step. I flattered myself that with such a manner as I felt sure I could assume those saucy maidens would forget my rosy cheeks and my curls and think only of my air of *grand seigneur.*

I glanced down to see that my costume was all right, and now I was glad that my doeskins fitted so perfectly, even if they were hard to get into in a hurry, that my high moccasins were so beautifully and elaborately beaded in purple and yellow, with broad slashes of fringe falling from the tops of them, and that my leathern doublet sat so well, as my peep into the mirror had convinced me it did.

As I started down, feeling well satisfied with my costume, yet trembling inwardly at the thought of the array of bright eyes I was to encounter, my glance fell on an untied lacing at one knee. I stooped to retie it, and at that moment heard what seemed to me the sweetest voice I had ever listened to, call:

"À moi, Leon, à moi," followed by a clear, soft whistle.

I was still clumsily fumbling with my lacers (my fingers have ever been all thumbs when there is any dainty task to be performed) when I heard a rush of soft, padded feet, and down the corridor behind me, in response to that clear whistle, bounded a great dog. Through the arch that my bent limbs made in stooping he saw the glow of the firelight from below

and made straight for it. But alas! the arch was nar-
rower than he thought, and dog and man went rolling
and tumbling down the staircase, bumping and bound-
ing from stair to stair, a wild mêlée of doeskin legs
and shaggy paws and clanging sword and wildly
brandished arms, making vain clutches at the air to
stay the headlong descent.

Deep-mouthed yelps voiced the terror of the dog at
this unexpected Sindbad who refused to be shaken off.
No words could voice the overwhelming shame of the
man at this unmannerly presentation of himself before a group of young maidens, when so dignified an
entrance had been planned.

As we struck the polished walnut of the hall floor,
I disentangled myself and sprang to my feet, where I
stood, scarlet with shame, head drooping, a pitiable
object indeed. There had been an amazed, and perhaps on the maidens' side a terrified, silence during
our noisy descent. Now from the maidens there arose
first a suppressed giggle and then an irresistible peal
of laughter, joined to the hearty guffaws of the men.
My shame was fast giving place to rising wrath, in
no degree appeased by the consciousness of the spectacle I presented. The dog, a magnificent mastiff, by
that time recovering from his confusion, and feeling
as keenly as I, no doubt, the derogation of his dignity,
and, with a dog's unreason, regarding me as the agent
of his humiliation when I was in fact the victim of
his own stupidity, sprang at me with a vicious growl.

Here was an occasion to vent my boiling wrath.
Quick as thought my sword sprang from its sheath

and came down flat-sided with a ringing blow on the brute's head. I have ever been a merciful man to all beasts, and dogs and horses I have loved and they have loved me; and even in my wrath and the quick necessity of defense I remembered to use the flat of my sword; yet such is the strength of my sword-arm from much practice, increased, I fear, by a venom instigated by those silvery peals of laughter, that I bowled the brute over as easily as if he had been a ninepin.

With a howl of mingled rage and pain he recovered himself instantly and crouched to spring upon me once more, with such bloodthirst in his eyes that I saw now I would have to defend myself in earnest. But as he was almost in the act of springing, from among the group of maidens there rushed what seemed to my dazzled vision a small whirlwind of satins and laces and velvets and jewels, and flung itself upon the dog with a ringing cry of "À bas, Leon! tais-toi, mon ange!"

The brute yielded obedience at once to the restraining arm and tones of command, though still regarding me with vicious eyes and uttering threatening growls.

As for me, I stood as if turned to stone, still in an attitude of defense, the weight of my body thrown forward on the right foot, the hilt of my sword pressed against my breast, the point presented to receive the onslaught of the brute. In that attitude I stood frozen, for never had I beheld such a vision of loveliness. The arm that encircled the shaggy neck of the dog was bare almost to the shoulder, the sleeve of finest lace having fallen back in the energy of her action, and never have I seen an arm so white, so round, or tapering so finely to the slender wrist and exquisite little hand clutching a lock of Leon's mane. Masses of wavy dark hair were drawn loosely back from a brow of dazzling whiteness into a cluster of soft curls on top of the head, where it seemed to be caught by a jeweled aigret, which yet permitted tiny ringlets to escape about the temples and the nape of the snowy neck. She had thrown herself with such abandon on the dog, and was holding him with such exertion of strength, that the narrow skirt of her satin gown, flowered in palest pink and silver, revealed every line of a most exquisite figure down to the little foot extending backward from her skirts and showing the high arch of the instep in its stocking of embroidered silk.

I had gazed with impunity, for the drooping white lids and the long, dark lashes sweeping the perfect curve of the cheek showed all her looks were for the dog, to whom she incessantly murmured in French mingled words of command and endearment. But suddenly she lifted her little head and flung it proudly back, with such a blaze of indignation and scorn in her dark eyes I felt withered under it. The scarlet curve of her lips fell away to disclose two rows of pearly teeth, close set, and through them, with a vicious snap, came the one word:

"Bête!"

I could not for a moment think that the word was meant for the dog, and such a rage slowly welled in

my veins as restored me at once to my self-command.
I dropped the point of my sword to the floor and
straightened myself to as proud a pose as hers.

"I pray you pardon, Mademoiselle," I said haughtily. The words were meek enough, but not the tone
nor the manner, and so enraged was I that I hesitated
not a moment over my French. My accent, I knew,
was good, for, my aunt having married Monsieur
Barbé Marbois, I was thrown much with French people; but I had been ever careless of my grammar,
and in a moment of less excitement I might have hesitated in venturing on the native tongue of so fair a
creature. But now my French poured from me in an
angry torrent:

"I pray you pardon. Danger alone is my excuse.
I do not doubt a dog is worth much more to Mademoiselle than the life of an American gentleman. I
make you, Mademoiselle, my compliments and my excuses."

Then returning my sword to its scabbard with an
angry ring, I made her a low and sweeping bow of
ironical courtesy and strode hotly from the room. I
was in such a tumult of rage and mortification that
not until I reached the landing on the banks of Cahokia Creek, where the boats were tied and the men
busily making ready for the departure, did I bethink
me that I had left the house without a word of adieus
or thanks to my host for his courtesy. I began to fear
that my sense of self-respect would compel my return,
and rather would I have faced a battalion of the British than another flash from those dark eyes; nor could
I hope to make another so masterly a retreat as I

plumed myself this one had been. But as I glanced back toward the house on the bluffs that had proved my undoing, to my intense relief I saw that the three gentlemen had followed not far behind me and were even now descending the pathway to the creek. I hastened to meet them and make my apologies.

A more courteous gentleman than Mr. Gratiot I never met. He spoke very good English indeed, his accent I believe not so good as my French one, but his grammar much better.

"My dear young gentleman, you acquitted yourself nobly," he was kind enough to say. "In the eyes of the young ladies, if I may possibly except Mademoiselle Pelagie, you are a hero. But they are much chagrined that you should have left them without giving them a chance to express their sympathy or their admiration."

The sound of those silvery peals of laughter was too vividly in my remembrance to permit me to accept Mr. Gratiot's compliments without a large grain of allowance for a Frenchman's courtesy, but I bowed low in seeming to accept them. Then he introduced me to his companion, who proved not to be Mr. Vigo after all, but Dr. Saugrain, the French émigré so renowned for his learning. I looked at him keenly as I made my bow, for I had heard something of him in Philadelphia, and in Kentucky there had been so many tales of the wonderful things he could do that I think most people looked upon him as a dealer in black arts. But he was in no respect my idea of a Mephisto. He was small and wiry of build, and dressed in black small-clothes, with ruffles of finest lace at wrist and knee.

Black silk stockings showed a well-turned calf in no whit shrunken with age, and his silver shoe-buckles glittered with brilliants. His hair, iron-gray and curly, was tied in a short queue with a black satin ribbon, and beneath a rather narrow and high brow beamed two as kindly blue eyes as it had ever been my lot to meet.

His greeting was most cordial, though there was a merry twinkle in his eye while speaking to me that made me feel he might still be laughing inwardly at my ridiculous descent of Mr. Gratiot's staircase. With a very grand manner indeed, and with much use of his hands, as is the fashion of Frenchmen, he said:

"My dear sir, it mek me mos' proud and mos' 'appy to know you. Vous êtes véritablement un brave. Le capitaine dîne chez moi to-day; I s'all be désolé and inconsolable if he bring not also his ver' dear young frien'." Then, with a sudden and entire change of manner, he laid his finger beside his nose and said in a loud whisper:

"My frien', I would not min' you kill that dog, moi! I lofe 'im not."

But while his words did not sound kind to me, who am such a lover of dogs that nothing but the necessity of self-defense would ever make me lift a hand against one, yet, all the time he spoke, his eyes twinkled more merrily than ever, and I wondered at the man whose manner could change so quickly from the grand seigneur's to that of a king's jester, and I puzzled my brains mightily to know what his connection with the dog could be.

CHAPTER II

I PROPOSE A TOAST

"The rose that all are praising."

"AND this is the village of St. Louis, sir?"
My discomfiture, my mortification, my rage, the vision of dainty beauty, the strange little savant— every remembrance of my brief visit to Cahokia had been swept away by the rushing waters of the great river of which I had read and heard so much.

My brain was teeming with tales of the Spanish adventurer De Soto; of the French trader Joliet; of the devoted and saintly Jesuit, beloved of the Indians, Père Marquette; and of the bold Norman La Salle, who hated and feared all Jesuits. I saw the river through a veil of romance that gilded its turbid waters, but it was something far other than its romantic past that set my pulses to beating, and the blood rushing through my veins so that I hardly heard my captain's answer, and hardly knew what I replied to him.

Through the months of my sojourn in Kentucky there had been one all-absorbing theme—the closing of the Mississippi to American boats by the Spanish, and their refusal to grant us a right of deposit on the

2   17

Isle of New Orleans. Feeling had run so high that there were muttered threats against the government at Washington.

There were two factions, each acting secretly and each numbering thousands. One was for setting off at once down the river to capture New Orleans and take exclusive possession of both sides of the river; and if the government at Washington would not help them, or, still worse, forbade them the emprise, they would set up an independent government of the West. The other faction, inspired by secret agents of the Spanish government, was for floating the Spanish flag and proclaiming themselves subjects of Charles of Aragon. Spain's secret emissaries were eloquent of the neglect of the home government in the East, and its powerlessness to help the Westerners if it would, and it was said they clenched their arguments with chink of Spanish gold. Treason and patriotism, a wild indignation at wrongs unredressed, and a wilder enthusiasm for conquest sent the blood of Kentucky to fever-heat. Passions were inflamed until it needed but a spark from a tinder to set them ablaze.

With me, friend and distant kinsman of the Clarkes, there was no possibility of being touched by the taint of treason. But while it would be treason of the blackest dye, and most abhorrent to my soul, to submit to Spain's rule, to my young blood there could be no treason in compelling Spain at the point of the sword to submit to our demands. I was all for war, and when the cooler judgment of General Clarke and his brother, my captain, prevailed to calm for a time the wild tumult of war, I was bitterly disappointed.

Now for the first time I was beholding the river that had aroused the mighty tempest in Kentucky, and it was not the tales of De Soto and La Salle, of Joliet and Père Marquette, that sent the blood rushing through my veins, but the thought that this was the mighty river forbidden to our commerce, that the swirling brown water at my feet was rushing down to the Spanish city on the Gulf, and I longed to be one of an army rushing with it to secure our natural and inalienable rights by conquest.

I knew that Captain Clarke was visiting St. Louis to make some arrangements for his brother's debts— debts incurred principally to Mr. Gratiot and Mr. Vigo for no benefit to himself, but in rescuing and protecting the people of Illinois from the Indians and the British; debts belonging of right to the government, but repudiated by it, and left to be borne by the noble man who, almost alone, by a heroism and genius for war unparalleled had saved all that Western country to the Union.

I knew this was my captain's errand, yet I hoped there might be some touching on the question of the river navigation with the Spanish governor of St. Louis, and I had visions of returning to Kentucky and, amid the acclaims of our fellow-citizens, announcing that Captain Clarke, assisted by his young kinsman, had succeeded in convincing the Spanish governor Delassus of the wrongs inflicted upon American commerce by the unjust interdiction; that Delassus had thereupon remonstrated with the intendant at New Orleans, and, as a result, the river was thrown open to the Gulf, and a port of deposit granted on the Isle of New Orleans where our merchants might store the goods they brought down the river for sale.

It was because my brain was teeming with such sweet dreams of glory that I answered my captain so absent-mindedly and so little to the point. It was still so early that the low morning sun at our backs had just begun to gild the bluffs before us. We could not have had a finer first view of the Spanish town of which we had heard so much. High and dry on its limestone bluffs, where no floods for which the great river is so famous could ever reach it, it extended in a straggling line for a mile and a half. Its dwellings, some of them of imposing size, were embowered in trees, and, at that distance, seemed to stand in the midst of large gardens. Behind the village rose another hill, on the summit of which stood a fort, and from the fort, in either direction, palisades curved around the town, interrupted at intervals by demi-lunes, and terminating at the bluffs in stone towers. Behind this second terrace the land continued to rise in a succession of terraces, covered partly with low bushes and shrubs and partly with high, waving woods, giving an impression of indescribable richness to the landscape, every detail of which the level rays of the bright morning sun brought out in strong relief. The whole made a most impressive appearance, more like the picture of walled towns on the Rhine than like anything I had seen in our country.

We were now so far out in the stream that the men could no longer use their poles, and were trusting to the great sail they had spread to catch a stiff south-eastern breeze, assisted by vigorous strokes of their paddles, and I could see that against the swift current they were straining every nerve and yet were steadily being borne below the village and the landing-place.

Paddling on the Schuylkill and the Delaware was ever a favorite pastime with me, and I doubt not I was a little proud of my skill. Forgetting my recent illness and the weak state it had left me in, I seized the paddle from a young fellow who seemed to me well-nigh giving over, and unceremoniously tumbled him out of his seat into the bottom of the boat, while I took his place. To my astonishment, I found this was an entirely different stream from the steadily flowing rivers of the East. My paddle was like to be snatched from my hand at the first dip into the powerful current, and though I saved it by a mad and desperate clutch, yet it felt like a feather in my hands, and I saw my captain (who had witnessed my peremptory usurpation of the paddle) trying to suppress a sly smile, while my mortified ears caught the sound of derisive snickers behind me, and Yorke, the impudent black, grinned openly from ear to ear.

The worst of it was, I myself could see we were losing ground more rapidly than before. Now, I had ever a horror of owning myself beaten (unless it were in argument, for I have no skill with words). I would fight to the last gasp, but I would never surrender, which is sometimes a foolish way, but more often wins

victory out of defeat. With my captain looking on, I
felt that defeat even in so small a matter would be a
disgrace I could never survive. And so, admonishing
myself to keep cool, and remembering a turn of the
wrist that an old Indian had taught me in Pennsylvania, I very soon caught the trick of the blade and
found myself holding my own. Hope returned, and
I gradually put forth more and more strength, until,
to my great satisfaction, I at last saw that we were no
longer drifting down-stream, but steadily making
head against the current, with fair promise of reaching our landing-place. Then, indeed, did I feel exultant, and such courage leaped through my veins,
and so swift and sure and strong were my strokes, that
I felt I could alone, with my single arm, bring the
great boat to harbor. But for the second time that
morning was my vanity my undoing. We did indeed
make the landing, where a great concourse of people
had gathered to meet us, among them a stately Spanish don (who, I had no doubt, was the governor) surrounded by a retinue of officers; but as the keel of our
boat grounded in the soft mud and my captain called
me to come with him to meet the governor, and I arose
in my place to obey him, suddenly a great blackness
and dizziness seized me, and I knew no more until I
opened my eyes to find myself being borne, on the
shoulders of four men, up the steep bluff toward the
village street. I insisted in the most forcible terms on
being put upon my feet at once, but as I spoke in English, and the soldiers were either Spanish or creole
French, my entreaties and imprecations were lost

upon them. Nor did my kicking and pushing avail me any better; they but held me the more firmly for my struggles. Then I called out lustily for help, and the ever-ready Yorke (but with the grin that I had learned at times to consider detestable) ran to my aid.

"Yorke!" I shouted to him; "make the rascals put me down this minute, and do you, sir, shut that *domtiferous* mouth of yours. I warn you, sir, you grin at your peril!"

My mother had ever a horror of the oaths with which gentlemen lard their conversation, and because I loved and honored her greatly, I had resolved that I would never, to use her words, "sully my mouth" with one. But often feeling the need of some more emphatic expressions than our language provides except in the form of oaths, I had coined for myself a small vocabulary to be used on occasions requiring great emphasis. Since these words all began with a *d*, I had the satisfaction of feeling that I was sufficiently emphatic without violating the respect due my mother.

Whether it was the strangeness of the form of my imprecations or the length of my adjective that scared Yorke, certain it is that he was sobered at once, and with the solemnity of the Spanish don himself he soon made the soldiers understand that they must put me down. Once on my own feet, though I still felt a little shaky, I was able, by availing myself of Yorke's arm, to climb the steep path leading up the bluff, and soon found myself in the main street of the village, which the *habitans* called the Rue Royale.

We had come out into a large square or market-

place, filled with the throng of people I had seen at
the landing and many more, so that, as the people
surged backward and forward to get a nearer view, the
whole open space looked like a great posy-bed of many-
hued flowers waving in a summer breeze. And if
St. Louis had had a foreign look to me when viewed
from a distance, still more did I feel as if I were in a
strange town in a strange land as I heard the babble
of strange tongues about me and saw the picturesque
costumes of the habitans, so unlike anything I had
ever seen in Philadelphia or Kentucky. Negroes were
chattering their queer creole patois, and Indians of
many nations were gathered into groups, some of them
bedizened with the cheap finery of the stores, some of
them wearing only bright-hued blankets, but with
wonderful head-dresses of eagle feathers, and all of
them looking gravely on with a curiosity as silent as
that of the habitans was noisy and babbling. The
presence of so many Indians and on such friendly
terms struck me as strange, for in Kentucky there
were no such friendly relations between Indians and
whites, and the presence of so many of them would
have betokened danger and caused much uneasiness.

It thrilled me much that our coming should have
made so great excitement in the village, and doubtless
my vanity would have taken fire again if I had not
known that it was my captain these people had come
to see, and not myself, of whom they had never
heard. Even my captain I knew must shine in a
reflected glory, as the brother of General George
Rogers Clarke, whom the people of St. Louis wor-

shiped as their savior in the affair of 1780, when the Osages surprised the men at work in the fields, and whom all the Indians of Illinois regarded with fear and reverence as the great " Captain of the Long Knives." Yet I could see that many of their curious glances fell on me also, and I let go of Yorke's arm and walked steadily with my head in the air, as befitted the friend of Captain Clarke.

We had stopped in front of a large stone building set inside a walled inclosure. My captain, who was in advance with the governor and his party, as he entered the inclosure turned and beckoned to Yorke and me to follow him. The throng parted to let us through, and as we entered the gates I saw that the governor had stopped on the wide gallery that ran round the four sides of the building, and with a stately flourish was bidding my captain welcome to Government House.

With Yorke close at my footsteps, I followed the governor's party through a wide door into a great room that extended through the house (as I could see by the open doors and windows at the rear), and that was almost as wide as it was long, with doors opening into rooms on both sides. Here I was presented to Governor Delassus, who received me cordially, and who, with his dark eyes and punctilious manners, was my idea of a Spanish don.

On either side of him stood two men who also greeted me cordially, but without the punctiliousness of the Spaniard. They were the two Chouteaus, Auguste and Jean Pierre. I had heard much of them, both in Philadelphia and in Kentucky, and I found it difficult to conceal the curiosity with which I regarded them. I had expected to find two rough frontiersmen, somewhat after the manner of Daniel Boone or Simon Kenyon, both of whom I had seen at General Clarke's; but they were very far from that. Auguste, the elder, and who, almost more than his stepfather, Laclede, was the founder of St. Louis, was the graver of the two, with keen, shrewd eyes that betokened the successful man of business. Pierre (as everybody called the younger) looked not at all like his brother: taller and slenderer of build, his flashing dark eyes and gay manners must have been inherited from his father, Laclede, for Madame Chouteau (whom I came to know very well later) was even graver and sterner in manner than her eldest son, Auguste.

But interested as I was in meeting these men,—and there were many others of whom I had heard, Manuel Lisa, Gabriel Cerré, Francis Vigo, and Josef Marie Papin,—I could not resist casting many a furtive glance toward a table set in the rear of the great room. My bowl of gruel in the early morning had satisfied me at the time, but I was still weak from illness and much fasting, and my hard pull at the paddles had left me famished indeed. It was now, I was quite sure by the sun and the shadows, nearly eleven o'clock, and I began to feel the dizziness once more, and to be seized with a terrible fear that I should again be overcome. It was with a great joy, therefore, that I began to observe black servants bringing in smoking viands and arranging them upon the table, and no words ever sounded more pleasant in my ears than the governor's invitation to breakfast.

As we were about to sit down, my captain on the governor's right, and I very kindly placed on his left, with Mr. Pierre Chouteau beside me, there was a noise at the door, and Mr. Gratiot and Dr. Saugrain entered. They were welcomed in such fashion it was easy to see they were both prime favorites in that society. In response to my captain's inquiries, they said they had left Cahokia very shortly after us, bringing the young ladies over in two small boats, and the boats being light and easily handled, they had nearly overtaken us.

At the mention of the young ladies I felt myself flush painfully, and I almost thought the little doctor regarded me with a wicked twinkle in his eyes. But I was not sure, and I resolutely put the thought of them out of my mind, while I devoted myself to the more serious matters of the table.

And, indeed, seldom has it been my lot to sit down to a more delicious meal. It was my first taste of French cookery, and I proved then, what I had often heard, that the French have a talent for savors and seasonings, and for dainty service, denied to us Anglo-Saxons. It may be, also, that my long fasting (for my light breakfast had hardly broken my fast) added a sauce to the viands more potent than any Frenchman's skill, for my appetite had come back with a rush, and for the first time in many days I ate like a well man, and a very hungry one. So well, for-sooth, did I ply my knife and fork that Pierre Chou-teau could not forbear congratulating me, in his polished French manner, on my prowess as a trench-erman; at which I had the grace to blush.

And now, having taken the edge off my hunger, I had leisure to enjoy the swift exchange of wit and repartee flashing back and forth across the table in mixed English, French, and Spanish. There had been many toasts, most courteously worded and delicately drunk, for I noticed these Frenchmen were not deep drinkers, and did not feel it necessary to drain their glasses at every toast, as is the manner in Kentucky. My captain's health had been drunk and he had re-sponded with the governor's (nor did our polite hosts forget to honor me), and the gaiety began to grow somewhat noisy, when a youngster, who had, no doubt, been drinking a little more than was good for him, sprang to his feet. Waving his goblet toward Yorke (who stood behind Captain Clarke's chair grinning delightedly at every flash of wit, whether he under-stood it or not), he called out:

" I drink to the health of Monsieur Yorke, gentle-men, tallest and most smiling of sable Mercurys. May his inches never be fewer nor his smiles grow less."

I saw my captain frown, and Yorke, who did not understand one word that was said, since it was all in French, easily understood the gesture toward him, and the hesitating glances in his direction, and the half-lifted glasses as their owners were in doubt whether the toast was to be taken in jest or earnest.

His eyes rolled in terror from the proposer of the toast to Captain Clarke, and back again. I knew my captain would never brook the indignity of having his health drunk at the same table and by the same people who afterward drank his slave's, and fearing an awkward *contretemps*, I sprang to my feet to avert it. I lifted my glass high as I cried:

"Listen to me, messieurs! Is there no fair lady to whose honor your young men would drink? For never could we drink to the ladies after drinking to a negro and a slave. I give you, messieurs, the fairest lady in St. Louis!"

As I said it, for one fleeting moment I had a vision of a round white arm bare to the shoulder, a slender hand grasping a tawny mane, and black eyes flashing with scorn. Perhaps it was due to that vision that my voice had a ring in it that brought every man to his feet, and as glasses clinked, each man drank to the lady of his love with a rousing cheer.

As we brought our glasses to the table, rims down, the young man who had proposed Yorke's health said, with a bow of apology to me:

"I accept my rebuke, and if the gentleman permit I would like to repeat his toast: To the fairest lady in St. Louis—Dr. Saugrain's ward!"

"Fill up your glasses, gentlemen, drain them to the lees, and throw them over your shoulders; 't is a worthy toast," cried the governor; and, filling his to the brim, and draining it at one draught, he flung it over his shoulder—an example which the others, benedict and bachelor, followed with ardor. In the midst of the crashing of glass, I thought I caught Dr. Saugrain's and Mr. Gratiot's eyes fixed curiously on me. I turned to Mr. Pierre Chouteau:

" Dr. Saugrain's ward must be fair indeed, to rouse such enthusiasm," I said.

"Vraiment," returned Pierre, "she is the Rose of St. Louis. But you dine with Dr. Saugrain to-day: you will see, and then you will know. Young Josef Papin yonder, who proposed the toast, is wild about her. And so are half the young men of the village."

"Vraiment," I murmured to myself, "if she is fairer than the scornful Mademoiselle Pelagie, she is fair indeed! "

And yet I found myself looking forward to Dr. Saugrain's dinner with suppressed excitement, while I puzzled my brains to interpret his and Mr. Gratiot's enigmatical glances in my direction.

CHAPTER III

"I am his Highness's dog at Kew;
Pray tell me, sir, whose dog are you?"

"ALLONS!" said Mr. Pierre Chouteau, "I will show you the village. There are yet two hours before Dr. Saugrain's dinner-hour arrives."

We were standing on the wide gallery of Government House, looking up the Rue de la Tour to the "Fort on the Hill" with its massive round towers of stone and high stockade. We had made our adieus to Governor Delassus, and we were quite ready to accept Mr. Chouteau's invitation. Mr. Gratiot and Mr. Auguste Chouteau excused themselves from accompanying us on the ground of pressing business, but Mr. Auguste Chouteau said he hoped soon to see us at his own house, and Mr. Gratiot promised to meet us at dinner at Dr. Saugrain's.

So it was only four of us who set out (or five, if you count the black as one), Mr. Chouteau and my captain leading, Dr. Saugrain and I following, with Yorke trailing in the rear; for Captain Clarke did not dare leave that ingenious black to his own devices, being well assured that it would certainly result in disaster to himself or to some of the habitans.

31

Diagonally across the street, at the corner of the Rue de la Tour and the Rue Royale, was a large garden, shut in by solid stone walls higher than a man's head. Over the top of the walls fell branches of fruit-trees, and grape-vines still with a few clusters of late grapes hanging from them. Beyond were the tops of lofty shade-trees, and between the branches, where the foliage was rapidly thinning, we could catch glimpses of the stone chimneys and dormer-windows of a great house.

We turned into the Rue Royale and walked by the stone wall stretching north a long distance. The morning had been frosty, but the noon sun was hot, and we were glad to shelter ourselves under the overhanging boughs. It was Auguste Chouteau's place, but Pierre said he would let his brother have the pleasure of showing it to us; and we were about to pass the wide entrance-gate half-way down the long wall when we were stopped by a strange procession. Out of the gate filed slowly, solemnly, one at a time, a long line of fantastically dressed Indians. The two in front were attired alike in shabby old United States uniforms, with gold epaulets much tarnished and worn, dilapidated gold lace on collars and sleeves, and wearing on their heads military hats with long draggled plumes. From thigh to the low moccasins their legs were entirely unclothed, and a more ludicrous combination than the civilized coats and the bare brown legs I had never seen. The two in military coats were evidently chiefs, and were followed by a long line of braves sweltering under heavy Mackinac blankets, each armed with a scarlet umbrella in one hand and a palm-leaf fan in the other, to protect them from the sun. Apparently they did not glance in our direction, but each one as he passed Mr. Chouteau saluted him with a guttural "Ugh!" to which Mr. Chouteau responded in the most military fashion.

"They are on their way to my place, and we will let them get well ahead of us," Mr. Chouteau said, as the last brave passed us. " It would hardly be dignified to be trailing in their rear; we will step into my brother's garden for a moment and give them time to get out of our way."

The massive gates, which, I saw, could be heavily bolted and barred, stood open, and we passed through into a park-like inclosure, beautifully laid out and kept in perfect order, with velvet turf and noble forest trees, and, in one part, a garden of vegetables and flowers. Set in the midst was a noble stone mansion some sixty feet in front, with wide galleries shaded by a projection of sloping roof, which was pierced by dormer-windows. Several smaller stone buildings were grouped around it, and from one to the other negroes were passing on various errands, giving a cheerful impression of industry and prosperity. I caught the flutter of a white dress disappearing through a wide door opening from the gallery into the house, and I would have liked to get a nearer view of the mansion and its inmates. But an exclamation from Mr. Chouteau put all thoughts of petticoats out of my mind.

3

"Diable!" he ejaculated, " 't is Black Hawk himself. Now what is the meaning of this, think you?"

I followed his glance, and saw coming from one of the outbuildings the noblest specimen of a savage I had ever beheld. Unlike the others, he was decked in no worn-out finery of the white man, bestowed upon him in exchange for valuable furs, but in the fitting costume of a great chief, his head-dress of eagle feathers falling back from the top of his head almost to his high beaded moccasins. He was far above the usual stature of Indians, and what increased his appearance of height was the lofty brow and noble dome, beneath which two piercing eyes and strong aquiline nose gave additional character to a most striking face.

I thought both Mr. Chouteau and Dr. Saugrain looked a little troubled for a moment, but as the savage stalked majestically toward us, Pierre advanced to meet him, and with a courteous but commanding wave of his hand stopped him.

"What has brought my brother from his island on the bosom of the Great Father of Waters?" he asked, after both had exchanged formal greetings.

Black Hawk turned his piercing eyes upon my captain. "It was whispered among my braves," he said, "that the great Captain of the Long Knives had sent his brother to St. Louis. I bring him a greeting from my people."

Most men would have been abashed by the ceremonial tone and gestures with which Black Hawk accompanied his speech, but if my captain felt any embarrassment he did not show it. With as ceremonious a manner as the chief's, he replied at once:

"The great chief of the Sacs has honored my brother and myself. I will bear your greeting to the Captain of the Long Knives, and it will fill his heart with happiness to know his red brother has not forgotten him."

Black Hawk only grunted approval, but I think he was pleased, for he turned to Mr. Chouteau with a more condescending manner:

"I will go with my brother to his wigwam. I will eat with him and sleep with him."

There was nothing for Mr. Chouteau to do but acquiesce, though when his back was turned on Black Hawk he made a queer grimace and said rapidly, in English, which probably Black Hawk did not understand:

"There will be trouble, my friends; my yard is full of Mandans, Arickarees, and Osages. They love not the Sacs, and Black Hawk is a turbulent fellow if any misunderstanding should arise. You see," he said to Captain Clarke, lapsing again into French, "these fellows have usually started back up the Missouri long before this time, but they have all waited this year to see the brother of the great Captain of the Long Knives. They planned their exit from Auguste's yard at the exact moment to get a good look at you."

My captain laughed his hearty laugh.

"And then they glanced not in my direction even, after all."

"Do not deceive yourself, mon capitaine; they looked you over thoroughly. Not one of them but would know you again among a thousand. But they timed their exit also with the hope of making an impression on you, and to that end, as you saw, had donned their finest toggery."

We had left Auguste Chouteau's yard and were going north again along the stone wall, Black Hawk stalking majestically beside Captain Clarke, upon whom he from time to time looked down and bestowed a grunt of approval. Across the street from us now was an open square (La Place Publique, Mr. Chouteau called it), and drawn up around it were many queer little French *charrettes*, loaded with cord-wood and drawn by small mustangs. The owners of the charrettes were most of them taking a noonday nap under the shade of the trees in La Place, and their mustangs were nodding drowsily in their shafts in sympathy with their owners. This was the same open place we had first come upon after climbing the bluff, and now, as we came to the corner of La Place, and the street leading down to the river (Mr. Chouteau said the street was called La Rue Bonhomme), I looked down the steep road and saw at the foot of it the landing-place, and our boats tied to great posts, with some of our men in charge.

I could distinguish on the great flatboat that had followed us, carrying our provisions and our horses, my own mare, Fatima, with her proudly arched neck. Before I had time to think of my manners I had put my fingers to my lips and uttered through them the shrill whistle with which I had used to call her. Instantly her head was flung swiftly up, and I saw her start as if to come to me, while up the bluff was borne her shrill whinnies, high above the shouts of the men, who had as much as they could do to keep her from breaking halter in her mad plunge for liberty to answer the call she had never disobeyed.

I was ashamed of my boyish trick, and apologized at once to the two gentlemen and to my captain. But Dr. Saugrain said it was a fortunate reminder: if we cared to send for our horses they could meet us at Mr. Chouteau's, for it would be a long and hot walk from there to his house at the extreme southern end of the village. So Yorke was despatched for the two horses, and right glad was I at the thought of being on Fatima's back once more, for it was a full two weeks since I had mounted her.

We were on the next block now, skirting another stone wall with overhanging boughs. Mr. Chouteau said it was his mother's place, and he would have to insist upon our stopping to pay our respects to her.

"You know," he said, "madame ma mère is a sort of mother to the village, and she would feel herself deeply aggrieved should such distinguished guests pass her by."

We entered another inclosure beautifully embowered in trees, and found a long, low building, not of stone, like her son's house, but built, in the French fashion, of upright logs. On the wide gallery sat Madame Chouteau herself, dressed in the style of the habitans who had filled the streets on our arrival, but in richer materials. Her petticoat was of black satin, and her short gown, or jacket, was of purple velvet with wide lace in sleeves and at the neck, and gorgeously beaded moccasins on her feet. But it was her head-dress which struck me as the most re-markable part of her costume, and Pierre Chouteau whispered to us, with a droll grimace:

"Regardez the head-dress of madame; she expects us, is it not? She is en fête."

It seemed to be a handkerchief of some thin mate-rial, purple in color, and worn like a turban, but entwined with ribbons and flowers until it became a gorgeous coronet, and added indescribably to the majesty of her presence. Already over seventy, with white hair, she was yet as erect as a girl, and her eye was as keen as an eagle's. Even my captain was abashed before its glances, which seemed to be taking a complete inventory of his physical, mental, and moral qualities. It was a bad quarter of an hour for me (whom she hardly deigned to notice), in spite of the good ratafia and delicious *croquecignolles* a small black boy brought out on a tray and placed on a stand at her side, and which she served to us with stately courtesy.

As for Black Hawk, it was more than he could stand when her severely questioning glance fell upon him. Without losing an ace of his dignified solem-nity of demeanor, he turned his back abruptly on the old lady, and stalked slowly and majestically down the path and out the gate. We hoped we had rid ourselves of him, but we found him waiting for us when we had made our formal adieus to madame. Just before we reached Pierre Chouteau's house he dropped back and walked beside Dr. Saugrain and myself. I thought he wished to pay me some of the respect he had been showing my captain, and I felt flattered accordingly. But I was mistaken; he had something to say to Dr. Saugrain. With many premonitory grunts he said it finally, and it had a startling effect upon the little doctor.

"Let great medicine-man watch," said Black Hawk, solemnly; "White Wolf will steal Little Black Eyes. Black Hawk has many ears and many eyes; he has seen White Wolf talking to Red Dog, and he has heard their whispers."

Such was the doctor's agitation that, although we were just entering Mr. Chouteau's great yard (so filled with all manner of buildings, warehouses, shops, and cabins for negroes and Indians that it seemed like a separate village of itself), he called to my captain and Mr. Chouteau and begged them to excuse him. He felt that he must return home at once and assure himself of the safety of his ward, he said, though we need not cut short our visit to Mr. Chouteau, but come to him later, in time for dinner. But Yorke coming up at that moment with our horses, and riding his own, Captain Clarke bade him dismount and give his horse to Dr. Saugrain, and insisted upon accompanying him home. Mr. Chouteau readily excused us, only courteously making a condition that the visit cut short now should be renewed at our earliest convenience.

As for me, I was a little sorry not to see more of Mr. Chouteau's place, for everywhere there were throngs of Indians in picturesque costume, and on the gallery of the great house a bevy of young maidens evidently awaiting our approach. But Fatima was calling me frantically with her delighted neighs, and the moment I was on her back, and felt her silken muscles stretch and tighten rhythmically beneath me, I cared no more for Mr. Chouteau's interesting place with its Indians and young maidens, and only longed for a right to leave my companions and have one good dash with Fatima across country, over fences and ditches. I would not have been afraid, in my present mood, to have put her at the high stone walls with which every one in St. Louis seemed to fence in his place, and so wild with delight was Fatima at meeting her master once more I think she would have taken them like a bird.

But the doctor was more impatient than I, and first taking Black Hawk aside for a minute's low-toned consultation, he made his hasty adieus to our host, and bidding us follow him, he was off. Turning off the Rue Royale into the Rue Bonhomme, he went up the hill a long block to the Rue de l'Église, and then, turning to the left, he called back to us:

"'T is a straight road from here on, messieurs; shall we race for it? It may mean more than life to a fair lady."

For answer I laid the reins on Fatima's glossy neck and whispered to her:

"Get up, Sweetheart!"

In a flash she had passed the two other horses and her dainty hoofs were flinging the soft dirt of the road in their faces. It was more a country lane than a village street, with scattered houses tree-embowered, and just back of Auguste Chouteau's place, which I recognized from the rear, was a church, and behind it the crosses of many graves, and beside it a priest's house with two black-robed priests taking a noonday siesta in comfortable chairs on the shady, vine-covered gallery. They awoke with a start as Fatima thundered by, and the two other horses, now well in the rear, pounded after, and I doubt not they thought it was the beginning of another 1780 affair, so frightened did they look.

It did not take Fatima long to cover that mile and a half, and when I saw that we were approaching the stockade at the end of the road, with only one house between (which, like the Chouteaus', was set in a great yard inclosed with high stone walls), I drew rein under a wide-spreading oak and waited for the others. And as I waited I began once more to wonder what kind of creature Dr. Saugrain's ward could be: the acknowledged belle of St. Louis and now in some extreme danger from a white villain and a rascally Indian, for so I had easily understood Black Hawk's figurative language—the White Wolf and the Red Dog.

I could hear the soft thrumming of a guitar, and a low voice crooning songs, of which I could now and then catch a word of the creole French. I did not doubt it was the doctor's ward who thus beguiled the hours with melody, and I grew vastly impatient to meet the loveliest lady in St. Louis and the sweetest of singers, if I could judge from the snatches of song that floated to my ears.

In a minute more the doctor himself rode up, shouting lustily before he reached the gate, ''Narcisse, Narcisse!'' which put a sudden end to the music. As a black boy ran out in answer to his call, the doctor sprang as nimbly from his horse as I myself could have done, and flung the boy his reins with a sharp command to take care of the horses. He started swiftly for the house, but stopped suddenly and turned to Narcisse.

''Where are your mistress and mademoiselle?'' he asked, in a tone so sharp and excited the boy was frightened and stammered as he answered:

''In the house, sir.''

''You are sure?''

''Yes, sir; 'fore God, sir, they're in the living-room this minute.''

''Thank God!'' ejaculated the doctor, and then I saw, to my astonishment, that he was all white and trembling. He recovered himself in a moment and turned to us with the suavity of a genial host:

''Gentlemen, I fear that rascal Black Hawk has played us a scurvy trick; very likely for reasons of his own he wanted to get rid of me. He has given me a bad quarter of an hour, but otherwise he has only given me the pleasure of welcoming you a little earlier to Émigré's Retreat. Let us go find the ladies.''

Before we had time to reply, round the corner of

the house sauntered slowly a huge mastiff, and as I caught a glimpse of him my heart sank into my boots, and there seemed to rise into my throat a tumultuous beating that was nigh to choking me: not from fear of the dog, though the moment he caught sight of me he stopped, every muscle tense, the hair on his mane erect, his eyes red, glowing, vicious, while he uttered one deep angry growl after another.

It was not fear of the brute that set my pulses throbbing painfully: it was the truth that flashed upon me for the first time—*Dr. Saugrain's ward was Mademoiselle Pelagie!* At that moment through the open door came a clear whistle and the sweetest voice I had ever heard, calling in ringing tones of command:

"À moi, Leon!"

CHAPTER IV

I MAKE AN ENGAGEMENT

"A rosebud set with little wilful thorns"

IT was too late to beat a retreat. I caught once more a merry twinkle in the little doctor's eyes as we followed the dog, who, obedient to his mistress's voice, had rushed before us into the house. I felt the red blood surging to the roots of my hair, and I knew when I stopped on the threshold beside my captain to make my grand bow that I looked more like an awkward country lout than the fine gentleman I was in the habit of considering myself.

I hardly dared raise my eyes, and yet I saw very distinctly that if Mademoiselle Pelagie in ball costume was bewitching, Mademoiselle Pelagie in simple morning dress was an angel. The room was a long, low one, cool and shady from the sheltering galleries outside, and with many windows, all open to catch the southern breezes that kept the dimity curtains bellying like white sails. On a low seat beside one of the open windows, looking out into cool depths of dusky green, sat Mademoiselle Pelagie. Her white dress, short of skirt

44

and reaching hardly to the daintiest of ankles, was just low enough in the neck to show the round, white throat, and just short enough in the sleeve to leave uncovered below the elbow the beautifully molded arm. Across her shoulders was a broad blue ribbon that held the guitar to whose soft thrumming I had been listening, and one restraining hand was laid on Leon's head, who sat beside her, erect on his haunches, regarding me with angry suspicion.

She rose as we entered, and still holding her guitar with one arm, while the other hand lifted her skirt daintily, she made us the deepest and most graceful of curtsies. Then she lifted her dark eyes shyly to Captain Clarke and with a ravishing smile bade him welcome in broken English. To me she vouchsafed not even a glance. I stood by stiff as any martinet while she made soft speeches to the captain in her adorable baby-English, and the captain responded in his most gallant fashion.

I grew more rigid and more gauche every minute, and I know not what would have become of me if the doctor, who had left the room to look for his wife, had not come to my relief. He came in, bringing Madame Saugrain with him, and a sweet and simple little old lady she proved to be. Her cap was almost as flowery as Madame Chouteau's, but she was as warm and cordial in her manner as the other was stern and forbidding. She greeted my captain first, of course, but she was as cordial to me as to him, and in her motherly way she called me "My son," which, after my icy reception from another lady, went straight to my heart. I was grateful to her in spite of the fear I felt that it was my very youthful appearance had called forth the endearing term.

We were all comfortably seated, Captain Clarke chatting gaily with Mademoiselle Pelagie, I pointedly addressing all my conversation to Dr. Saugrain and madame, when Narcisse came in with a tray of cooling drinks—a mild and pleasant beverage made of rasp-berry conserves and lime-juice mixed with some spir-its and plenty of cold spring water. I liked it well, and would have taken another glass, for I was thirsty and our ride had been a warm one, and Madame Sau-grain urged it upon me, but as I was about to take it I heard a saucy voice saying:

" 'T is no wonder that you empty not your glass, Captain Clarke; 't is a drink much more suited to maidens and to young boys than to men."

My glass was half extended, but I drew it back has-tily, and then was angry with myself, for I heard a mocking laugh that I was sure was intended for me, and for the life of me I could not refrain from glan-cing quickly in mademoiselle's direction. Her eyes met mine with more of scorn in their dark depths than I could well stand. I gazed steadily into them for as much as half a second with all the defiance in my glance I knew how to convey, and then I turned again to Madame Saugrain:

"If you will permit me to change my mind, ma-dame," I said, "I would like another glass of your delicious beverage."

And then, lifting it to my lips, I added:

"I drink to the ladies: they add fragrance and beauty to our lives, like the red berries; comfort and strength, like this good ratafia; sweetness, like the sugar; and if sometimes they also add bitterness and acid, like the limes, it is doubtless for our good."

The gentlemen both touched glasses with me as they drank to my toast, the little doctor preternaturally solemn, and my captain almost as grave, but for a wicked twinkle in his eye. I knew they thought my toast a boyish one, and doubtless understood its inspiration, while they struggled to preserve their gravity out of courtesy to me. Whether mademoiselle's eyes were more mocking than ever I did not know, for I looked not in her direction. But madame glowed with genuine pleasure and declared 't was a pretty toast, and she thanked me for her share in it. Whereupon mademoiselle said in the gravest voice:

"I also, monsieur, thank you for my share in it, for I suppose the lime-juice is mine," and, to my amazement, when, as in duty bound, I glanced at her, since she spoke directly to me, I saw that her eyes were downcast, and the richest color had flamed into the warm white of her cheeks.

I know not what I might have said or done, so repentant was I at once for having caused her annoyance, had not a short, sharp exclamation from Dr. Saugrain startled us all:

" 'T is that skulking Osage again. What does he here, Narcisse?"

"He bring note, m'seh, for La Petite," answered

Narcisse, rolling his eyes at the unwonted sharpness in his master's tones.

Dr. Saugrain turned at once to mademoiselle.

"Pelagie," he said, "what does this mean? Who is sending you notes by Red Jean?"

Mademoiselle looked up half defiantly, half inclined not to reply to such peremptory questioning in the presence of strangers. But on second thought she answered quite submissively:

"It was the young Chevalier Le Moyne who is staying at Gabriel Cerré's."

"Now, I like not that," said the doctor, hastily; and then bethinking himself, he ordered Narcisse to take away the empty glasses and keep an eye on Red Jean.

"Don't let him get out of your sight as long as he stays about the place; he will be stealing the horses if you don't watch him."

The moment Narcisse had left the room the doctor repeated:

"I like not that; I begin to think Black Hawk may have had good reason to warn us against the White Wolf and the Red Dog."

Then, turning to mademoiselle, he added more gently:

"I like not to inquire into mademoiselle's little affairs, but this is of the gravest importance. Will you tell us the contents of that note, ma chère?"

Mademoiselle hesitated, and glanced almost unconsciously at the captain and at me. We both sprang to our feet at the same moment, and the captain spoke:

"The lad and I will step out on the gallery, where, if you permit, we will light our pipes."

But with a quick gesture of dissent, mademoiselle also sprang to her feet.

"No, no! mon capitaine, no, no! Meestaire, it is not'ing, not'ing. I will say all before you. 'T is only that the chevalier asks may he escort me to the peek-neek on Chouteau's Pond."

"Sit down, gentlemen, if you please," said the doctor; "I think it wise for us to hold a council of war. I shall need your advice much, possibly your help. First, I want to say that some weeks ago I received letters from France warning me of a plot to capture Mademoiselle Pelagie and carry her back to France. A week ago this mysterious stranger arrived in St. Louis. Gabriel Cerré picked him up in Ste. Genevieve and brought him home with him, and that is about all any one knows of him, except that he claims to be of an old French family, who has saved enough from the wreck to permit him to travel and see the world. When he has finished this trip he declares he will return and settle on his estates on the Loire which he says have been returned to him by Bonaparte. Whether Black Hawk meant him when he bade me beware of the White Wolf I know not. I could get very little information when I spoke to him before leaving Pierre Chouteau's, and I am not sure he had any to give me, yet I think he knows something. I confess I have been suspicious of this fellow from the first, arriving, as he did, on the heels of my letter of warning. And now what think you 't is best to do?"

4

I was eager enough to say what I thought best to do, but I knew my place better than to speak before my elders, and so I waited for my captain. Mademoiselle was not so modest, or perhaps she thought no one had a better right than herself to speak on a subject so nearly concerning her.

"I think, sir," she said, lapsing into her native tongue, "you wrong the Chevalier Le Moyne. I have seen much of him in the week of his stay at Gabriel Cerré's, and he has been invariably respectful and most gentleman-like in all his demeanor."

"'T is the very fact of his seeing so much of you, my child, that first roused my suspicions. He is for-ever hanging round you at dance and dinner; not even Josef Papin gets much chance to come nigh you."

Mademoiselle flushed slightly at the mention of Josef Papin's name—a name I was beginning, for some reason, to dislike.

"I should think," she said demurely, "there might be other reasons for that than suspicious ones"; and then she laughed merrily when I murmured, "Vrai-ment!" and touched my heart with my handkerchief. I thought she was mocking me again.

"Mademoiselle is quite right," said Captain Clarke, gravely; "there are doubtless very natural reasons for the chevalier's devotion, yet I think it would be well, nevertheless, to act on Dr. Saugrain's suspicions. May I inquire whether mademoiselle has accepted the chevalier's offer of escort?"

We all listened eagerly for the answer.

"No," said mademoiselle; "I had just received the

note when you arrived, and I would not answer it until I had consulted my guardian. He is very stern with me, messieurs,'' turning to us with a witching smile that I could see pleased the good doctor greatly.

"Then," continued the captain, "it would be a very easy matter, I suppose, to decline his escort."

But La Petite pouted.

"Not so easy, mon capitaine. I have no reason to offer, and it would shut me off from accepting a second invitation."

"I think," said Dr. Saugrain, "it would be better that you should not go to the picnic. Chouteau's Pond is beyond the stockade, and shut in by the woods; it would be an ideal spot for a surprise and a capture. There are always plenty of rascally Osages to be hired for a trifle to carry out any such villainy."

"Not go!" exclaimed mademoiselle, in dismay. "But it is given for me! It is my fête! Josef Papin planned it entirely for me, he said."

Mademoiselle was now growing rosy red, for, with a child's eagerness to carry her point at all hazards, she had said more than she meant to.

"Then why did not Josef offer himself as your escort?"

"He will, probably, later; but," and she tossed her head like the spoiled beauty she was, "it will serve him right, for being so slow, to find that I have accepted another. Besides which," and she shrugged her shoulders with all the airs of a Parisian dame, "you know your bourgeois etiquette. I cannot accept

another: it would be a just cause for a duel au pis-
tolets.''

"'C'est vrai,'' said the doctor, with an answering
shrug, and looking woefully perplexed.

"Now, if you will permit me,'' suggested the captain, "since mademoiselle is so sure Mr. Papin will ask
her later, why can she not plead to the chevalier a
previous engagement?''

But not for a moment would mademoiselle listen to
that.

"And be the laughing-stock of all St. Louis when
it gets about, as it surely will. I refuse the chevalier
because I prefer to wait for Monsieur Papin. Monsieur Papin hears of it and invites some one else to
teach me not to be so sure, or,'' primly, "I have given
him undue encouragement.''

"Then,'' said the doctor, gravely, "I see nothing
for it but that you stay away from the picnic and
write the chevalier that you have decided not to go
Unless,'' he added hastily, seeing the gathering storm
on Pelagie's brow, "unless—'' and then he hesitated,
much embarrassed. "Perhaps our young friend here
would like to attend one of our rural picnics, and
would be willing to look after you and give you the
opportunity of writing to the chevalier that you have
a previous engagement.''

It was now my turn to blush. I had been ardently
longing to offer my services, but not for a moment had
I thought of daring. Now it was thrust upon me.

"If mademoiselle would be so good,'' I murmured,
bowing low, "I am her obedient servant.''

But mademoiselle was speechless. One moment she turned white, and the next she turned red, and then white again. When she found her voice she said, looking not at all at me, but straight at Dr. Saugrain:

"I will remain at home, monsieur. I care not to be a burden upon unwilling hands."

And then rising to her feet, with her head held high, her guitar on one arm, and the other hand still on the mastiff's head, she said:

"Allons, Leon!" and was sweeping proudly from the room.

I was in such consternation that probably I would have sat like any bumpkin and let her go, if not that, as she passed me, although her head was turned from me, it was not quite so much turned but that I caught a sudden quiver of the little chin, held proudly in air, and something bright glistening on the long, dark lashes. I sprang quickly before her. There was an angry growl from Leon, who no doubt thought I intended to serve his mistress the same trick I had served him, but I did not heed it.

"Mademoiselle!" I entreated, "I beg you will reconsider. Nothing could give me more pride and pleasure. Besides," adopting an argumentative tone, "you know it would be my only chance for attending the picnic, and I have a vast desire to engage in some of your St. Louis festivities, and to meet some of the young maidens I was deprived of meeting last night."

She was compelled to stop,—I barred her way; but for a few moments she showed no signs of relenting. She dashed away the shining drops from her lashes, and quieted Leon with a low "Taise-toi." But gradually I saw her face change, and then, still holding herself proudly, and with the air of a queen graciously condescending to bestow a favor upon a suppliant, but also with a smile of radiant sweetness, she spoke, and her voice was like the song of the thrush beside running waters:

"Very well, monsieur; if I am not to be considered as putting myself under obligations to a stranger, I will go and write the chevalier that I have a previous engagement."

CHAPTER V

"Many a youth and many a maid
Dancing in the chequered shade."

THE good doctor uttered a sigh of relief as mademoiselle left the room, followed by madame, who no doubt, in the goodness of her heart, went out to praise the young lady for having done as she ought, and to condole with her for being obliged to go to the picnic with a man she knew so slightly, and knew but to dislike.

The sigh was quickly followed by a frown.

"I wish that my ward had not so strong a will of her own. I scarce think it safe for her to go to Chouteau's Pond at all if, as I fear, her enemies are plotting to capture her."

"I will defend her with my life, sir," I hastened to aver, "since you are so good as to intrust her to me."

The doctor smiled at my boyish ardor, but said kindly:

"I would trust her with you sooner than with most, my lad, for I believe I have seen enough of you to know that you are brave to a fault, and entirely trustworthy. But you know not the wiles of these treacherous Osages, and if this Chevalier Le Moyne is the man I fear he is, he is a much to be dreaded villain.''

"Whom do you fear him to be?" the captain and I uttered in one breath.

The good doctor hesitated a moment and then seemed to take a sudden determination.

"I am afraid I have no right to be letting you into my confidence, for it is not mine alone. In what I am about to say to you it is my country reposing a confidence as well. But our brief acquaintance has inspired me with trust in you both, and I have need of advice and help in this emergency, and perhaps of a good sword, if one of you be free to offer it. It is not the fortunes of a simple maid, such as my little Pelagie seems to be, that are alone involved, and yet I am not at liberty to tell you what great issues are at stake. We will say, by way of illustration, it would be to the advantage of an Orleanist to get rid of all possible Bourbon claimants to the throne of France, would it not? Merely by way of further illustration, suppose there were some young Orleanist, far removed from any pretensions to the throne, who by marrying a young Bourbon maid much closer to the throne, but, of course, barred from it by her sex, should prevent her marrying royalty and so having a son who might succeed to the throne. Do you follow me?"

We both bowed our comprehension, for we were too eager to interrupt him by a word. The doctor went on:

"And suppose by such a marriage he removed one

more obstacle from the path of a powerful kinsman in his progress toward the throne. And if this young Orleanist were penniless and the Bourbon maid rich in prospect, he would save his kinsman the necessity of providing for him. And if he were dissolute and unprincipled, he would hesitate at no means to accomplish his ends. And if he were handsome, after a fashion, and accomplished in all Parisian arts, there would be reasonable chance of his success with a young maiden but little versed in the wiles of the world. Although I have used this merely as an illustration, this is very much the situation that confronts Pelagie's friends. You see, I have some reason to feel alarmed, and I fear I have no right to permit her to go to this picnic. Yet,'' with a grimace, '' what can I? Where a wilful maiden will, a man is helpless.

'' And now, messieurs, you see how fully I have trusted you, not only with my affairs, but the affairs of France. I am not asking for a pledge of secrecy, for I feel no such pledge is necessary. Pelagie and her interests and the interests of her house in France I believe to be as safe in your hands as in my own.''

As the doctor uttered these last words he sprang to his feet, and betrayed the intensity of his feeling by the mist in his eyes, the tremor in his voice, and the dramatic clasping of his hands.

By a simultaneous emotion of sympathy, both the captain and I found ourselves on our feet also. The captain extended his hand, and, like the straightforward, simple-minded gentleman he is, said only:

"Your trust is not misplaced, Dr. Saugrain; your secret is safe."

I was almost too deeply moved for words; I could only murmur as I bowed low over the hilt of my sword:

"Safe as my honor!"

I know not with what emotions my captain had listened to this long recital. As for me, I had been intensely interested. Yet I could not tell why it should not please me to find that this scornful little lady was presumptive heiress to wealth and titles, probably even of royal rank, for so I could not but understand the doctor's illustration.

"Does Mademoiselle Pelagie know all this?" inquired the captain. "Does she know her rank and prospects? Is it permitted to speak of them to her?"

"Oh, no, no, no!" uttered the doctor, rapidly, with vigorous protestations of head and hands. "Pelagie knows nothing but that almost longer ago than she can remember she lived in a beautiful house with many servants, and with a father and mother who idolized her, but who went away from her one day never to return. Of course she knows now why they never returned, but that is all. She has lived with us in America nearly ten years, and I think she has learned to love Madame Saugrain and me almost as if we were indeed her father and mother, and we could not love child of our own more tenderly.

"And so you see, my dear young sir," regarding me with affectionate concern, "what a weighty responsibility I have put upon your young shoulders.

If the burden is too great for you, I absolve you from your offer as escort, and Pelagie shall stay at home whether she will or not. I think it would be far the better way."

"Oh, no, no, sir!" I protested eagerly. "I am proud you think me worthy such a responsibility. I will never let her out of my sight for one moment, and I promise to bring her back to you in safety."

"Thank you," said the doctor, gravely; "that is what I would wish. Do not let her out of your sight if it is possible. Even if she seems to be fretted by your espionage I hope you will bear with her temper, —which I know to be a royal one,—and persist in your watchfulness. I shall be deeply grateful to you."

By the time the day of the picnic arrived, I flattered myself I had made some slight progress in Mademoiselle Pelagie's regard. Very slight, to be sure, yet I thought she did not treat me with quite the disdain she had shown at first. Indeed, I even thought I sometimes detected that she was listening with interest when Madame Saugrain or the good doctor was questioning me about my life at home in Philadelphia.

Twice a day at least we were brought together at the table, for the captain and I had taken up our abode at Dr. Saugrain's. It was not without much demur that we had, at last, accepted the doctor's urgent invitations to do so. To be sure, there was no hostelry in the village, except the low tavern where the disreputable Indians and rough river-men congregated, and we would have been obliged to accept some of the

many hospitable invitations extended us by the Chouteaus, the Papins, the Cerrés, indeed by nearly every
leading citizen of St. Louis, all eagerly vying with
one another for the privilege of entertaining General
Clarke's brother. I think the captain's hesitancy
arose from the feeling that he ought to accept Émile
Yosti's or Manuel Lisa's hospitality, since his business
was chiefly concerned with them; but with me it was
the feeling that it would be intolerable to dwell under
the same roof with my Lady Disdain, and be subjected
to countless little ignominies at her hands. Yet when
the doctor presented it to us as a very great favor
to him at this time, when he might need our assistance
as well as our advice in protecting Mademoiselle Pelagie, we could object no further, and I, at least, was as
eager to stay as I had before been unwilling. To me it
seemed the more reasonable that he might easily need
what assistance our swords could give him, if there
were really on foot a plan to capture mademoiselle,
because the doctor's house was set in a large garden,
at the extreme borders of the village, next to the
stockade and with no neighbor within hearing.

The day of the picnic rose clear and bright, changing soon to the purple haze and soft air of a day in
late November. Breakfast was hardly over when the
picnickers began to pass the house, some of them walking in merry groups, some in little French carts
drawn by oxen or small, hardy ponies, but many of
them, I noted with a beating heart, on horseback carrying double, the maiden on a pillion holding fast
with her arm around her escort's waist. Was it thus

my Lady Disdain expected to be carried to the picnic, I wondered, and could not tell for the life of me whether I most hoped it or dreaded it.

But my hopes and fears were alike vain. I sat smoking on the shady gallery, and was beginning to wonder when my lady would see fit to start, for by now the procession had thinned out to almost none, only a straggling couple occasionally hurrying by as if they feared they were late and must hasten to be in time for the sport. I began to think it possible she had changed her mind and would stay at home rather than go with an undesired escort.

I had risen early, and though I had made an unusually careful toilet, calling Yorke to my aid to see that every lacer was fresh and securely tied, and my buckles shining, yet I had made much haste also, not knowing at what hour mademoiselle proposed starting, and fearing greatly to annoy her by being one moment tardy. So here had I sat smoking on the shady gallery a good two hours awaiting my lady's pleasure, and beginning inwardly to fume, for my temper was not such as to bear meekly even the caprices of a beautiful maiden—no, not though she might be also some great lady in disguise.

But when I had for the tenth time started up to stride angrily up and down the gallery, I heard the creaking of wheels, and around the corner of the house came a little French charrette, its wooden wheels making a great noise, drawn by one ox and Narcisse walking beside it, driving. I was filled with dismay, for to me it seemed not a mode of conveyance suited to the dignity of the son of one of the proudest families of Philadelphia, to say nothing of Mademoiselle Pelagie. Besides, I had had visions of the fine figure I was to cut before the St. Louis beaus and belles on my prancing and curveting Fatima, whose glossy coat was like satin this morning from the extra rubbing I had ordered Yorke to give her.

But as Narcisse passed me and pulled off his hat with an amiable grin, I saw a great hamper in the charrette, and from a spicy whiff borne to my nostrils by a passing breeze I knew he was conveying our dinner to the picnic-grounds, and I was duly thankful that neither Fatima nor I was to be hampered ('t is a poor pun, and my father hath ever taught me 't is the lowest form of wit) with clumsy packages dangling from saddle and arm.

In a moment more, around the corner of the house again came a black, leading a small Indian horse gaily caparisoned, and fitted with a lady's pillion, and immediately behind, Yorke, leading my own Fatima. I knew then we were about to start, and my heart began once more its silly thumpings. Yet would I not move from my seat, where I had assumed an attitude of indifference, until I suddenly heard behind me a cool and haughty voice:

"Are you not ready, sir? It is high time, I should think, we were on our way, or we will be too late for the déjeuner."

Now was I in wrath indeed, to be spoken to in tones of reproach when I had every reason to expect at least an excuse, if not an apology, for having been kept so

long waiting. I rose to my feet in leisurely fashion
and made mademoiselle a most elaborate bow, as I replied in a voice as cool and haughty as her own:

"Had I been informed at what hour mademoiselle
would require my presence, I should have been belted
and hatted and not have detained your ladyship for
even a moment, to say nothing of having wasted two
good hours of my own time in idle waiting."

As I spoke I stooped to pick up my sword-belt from
the floor beside my chair, and began slowly to buckle
it on. My eyes were on my belt, but not so closely
but that I could see a little smile hover around mademoiselle's lips, and I thought she was not displeased
to find I had a little spirit of my own and was not
always to be cowed by her scornful airs. I was so
elated by the discovery that I, foolishly, prolonged
the buckling beyond all possible necessity, and mademoiselle's good humor was quickly exhausted. She
tapped her little foot impatiently for a moment and
then spoke as icily as before:

"Since monsieur finds difficulty with his belt, I will
ask Yorke to put me on my horse and then send him
to your assistance."

All my foolish elation was gone in a moment, and,
between my mortification and my impatient haste, I
fumbled in earnest. I was in desperate haste; for not
for a moment did I intend to let Yorke put her upon
her horse: yet so swiftly had she swept down the long
gallery and the steps to the driveway a little distance
off, and so slow had I been with my buckle, that I
reached her side just in time to hear her say:

"Yorke, put me on my horse, and then go at once and buckle your master's belt. We are like to be all day getting to Chouteau's Pond."

"Yes, missy," said Yorke, and flinging Fatima's reins to Narcisse, prepared to obey her, though he could only have comprehended by intuition, for not a word of her tongue did he understand.

I was restored at once to my equanimity by her impatient tones, and I spoke to Yorke with a calm authority he dared not disobey:

"Take care of Fatima, Yorke; I will attend to mademoiselle," and without giving her time to object I coolly lifted her to her horse. She was only a feather's weight, but I think she liked not that fashion of mounting, and was minded for a moment to kick and scream like an angry child. But she thought better of it, and though the quick flame sprang into her cheek, she bowed her thanks in stately fashion, and I springing on Fatima's back and bidding Yorke to follow at once, we set forth at a round pace.

Not a word did she speak as we galloped side by side down the driveway, through the gate, and along the short bit of road that extended to the stockade. When we had passed through, there was not much more than a rough foot-path, that began to descend very soon from the high bluffs, sometimes by a gentle incline, sometimes by a steep and rocky descent, to the valley of La Petite Rivière.

The path was no longer wide enough for two horses, and we were compelled to ride in Indian fashion. Fatima was ahead and was picking her way daintily and surely, but slowly. The little Indian horse, being much more used to such rough paths, would have gone on more rapidly, and fretted at being kept back by Fatima. So, no doubt, did his rider, for presently, in her formal way, she said:

"If monsieur will permit, I will take the lead. I think my pony knows the path better and can show you the way."

But I had been specially warned to keep ever in advance, and it did not add to mademoiselle's good humor that I was compelled to refuse her the *pas*. I was beginning to feel that my task was a thankless one, and the picnic on Chouteau's Pond did not look to me quite so alluring as it had looked a few days before. Perhaps my face betrayed my feeling; for when we reached the foot of the incline and our path broadened out as it turned to follow the windings of the little river toward the pond, mademoiselle rode up beside me, and with a very pretty air indeed, half arch, half shy, wholly sweet, she said:

"I pray monsieur will not think me ungrateful. I do not forget that but for his courtesy I could not have gone to my fête."

Then she added roguishly:

"But I will make amends. I will introduce you to many St. Louis belles, the fascinating Pelagie Chouteau, Émilie Gratiot, who dances like a fairy, and Marguerite and Marie Papin, the beautiful sisters. And there are many more just as beautiful."

I bowed gravely:

"I thank you, mademoiselle. I have heard much of

5

the beauty of the St. Louis demoiselles, and have desired much to meet them. You remember it was largely for that inducement I consented to undertake the difficult task of looking after your ladyship.''

Pelagie pouted.

''Why do you persist in calling me 'your ladyship'? I am only mademoiselle.''

''Indeed!'' I said, with affected surprise: ''your manner has led me to suppose you marquise at least, if not duchesse.''

Mademoiselle reddened, but spoke very seriously and very sweetly :

''I am afraid I have very bad manners, and a very bad temper. But I intend to be good now, and to remind me I give you permission when I am haughty or disagreeable to call me comtesse.''

The sycamores and cottonwoods that bordered our path had lost more than half their leaves, and the soft haze of the late November sun filtering through flecked mademoiselle with pale gold. It touched her dark hair and turned it to burnished bronze, it brought a faint rose to the warm white of her cheek, and made little golden lights dance in the shadows of her eyes uplifted to mine. The mysterious fragrance of late autumn, of dying leaves and bare brown earth, and ripening nuts and late grapes hanging on the vines, and luscious persimmons on the leafless trees, rose like incense to my nostrils and intoxicated me. I hardly knew how I answered as I looked deep into her shadowy eyes, and I was almost glad that, our way crossing the little river by a steep path leading down to a shallow ford, I was compelled once more to take the lead.

Half-way across we stopped to let our horses dip their noses in the cool water dashing merrily over the stones. Fatima only played with it, swashing her muzzle well, and flinging the bright drops over mademoiselle's horse, who drank steadily. The opposite bank was more heavily wooded, and I became aware, as I sat idly flecking the foam from Fatima's flanks with my riding-whip, that I had for some time been hearing a whippoorwill calling and its mate replying. The woods looked dense enough to be the haunts of the lonely birds, but, nevertheless, I felt uneasy and began to listen—for rarely, indeed, does one hear a whippoorwill in the daytime. I knew birds well, and I soon became convinced that these whippoorwills were like none I had ever heard. They were too deliberate in their calls and replies, and the varying number of each sounded like a system of signals. I began to wish mademoiselle had not been so tardy in starting, that we might have had company on our way, and I strained my ears if I might hear anything of Yorke, who should be not far behind.

But there were no signs of Yorke; and mademoiselle's horse had finished drinking, and there was no excuse for our delaying longer. I would not alarm mademoiselle with my suspicions, yet I wanted my firearms ready to my hand. I drew my pistol from its holster and laid it across my saddle-bow, saying carelessly that if I caught a glimpse of that whippoorwill in the woods I should shoot it for my aunt in

Paris, who was making a collection of American birds.

Mademoiselle Pelagie accepted my explanation without comment, and I led the way up the steep bank opposite. Once up, I saw, to my satisfaction, that the path was still wide enough for two. I put mademoiselle on the side nearest La Petite Rivière, and I rode next the woods; and though mademoiselle had suddenly grown talkative, and was full of a saucy French wit, I fear I must have seemed very stupid to her, for all the while I was trying to keep up my share of repartee and quip I was listening, listening. Mademoiselle noticed at last that I was somewhat distrait.

"Why do you keep your eyes turned upon the woods, monsieur? In France we are taught that it is polite to look at a lady when she speaks."

"Pardon, mademoiselle," I stammered. "I am looking for that whippoorwill."

"Your apology is more than sufficient, monsieur," in her haughtiest tones. "There will, no doubt, be no other opportunity so suitable for adding to your aunt's collection."

I had kept my eyes fixed on the woods even while speaking to her, not daring to turn them away, but at her tone I turned quickly toward her.

"Pardon, mademoiselle la comtesse," I began saucily, but went on seriously. "Permit me, I beg, to seem rude, though it is farthest from my desire to appear so. It is more than the whim of my aunt that is at stake. Some day I will explain to you."

Even as I spoke I was startled by a sharp crackle followed by a stealthy rustle, as if some one had inadvertently stepped upon a dry twig and had then glided quickly away. I turned at once to the woods, and could almost have sworn I caught a fleeting glimpse of a copper-colored hand and the flash of a rifle-barrel. But as I gazed longer I saw nothing but the dense foliage of the low scrub-oaks that grew under the tall forest trees, and I hoped I was mistaken.

A level bit of road stretched ahead of us.

"Will you race with me, mademoiselle, to yonder tree?"

The quicker we got to Chouteau's Pond the better, I thought, and the faster we left the whippoorwills behind the better also.

"I will race you and beat you," she said gaily; "my little La Bette is fleet of foot. But what shall be the prize?"

"If I win," I said boldly, "the first dance to-day."

I thought a shadow of annoyance passed over her face, but it cleared and she answered slyly:

"And if I win, I claim the first whippoorwill you shoot; the second may go to your aunt."

"Done!" I said grimly. "Are we off?"

It was evident that fleet as La Bette might be, Fatima was far fleeter. But not for worlds would I have left mademoiselle behind; so, while seeming to urge Fatima forward, I was, in reality, giving her the constant little touch that meant a check. Still I was mindful of my prize, and when we were not more than twenty yards from the tree, and I thought we were safe, I gave Fatima the rein and passed the tree a full length ahead.

I felt a little more comfortable now, for I thought if I had really seen a redskin with a gun lurking among the bushes, we must have left him well behind, and we fell into a comfortable little jog-trot, side by side again. Suddenly I heard once more the ominous crackle of a dry twig, and turning quickly, I looked full into a pair of dark eyes peering through the bushes. I hesitated not a moment, but raising my pistol, leveled it straight at the eyes, and would have fired but that a voice called to me in good English:

"Hold, monsieur! Do not fire!"

And from behind the clump of bushes sprang a more elaborately dressed man than any I had yet seen in St. Louis. In truth, I thought him too foppishly arrayed for the woods, for there were fine ruffles at wrist and knee, and beneath his leathern doublet peeped the edges of a satin waistcoat, canary-colored. His hair was long and curled and tied with a ribbon, but it was not powdered, and over his forehead it fell in short, black curls that made his skin look very white and pink; indeed, I was not at all sure but the pink of his cheeks and the red of his lips were more of art's cunning than nature's mingling. A soft, dark mustache on his upper lip, carefully trained and curled, proved him a Parisian of the latest mode, and I at once felt an instinctive dislike and distrust of him. I had never seen him before, but I was not at all surprised when mademoiselle addressed him as Chevalier Le Moyne and paid me the compliment of presenting him to me.

There was just a little disapproval in mademoiselle's

manner, for the chevalier had certainly been caught spying, if nothing worse; and he had the grace to be embarrassed, and hastened to make his apologies in voluble French, which he seemed to take for granted I did not understand.

"I missed mademoiselle from the fête, and I sauntered out to see if there were any signs of her approach. Mademoiselle must know that it is no fête for me when the queen is away, and the day is *triste* indeed that is not lighted by her eyes. I was not sure it was mademoiselle when I heard voices, and so I looked through the bushes to see before addressing her."

"You spoke just in time," mademoiselle replied. "Monsieur took you for a whippoorwill, and a moment more," with an arch glance at me, "he might have added you to his aunt's collection."

I thought at first my lady must be heartless indeed to make a jest of a very narrow escape from death, but as I glanced at her, I saw little tongues of flame leaping in and out of her cheeks, and a great pulse beating in her throat, and I knew the light manner was only a mask.

I watched the chevalier narrowly as she spoke of the whippoorwill, and I saw him look quickly at her with a startled glance, but her evident innocence reassured him. I spoke to him in his own tongue, partly to show him I understood it very well and he must be careful what he said before me, and partly because I was not sure he understood mine. Indeed, I had many times been thankful that my French was

almost as natural to me as my English, for in this
French- and Spanish-speaking town there was almost
no one could speak my tongue. Once in a great while
(but not often) mademoiselle attempted it, either to
practise her English or out of compliment to my captain, who was not quite so fluent with his French
as I. (And when she did, her pretty broken ac-
cents made our rough language sweet as the song of
birds.)

"Monsieur was fortunate to speak so soon," I
said. "I am looking for whippoorwills, and I took
you for one. A moment more would have been too
late."

But as I spoke I looked straight into his eyes with
a meaning he could not misunderstand. His glance
fell, and a deep red slowly mounted from beneath
the artificial pink of his cheeks and spread over his
face. He recovered himself in a moment, however,
and answered me gaily:

"Thanks, monsieur, for a narrow escape. 'T is the
luck of the Le Moynes. Perhaps you know the motto
of our house?—'By hairbreadth escapes we *always
win.*'"

And this time he looked straight into my eyes, and
conveyed by his glance a haughty challenge.

I bowed a mute acceptance of it; and mademoiselle,
conscious from our manner we were not particularly
amiable toward each other, hastened to avert any
threatening unpleasantness.

"I think the chevalier will excuse us if we hasten
on. We are already late, and I fear we will keep déjeuner waiting."

"For the chevalier had certainly been caught
spying, if nothing worse"

The chevalier bowed low, with his hand on his heart, and stepped aside to allow us to pass.

It was but a five minutes' ride till we left the woodland path and the merry company of the little river and stood on the shores of Chouteau's Pond. I had not expected to find such a beautiful woodland lake, and at my exclamation of delighted surprise, mademoiselle looked pleased indeed.

"We are proud of our pond, which Mr. Auguste Chouteau has made for us," she said. "Is it not as beautiful as your Pennsylvania lakes?"

"I have never seen a more beautiful!" I ejaculated fervently, and I spoke truly.

We had drawn rein on a point of high land, and at our feet the waters of the little river, in foaming rapids and tumbling cascades, stretched up to the foot of a high dam, where the waters of the lake poured over in a silver flood. To the right, embowered in trees, were the vine-covered stone towers of Chouteau's mill, and beyond, gentle grassy slopes, with drooping trees dipping their branches in the water. To the left rose high banks with overarching foliage, and then for a mile or two the lake wound from one embowered cove to another, till it was lost in the hazy distance. Directly below us, it lay a glorious topaz in the soft November sun, for which the dark porphyry of oaks, the tawny gold of cottonwoods, and the emerald of turf and darker green of cedars made a jeweled setting richer and more harmonious than would have been the flaming scarlet and gold of our Eastern woods. On the bosom of the little lake a white sail was floating lazily, for there was but little breeze, and two or three canoes were darting swiftly from shore to shore, the dip of their paddles breaking the lake to flashing silver.

There were no other signs of life, and now mademoiselle took the lead and we followed the right shore of the lake behind the stone mill, along the shady, grassy slopes, until, after several windings, we came out on a little cove where a silvery fountain bubbled up and flowed down in a tiny rivulet to the lake. Around the fountain was soft green turf, with natural seats of rock, shaded by lofty trees, where the deep forest came down to the shores of the cove, and here we found our party of merry revelers. Horses, ponies, and oxen were all tethered deep in the forest, while young men and maidens were running to and fro, arranging tempting piles of broiled fowl, venison, and game pasties on the white cloth, spread on the green grass. A delicious odor of coffee came from a great caldron, hung over a stone fireplace on an improvised crane, and two young men were mixing, in a great bowl, a spicy compound of spring water, ratafia, sweet spices, and raspberry wine.

They hailed the arrival of mademoiselle with delight, and young Josef Papin came running up, and took hold of her horse's bridle-rein, and led her to the head of the table, where they had made a throne for the queen of the fête out of a flat rock, covered with bright-colored capotes, and wreathed with garlands of bright-leaved vines.

He claimed it his due, as giver of the feast, to sit at her right, and awarded to me, as a courtesy due her escort, the seat on her left. In the merry scramble for places that followed (there was nothing rude in it: these French folk are gentle and courteous in their gayest frolics) the chevalier was forgotten. When he came in, late (somewhat flushed, as if he might have been running when no man was looking, but debonair and smiling, with many apologies), there was no place for him near mademoiselle, and I was not sorry. Neither, I confess, did he seem to be, for he devoted himself pointedly to Mademoiselle Chouteau, as fascinating a little coquette as mademoiselle had described her.

Half-way through the meal the chevalier made an excuse for going for a cup of water to the spring, and, in passing behind mademoiselle, he stopped a moment to ask her, in a low tone, for the first dance. It was not so low but that I overheard, and I heard, too, the tone of regret with which she told him it was already promised. I might have thought the tone only a tribute to politeness had I not caught her glance, which said louder than any words, "I had much rather it were you," and I said to myself, "Either mademoiselle is a most dangerous coquette, or the chevalier has already succeeded in at least winning her interest," and for a moment it sprang to the tip of my hasty tongue to release her from her promise. But I shut my lips firmly before the words were out.

"Ce garçon-cà! The second, then?"

I turned away my head and did not willingly hear any more, but I could not quite help overhearing the chevalier once again, in a tone intended to be quite cutting, and for that reason, no doubt, more distinct:

"If mademoiselle's dances are not taken for the entire afternoon, perhaps she will be so kind as to say which one she will graciously grant me?"

I did not hear her reply; but I heard his joyful response to it:

"A thousand thanks, ma belle reine; au troisième, donc!"

I was in two minds through the rest of the meal: should I hold mademoiselle to her promise, which was, evidently, irksome to her, or should I free her from it? I resolved, finally, that the dance was fairly mine and I would hold her to it. Yet when the music sounded and the line was forming I was a little late in reaching her side, for I had been following the chevalier's example and getting my dances promised ahead, and Mademoiselle Chouteau had been so full of her little French coquetries I had found it hard to get away in time to claim mademoiselle's hand. I found her tapping her little foot impatiently, and an ominous line between her dark eyes. I made my apologies humbly, but mademoiselle was coldly scornful.

"Had I known monsieur would find it so irksome to keep his engagement I could have released him. There were others who would have appreciated the honor, since it is my duty to open the dance."

"It is inexcusable," I murmured, "but it was unavoidable"; and without waiting for further recriminations I led her to the head of the line.

I had never seen the minuet danced with more grace

and spirit. These Frenchmen have winged feet, and though I knew my steps well and had not thought myself particularly awkward, yet now it seemed to me impossible, with my great size, not to seem, to mademoiselle at least, a clumsy giant. It made me more conscious of my awkwardness that I was leading the line with mademoiselle, reine de la fête, and a perfect fairy for grace, and that, opposite us, with Mademoiselle Chouteau, was the chevalier, full of Parisian airs, which looked a little ridiculous to me, but were, no doubt, the admiration of all the maidens.

And if anything could have made me more clumsy it was the accident that befell me in the sword-figure. It fell to my lot to cross swords with the chevalier, and I cannot be sure that he did it wilfully, yet so it seemed to me. By a twist of his wrist he loosened my sword from its grasp, and it fell clattering to the ground at the very feet of my lady. Had I been expecting anything more than the usual crossing of points my grasp would have been firmer, and I really think I was not to blame. Yet I was covered with confusion, and as I stooped to pick it up, necessarily delaying the progress of my lady, who was leading her line of maidens under the arch of swords, I glanced at her face, expecting nothing less for my gaucherie than the mocking smile I had learned to dread. To my amazement, my glance was met with the sweetest of smiles, and it was the chevalier who winced this time.

"I hope monsieur will pardon the chevalier's awkwardness," she said; "he is, no doubt, more at home in a Parisian ball-room than at a rustic dance on the turf."

After that, you may be sure, I carried myself proudly, and so elated was I by her unexpected sweetness that I lost all sense of awkwardness, and I began to hear murmurs of admiration that I knew were intended for my ears, and lent wings to my feet, also.

"A handsome pair!" "What grace!" "He carries his head like a grand seigneur!" and Mademoiselle Chouteau was wicked enough, as we crossed in the dance, to look up at me and whisper saucily:

"I die with impatience, monsieur, for la troisième!"

CHAPTER VI

WHIPPOORWILLS

"Is this that haughty, gallant, gay Lothario?"

IT was in the third dance, in the middle of an intricate figure (and Mademoiselle Chouteau was proving herself a most bewitching partner), that I suddenly discovered that neither mademoiselle nor the chevalier was dancing; nor could I see them anywhere, though my glance shot rapidly into every leafy nook and corner.

An unreasoning terror seized me, and with all my might I tried to think what I could do. Should I leave my partner and fly in pursuit, as I longed to do, the figure would be broken up, and should my fears prove unfounded I could never again hold up my head among the St. Louis maidens. Yet I thought if I waited until the dance was over there would be time for the worst to happen, and I had promised not to let mademoiselle out of my sight. Now did I curse my folly (with many of my big *d*-inventions) that, since I had come to the picnic solely to look after mademoiselle, I had allowed myself to make any engagement with any other maiden, however bewitching.

In my agony of indecision, though I was still going

through the figure in a dazed fashion, great drops of perspiration started out on my brow. At that moment there came a pause in the dance, while the figure was changing, and above the babble of talk that broke forth I heard the distant call of a whippoorwill. It was enough. I bent low and whispered to my partner:

"Mademoiselle, do you think you could invent a pretext by which we could both be excused from the dance? Could you be taken suddenly ill?"

Mademoiselle Chouteau looked up at me quickly; I think for a moment she thought I wanted to get her away for a cozy flirtation in a quiet little nook, such as some of the other young couples seemed to be enjoying. But when she saw my anxious face she spoke quickly, with the prompt resource I have ever noted in young maidens:

"Certainly, monsieur! In a moment you will see me grow quite pale, and then we will go and ask Gabriel Cerré and Marguerite Papin to take our places."

She was as good as her word: in a moment she really seemed to me to turn pale, and she said, quite distinctly, so that those standing near could hear:

"I am very tired, monsieur; I will have to ask you to excuse me from dancing. Perhaps we can persuade another couple to take our places."

I think Gabriel Cerré and Mademoiselle Papin were a little loath to give up their pleasant chat, but on Mademoiselle Chouteau's representing that the dance would be broken up, and she was really not able to take another step, they very amiably consented to take our places.

Then I had to explain to Mademoiselle Chouteau, very hurriedly, the reason for my strange request, and in doing so I was compelled to confide to her somewhat of my fears, and beg her to be silent if any one should notice that I too had disappeared. She proved a good ally, and, on my expressing my perplexity as to where to look, she suddenly remembered that she had seen mademoiselle and the chevalier, as the dance was beginning, enter the woodland path that led on around the lake to Rock Spring at its head.

"A favorite resort for young people, and especially," she added slyly, "les amants."

The dance had been moving rapidly and it was not yet over; they could not be so far away but that I could overtake them, and I felt a little relieved. Yet I must see Mademoiselle Chouteau disposed of among her friends; I could not leave her discourteously, and every second of delay fretted me greatly. When that was accomplished, I caught Yorke's eye (for he had arrived very shortly after us, and having made himself generally useful at the déjeuner, was now watching the dancers with grinning delight), and motioned to him to follow me.

I slipped into the woodland path, and Yorke did not keep me waiting long. As rapidly as possible I told him my suspicions, and bade him slip into the woods where the horses were tethered and bring his own horse and Fatima by some roundabout way, so as to be unseen, and follow me on the path to the head of the lake.

6

It was a comfort to feel that Yorke would not be many minutes behind me, for impatient as I often was with his pranks and his eternal grin, I knew him to be a good fighter, and true as steel. Still more of a comfort was it to know Fatima would be within calling of my whistle, for I knew not into what I was going, and if those dark forests overhanging the cliffs on the opposite shore of the lake were as full of the treacherous savages as the frequent call of the whippoorwills had led me to think, I might find that the only road to safety for both mademoiselle and myself was on Fatima's back.

So it was with better courage (though I will not deny that my heart was beating fast) that I set off at a round pace on the woodland path toward the head of the lake. I had ever an eye for the beauties of nature, and an ear attuned to all its voices, yea, and a nostril for its sweet odors, and engrossed as I was (rushing on lest I might be too late, yet dreading every step that I fall into some ambush of whippoorwills), I still could not but note how softly the November sun fell through the half-bare branches, flecking the path with shine and shadow; how glowing cardinals and flaming orioles, not yet started south, flitted through the trees in rollicking sport; and how the sweet odor of dying leaves mingled with the soft call of woodthrushes. The cottonwoods had laid down a path of gold for me to walk upon, but, fortunately, it had rained the night before and the leaves were still damp and so did not rustle to my tread.

I had hurried on at a breathless pace, following the

path that in its turn followed the windings of the lake for nearly a mile, when suddenly I heard voices at no great distance ahead of me. I stopped for a moment, my heart beating so fast I could scarce listen. Yes, it was a man's voice and a maiden's, speaking in low tones as if for each other's ears alone, and I did not doubt it was mademoiselle and the chevalier.

Now it was most distasteful to me to think of playing eavesdropper, and I was of half a mind to stop where I was and wait until they had finished what they had to say and were ready to return. I would at least be near enough at hand to prevent a capture should it be attempted. But as I waited, mademoiselle's voice was suddenly raised, and I heard her say in a tone of pain:

"Do not make me distrust my guardian! I can believe no wrong of him! He has been the only father I have known."

I caught nothing of the chevalier's reply but the two words "interested motives"; but I thought, since it was evidently no tender interchange of sentiment to which I would have to listen, but the rascal was maligning my good friend Dr. Saugrain, it was my duty to listen with all my ears. I crept forward softly, fearing lest a crackling twig or a dry leaf might betray my presence, and fearing, too, since I could not discover whence the voices came, that I might come upon them unawares and so reveal myself.

Which I came very near doing. Another step, and I would have stepped over the brink of a low bluff which encircled a cup-like depression. A cluster of tall oaks rose from the center of the little glen thus formed, sheltering a silvery fountain gushing from a great rock and then, in a bright rivulet, dancing merrily over moss and stones to the lake.

This, then, was Rock Spring, and the source of Chouteau's Pond! A sylvan retreat indeed for lovers, and I had heard it was much frequented by them. A fringe of crimson sumac-bushes screened the edge of the bluff and effectually screened me from two people just below me. I liked not to be spying, but I felt that duty and honor both, and my pledged word to the doctor, demanded that I keep mademoiselle in sight. So I cautiously leaned forward and looked.

Mademoiselle was seated on a boulder with her face turned toward me and uplifted to the chevalier, who was standing with his back to me, looking down on her. Her dark eyes were wide and startled, full of surprise and pain; I was not sure but there were tears in them. Her straight brows were drawn together in a deep furrow, and the scarlet lips, usually so like a Cupid's bow, were set and stern. I wondered what the chevalier could be saying in that low voice of his to move her so deeply. As he finished, mademoiselle sprang to her feet, generous indignation in her flashing eyes and ringing tones.

"I can never believe it! Either I have no such prospects, or he has some good reason for not telling me yet. I will never doubt his truth and honesty!"

Then I heard the chevalier's reply, low and distinct:

"Mademoiselle, your friends in France doubt both

the friends of your father and mother. They have sent me here to find you and bring you back with me to your rich estates, to your rank and position, and to the friends who love you. But they know well Dr. Saugrain will never let go his hold on you, until he can get control of your property himself, and so they have instructed me to use all caution and secrecy.

"In the woods yonder, on the other side of the lake, is a trusty escort to ride to Cape Girardeau, where a boat is waiting to take you to New Orleans. In New Orleans is a ship ready to sail the moment mademoiselle puts her foot upon its deck, and in a little more than a month you will be in Paris, among friends who will receive you with outstretched arms, surrounded by every luxury, living the life of grande dame as you ought to live, among the great nobles where you rightfully belong, and not in this rude, rough country among Indians and boors. And mademoiselle will permit me to add, there is no great lady in France so fitted by nature to adorn her high station as she. She will have all Paris at her feet. Come with me now, mademoiselle! There is no time to be lost! Any moment we may be interrupted and it may be too late."

My eyes did not leave mademoiselle's face through all this long speech, and I saw her expression slowly change. The generous indignation was still there, but I saw that the picture that he presented of the life that awaited her in Paris began to fascinate her. She spoke slowly and doubtfully:

"I will tell Dr. and Madame Saugrain all you have

told me, and if it is right, they will let me go with you. I will not doubt my friends.''

The villain saw that he was gaining ground:

''They are not your friends! They are your bitterest foes. They are keeping you from everything that will make your life grand and beautiful, with the hope of their own gain some day. They will never let you go! If home and Paris and friends and wealth and rank and power are to be won at all, it must be at once. Five minutes more may be too late. That boy [with infinite scorn] may have discovered your absence and come to seek you.''

Suddenly the chevalier dropped on one knee, his hand on his heart. I turned quickly away (for I would not listen to what I feared would be a declaration of love), and, as I turned, I saw Yorke coming up the path, leading the two horses, who were picking their way as cautiously as if they knew the occasion demanded the utmost secrecy. I motioned to Yorke to leave the horses where they were (I knew they were so trained they would stand perfectly still without tying) and to come silently to me. I felt that the moment of rescue could not be far distant.

He had crept cautiously up just as the chevalier ceased speaking. I was intent on noting the position of the horses and forming a plan of rescue, and so did not observe Yorke, or I might have prevented what followed. He had stolen up softly behind me, and, unconscious that he was on the edge of a bluff, had stepped a step beyond me. Of course he went over at once, heels over head, turning a complete somersault, and alighted erect, astride the neck of the kneeling chevalier.

At his terrified cry I turned quickly, just in time to see him alight; and if it had been a time for laughing it would have been a funny sight indeed: the look of startled terror on mademoiselle's face gradually changing in spite of herself to one of convulsive merriment; the chevalier, his nose ground in the dust, squirming helplessly and sputtering vigorously in French; and, lastly, the big black, the white balls of his eyes almost starting from his head in amazement and fright, and a ceaseless torrent of ejaculations pouring through his white teeth!

"Oh! Oh, Lordy! Oh, my gracious! Oh, de good Lord! Oh, massy!"

Yet he made no effort to rise, and I began to suspect he was enjoying the situation, for the more vigorously the Frenchman sputtered the louder the negro bellowed.

It was time for me to interpose, but I wished to avoid the appearance of having been spying on them, with Yorke, from above, otherwise I could easily have leaped down the low bluff. Looking around hastily, I discovered, what I had not noted before, that the main path led around the foot of the bluff into the little glen from below. I had followed a branch of it in coming to the top of the bluff. I ran quickly down to the lower entrance of the glen, but there I stopped a moment to assume an air as of one leisurely strolling. I did not pretend to see the group until I was well into the glen where I could also be seen. Then I struck an attitude of intense surprise for mademoiselle's benefit (who by this time had caught sight of me), and when I had sufficiently recovered from the surprise for utterance, I spoke to Yorke in tones of stern command:

"What are you doing, sir, on monsieur's back? Have you taken him for a horse? Or a donkey? Off, sir, this moment, and make your humble apologies to the chevalier."

Yorke was not much afraid of my stern tone. Still yelling bloody murder, he contrived a most audacious wink with the eye next to me, but he tumbled off slowly, and then I hastened to help the chevalier to his feet. He was a sorry spectacle, and I saw mademoiselle's look of suppressed amusement change to pity and concern. Blood was gushing from his nose all over his fine clothes, and his face was so begrimed and gory it would have been impossible to guess it was the dapper Parisian.

But he was in such a blind rage that for once he ignored his clothes. Stanching the blood as best he could with his flimsy lace handkerchief, he poured out a torrent of abuse in mingled French and English, on Yorke and on me, but principally on me. I tried to interpose a polite word of regret, but he would not listen to me.

"You air a sneak, a cowaird, sir! You spy on mademoiselle and me! Cowair-r-r-d! I will have the satisfaction! Sacré Dieu! You have no doubt told the negro to leap upon my back! I will have r-r-r-evenge!"

And as if reminded by that last word, he turned to mademoiselle and spoke in French:

"Fly with me at once, mademoiselle! You will not stay to be at the mercy of a sneaking spy. See! I will call my red friends. Do not be afraid! They will carry you off, but I will be with you, and we will find horses and fly."

And without waiting for an answer he turned and imitated three times the call of a whippoorwill.

I knew what that meant—that in a moment the Osages would be upon us; and hardly had his first call left his lips before I too had turned and uttered the shrill whistle that always brought Fatima to my side.

As I knew, the last whippoorwill call had not died away when from the woods on the opposite side of the lake, silently, swiftly stole first one dark figure and then another, until at least a dozen savages, armed and painted, were bearing down upon us with the fleetness of deer. In a moment more they would be upon us, and neither Yorke's life nor mine would be worth the asking, and, what was far harder to contemplate, mademoiselle would be captive in their hands.

She stood for a moment petrified with horror at the sight of the swiftly advancing savages, and then she turned to me in an agony of entreaty.

"Oh, fly, fly at once!" she said, "you and your black man, before it is too late."

I turned to Yorke:

"Go as mademoiselle bids you; get your horse and fly."

Yorke tried to remonstrate, but I would not let him open his lips.

"No; you will only hinder me now. If worse comes

to worst, you can at least bear the news. Go at once!"
And without waiting for further orders, Yorke
turned, scrambled up the face of the bluff, and was
off.

"But you will go, too!" she cried, as I turned again
to her.

"And leave you?"

"Oh, do not mind me! They will not hurt me!"
And then, as I stood perfectly still, with my pistols
ready, but with no intention of leaving her to the
tender mercies of the savages and the savage mercies
of the chevalier, she grew desperate, grasping my arm
and trying with her feeble strength to push me toward safety.

"I implore you," she entreated, "if you have any
feeling of friendship for me, fly before it is too late!"

"Mademoiselle," I said, "I stir not one step from
this spot unless you go with me."

"I will but hinder you," she cried, "and prevent
all possibility of escape. Oh, do not stay for me!"

"Mademoiselle," said the chevalier, who had been
enjoying this scene, with no attempt at concealing his
relish for it, "go with monsieur, since he desires it."

Even as he spoke, the first of the Osages darted into
the glen; the others were close at his heels; but at the
same moment from the entrance of the glen nearer to
us came the thunder of hoofs, and Fatima was at my
side, her eyes flashing, her hoofs pawing the earth, her
nostrils snorting with rage: for well she guessed that
painted savages meant danger to her master.

I was on her back in a moment, and, stooping, lifted
mademoiselle swiftly to the crupper in front of me.

Holding her there with my left arm, I wheeled Fatima with the one word of command, "Go!" and turning my head as she flew over the rough earth, I leveled my pistol at the chevalier.

"Do not stir, monsieur, at the peril of your life!" I called to him, and kept him covered as we flew. I knew the savages were running to try to head me off, but I paid no attention to them until, rounding a great boulder, the chevalier (his face ghastly with rage and disappointed revenge, for so sudden had it all been he had had no time even to draw his pistol to prevent the rescue until too late) was out of my range, as we were out of his. Then, turning my pistol swiftly on the Osage in the lead,—none too soon, for his rifle was leveled at us,—I fired. The poor fellow fell forward with a wild yell that turned my heart sick; yet none the less, the others rushing on with their wild whoops to avenge him, I drew my second pistol and fired once more.

But I knew not with what result, for mademoiselle, with a convulsive shudder and a look of mortal woe, cried out:

"You have killed the chevalier!"

"No, mademoiselle," I answered grimly; "I have killed the poor whippoorwill you asked me for"; and then had all I could do without paying any more attention to the savages, for mademoiselle had fainted and lay like one dead on my arm, her white face upturned to mine, her long black lashes sweeping the marble cheeks, and the dark curls falling backward from the white brow and floating on the wind, as Fatima flashed along the woodland path like a swallow on the wing.

CHAPTER VII

I TWINE CHRISTMAS GREENS

" Woman 's at best a contradiction still."

YORKE had reached the picnic-ground just long enough ahead of us to create pandemonium. He had reported both mademoiselle and me as killed and scalped by this time, and a band of a hundred savages, with the chevalier at their head, on their way to the picnic.

The massacre of 1780 was still fresh enough in the memory of St. Louis folk to make this seem no improbable tale, and the utmost confusion ensued. Some of the young men, with Josef Papin and Gabriel Cerré at their head, were for going at once to our rescue; but the maidens implored, and Yorke averred it was too late, and reported the savages in such numbers as would make such an undertaking only foolhardy. (And by this you must not judge Yorke a villain and a coward; he would have been the first to volunteer and the loudest to urge on the others, but he had heard Fatima's hoofs behind him, and knew we were safe, and, rascal that he was, could not resist his practical joke nor his negro love of producing a great effect.)

Into this wild pandemonium of women screaming

unintelligible cries to each other as they hastily got together their belongings and packed them into charrettes and saddle-bags, amid sobbings and wailings, and men shouting hoarsely to mustang and pony as they struggled with bit and bridle, mademoiselle and I rode; and their joy at seeing us alive, and our hair still on our heads, knew no bounds.

I told them the true state of the case—that there were not more than a dozen or twenty of the savages at the most, and I hardly thought the chevalier would bring them down upon us. Yet, knowing that he might be in a mood for risking everything to recapture mademoiselle, I recommended that the men form themselves into two bands to ride in the front and in the rear, with the maidens between the two, and to start at once. We could go no faster, of course, than the charrettes could go, and the savages could easily overtake us if they desired; but I did not believe they would dare, for our numbers were greater than theirs, and the young men were all well armed.

Mademoiselle had recovered from her fainting, but was still white and weak. And because I did not believe she was able to sit La Bette, I recommended that she ride in Josef Papin's charrette with Mademoiselle Chouteau and let Josef ride her horse. We two, young Papin and I, brought up the rear; and I did not see mademoiselle again except once, for a moment, when we were crossing La Petite Rivière, and I rode up by her side to see that the charrette went steadily through the water. Her head was on Mademoiselle Chouteau's shoulder, who was supporting her with her arm. Her eyes were closed, and Mademoiselle Chouteau whispered to me, "She is asleep!" but at that she opened her eyes quickly and looked up at me. She tried to smile, but I think the terror of it all was still strongly with her. She said:

"I have not thanked you, monsieur.; but I know I owe you my liberty, if not my life, and I am not ungrateful."

It was very sweetly said, but there was a horrible fear at my heart that she would rather have been captured by the redskins, and gone away with the Chevalier Le Moyne, than to have been rescued by me.

Just at the stockade we met a party of horsemen. Dr. Saugrain and my captain were in the lead with Black Hawk, who had reported Red Jean with a band of Osages lurking in the woods, and they were on their way to clear them out, lest they molest the picnic or the village. Amid a babble of excitement, every one trying to talk at once, our tale was told. And as Dr. Saugrain and my captain thought it was best to go on and try to capture the chevalier and his band, and as our escort was no longer needed for the maidens, I turned my horse and rode back with them to find the chevalier.

I confess it would have done me good to bring him in a captive, but I was doomed to disappointment. We scoured the woods, and the only traces we found of him and his band were the prints of horses' hoofs going south,—a dozen horses, I should think,—and, just where Rock Spring bubbles up in a silver fountain, a torn and bloody lace handkerchief. I gave the good doctor a full account of the conversation I had listened to, and he ground his teeth with rage at the chevalier's duplicity. He was much touched at Pelagie's chivalrous defense of him; yet, as delicately as I could, I tried to tell him that at the very last I feared the chevalier had succeeded in insinuating some seeds of doubt and suspicion in mademoiselle's mind. The doctor and my captain both agreed that it was time to tell Pelagie the full truth of the matter. She should know all about herself and her expectations, and who were her friends and who her foes.

I was curious to see what effect the revelation would have upon her; or it could hardly be called a revelation, since the chevalier had already revealed it— rather the confirmation of his tale. But in that, too, I was doomed to disappointment. She was ill for several days and confined to her room,—the effect of the excitement she had passed through,—and before she was well enough to be about again, my captain and I had set off, with Black Hawk as guide and Yorke as factotum, to make a visit to Daniel Boone at his home on the Missouri River.

We found the grand old man as happy as a child in the beautiful home he had at last made for himself and his family at the very outposts of civilization. We were gone four weeks, exploring the woods and mountains and rolling prairies of the beautiful country, and coming home on a great flatboat down the swiftly rolling Missouri, past Fort Bellefontaine, where the Missouri empties into the Mississippi (where we were royally entertained by the Spanish comman-

dant), and so at last by the Mississippi back to St.
Louis.

I found myself trembling with a mingling of fearful and pleasant anticipations as I rode up the steep
bluff on Fatima's back, and we took the Rue de
l'Église to Dr. Saugrain's house.

It was the day before Christmas, and I had not remembered it; but as we passed the church in the rear
of Auguste Chouteau's place, through the open doors
we could see young men and maidens winding
long garlands of Christmas greens and festooning
them over doors and windows, while shouts of merry
laughter floated out to us. I was for drawing rein
and going in to help with the trimming; but my captain (who, I believe, was shy of the maidens) insisted
we must first pay our respects to our host.

The little doctor met us at the gate with a beaming
face, and when Narcisse and Yorke had led away our
horses we entered once more the long, low room we had
first entered nearly two months before. The windows
were no longer open, looking out into cool green foliage, with white muslin curtains stirring in the
breeze, and there was no maiden in a white robe, with
the blue ribbon of a guitar across her shoulders, singing creole love-songs. Instead, crimson damask curtains were falling over the white ones, and a great fire
of logs was blazing in one end of the room, looking
cozy and cheery enough on this crisp December day.

Yet, in spite of its coziness, I thought it had a dreary
look. Leon was lying before the fire, and though he
looked at me a little doubtfully, as he slowly rose and

shook himself, I felt a rush of friendliness toward
him, and showed it so plainly, as I called him to me,
that at last he capitulated, and we have ever since been
the best of friends.

Then Madame Saugrain came running in, flushed
and rosy from the kitchen, where she had been super-
intending the baking of Christmas tarts and croquecignolles, and bringing with her appetizing whiffs of
roasting and frying. My captain laughingly told her
that the good smells made him hungry.

"You shall come and see," she said; and led us into
the great kitchen, where, on tables as white as snow,
were piled heaps of golden-brown croquecignolles, cut
in curious patterns, and the big black cook was drop-
ing still more into the kettle of boiling fat, and bringing out puffy and wondrously shaped birds and beasts.
Narcisse, on his knees on the hearth, was turning two
great fowls suspended before the fire, from which
oozed such rich and savory gravy as made one smack
his lips. On another table a huge venison pasty and
tarts and cakes of many kinds were temptingly arrayed, and madame's pride in her housewifely preparations for the Christmas feasting was pretty to see.
She would have us taste her croquecignolles and little
cakes, and had a glass of gooseberry wine brought out
of the store-room for each of us, and we drank it
standing in the kitchen, and helping ourselves from
the pile of croquecignolles.

But kind and charming as was madame, and toothsome as were her cakes, and much as her gooseberry
wine tickled our palates, I was yet on nettles to be

7

gone and join the young people at the church.
Whether madame guessed it or whether it was just
one of her kindly thoughts, she said in her motherly
way:

"But, my son, you should be at the church. The
maidens will be vexed with me if I keep you talking to
an old woman, when they might be having your help
with the wreaths."

"If you think they need me?" and I tried to look as
if only a stern sense of duty could induce me to go.

Madame Saugrain laughed, with the merry twinkle
in her eye that made her as captivating as a young
maiden.

"Allons donc!" she said. "Quel garçon!" And
with my best bow to her and a salute to my captain
and the good doctor, I whistled to Leon to accompany
me and strode quickly down the road toward the little
church.

But as I neared it I slackened my pace, and but for
very shame I would have turned and fled again to the
shelter of madame's motherly smile. I had not seen
Mademoiselle Pelagie since the day of the picnic, and
I was much in doubt whether she regarded me as her
rescuer to be esteemed with grateful and friendly feeling, or as the cause of the loss of a dear friend, perhaps
a lover. I felt very sure I would be able to tell at our
first meeting in which light I was held, and, screwing
up all my courage, I made a bold dash for the church
door.

Scarcely had my shadow darkened the doorway
when I was surrounded by an eager group, saluting

me with every form of friendly welcome back to St. Louis; but the face I looked for was not among them. Mademoiselle Chouteau and Mademoiselle Papin seized me, one by either arm, and led me to a great pile of greens, and would have set me at once to work in tying them to long ropes. But I begged them to permit me first to pay my respects to the rest of my friends; for over in a dark corner I had seen Pelagie at work, with two or three young men around her, supplying her with greens for her nimble fingers to weave into garlands, and she had not come with the others to greet me. I thought at least that little courtesy was due me, for, whether she liked or resented my rescuing her, I had risked much in the doing of it.

I was filled with bitterness toward her, but could have no more kept away from her than the moth from the flame. My bitterness now gave me courage, and I sauntered up to her with what I flattered myself was quite as grand an air as the chevalier's might have been. Hand on the hilt of my sword, hat doffed, with its plume sweeping the ground, I bowed low.

"If mademoiselle has not forgotten an old acquaintance, will she permit me respectfully to salute her?"

She had been seated on a low seat with the side of her face toward me, and may or may not have been aware of my approach. As I spoke, she rose quickly and turned toward me, the rich blood rushing over her face and neck for a minute, and receding and leaving her almost as white as when I had held her in my arms and she had thought the chevalier killed.

She did not speak, but she held out her hand, and I

bowed low over it, and barely touched it with my lips.
The young men (among whom was of course Josef
Papin) crowded around me with friendly greetings,
and for a few minutes we talked fast, they asking and
I answering many questions about Daniel Boone and
our adventures in the far West.

I did not look at mademoiselle as we talked, but—it
is a way I have—I saw her all the time. I think it must
be because I am so much taller than most people that
I can see all that goes on around me (or, perhaps
more truly, beneath me) without seeming to look. I
saw mademoiselle regard me with a strange glance, as
if she were looking at some one she did not know, and
was trying to explain him to herself. Then she sat
down and quietly went on with her work, her head
bent, and not looking at me again.

I talked on for a few minutes, and then turned to
make my adieus to mademoiselle. She looked up at
me with a friendly smile and I saw, what I had not
noticed before, that she was paler and thinner than
when I had seen her last, and there was a look in her
dark eyes as of hidden trouble.

"Will you not stay and help us, monsieur?" she
said in that voice which, from the first time I had
heard it, had always seemed to me the sweetest in the
world. Of course it set my silly pulses to beating
faster, but I answered steadily and with an air of cold
courtesy:

"I regret that I cannot accept mademoiselle's invitation; I have promised my services elsewhere"; and
with another low bow I turned on my heel and, hold-

ing my head high, went back to weave garlands with Mademoiselle Chouteau and Marguerite Papin.

And because I was so big and they were so petite, they delighted in ordering me around (and I delighted in obeying), and they made me mount to the highest beams to suspend garlands, and applauded me when I arranged them to suit their fancy, and laughed at me or scolded me when I was awkward and stupid, until my back ached and my heart grew light; for I forgot for a time that mademoiselle, for whom I had risked my life, had not even cared to give me a friendly welcome back to St. Louis.

The last garland was fastened in its place, the last stray bit of evergreen and rubbish swept from the doors, the church garnished and beautiful to behold. There was the noisy bustle of preparing for departure and the calling back and forth:

"Be sure you are at midnight mass, Gabriel."

"Au revoir at midnight mass, Pelagie."

"I will see you at midnight mass, monsieur."

And for me there was a moment of embarrassment. Was it my duty to offer myself as escort to any of the maidens? For though the hour was early it was already dark. Or, since I was going direct to mademoiselle's house, would I be expected to accompany her? I glanced over to her corner; she had already left the church. I looked through the open doorway; she was walking down the Rue de l'Église with Josef Papin.

"Mademoiselle Chouteau," I said, "may I have the pleasure of walking home with you?"

But all the way up the Rue de l'Église and down the steep incline of the Rue Bonhomme, and up the Rue Royale to the great barred gate that led into the stone-walled inclosure of Pierre Chouteau, while Mademoiselle Chouteau, with her nimble tongue, was flitting from one bit of village gossip to another, like a butterfly among the flowers, I was saying bitterly to myself:

"And she had even the discourtesy to walk away without waiting to see whether the guest of her house was going home or not."

It was a long mile and a half from Pierre Chouteau's house to Dr. Saugrain's, and it was a frosty December evening. It was only five o'clock, but the stars were out, and through the leafless trees I could see lights twinkling from the houses as I passed. Faster and faster I walked, as my thoughts grew more and more bitter toward mademoiselle, and by the time I had reached the cheery living-room, with its blazing lightwood fire, I was in such a glow from exercise and indignation as made the fire all unwelcome.

I had quite made up my mind, on my long walk, that mademoiselle should find me as cool as herself; and through the evening meal I scarce looked at her. But if I had fancied mademoiselle suffering from some secret trouble, I changed my mind at supper. She sat between my captain and her guardian, and was in such merry mood that she had my captain alternately laughing uproariously at her wit, and making fine speeches about her beauty, in a fashion that quite amazed me, for I had ever considered him a sober-minded fellow, above all such light ways.

Nor did she refrain from a slight stab at me whenever it was possible to get it in. I took no more notice of these than I could help, yet I felt my cheeks, already burning from my frosty walk, grow hotter and hotter, until the very tips of my ears were on fire; and I felt it the unkindest cut of all when she said, with her pretty accent and air of polite condescension to a very young boy:

" 'T is a long walk from Mademoiselle Chouteau's, monsieur, but it has given you une grande couleur. What would not our St. Louis belles give for such roses! "

I turned toward her just long enough to say gravely, "I thank you, mademoiselle," and then renewed at once my conversation with madame. But I could see from the tail of my eye that she had the grace to blush also, and to be ashamed of her petty persecutions, for she left me to myself the remainder of the meal.

CHAPTER VIII

"Tender-handed stroke a nettle,
    And it stings you for your pains;
Grasp it like a man of mettle,
    And it soft as silk remains."

IN our room, making ready for midnight mass,
which all the family, including guests, were expected to attend, my captain told me what Dr. Saugrain had said to him about mademoiselle. He had
told her fully her history and expectations (save only
her exact rank and title, which he had thought best
still to withhold from her), and the plans of her
friends for her future. He had also told her very
plainly that he had suspected the chevalier of just
such an attempt at her capture as he had made, and
for that reason had been so unwilling that she should
go to Chouteau's Pond.

Mademoiselle had listened, and had asked him many
questions, and had at last said that she could not
doubt the truth of her guardian, but she thought it
possible the chevalier was honest also, and misjudged
Dr. Saugrain because he did not know him. The
doctor had tried to convince her of the chevalier's duplicity, and showed her the letter of warning from

France concerning him; but the doctor was not sure that mademoiselle was convinced, and he had determined, as soon as safe convoy could be found, to send her to her friends in Paris.

In the meantime mademoiselle did not seem happy, and the good doctor was much puzzled to know whether it was, as he hoped, regret at leaving his wife and himself, who had been father and mother to her, or, as he feared, a secret regret for the chevalier, and a lurking doubt of the Saugrains.

And now all my bitterness toward mademoiselle had suddenly vanished. I seemed to understand fully the state of mind the poor girl was in, and there was no room in my heart for anything but a great pity for her. The remembrance of her face as I had seen it when the chevalier was talking to her, the generous indignation changing to doubt, and then the gradual kindling of a desire for the life depicted to her by the chevalier (and, perhaps, a touch of a softer emotion for the chevalier himself),—it was like reading an open book, and I said to myself:

"Mademoiselle is torn by conflicting emotions: her love for her friends here whom she is to leave, and longing for the life in Paris which may soon be hers, and, perhaps, love for the chevalier, whom she feels she ought to despise. What does it matter if she sometimes vents her irritation with herself upon me, whom she regards as but a boy? I shall not resent it; but if I find a chance I will try to let her know I understand."

But I had no chance on the way to mass. Madame

Saugrain seemed to take it for granted that Captain Clarke and the doctor would walk with mademoiselle, and I was her peculiar property; and I suppose I had given her the right to think so by always pointedly devoting myself to her.

It was a solemn service at that midnight hour: the bare little church made beautiful with our garlands of green, and the twinkle of many candles around the altar; the heads bowed in prayer; the subdued murmur of voices making the responses; the swelling note of triumph in the Gregorian chant; and then coming out under the quiet stars and exchanging greetings with friend and neighbor.

And last of all the quiet walk home, and, to my surprise, I was walking by mademoiselle's side. I was surprised, for it was not of my arranging, and it set my blood to leaping to think it was possibly of hers. I made up my mind that no word of mine should mar the friendliness of the act, and I plunged quickly into a lively discussion of the ball that was to take place at Madame Chouteau's on Christmas evening. But she interrupted me almost in the beginning, and, as was her habit when she talked with me, she spoke in French. It was only rarely she tried her English, though, when she did, it was with such a witching grace I could have wished it oftener.

"Monsieur," she said, "I have been so unmaidenly as to inflict my company upon you for the walk home when you had not solicited it, but I had a reason for so doing. I hope," as if a sudden thought had struck her, "I have not interfered with other plans. Had you desired to escort some one else home?"

"Certainly not," I said coolly, for I was unaccountably irritated by the suggestion. "And I did not solicit the honor of being your escort only because I had reason to suppose it would not be agreeable to you."

"It was for that I am here without an invitation," she answered quickly. "I have many times given you occasion to think me entirely without manners. I have often been very rude to you. I wish to ask your pardon for my silly speeches at the table, and for all my unamiability, and to assure you I have not forgotten your great services to me, and I am not ungrateful. It is because I have naturally a very bad temper; and now I believe I am not quite well, I am so irritable of late."

Several times I had tried to interrupt her; I could not bear to have her humiliate herself to me (for I was sure it must be a humiliation to one of her haughty temper). But she would not listen to my interruptions; she went steadily on with a voice so low and sweet and sad it quite unmanned me.

Yet because I thought her voice trembled, and in the moonlight (for the late moon was now well up in the sky) I was sure I saw something bright glistening on her long lashes, and because my heart was torn for her, and I was seized with a horrible fear that she might weep, and I would not know what to do—for all these reasons I spoke quickly and lightly :

"Mademoiselle, you have the temper of an angel, and if sometimes you lose it, I fear it is because only an angel with wings could be patient with a blundering giant like me."

"You are no blunderer, monsieur," she said

gravely; "and if you are a giant, you are one of the good kind who use their strength and their courage in rescuing distressed damsels. I hope they will not all requite you as badly as I have done."

"Mademoiselle,"—I spoke as gravely as she had spoken,—"I hope you will not let the remembrance of any service I have been able to render you prove a burden to you. I would risk much more in your service, if the occasion offered, than I risked then, and find my delight in so doing." And then I added: "I wish you would promise me that if you should ever need such service again—if you are ever in peril of any kind, and I am in reach—that you will call on me."

Mademoiselle hesitated a moment before she replied:

"You are heaping coals of fire on my head, monsieur; you are far kinder to me than I deserve, but—I promise."

"Thank you, mademoiselle; you have given me my reward, and if you were ever unamiable to me, you have fully atoned. Sometimes I think, mademoiselle," I went on, inwardly trembling but determined, "that you did not esteem it so great a service that I rendered you—that perhaps you had rather not have been rescued. Am I wrong?"

I was looking down on her and watching her narrowly as I spoke. I could see, even by the uncertain light of the moon, that she went suddenly white, and there was a perceptible pause before she spoke.

"I hardly think, monsieur, that you have any right

to ask me such a question, but I am going to answer your question by another." And slowly the color crept back into her face, and grew brighter and brighter, but she went steadily on. "Did you overhear what the Chevalier Le Moyne was saying to me in the glen?"

It was my time to wince. Must I confess to eavesdropping? It was hard enough to do that under any circumstances—but she might think I had listened too to the chevalier's wooing; it seemed to me I could not so outrage her sense of delicacy as to let her think that. I had been reared to revere the truth, but for once I thought it not wrong to chip a little from its sharp edge.

"Mademoiselle," I said, "I will confess to you. I missed you and the chevalier from the dance. I had been warned that the chevalier might attempt to carry you off, and I had given my word not to let you out of my sight. Of course I went at once in search of you, and because I believed the whippoorwills we had heard in the woods to be signal of savages, I bade Yorke follow me with the horses. I heard voices, and in following them came to the top of the bluff encircling the glen. I would scorn to be an eavesdropper under ordinary circumstances, but a chance word caught my ear, and when I found the chevalier was not pleading a lover's cause, but maligning my friend Dr. Saugrain to the maiden he loves as his own daughter, I felt it my duty to listen. Your rejection with scorn of the chevalier's base insinuation against Dr. Saugrain delighted my heart, but when I found

that he was continuing with devilish ingenuity to seek
to undermine your faith in your guardian, I concluded
it was time for me to interfere. I told Yorke to be
ready with the horses, and myself went down to the
entrance of the glen, intending to interrupt the chevalier, and use my pledge to your guardian as authority
for requesting your return. Imagine my astonishment to find Yorke, whom I had left in charge of the
horses, astride the chevalier's neck! What followed
you know, and now you know what I heard and why
I listened. Was it wrong?''

Mademoiselle was silent for a minute. I think she
was not quite sure that I had not heard more than I
confessed to, but she was willing to hope I had not.

''Monsieur,'' she said, ''you were no doubt justified
in listening, if one can ever be justified in listening to
what is not intended for his ears. But you have used
some harsh expressions concerning the chevalier, and
I think it is possible you wrong him, even as he
wronged my guardian. I do not for one moment believe that my guardian has had any but the best of
motives in keeping from me all knowledge of my rank
and wealth; but I might still be ignorant of it, and I
know not for how much longer, if the chevalier had
not revealed it to me. Dr. Saugrain corroborated all
that he has said. He only refuses to believe that the
chevalier was sent by my friends to take me back to
Paris. He accuses him of being in a plot to get possession of my person and of my wealth. Yet that is
exactly the accusation made by the chevalier against
Dr. Saugrain. Dr. Saugrain admits that all the

chevalier said about my present rank and future prospects is true. Why should not the rest be true—that he had been sent by my friends to bring me back to Paris? Can you not see that he does not necessarily seem to me so black as he does to you and my guardian? And it seems a hard thing to me that he should be a refugee among savages, leaving a blackened reputation behind him (for there is no one in St. Louis who does not vilify him), when he was actuated by most chivalrous motives, however mistaken they might be; for he thought he was rescuing a wronged maiden from those who had unlawful possession of her, and restoring her to her friends. I cannot but feel shame and regret that I should have caused the chevalier so great a journey, at such cost of money and fatigue, in vain, and that he may be even now suffering all kinds of exposure from wild savages, if not in peril of his life.''

Now here was the opportunity I had desired to assure her of my sympathy, and tell her that I understood the difficulties in which she was placed; but my tongue clove to the roof of my mouth. When I thought of that villain (for whatever mademoiselle might think, I never for a moment doubted his villainy) my blood boiled, and, instead, I blurted out roughly:

"Mademoiselle, 't is incomprehensible to me how you can for one moment give the word of such a man as the chevalier, whom you have known so short a time, equal credence with the word of such a man as Dr. Saugrain, thorough Christian gentleman in every

fiber of his being, and your lifelong friend and bene-
factor, your more than father.''

But I had spoken beyond my right. Mademoiselle
turned on me with cold fury:

"Monsieur, I have not sought this interview that
you should teach me my duty to my guardian, nor
criticize my attitude toward the chevalier. I am sorry
we have allowed the others to get so far ahead of us,
but if we hasten we may overtake them and I will relieve you from further attendance.'' Whereupon she
started ahead at a round pace.

"Mademoiselle!'' I called to her, "I entreat you to
listen to me for a moment.''

Mademoiselle stopped and turned toward me, and
we stood facing each other in the middle of the road,
alone in the white moonlight, for the others were quite
out of sight around a bend in the road, and there were
no houses near. Below us lay the Mississippi, a white
flood in the moonlight, and far across the river the
twinkling lights of Cahokia, one of them, no doubt, in
Mr. Gratiot's house, where I had first seen mademoiselle. Her eyes were flashing scorn at me now, as they
flashed at me when she knelt with her arms around the
great shaggy brute, and, looking up in my face, called
me "Bête!'' There was no doubt about it, mademoiselle could be a little fury at times, and no
doubt she would have liked to call me once more,
"Bête!''

"Mademoiselle,'' I said, "I am so unhappy as to be
always offending you. From the moment when I
made my descent of Mr. Gratiot's staircase on the

back of your dog, to the present moment, I seem to have been able to make myself only ridiculous or offensive to you! I beg you to believe that it is a matter of the deepest regret to me that this should be so, and to believe that to offend you is ever farthest from my desire. I realize that I was over-zealous for Dr. Saugrain, whom I greatly admire and love, and that you certainly had never given me any right to take such interest in you and your affairs as I just now displayed. I beg you to believe that I shall never again offend in like manner, mademoiselle la comtesse.''

I saw her face slowly change from its expression of scorn to that same wondering look I had noticed in the church, as if she were regarding some one she did not know and was trying to understand. As I uttered the last words, ''mademoiselle la comtesse,'' another and a swift change came over her. Her eyes fell, her head drooped. Still standing there in the moonlight, she suddenly buried her face in her hands and sobs shook her slender figure.

''Mademoiselle, mademoiselle!'' I cried. ''I beg, I implore, you to forgive me. I am, indeed, a brute!'' And as she continued to sob drearily, I was beside myself. What could I do? She looked so like a little child, and I was so big, to have hurt her seemed cruel and shameful. I was in a state of desperation. I begged her and implored her not to weep; but it seemed to me she only sobbed the harder. What did one do, I wondered, with a weeping maiden? Had it only been a child I would have known, for I had ever

8

a way with children; but before a weeping maiden I was helpless.

And still mademoiselle sobbed on, her sobs coming faster and harder, until, in a paroxysm of grief (or I know not what), she flung herself upon a low bank beside the road, moaning and crying aloud.

Instantly my courage returned to me. Mademoiselle was acting like a child; I should treat her as one.

"Mademoiselle," I said firmly, "I cannot permit you to sit upon the cold ground. I am very, very sorry for you, but you must at once arise and dry your eyes and tell me what is the matter, so that I can help you."

Mademoiselle but wept the louder. There was no help for it; at the risk of being rude I must stop her weeping and make her rise from the ground.

"Mademoiselle!" I said sternly, "you will oblige me by rising at once from that cold ground or you will compel me to go for Madame Saugrain and deliver you into her hands."

For a second, amazement at my tone of authority kept her silent, then followed a storm of sobs and tears more violent than before.

"I am sorry, mademoiselle," I said, in a tone purposely cool and cutting (though it was my own heart I stabbed with my coldness), "that you compel me to treat you *comme enfant*. I shall wait one minute, and if you do not rise from the ground in that time I shall call your friends." Then I drew myself up tall and stiff, like a sentinel, turned my back on mademoiselle, and took out my watch to note the time by the moonbeams.

There was no answer, but the sobs grew less until there was only an occasional convulsive catching of the breath. Then came a moment of quiet. There were neither sobs nor moans. Then a small and plaintive voice said gently:

"Monsieur, I will be good now."

I turned quickly. Mademoiselle was starting to rise from the low bank; I grasped her hands and helped her to her feet and looked down upon her. Her face was flushed with weeping; her hood had fallen back and her dark curls were in wild disorder; she might have been a beautiful child who had been naughty but was now subdued. She adjusted her hood and her curls as best she could, and then walked quietly along beside me. We neither of us spoke, and we walked rapidly and in a few minutes overtook the others and came up to the house together, and into the big living-room, where fresh logs piled in the great chimney-place were blazing and crackling, and lighting every cranny of the long room.

Mademoiselle was paler than usual, but otherwise there were no signs of the tempest she had just been through, and I looked at her with wonder. Madame Saugrain, noticing her pallor, and thinking she was cold, put her down on the wooden settle in the chimney-place to warm by the glowing fire, and bustled about helping Narcisse to bring in plates of croque-cignolles and cups of hot mulled gooseberry wine, which was much to my satisfaction, for the frosty air and the lateness of the hour had put a keen edge on an appetite that was ever ready for trencher service.

Now the settle on which mademoiselle sat had a high back and was turned away from the rest of us, so that, as we engaged in helping Madame Saugrain, we might easily have forgotten the little figure hidden away upon it. Perhaps the others did, but I did not. My mind hovered around it all the time; but I was divided between a desire to take her some cake and wine, which I was sure would do her good, and a fear of my reception if I did, and a baser fear that I might thereby lose my own toothsome cake and fragrant wine, which was at that moment making most potent appeals to my inner man by way of the nostrils. "For," I said to myself, "I know the ways of maidens. They like not to see men eat. It seems in their minds a greater compliment to them if a man do but nibble and sip and seem to be careless of his victuals and drink, which I maintain is a great mistake, for a good trencherman is ever a good lover, and a man to be trusted in all the serious business of life."

To ease my conscience and my appetite at the same time, I disposed of a croquecignolle and my steaming cup of wine with such haste that the one stuck in my windpipe and liked to choke me, and the other burnt my mouth well and might as well have been boiling water for all the pleasure my palate got out of it. Then I pretended to suddenly remember mademoiselle, and carried her a plate of cake and a cup of wine with fear and trembling.

She refused them, as I thought she would, but looked up at me very sweetly and asked me very gently to sit down beside her for a moment, and I remember thinking as I did so that I had been wise to secure my cake and wine first, else would I have gone hungry, since I could scarce have the face to eat if mademoiselle would not eat with me. But I still thought it would do her good to have at least a little of the wine, and, remembering how well she had yielded to discipline when she found she must, I set the wine on the hearth where it would keep warm for further use, and then turned to hear what she had to say.

"I only want to say to you, Monsieur, that I am very much ashamed of myself this evening, but I am very unhappy, and I have brooded upon my unhappiness until I have become nervous and irritable, and, as you saw to-night, incapable of self-control. Is that a sufficient excuse for behaving like a spoiled child?"

"Mademoiselle," I said, "it is far more than sufficient, but I am more distressed than I can tell you that you should be so unhappy. If you would but tell me the cause perhaps I could help you. Is it anything you can tell me?"

"Oh, no, no, no!" said Pelagie, hastily, and then seeing perhaps by my face that it hurt me that she should think it impossible I could help her, she added hesitatingly: "That is, I think not. Perhaps it might be possible. I will think about it to-night and to-morrow, and perhaps at Madame Chouteau's dance, if I have an opportunity, I may tell you. I believe," still more slowly, "if any one could help me, you could."

I am sure I thanked her more with my eyes than with my voice, but I know she understood, and then, thinking she had had more than enough of serious converse for one evening, I resumed my rôle of stern disciplinarian and made her eat a little of the cake and drink most of the wine, pretending all the time that she was a naughty child to be sternly dealt with. And I could see that the warm wine and the foolish play were bringing back the color to her cheeks and the brightness to her eyes and the gay ring to her voice, which pleased me greatly. Then my captain called to me that it was high time to be saying good night to the ladies, or rather good morning, and I rose to go, but I turned first and leaned over the back of the tall settle:

"Mademoiselle, at the picnic on Chouteau's Pond I won the first dance with you, I think somewhat against your will. If I should ask you for the first dance to-morrow night, would you give it to me willingly?"

"Willingly, Monsieur," with a glance into my eyes (which were very near her own) by far the sweetest I had yet had from hers.

CHAPTER IX

MADAME CHOUTEAU'S BALL

"The uncertain glory of an April day."

WE met at reveille the next morning at nine—
the great Christmas feast when kinsfolk all
gather at the house of the head of the family and
make merry together. Then I saw for what all the
mighty preparations of the day before were intended.
The roasted fowl and venison pasty, smoking hot,
were flanked by tarts and cakes and jellies and cor-
dials beyond my power to inventory, for I had ever
less of a talent for the description of such things than
for making away with them.

It was a goodly feast, and we lingered at table for
over an hour, mingling with our enjoyment of Madame
Saugrain's good things such pleasant converse as
Frenchmen excel in. Dr. Saugrain himself had always
something wise and witty to say, and being a man of
deep learning and much science, was often, also, most
instructive. An hour, therefore, passed quickly
enough, and I was glad to see that mademoiselle was
looking more as she had looked before the picnic on
Chouteau's Pond than I had seen her since my return.
But I had chance for little more than the good wishes

of the day with her, for the company was large and my seat, as usual, was near Madame Saugrain, at the other end of the table from hers. My thoughts had dwelt much upon her when I lay on my bed the night before, a long hour ere sleep visited my eyelids. I had lived over the events of the evening, and of the weeks that I had known her, and she had seemed to me not one, but many maidens. Haughty, meek, scornful, merry, mocking, serious, sad, sweet—in how many moods had I not seen her, and in each in turn she had seemed to me the sweetest. I always forgot, when I was with her, that she was a great lady in France and destined soon to return to her home land and her rightful position. I never could think of her as anything but Dr. Saugrain's ward: wilful, sweet, and capricious, the belle of St. Louis, the toast of the young men and the idol of the young maidens. That as a rule she had treated me with scorn or indifference did not in the least detract from her charms for me, but the unwonted sweetness of the night before had quite gone to my head, and I was henceforth her willing slave.

From the breakfast-table we separated; the captain and Dr. Saugrain going to the doctor's laboratory, where he was making some wonderful experiments with phosphorus, by which one might at any moment obtain a light, without the aid of tinder, by means of little sticks of wood dipped in the phosphorus! 'T is not to be wondered at that many people think Dr. Saugrain a dealer in black arts when he can accomplish such supernatural results by the aid of science!

As for me, I had an engagement with Josef Papin and Gabriel Cerré and some other young men to go duck-shooting on the Maramec, a good day's tramp, and we did not expect to be back until nearly time for Madame Chouteau's dance. I think the matrons and the maidens expected to spend the day in going to church and in making visits, which seemed to me a dull way to spend Christmas, but no doubt they liked it.

It was a grand day for shooting, the air so clear and dry, just frosty enough to send the blood leaping through our bodies; and we came home with a great string of prairie-chicken and duck and partridge— enough to supply the village for a week. We were a little later than we had intended in getting home, and tired enough to go right to bed, but I, for one, would not have missed this my first opportunity to appear in *grand costume du bal,* to say nothing of the joys of the dance.

There was a hot supper waiting for me, which rested me wonderfully; and then, with Yorke's help, I had a quick bath and was into my ball dress in a shorter time than I had dared to hope. Yorke had laid out my dress for me and looked to the lace ruffles and lacers, so that I had only to jump into it and let him tie me up, and I was ready.

I was glad that I had such a becoming costume with me, for, without being unduly vain, I knew that the rich plum-colored coat and breeches and the lilac satin waistcoat with fine lace frills and a touch of gold here and there were a good offset to my yel-

low hair and rosy cheeks, which, much as I despised
them at times, I was yet at other times well satisfied to
endure. I liked, too, the looks of my leg in a fine white
silk stocking and low pumps with shoe- and knee-
buckles of brilliants, and was not above being proud
of a well-turned calf and ankle.

Madame and mademoiselle had gone on ahead in
a charrette, as better suited to their *costumes du bal*
than horseback-riding, and Dr. Saugrain and Captain
Clarke had ridden by their side, leaving me to finish
dressing and hurry after them as soon as I could.

A mad haste seized me before I reached Madame
Chouteau's lest the first dance should be over and I
lose my promised honor. I reflected, too, that mademoiselle would think me always tardy in keeping my
engagements with her, and the thought lent spurs to
my movements. I entered the great ball-room in
breathless haste. The walnut was waxed to the last
perfection of slipperiness, and not taking heed to
my steps, my feet slipped up. But I caught myself
from falling, though not without as many gyrations
of long arms and long legs as a Dutch windmill might
accomplish on a windy day.

My remarkable entry was greeted with a shout of
laughter by the young men and maidens, who by this
time had come to know me well. I did not mind that,
but I looked hastily toward Mademoiselle Pelagie, and
there, between the straight black brows, was the ominous little frown I had learned to dread. What
availed my beautiful plum-colored velvets and laven-
der satin, lace, and buckles, if I only succeeded in

being an awkward hobbledehoy? I must retrieve my-self!

I drew myself up in my grandest manner and walked up to Madame Chouteau, sitting in state in a great arm-chair near the chimney-piece. With my courtliest bow, in my best French, I made my com-pliments to her as if I had been accustomed to enter-ing rooms in no other fashion. Then I made the cir-cuit of the room, talking for a minute or two to each of my acquaintances, lingering longest by Mademoi-selle Chouteau, whose eyes were dancing with mirth, and so round the circle, head thrown back (but being careful of my steps), until I came to mademoiselle. There I stopped, with another low bow. Looking down on her, I was glad to see the frown was no longer there, but a look of something far pleasanter, almost like admiration, had taken its place.

Of course she was surrounded by young men—that did not displease me: I liked to see her admired. She was wearing the same gown she had worn at Mr. Gratiot's the first time I saw her, and I said to my-self: " I know not what her rank in France may be, —comtesse, marquise, or duchesse,—but I know she looks every inch la reine." I think my pride in her lent stateliness to my steps as I led her out in the dance. I know that for her sake I wished to look as much le roi as it was in me to look.

But there was no chance during the minuet for mademoiselle's promised confidence, and as the even-ing went on I began to think there would be none at all. There had been the old folks' minuet, when Dr.

Saugrain led out Madame Chouteau on the floor, and his plump little calves, silk-robed, had twinkled beside her stately steps in wondrous fashion. And then had come supper,—a bounteous feast of delicate cakes and sweetmeats and rich salads and cold fowl, with gooseberry wine and a sweet punch brewed from New Orleans ratafia,—and I feared that would put an end to the festivities, and still there had been no chance.

But 't is a wonderful thing on what a small matter great matters will sometimes turn! Though there may be those who would think it no great matter that I should find myself riding home in the moonlight with mademoiselle on a pillion behind me, and Fatima going at so slow a pace as put her in a constant fret of wonder as to what could be the reason that her master kept her down so, and mademoiselle telling me her story in a low tone (for being so near my ear she did not have to raise her voice), and sometimes trembling so much that the little arm which was pretending to circle my great waist to hold on by (but which only reached by uttermost stretch a quarter-way around) would almost lose its grip.

It seemed a great matter to me, and it happened in this wise: I had barely spoken to mademoiselle since our dance, when just as I was getting a glass of gooseberry wine and a croquecignolle for Mademoiselle Chouteau (she said she had no stomach for salads and meats at a dance) mademoiselle came up to me, inquiring most anxiously had I seen her capote. 'T was of heavy silk, and lined with the skins of beavers, and would have been very costly in Philadelphia, and handsome enough for our greatest dames. I had not seen it, but offered to go at once in search of it as soon as I had carried the wine and croquecignolle to Mademoiselle Chouteau.

We hunted together in all the most impossible places, and mademoiselle growing every moment more anxious, because she was keeping madame and Dr. Saugrain waiting. They were tired and longing to get home, and I said, half in jest:

"Had I a pillion, Mademoiselle, we would tell madame not to wait, and when we had found your capote I could bring you home with me on Fatima."

But mademoiselle answered quickly:

"Would you be so good, Monsieur? I doubt not Madame Chouteau would lend us a pillion, and it would greatly relieve my anxiety in keeping madame waiting."

I hardly knew whether I felt more joy or consternation, but mademoiselle gave me no time to decide which, but hurried me with her to persuade her guardians not to wait. I thought the arrangement did not altogether please the doctor, and he demurred greatly; but his good wife, who never differed with mademoiselle (whether through being over-fond or a little in awe, I am not sure), persuaded him that it was all right and quite the best way.

And five minutes after the charrette, with my captain and the doctor accompanying it, drove out of Madame Chouteau's gate, the capote was found, mademoiselle herself suddenly remembering where she had laid it.

I have never felt quite sure that mademoiselle had not known all the time where it was. But I admired so much the cleverness that could contrive to accomplish her end (for myself, I could never plan or scheme, though quick enough to act if occasion presented) that I forgave the little deceit, if there was any—maidens not being like men, who must be true and straightforward in even the smallest matters, lest their honor be attainted.

But when I had mounted Fatima and lifted mademoiselle to her pillion, and felt her little arm steal round my great waist (as it needs must, to keep her from falling), my stupid heart began to beat so fast and to thump so hard against my waistcoat I feared the buttons would give way, and was greatly shamed lest mademoiselle should feel it thumping and guess the cause. Yet presently Fatima, not being accustomed to petticoats falling over her flanks, pranced on two feet in such a fashion as to cause mademoiselle to clutch me convulsively with both arms, whereupon I found myself suddenly calm and master of the situation. It was the work of a minute or two to reduce Fatima to order and make her understand that petticoats and a pillion were entirely proper. That being accomplished, and Fatima made to understand also that she was to go at her slowest pace, I was ready to hear mademoiselle's story, which finally she began:

"Monsieur, I feel that I must take advantage of this opportunity so providentially offered me. I had not thought to confide in any one, but I am in sore need of advice, and I know not where else to turn."

"I know not, Mademoiselle," I answered, "whether I am good at giving advice. I had rather you would ask me to do for you some perilous and arduous service. But if it is advice you need most, then such as I can I will give you truly and faithfully."

"I thank you, Monsieur"; and then mademoiselle was silent for so long a time that I half turned in my saddle to look at her. She looked up at me with a pitiful little smile.

"Have patience, Monsieur—I will soon find my courage; but I have need to trust you greatly, for I am trusting you with the safety, perhaps the life, of a friend. You will not let any harm come to him through my betrayal?"

"I promise, Mademoiselle," I said, "to do nothing you will not approve. But there should never be any question of a betrayal. If a trust has been given and received, then it is sacred, but it is not betrayal if it has been forced upon one without his consent."

I said this because I began to have a glimmering of the truth, and I did not want mademoiselle to violate her conscience. No good can ever come from that, I have found, and much as I wanted to hear what she had to tell me, I could not listen comfortably if I thought she were really betraying a trust. I was still turned in my saddle, watching her face, and I saw it lighten at once, and something like a great sigh of relief seemed to come from the depths of her breast.

"I see, Monsieur," she said, "you men understand

right and wrong better than we maidens. It has troubled me greatly that I should prove unfaithful to a
trust, and yet I saw no other way. And now, for fear
my courage will ooze out, I must tell you quickly.

"Two weeks ago I received a letter from the Chevalier Le Moyne, a week ago I received a second, and
yesterday I received a third. The purport of all these
letters is the same. I have returned no answer to any
of them, though each has begged for an answer and
given me full instructions as to how to send it.

"The chevalier has gone no farther south than Cape
Girardeau. He is waiting near there, in an Osage
camp, to seize an opportunity to rescue me, he says,
and restore me to my people. If I had replied to
either of these letters, professing my willingness to
go with him, then I should have received a note of instructions as to where to be on a certain day and at a
certain hour. But I have replied to none, and the last
letter has grown desperate. In it he says if he does
not hear from me he shall return to St. Louis on the
evening of the Jour des Rois and be present at the
dance, which is by custom a masked dance, and will
then find means to carry me off. If I am not willing
to go with him, then I must send him a letter before
the Jour de l'An, telling him so finally, when he will
return to New Orleans and leave me to my fate. Now,
Monsieur, it will seem to you an easy matter that I
should write him, finally, that I will not go with him.
But a woman's heart is a strange thing. I want to
go with him, with all my heart, and yet I shudder at
the very thought of going with him. When I let my

thoughts dwell on the glories that await me in Paris,
wealth and power and luxurious living, and the society of the great and the noble, such as the chevalier
has described it, I feel as if I must go, and all this life
which has been so sweet to me here on the very borders
of civilization grows utterly distasteful. Yes, even the
friends that have been so dear to me begin to seem
rude and boorish, as the chevalier called them. Sometimes, in some of my wayward moods, the very perils
of the journey attract me with a strange fascination.
The ride through the forest with savages for guards;
the long journey in an open boat on the bosom of the
great Father of Waters; and at last the perilous voyage by sea, all draw me strangely. At such times the
chevalier seems to me an angel of light, and my only
hope of escape from my narrow confines to a broad
and beautiful life. But there are times when it all
seems very different: when the thought of leaving my
two dear guardians is unbearable, and the life I have
known and loved from childhood, among sweet, true
friends, the only life I desire. Ah, Monsieur, I am so
torn by these conflicting states of mind that what wonder my guardians think me changed! They believe
the chevalier's tales have spoiled me for my life in
St. Louis, and that I would gladly leave them. When
I see them sad over what they believe to be my heartlessness my own heart is like to break, but I say nothing, and they believe me to be entirely ungrateful
and unfeeling.

"So you can see how unhappy I have been and am,
and how sometimes I am tempted to break away from
9

it all and fly with the chevalier to new scenes, whether they bring joy or sorrow.''

Mademoiselle did not tell me all this without much hesitation, sometimes stopping entirely until she could find courage to go on again, and, as I said before, often trembling so much that the little arm about my great waist nearly lost its grip. I did not interrupt her once, but waited, even after she had finished, for fear she might have more to say. And presently she added:

"If I do not answer the chevalier's letter he will be here on the Jour des Rois, and it is more than likely he will lose his life in the attempt to carry me off, even if I were willing to go with him.''

"Mademoiselle," I said slowly, "it is a hard thing you have asked me, and I feel sure that whatever I may say I will make you angry, as I did last night. Of course you know that what I would most like would be that you should let the chevalier come on the Jour des Rois, and we would capture him, and there would be an end to all this trouble. But you know, too, that since you have trusted me with his secret I would feel in duty bound to save him and get him safely outside the stockade again, even, if need were, at the risk of my own life. The thing, therefore, that I wish you would do, and that seems to me the only thing to do, is to write him at once, telling him you will never go with him, and bidding him return at once to France since his task is a hopeless one.''

"And cut myself off from seeing France and recovering my possessions!''

" 'T is not cutting yourself off.'' (I spoke a little

sternly, for I was beginning to feel irritated that she could not see the utter folly of thinking for a moment of going with the chevalier.) "Your guardian is only waiting for two things, and as soon as they are accomplished he will send you to Paris. He is awaiting letters from your friends to say the time is ripe for your return, and they are ready to receive you, and he is waiting to find a proper person in whose care he can place you to make the voyage."

"Then here is the time and the opportunity," said mademoiselle, eagerly: "my friends have sent the chevalier for me, and he is waiting to conduct me there."

I could have shaken her, for a minute, her stupidity seemed so vast to me. Then I remembered she was really only a child, and that there are many things maidens do not understand so well as men. So I tried to speak gently, but so plainly that once for all she might understand.

"Mademoiselle," I said, "do you not see that the very fact that the chevalier is trying to induce you to go to France alone with him is proof either of his villainy or of his colossal stupidity? Were he the angel of light he has sometimes seemed to you, and should he carry you safely to France and deliver you into the hands of your friends, yet who, in gay and skeptical Paris, would not be willing to believe the worst of both of you? The society that he has painted to you as ready to fall at your feet would be only ready to spurn you. Forgive me, Mademoiselle, for speaking thus plainly, but there is no man in the world who would not believe that the very fact of the chevalier's trying to persuade you to go with him to France proves him a villain of the deepest dye.''

Mademoiselle did not answer; but her arms slipped from my waist, and presently I felt her little head resting on my broad back, and sobs were shaking her little figure. I did not dare stir, for fear of disturbing her, but it was very uncomfortable to sit so rigidly erect, not daring to move, because a beautiful little black and curly head was resting a little above the small of one's back, while tempests of tears were drenching one's military cloak, and the shaking from the sobs was making queer little shivers run up and down one's backbone.

Now this was the second time my brutality had brought mademoiselle to tears. This time I thought it was good for her, and was of a mind to let her weep it out, though all the time longing to turn around and take her in my arms and let her weep upon my breast instead of on my back.

But presently I was aware of heroic efforts to stifle the sobs and stay the tears, and then I heard a most woebegone voice:

'' Oh, monsieur, what shall I do? what shall I do? ''

Now, I had brought Fatima to a standstill, for I was afraid to let her go even at a slow walk when mademoiselle had no arm to hold on by, and her head bobbing at every step of Fatima's into the ticklish part of my back. And by chance we had stopped where the Rue Bonhomme climbs down the bluff to the river, and our boats lay moored at its foot. Suddenly an answer to her question flashed into my head. It seemed to me a perfect solution of all difficulties, but in the nature of the case I could say nothing to mademoiselle until I had consulted Dr. Saugrain and my captain.

One thing I could say, however, and I reiterated what I had said before:

"One thing you can do at once, mademoiselle: write to the chevalier so firm and positive a refusal that he will never trouble you again, and then go and tell your guardian all about it. He deserves this confidence from you, and I think you will never be very happy until you have made him feel that there is no change in your grateful affection to him."

There was another moment of silence, and then, in the meekest of tones:

"I will do all you tell me, monsieur."

I could not believe it was the same haughty mademoiselle who had so scorned "ce garçon-çà." But I was not going to show her the elation I could not help feeling in her change of attitude; and being also most sorry for her, and everything settled as far as it could be about the chevalier, I thought it time that she should be diverted from her unhappy thoughts, and so I bade her look down on the great river, now rolling, a silver flood under the moon, straight to Cape Girardeau, where the chevalier was lingering, and past fort and forest on to the rich city of New Orleans. For a moment the old longing returned to be one of a great army borne on its swift waters to capture the haughty city that held the gateway to the sea. I thought it no harm to tell mademoiselle what my dreams had been, and we both laughed merrily at the audacity of them.

But the night was passing, and gently lifting mademoiselle's arm and placing it so that it should once more hold her secure on her pillion, I put Fatima to a gentle canter; and as I felt Pelagie's clasp tighten, my pulse leaped faster in my veins, and I gave Fatima full rein, and we went thundering down the Rue Royale, past Madame Chouteau's place, with the last revelers just coming through the great gates; past Auguste Chouteau's house, standing dark among its trees; past the Government House, still brightly lighted, for Governor Delassus and his retinue were just entering the great hall; turned up the Rue de la Tour, with the tower at the top of the hill shining white in the moonlight, then down the long stretch of the Rue de l'Église, faster and faster, as mademoiselle clung closer, until we reached the gate of Émigré's Retreat, and a great dog came rushing to meet us with mighty bounds and joyous barks, and would have overpowered us both with his clumsy caresses but that a sweet voice (never before one half so sweet) called:

"À bas, Leon! Tais-toi, mon ange!"

CHAPTER X

LA GUIGNOLÉE

"By sports like these are all their cares beguiled."

I WOKE the next morning with a feeling of elation
that for a moment I did not understand; then I
recognized that it was a feeling that mademoiselle and
I would never again be on any but the friendliest of
terms. No more fear of merry scoffing or haughty
disdain! I had a right to look now for only kindness
and friendliness.

But I did not know mademoiselle. The morning
was bleak; a fine drizzle of rain, freezing as it fell,
was hanging jeweled pendants from every twig and
branch. I went down-stairs, to find that morning coffee was being served in the living-room, on a small
table drawn up before a blazing fire of logs. Mademoiselle, who did not often come to early coffee, was
serving it, in a warm-looking gown of some wool stuff,
deep red in color, and I thought it suited well her dark
beauty and the bleak morning. I stopped at the threshold to make my low bow, and then went forward,
expecting a less formal greeting. But she only looked
up from the silver urn, whence she was drawing a
cup of coffee for the captain, long enough to say,

" Good morning, monsieur," in her iciest tones, and then went on talking gaily to the captain of the ball the night before. I did not understand at all, but I thought it quite possible I had imagined her coldness; and so, without seeming to push myself unduly, I sought to join in the conversation when opportunity offered. I think the captain seconded my efforts out of the courtesy natural to him; but mademoiselle made it so plain that she desired to ignore me that I soon took my cup and withdrew to a corner of the fireplace. I hope I did not do anything so boyish as to sulk there, but of that I am not sure.

When the good doctor came bustling in from his laboratory a few minutes later, half frozen, but burning with enthusiasm over some experiments he was making with quicksilver, he brought his coffee to my warm corner, and I at once simulated the deepest interest in his account of his morning's work— though I confess I have never taken any great interest in science, and from what he seemed to expect the quicksilver to do I did not feel altogether sure that he was not, in truth, dabbling in black art.

There was a long mirror at the other end of the room—one that Madame Saugrain had brought from France, and the pride of her heart. As we talked I could glance in it and see mademoiselle perfectly without seeming to look at her. I observed that she grew more and more distrait, only half listening to the captain, and very evidently trying to overhear our conversation. I had not known that mademoiselle was so interested in science, and I began to make deep and learned speeches (or, at least, I hoped they sounded so) on quicksilver and on every subject allied to it. I did not hesitate to make some remarkable statements, for whose truth I modestly said I could not vouch. The doctor was too courteous to show the surprise I think he must have felt at some of them, but if I had not been so interested in my investigations in the mirror (which, I am sure, is closely allied to quicksilver) I would have noticed without doubt that knowing twinkle of the eye that I had seen at least twice before. My glances in the mirror, however, showed me that my learned speeches had produced their intended effect on mademoiselle, at least, and once more I caught that wondering glance fixed upon me.

I did not see mademoiselle again until the evening supper-hour. After breakfast Dr. Saugrain invited the captain and me to ride with him up to Pierre Chouteau's, and on the ride he told us that mademoiselle had come to him that morning in the laboratory and had told him all about the chevalier. I was much touched that she had acted upon my advice so promptly, and half forgave her for her treatment of me at coffee, though I understood it the less. The doctor did not say so directly, but I judged from one or two little remarks that he and Pelagie had had a thorough clearing up of all their misunderstandings and were once more on the old confidential terms. He spoke especially of her " sweetness," and said his advice had been, like mine, to write the chevalier at once a firm refusal. But the good doctor was greatly troubled.

"I shall never feel quite secure again," he said, "till I have Pelagie safe with her friends in France; so I shall seek the first opportunity of sending her there. 'T is for that I am going to consult Pierre Chouteau, and I thought you might have some suggestion, one or both of you, as to how to find an escort for her."

I was so eager with my plan that had flashed on me the night before that I could not wait to show the proper courtesy to my captain. He certainly had a right to speak first, but I broke forth, "I have a plan, sir—" and then was abashed and stopped short.

The doctor understood, and nodded to me.

"Yes; let the captain speak first, and then we will hear your plan."

"Nay," said the captain, with his friendliest smile; "let the lad speak. He has a plan that seems to me not wholly unpracticable and may prove the very thing."

Thus encouraged, I rushed ahead:

"I have been talking to Captain Clarke about it, sir, and he thinks it can be done. My last letter from home said that Colonel Livingston was about to join his father in Paris. My family know Colonel Livingston well, and a letter from my father would insure the protection of both Colonel and Mrs. Livingston for mademoiselle on the voyage."

But the good doctor shook his head.

"I could never get Pelagie to New York, I fear; to both Madame Saugrain and myself, such a journey seems an almost impossible undertaking."

"But Captain Clarke has that all arranged," I cried.

The doctor looked at the captain, who answered, smiling:

"It is my good Achates who has arranged it, but I heartily approve of his plans. It is time we were getting back to Kentucky, and he proposes that we take mademoiselle with us to my sister, Mrs. O'Fallon. There she can stay until we can find a suitable escort up the Ohio to Fort Duquesne, and across the mountains to New York. There are boats going up the river every week, and always some one going back to the old home to whom we could intrust mademoiselle. I think it a good and feasible plan."

But we had quite reached Pierre Chouteau's before we had persuaded the doctor that our plan was at all a practical one. Not, as he assured us, that he could not trust mademoiselle with us, but the difficulties, dangers, and inconveniences of such a trip, for a young maiden with no woman in the party but her colored maid, seemed to him almost insurmountable. However, he was so nearly convinced by my eloquence and the captain's logic that just as we were turning in at Mr. Chouteau's he said:

"Well, well, my dear friends, it may be possible. We will see! I must take time to consult Madame Saugrain, and, until then, not a word to mademoiselle, I beg of you both."

We both readily promised, though I was so elated at what I considered the already assured success of my plan that I might have found it difficult not to speak to mademoiselle about it if she had not been in the same icy mood to me at supper (though sweet and most charming to the captain and her guardian) as she had been at breakfast.

The next day Dr. Saugrain told us that he and his wife had talked far into the night about Pelagie, and they had come to the conclusion that our plan was the best solution of the difficulties. He said madame had wept much at the thought of parting with Pelagie, and of all the difficulties and dangers she must encounter, before she could become reconciled to the thought of it; but now she was quite resigned, and had already begun to plan what clothes and other conveniences it would be necessary for Pelagie to take with her, and how they could best be got ready.

"And, after the manner of women," the doctor said, "from the moment she began to think about clothes, she began to grow cheerful. And she has such confidence in Clotilde, who will go with her, and who has had entire charge of her since her babyhood, that she thinks she will be as well taken care of as if she were with her herself. But we both think," he added, "that it will be wiser to say nothing to Pelagie about it until it is almost time to make the start. If, for any reason, our plan should fail, her mind will not be unsettled by it, and she will be no worse off than if we had not thought of it. Moreover, the fewer we take into our confidence the better, for I am assured the chevalier has spies and secret emissaries that we do not suspect. We will give him no chance to thwart our plans!"

The good doctor spoke the last words so grimly that it was easy to understand in what esteem he held the villain, and both the captain and I heartily approved his precaution.

There followed busy days for me. The captain, who was much engaged in settling up the business for his brother which had brought him to St. Louis, had little time for aught else, though Governor Delassus, the Chouteaus, and Mr. Gratiot made many demands upon him for counsel and for social festivities, in which last I was courteously included. When these fell upon the evening I was very ready to join in them, but my days were more than full. All the arrangements for mademoiselle's comfort on the boat my captain had intrusted to me, and I was determined that nothing should be left undone to make her voyage on the Great River as comfortable as possible. The cabin, a rough affair at its best, was partitioned into two, and the larger one made as clean as six blacks scrubbing hard on hands and knees could make it. Then I got from Pierre Chouteau a small stove such as he often used on his boat in winter trips up the Missouri, and set it up in the cabin, cutting a hole in the roof to give egress to the stovepipe. From Madame Saugrain I got some strips of warm, bright carpet and some clean warm bedding, and I set Yorke to work, under my careful supervision, to make the two beds for mademoiselle and her maid, to tack down the strips of carpet, to put up some white ruffled curtains (also Madame Saugrain's gift) at the square bit of window, and to polish up the brass handles of the portable locker that was to hold mademoiselle's wardrobe. I thought, when all was done,—the small table covered with a white cloth, and two shining candlesticks on it, and the three comfortable chairs arranged about it,— I thought it cozy and complete enough for a trip to France; and my heart beat high when I thought of the tête-à-têtes with mademoiselle that must almost necessarily fall to my lot on a voyage of at least a week. But, in the meantime, I was seeing very little of her, between being busy all day and often invited out in the evening—and not getting much satisfaction when I did; for either she was incased in her icy hauteur, or, if she chanced to be kind, I was so brimming over with my secret, so afraid I should let it slip, I was unnaturally constrained with her.

Before I knew it the Jour de l'An was upon us, and the doctor and the captain had both agreed it would be wise to set out on the day before the Jour des Rois. On no account would it do to risk remaining over the Jour des Rois, lest the chevalier should accomplish his purpose in spite of mademoiselle's letter of refusal.

Now, as its name signifies, the Jour de l'An is the greatest of all days to these St. Louis Frenchmen. Preparations had been making for it all the week. The governor himself was to give a grand ball at Government House, and I had heard mademoiselle telling Captain Clarke, as we sat at supper on New Year's eve, how that would be only the beginning of a round of festivities, and that Marguerite Papin, Pelagie Chouteau, and she had been making the beancake that afternoon.

"And what is the bean-cake, pray, Mademoiselle?" I inquired, determined to take matters into my own hands and be no longer shut out from conversation as if I were infected.

Mademoiselle looked up in surprise at my audacity, and for a moment was of half a mind not to reply to me; but she thought better of it, and answered coolly and formally:

"'T is a cake, Monsieur, with four beans baked in it. It will be cut to-morrow night at the governor's ball, and the four maidens who receive the slices with the beans will be the queens of the ball. They will choose four kings, who will then be obliged to get up the ball for the Jour des Rois, and at that these four kings will choose four queens, who will choose four other kings, who must give the next ball. 'T is an endless chain of balls till Shrove Tuesday arrives, to finish it all up with one grand carnival ball; and so you see, sir, if you stay in St. Louis I can promise you a merry winter."

I almost laughed as I thought how little she dreamed that she would not be here herself. Yet the prospect sounded alluring, and I could have been well pleased to spend the winter in the gay little village, if the fates had ordained. I answered her to that effect, and then I added:

"If you could but give me any hope that I should be chosen a king, I might take fate into my own hands and stay anyway."

"There is much ground for hope, sir," she answered demurely, "since both Pelagie Chouteau and Marguerite Papin are almost certain to be queens."

Then, with a quick beat of the heart, I thought perhaps she had not liked it that they had been friendly and I had been polite. If her manner to me could be so accounted for I was well content, for at least it did not argue indifference.

But before I could reply there was a great noise, outside on the gallery, of shuffling feet and smothered whispers, and mademoiselle clapped her hands and cried:

"La Guignolée!" And at the same moment there arose, to the quaintest air, a chorus of men's voices:

> " Bon soir, le maître et la maîtresse,
>   Et tout le monde du logis!
> Pour le premier jour de l'année
>   La Guignolée vous nous devez.
> Si vous n'avez rien à nous donner,
>   Dites-nous le;
> Nous vous demandons pas grande chose, une échinée—
>   Une échinée n'est pas bien longue
> De quatre-vingt-dix pieds de longue.
>   Encore nous demandons pas de grande chose,
> La fille ainée de la maison.
>   Nous lui ferons faire bonne chère—
> Nous lui ferons chauffer les pieds."

Horrified at these last words of the song, I scarcely dared glance at mademoiselle; but when I did dare, to my amazement, she was smiling good-humoredly, and I saw the words meant nothing to her. But the chorus was interrupted at that moment by a single voice which I recognized at once as Josef Papin's, singing a ditty about doves and cuckoos and nightingales, and winding up by declaring that he was dying for the soft eyes of his mistress. I saw that mademoiselle recognized the voice, too, and I was vexed to see the bright color and downcast eyes that betokened she understood these words perfectly.

But the chorus began again immediately:

> " Nous saluons la compagnie
>   Et la prions nous excuser.
>   Si l'on a fait quelque folie."

(I thought this apology most becoming.)

> " C'était pour vous désennuyer;
>   Une autre fois nous prendrons garde
>   Quand sera temps d'y revenir.
>   Dansons la guenille,
>   Dansons la guenille,
>   Dansons la guenille ! "

And then the doors were flung open, and there burst in upon us a motley crew of grotesque and hideous masks, each one bearing a basket or bucket or sack, and all singing and shouting in every key and in no time:

> " Bon soir, le maître et la maîtresse,
>   Et tout le monde du logis ! "

Madame Saugrain and mademoiselle sprang up from the table and ran to the kitchen, returning with both hands full, and followed by a procession of servants bringing eggs and sugar and butter and flour and poultry and wine—a goodly donation indeed for the Jour des Rois ball, and for which the maskers showed their thanks by dancing *la guenille,* a truly

10

Saturnalian performance, somewhat shocking to my Eastern notions of propriety. But evidently neither the doctor nor his wife nor mademoiselle saw any harm in it, for they applauded it greatly, after the French fashion, by clapping of hands and crying "Encore!"

Yorke had come in with the other servants from the kitchen, and it was a sight to see his great eyes rolling in ecstasy and his white teeth displayed from ear to ear as he watched the mummers, and I was not surprised to see him follow them like one bewitched as they went up toward the Rue des Granges to Paschal Cerré's house, singing:

> " Bon soir, le maître et la maîtresse,
>   Et tout le monde du logis ! "

"You will be having Yorke dancing la guenille," I said to the captain, "when he gets back to Kentucky."

"An he does," answered the captain, with a grim smile, "I will bastinado him." For I think the captain did not like some of the figures of la guenille any better than did I.

CHAPTER XI

"She moves a goddess and she looks a queen."

LE Jour de l'An was a full day with me. Though I did not go to early mass with the family, I left the house when they did and had a fast gallop on Fatima's back through the gray dawn down to the boat, for there were still a few finishing touches to be put to my decorations and arrangements for mademoiselle's comfort, and I was in feverish haste that all should be in readiness. Captain Clarke and I spent the day in visits of ceremony made at the houses where we had been so often and so kindly entertained during our stay. They were really farewell visits, though for prudential reasons we said nothing of our approaching departure. At every house we were served with croquecignolles and wine or ratafia by the young maidens and their mothers, and we were so hospitably urged to eat and drink that had we done anything more than make the merest pretense for the sake of good fellowship we would have been in no condition for the dance in the evening.

Frenchmen know better how to manage their drinking than do we Anglo-Saxons. I know not how they

147

do it, but I know not a young fellow appeared at the governor's house in the evening who had apparently taken more than was good for him; and yet had our Philadelphia lads been through the ordeal of proffered glasses all day long, I warrant there would not have been a corporal's guard able to line up in good order at the governor's ball. But all these young St. Louis Frenchmen were out in fine feather, and carrying themselves grandly, eyes bright and heads steady, ready to lead out to the governor's table the belles of St. Louis, dazzling in brocades and feathers, lace, and powder and black patches.

It was a goodly feast, ragout and roast fowl and venison pasties, and cakes and tarts and rich conserves making the tables groan; but the crowning moment was when the governor's stately butler brought in the bean-cake (almost as much as he could carry) and set it down before the governor. 'T was a breathless silence as the governor cut each slice and sent it first to the maiden nearest him and then to the next in order. I was not in the least surprised when one of the four beans fell to mademoiselle's lot; I would have been surprised if it had not. There was a burst of ringing cheers, led by Josef Papin, when the lucky slice came to her, and I thought, "He knows he will be chosen king," and smiled with bitterness at the thought.

I had not seen mademoiselle all day. As I glanced at her now, smiling and coloring with pleasure at the cheers that betokened her popularity, it flashed into my mind that she would reign a queen indeed

when she came into her own in France, for I was very
sure there were no court ladies could compare with her
for beauty and grace.

The governor himself crowned the four queens, and
then they had to retire into the background for a
space while their elders danced the first minuet, in
which the governor led out Madame Chouteau in
stately measure. But after that formal opening of
the ball the young people had it all their own way,
and the four queens queened it royally each with a
flock of suitors around her. I said to myself proudly,
" I will not hang on to any of their trains." There
was no possible doubt but that mademoiselle would
choose Josef Papin (since the chevalier was not there),
and while I would have liked it well if one of the others
had chosen me, just to show mademoiselle that all did
not scorn me, I would not seem to sue for favors. So
I attached myself to Mademoiselle Chouteau (who had
not been so lucky as to draw a bean); and she being
in the sauciest mood (and looking exceeding pretty),
and I feeling that I was at least as well dressed as
any other man (since I had on my plum-colored velvets
and my finest lace), and therefore at my ease, we made
ourselves so entertaining to each other that I began
in my heart to feel a little regret that this was to be
my last ball with her.

I would not so much as look at mademoiselle, whose
silvery laugh sometimes floated to my ears, for she had
treated me shamefully of late, and, as far as I could
see, without the least reason. Just once I caught her
eye, however. I do not know how it happened, but

there was a moment of almost silence in the crowded
room. The violins were not playing, no one was dancing, and for one fleeting moment, every one, or nearly
every one, seemed to have ceased talking. Into this
strange silence, through the open windows, there
floated the clear call of the whippoorwill,—only one,
for the buzz and clamor and clatter of many voices
surged up again instantly, and the violins began to
scrape and screech themselves into tune, and no one
seemed to have noticed either the silence or the whippoorwill. But I could not for the life of me help one
swift glance toward mademoiselle, and I met her eyes
seeking mine in a look of startled alarm that was almost terror. I held her glance long enough to say to
her with my eyes, "Do not be afraid; I will see what
it is," and I had the satisfaction of seeing, before she
turned away, that she understood and was reassured.

A few minutes later I slipped outside. I was not
entirely at ease about that call, it had meant so much
once. And I was not at all sure of the chevalier. A
ball like this, with every one off guard, would be just
his opportunity. Outside there was a motley throng
of negroes, river-men, and Indians, hanging around to
get glimpses of the dancers and the guests coming and
going. The yard was brightly lighted in spots by
flaming lightwood torches, which left the other parts
in deepest gloom. I noticed among the throng a little
group of mummers, such as had been at Dr. Saugrain's the night before in hideous masks. This did
not at first seem strange to me, but afterward I

thought it must be unusual, for they belonged peculiarly to New Year's eve.

Leaning against a post that held a lightwood torch,
a little withdrawn from the others, in solitary dignity,
stood Black Hawk. I knew if there had been anything
unusual in the whippoorwill cry he would know it.
I sauntered up to him carelessly (for if there were
spies about, I did not want to arouse suspicion), and
stopped where the light fell full on me, for I knew
well the value of impressing Black Hawk with the
splendor of my dress. For the benefit of any possible listener, I told him that the governor's halls were
hot and I must needs get a draft of cold air before I
could go back to my dancing. Then I talked to him of
Daniel Boone, for he had been with us on our trip
to his home, and I knew his admiration for that wonderful man. His only responses were a series of
grunts, but they were amiable ones (I think the old
savage rather liked me), and as I talked I gradually
drew nearer. When I was quite close to him, I said
suddenly, in a low tone:

"Does the Great Chief of the Sacs think there are
any White Wolves or Red Dogs about to-night?"

I saw a sudden glitter in his eye, but that was the
only response except the invariable "Ugh!" Then
I said again in the same low tone:

"If Black Hawk will watch and let his white
brother know what he finds out, it will greatly please
the brother of the Captain of the Long Knives."

There was another "Ugh!"—this time with half
an inclination of the head, and I went back to the

dance satisfied that if there was anything wrong, Black Hawk would discover it.

It was half an hour later when Yorke came to me between the figures of the dance and begged a word with me.

"Jes as soon as yo' can slip out unbeknownst-like," he said, " that thar decent redskin 's waitin' to speak to yo'-all at the kitchen doah. Yo' 's to go down through the house, so 's nobody outside won't see yo'."

I found an opportunity as soon as that dance was over, and going down through the house, with Yorke as my guide, I found Black Hawk waiting, and without a preliminary word, in slow, sententious fashion, he delivered his message.

" Black Hawk say to White Brother, Beware of White Wolf and six Red Dogs. Wear devil's faces. All gone now. Wait for Little White Fawn going home. Black Hawk go home with White Fawn and Fine Dress and Long Knives' brother and Little Medicine-man and Big Black."

I understood his broken sentences very well. The mummers were, as I had half suspected, the chevalier and a band of Osages. They would lie in wait for Pelagie on our way home and capture her if we were off guard. Black Hawk offered his services to guard her on the way home, and I gladly accepted them, for even then the chevalier's band would outnumber us; and while in a hand-to-hand fight I did not doubt we were much the better men, they would have greatly the advantage of us in being able to spring upon us from ambuscade and get the first shot.

"In solitary dignity stood Black Hawk"

Black Hawk had planned our forces well, but I did not like his title for me, " Fine Dress "; I would rather he had called me "Straight Shoot," the name he had several times given me on our trip together up the Missouri. I had a lurking doubt that he was rebuking me for my vanity.

But there was no time to quarrel about titles. I hunted up Dr. Saugrain, whom I found in the wide chimney-corner, the center of a group of choice spirits,—the two Chouteaus, Mr. Gratiot, Mr. Cerré, Francis Vigo, and Manuel Lisa,—and he was telling them all, with great enthusiasm, about his experiments in quicksilver, and, to my surprise, they were listening as eagerly as if he had been telling tales of war and adventure—which was a marvelous thing to me, to whom science was ever dull and dry-as-dust. I liked not to interrupt him, but the need was pressing, and when I had called him to one side and told him of the presence of the chevalier and his Osages, he was greatly excited.

The thing that troubled me most was that we were without firearms. I had my sword on, of course, and so had the captain, but swords would be of little use, for the savages would not wait for a hand-to-hand encounter, but would fire at long range. The only thing to be done was to borrow from the governor; and in his grand Spanish manner he pressed all the guns of his armory upon us, and said he would send a messenger at once to the fort to have a troop despatched to scour the town and rid it of every suspicious character; which was somewhat of a relief to me, but would have been more so if I could only have felt more confidence in his slow-moving Spanish soldiers.

But the governor begged, since it was a matter that required no haste, that we would say nothing to alarm his guests and so break up the dance in undue time, for, as he said, the kings had not yet been chosen, and it would be a great pity to interfere with that pleasant ceremony. As for me, I would have been quite willing to dispense with it. There would be no pleasure to me in seeing mademoiselle pin her bouquet on the lapel of Josef Papin's coat, thus choosing him her king; but there was nothing to do but go back to the ball-room and see it out.

As I entered the room, there happened to be a little break in the coterie of young men surrounding mademoiselle, and through it I met her glance of eager inquiry. She had evidently missed me from the room, and had her suspicions as to the cause of my long absence. I returned her glance with an assuring smile that all was well, and went on to where I had left Mademoiselle Chouteau a half-hour before. I could not have expected her to sit in a corner waiting for me all that while, yet when I found that she too had her little coterie, and I was evidently not missed, I felt unaccountably hurt and forlorn: as if there was no place for me, an alien, among these St. Louis French people. As I had done many times before, I turned to Madame Saugrain for comfort.

It was nearing midnight, and I had wondered as I came in why they were not dancing. Now I saw the reason of it. Down through the center of the floor came the governor, followed by his tall butler bearing a silver tray with four small bouquets upon it. He went directly to mademoiselle first, and then to the three other queens in turn, presenting each with one of the bouquets and making to each a gallant little speech, which the four maidens received with smiles and blushes and curtsies as became them, but mademoiselle also with a stately grace befitting a queen.

Then there was a moment of intense expectancy, for it was mademoiselle who was first to place her bouquet on the lapel of the coat of the chosen king. I would not look at her. I did not want to see her put it upon Josef Papin's coat, though there was no other there more fitting to receive it or who would make a more royal king for such a queen. So I half turned my back and talked busily to madame, who listened to me not at all, so engrossed was she in the spectacle. It seemed to me a long time in the doing, and presently I saw in madame's eyes a light of eager surprise.

"Look, m'ami, look!" she cried to me. But I would not look; no, not even when I began to feel a suspicion of what was going to happen, from a queer feeling in my backbone, and my heart beating like a trip-hammer, and the blood rushing to the roots of my hair.

"Look, look! I beg you to turn!" madame cried again. But I would not turn, though I heard a subdued murmur of voices all around me, and a soft rustle of silken skirts coming nearer and nearer—not until the soft rustle stopped close beside me, and a sweet voice said:

"Shall I pin my bouquet upon Monsieur's back? I believe it is usual to pin it upon the lapel of the coat."

Then I turned quickly, and for all the answer I made I dropped on one knee and held toward her the lapel of my coat, and as she stooped to pin it on I looked straight into her eyes. And what my eyes said to hers I know not, but quickly the white lids drooped over hers and shut me out from heaven, while the long black lashes lay upon her cheek, and the rich blood swept in a slow flood from the snowy throat to the dark waves of hair that crowned her white brow.

And now her fingers trembled so in pinning on the flowers that she was long in the doing of it (though I could have wished it much longer); and when she had finished I seized the hand that trembled, and for the first time I had ever dared I pressed my lips upon it. I saw another wave of color sweep her face, and then she bade me rise, and as I stood beside her a burst of acclaims came from every lip, "Vive le roi! Vive le roi!" and from one, "Vive le roi et la reine!" and I could not have been prouder had I been king indeed, and she my royal consort beside me!

CHAPTER XII

A MIDNIGHT FRAY

"Out of this nettle, danger, we pluck this flower, safety."

JOSEF PAPIN was the first to bow the knee to me in mock homage, and as his laughing eyes met mine he said, in a tone not so low but that mademoiselle might have heard if she had listened:

"I owe you a grudge, sire. You have stolen the honors I so dearly coveted."

A sudden impulse seized me.

"Would you like to be detailed on some special service to your king and queen?" I asked.

"Most certainly, sire."

"Then stay by me, and when the ceremony of choosing the next king begins I will tell you about it."

Here was a heart as true as steel, ready to be generous to a successful rival and loyal unto death to his queen. It would not hurt to have one more guard for mademoiselle on our midnight ride; we would then more nearly match in numbers the chevalier's band, and by numbers alone might intimidate him from even making the attack. Which was much to be desired, since there would be two ladies in our party, and fighting and bloodshed are not for tender hearts like theirs to know.

But more than that, I thought I could give him no greater pleasure than the chance to prove himself of some real service to mademoiselle, and I would like to atone for stealing the honors he had felt so sure of. And more still: we had decided, in our hasty conference a little while before,—Dr. Saugrain, my captain, and I,—that it would not do at all to wait until the day before the Jour des Rois, as we had at first intended. Since the boat was in readiness, and the captain's business finished, there was no reason why we should not start at once. We had decided, therefore, on the next morning for our departure, for we all felt that as long as the chevalier was lurking about there was no safety for mademoiselle until she was well on her way to France.

To spirit mademoiselle away without a chance of saying good-by to so good a friend as young Papin seemed to me unkind to them both. We could trust him fully, and he should have his chance to say good-by. The captain and Dr. Saugrain had intrusted me with the entire arrangement for mademoiselle's safety and given me command of our little force, so I could make my offer to him with authority. When the opportunity offered to explain to him, a very few minutes sufficed to tell him our fears for mademoiselle's safety. His eyes flashed fire as he listened, and when I said to him, "Would you like to make one of our guard on our way home?" he grasped my hand and wrung it.

"I thank you, monsieur," he said, and then he muttered in my ear:

"What would I not give for one good chance at the chevalier!"

Half an hour later our little cavalcade set off from the governor's house, the governor himself waving us an adieu from the gallery steps. We had placed madame and mademoiselle in the center, with Josef Papin on one side and myself on the other. Black Hawk and Yorke were in the van, and Captain Clarke and Dr. Saugrain brought up the rear.

It had been necessary to make to the two ladies some explanation of these warlike arrangements, but we had said nothing of the presence of the chevalier. I knew it would distress mademoiselle, nor was I sure that her heart would not dictate a surrender, and he would at last accomplish his purpose and bear her away with him, a willing captive, to France. We had only said that a suspicious band of Osages was lurking about, and we thought it wise to take some precautions.

There was, on the Rue de l'Église, which was our direct way home, one spot peculiarly fitted for an ambuscade, where the road dipped suddenly into a deep gully and rose again on the farther side, and where, owing to the marshy nature of the soil, the forest had not been cleared away. It was a lonely bit of road, without houses on either side for a quarter of a mile, and I thought it more than likely that the chevalier would select this spot for an attack, if he intended to make one.

To cheat him, if possible, we rode up the hill of the
Rue de la Tour and turned to the left at the fort,
which was dark and silent, a proof to me that the
troops had left it, and had, no doubt, ere this rid the
village of our enemy. The Rue des Granges, down
which we rode, ran along the crest of the hill, and
there was no marsh here to be crossed, and the gully
had run out to a mere depression. We bore no torches,
and moving as silently as possible through the blackness of the night, we hoped we might escape detection. But as we came to the head of the gully I
glanced down, and at that moment a swift spark as
from a tinder flashed into the air, followed by a steady
glow, and I knew the chevalier was there and that,
deeming himself securely hidden among the trees, he
had just lighted a cigar to keep him company in his
stealthy watch. And I knew, too, that if I but drew
my pistol and took steady aim at that glow-worm in
the dark there would be no more trouble or anxiety
for any of us on mademoiselle's account. For one
moment I hesitated, and Fatima, feeling the involuntary grasp of her bridle-rein, half stopped. But could
I have brought my mind to the committing of a cold-
blooded murder like that, the memory of mademoiselle's plea for the chevalier's safety would have pal-
sied my arm. Yet my generosity had like to have been
our undoing. What it was that betrayed us I know
not. It may have been the tramp of our horses' feet,
conveyed down the gully as by an ear-trumpet; or it
is possible that in spite of the darkness our moving
figures were silhouetted against the faint light in the

western sky; or a stone, loosened by one of our horses, may have rolled down the gully to the chevalier's feet. Whatever it was, I knew we were discovered. There was suddenly a soft call of a whippoorwill from below us, answered quickly and softly by a half-dozen others, and then a sound as of hasty but cautious stirrings. I knew what it meant: they had seen us, and they would cut us off before we reached our gates. I gave a quick word of command:

"Ride as hard and as fast as you can; never mind the noise you make. We are discovered! Our only hope of avoiding a fight is by reaching the gates first."

Black Hawk and Yorke were off like a shot: Yorke, I have no doubt, with the intention of getting to cover as quickly as possible, but Black Hawk, I believe, after a scalp or two. I had to call to them both to come back and keep close to the ladies. Mademoiselle had uttered not a word, only urged her little La Bette to do her utmost, but madame, since the embargo of silence was removed, did not cease to utter a string of prayers and entreaties to "le bon Dieu" to save us all from the savages.

We were on the crest of the hill, and looking down to the Rue de l'Église I could get an inkling of what progress the savages were making from an occasional flash of shining metal in a ray of light from some window; for though the hour was late the town was still astir from the governor's ball, and lights were in most of the houses. As yet they were some distance behind us, but though we were on horses and they afoot, they

11

had a much shorter distance to travel and they were
fleet runners. We were like a chain, only as strong
as our weakest link; we were only as fleet as our slowest horse, and that was the one that bore madame's
plump figure. La Bette was not much faster, and
I began to get in a fever of impatience, as I could see
the savages were steadily gaining on us. Should we
meet them in that dark lane leading down from the
Rue des Granges to the Rue de l'Église we were almost certainly at their mercy. In a few minutes it
was evident to me that at our present rate of progress
they were sure to meet us there, and there seemed no
possible way of hurrying our two slow ponies. I
would have turned back but that I believed the chevalier was sharp enough to have sent part of his men up
the gully to cut off our retreat, should we attempt
one. There was but one thing to do: Fatima had
saved mademoiselle once; she should save her again.
I leaned back of mademoiselle and spoke to Josef
Papin:

" We will never reach the house before the savages
at this rate. I shall take mademoiselle on Fatima and
get her safe inside the gates. You and Black Hawk
follow me as quickly as possible, and the other three
will remain to protect Madame Saugrain."

Then I called a halt and explained my plan to the
others. It needed but a word, and there was no
demur but a low wail from Madame Saugrain, who,
I make no doubt, believed Pelagie was going to certain
death. Mademoiselle herself said nothing; I think for
the first time she realized that the chevalier was lead-

ing the Osages and that their only aim was to get possession of her.

My explanation had not consumed a minute, and as I finished it I turned in my saddle.

" By your leave, Mademoiselle," I said, bent over and lifted her from La Bette's back (and never was I more thankful for my great strength and that she was but a feather-weight, else had the feat proved a difficult one) and placed her securely in front of me on Fatima. 'T was not so comfortable a seat as at my back, no doubt, but I dared not risk her where I could not see what befell her. One word to Fatima:

"Sweetheart, for our lives!" I laid the reins low on her neck, and we were off with a long swinging stride that soon left even Black Hawk and Papin far behind, though they were urging their good horses to the utmost.

There was not a moment to be lost, for I could see that the savages were nearing the junction of the lane and the Rue de l'Église, and we must pass that point before them and ride some twenty paces down the Rue de l'Église before we should reach the gates and a safe refuge behind the walls of Émigré's Retreat. I did not cease to urge Fatima by my voice, though never touching her reins. One arm held mademoiselle securely, and my right hand lay on the holster of my pistol, ready for instant service.

Out of the Rue des Granges we shot like a bolt, into the steep and rough lane leading down the hill. Had I not held mademoiselle so firmly I think that swift swerve at the sharp corner might have unseated us both. Faster and faster we flew, like a swallow on the wing, Fatima's dainty feet as surely placed among the rocks and holes of the rough road as if she had been pacing in Rotten Row. Well she knew that a misstep of hers now might mean death to all three of us, and well she knew that her master trusted her perfectly.

I could feel mademoiselle's heart fluttering like a caged bird for terror; my own was beating like a trip-hammer, for I was near enough now to perceive that the savages too were redoubling their efforts and it was still a chance which of us would reach the corner of the Rue de l'Église first.

" Faster, Sweetheart, faster! " I urged in an agony of apprehension as I pressed my knees close to Fatima's hot sides, and felt her breath beginning to come in long laboring moans as my great weight (with mademoiselle's added one, which might yet prove the last feather) began to tell on her. Bravely she responded to my voice and stretched out farther and faster at every stride, and in another moment, with another tremendous swerve, we had turned the corner into the Rue de l'Église with the foremost of the savages not twenty feet behind us. I expected nothing less than a bullet in my back, and was glad indeed that mademoiselle was in front of me, fully shielded by my broad shoulders, for I knew whatever befell me Fatima would carry mademoiselle into the garden and to the very door of Émigré's Retreat before any savage could possibly reach her. But I felt no bullet, nor did any whistle by my ears, and I wondered why, until I saw, what the savage possibly saw too in the dim light, that mademoiselle (whose head had been cowering on my breast like a child in great terror trying to hide from the sight of danger) had, as we turned into the Rue de l'Église, raised her head and looked boldly over my shoulder.

I have no doubt the savage feared to shoot, lest he should hit that white face, and I did not doubt that was mademoiselle's plan, to use herself as a shield for me. I was very angry with her, but I had only time to draw her head roughly down on my shoulder again when we were within the gates and, in a dozen mighty strides, at the very door of Émigré's Retreat.

At the sound of clattering hoofs, Narcisse and half a dozen servants, among them mademoiselle's maid, Clotilde, came running out on the gallery. I sprang from my horse and lifted mademoiselle down, in too great haste to be gentle, I fear.

"Take your mistress into the house and bar every door and window!" I cried sharply. "The savages are after us!"

It needed but that word "savages" to lend wings of terror to the usually slow and lazy movements of the negroes. With shrieks of women and shouts of men, they dragged mademoiselle into the house, and I heard the hasty putting up of bars. Then I turned to meet that one savage who was so far in advance and who must by this time have reached the gates. I had no fear, now that I was free of mademoiselle, for I felt myself good for two or three of them, and I could even now hear the clattering hoofs of Josef

Papin's and Black Hawk's horse coming down the lane, and they were a host in themselves. But by the time I had reached the gate there was a great noise of shouts and firing and wild halloos at the corner, and I ran on, knowing that Papin and Black Hawk must have met the savages, and knowing that the two would be outnumbered and greatly in need of my assistance.

But I had hardly got into the thick of the mêlée, cutting and slashing with my sword for fear a shot would go astray and hit one of my friends should I use my pistol, when the savages suddenly turned tail and ran off, disappearing in the night like shadows. For a moment I thought it was my prowess that had put them to flight, and I began in my heart to plume myself thereon. But only for a moment, for up the Rue des Granges and down the steep lane there came charging the belated troops of Spanish horsemen (they had stupidly been scouring the other end of the village, it seems), and would have charged full upon us, no doubt,—since in the dark one could not tell friend from foe,—had not young Papin called out in Spanish that we were friends and belonged to Dr. Saugrain's party. Whereupon the officer halted long enough to inquire in which direction the savages had fled, and with many a round Spanish oath that he would not leave one of the red dogs alive if he had to follow them to Cape Girardeau, he led his troop clattering off toward the stockade. And no sooner had they disappeared than down the steep lane came the rest of the party, Madame Saugrain half dead with fright (for she had heard the sounds of firing and of fighting, and feared the worst for Pelagie), the doughty doctor and my captain not a little disappointed that they should have missed the fray, and Yorke almost as much so, since it had turned out to be such an easy victory.

But when I had told madame that Pelagie was safe in the house and the savages had fled and, except for a scratch on my forehead that scarce drew blood, no one was hurt (though at that very moment Black Hawk came creeping back out of the darkness hanging a dripping scalp to his belt, which when I perceived I was nigh sick unto death for a moment)— when I told her all this (and, fortunately, madame did not see Black Hawk's ugly trophy), she broke forth into a Te Deum and went happily up to the house, where Pelagie herself came running out to meet her, and they fell into each other's arms and, after the manner of women, wept long and loud for joy, though they had shed no tears when there might have been occasion for them.

CHAPTER XIII

"A PRETTY BOY!"

> "And to be wroth with one we love
> Doth work like madness in the brain."

AT the door of the house, Black Hawk and Yorke branched off to the servants' quarters, and I followed them to see what had become of Fatima, for I had left her standing beside the gallery when I ran back to meet the savage. I found her standing patiently by the stable door waiting to be let in, and she whinnied with delight as she heard my step. I called to Yorke to come and take care of her (for I was in haste to get back to the house), and at the sound of my voice Leon came rushing, in great bounds. Together we walked down to the well, that I might wash the blood from my face before presenting myself to the ladies. The well was in a low part of the grounds, some little distance from the house, and it was while I was vigorously splashing my hands and face that I heard a low growl from Leon. I looked up quickly and thought I caught the glimpse of a gun, and instinctively I sprang to one side, that if any one was aiming at me I might cheat him of his aim. At the same moment Leon sprang with a terrible roar

straight at the spot where I had fancied I saw the
metal shining and where now I was sure I heard the
rustle of some one fleeing. I followed quickly after, for
the thought of any human creature in the power of
that great beast in rage was awful to me. Enemy or
no, I would if possible save him from being torn to
pieces by a furious dog.

As I ran, I called to him as I had heard his mistress
call, and in French, lest he might not understand
English:

"À bas, Leon! Tais-toi, mon ange!" But the
words had no meaning for him in my gruff voice: it
was the soft music of his mistress's tones he understood and obeyed. I heard another furious roar, a
wild shriek as of a creature in mortal fear or pain,
and then a shot. I was on the spot almost before the
shot had ceased to ring in my ears. There lay Leon on
the white snow, a dark mass writhing in what I feared
was a death-struggle, and above him stood the chevalier, his smoking pistol in his hand. I knew as soon
as I saw him in Indian costume that he was the savage
who had been the foremost of his band, who had followed us so closely and had disappeared when I had
gone to seek him. It was in the doctor's garden he
had disappeared and lain in hiding to accomplish the
capture or execute a revenge later.

My own pistol was in my hand, and I covered him
with it. In that moment of rage when Leon, whom
I had learned to love and who loved me,—Leon, *her*
dog,—great, beautiful, tried and trusty companion
and friend,—lay dying from a shot from that villain's

hand: in that moment of rage I came near putting an
end at once and forever to a life that I believed could
never be anything but a curse to any mortal associated with it. But the words of Pelagie rang in my
ears and stayed my hand:

"If it is in your power, save the chevalier!"

His own pistol was empty and he knew himself to
be at my mercy, and that his life was worth no more
than the snuffing out of a candle; yet, to do him justice,
he held his ground and returned my gaze as fearlessly
as he might have done had we stood with drawn
swords, each ready for the thrust and parry.

The old moon had but lately risen, and, hanging
low in the eastern sky, her level rays fell full on the
chevalier's face. It was white enough, but that might
have been the effect of her sickly light reflected from
the ghostly snow; the daredevil in his eyes said plainly
as words, " Do your worst! "

For a full half-minute I kept him covered, and for
a full half-minute he returned my steady gaze. Then
suddenly there arose from the house the noise of
doors opening and shutting and the hurried tramp of
feet. I knew what it meant. The shot had been
heard and they were coming to see what had happened.
In a moment they would all be upon us,—my captain,
the doctor, young Papin, yes, and Yorke and Black
Hawk too,—and there would be no possibility of sav-
ing the chevalier.

He heard the noise, also, and he too knew what it
meant. For one instant his eyes wavered and he
looked as if he would turn and run, spite of my threat-

ening pistol. Only for an instant, and then he drew himself up proudly and threw back his head.

"Fire, Monsieur," he said. "Why do you wait to let others share the glory?"

For answer I lowered my pistol.

"Monsieur," I said, "you richly deserve death, and for a moment you were in deadly peril; but Mademoiselle Pelagie, whom you would basely wrong, pleads for you, and I spare your life at her intercession. If you will turn and run directly south, there is a low place in the wall, and on this side a pile of logs by which you may easily scale it, and almost directly opposite a narrow opening in the stockade through which you can force your way. But you must run for your life. I will remain here and do what I can to prevent pursuit; 't will be no easy matter to keep Black Hawk off your trail."

Yet he did not start at once. He hesitated and his eyes fell; then he looked up quickly and half extended his hand.

"Monsieur, you have been a generous foe; will you permit that I clasp your hand?"

But a flood of memories rushed over me: his unswording me in the dance; his attempt to steal mademoiselle at the picnic and to poison her mind against her friends; this second attempt, where it was through no fault of his that we were not all dead men and mademoiselle far on her way to Cape Girardeau, in the power of savages and a villain more to be dreaded than they. I put my hand behind me and said coldly:

"My hand belongs to my friends and to a foe whom

I can honor. Monsieur, if you tarry longer, I will not
be responsible for your life.''

Even in the pale light I could see the deep flush
sweep his cheek and his hand spring involuntarily to
his sword-hilt. But he thought better of it, turned,
and strode quickly away toward the low spot in the
stone wall.

Then I had leisure to think of poor Leon. I knelt
down beside him, where a dark pool was rapidly wi-
dening in the white snow. I could see where the red
fountain gushed from a wound in his shoulder. It
was possible no vital part had been touched and he
might be saved could that gushing fountain of life-
blood be stanched. As it was, his eyes were already
glazing and his limbs stiffening and his breath coming
in long-drawn sobs, like a man in extremity. He
was like to breathe his last before even those hurrying
feet, fast drawing near, should reach him. I knew
enough of surgery to know that I must apply a tight
bandage above the wound; but where should I find a
bandage? My flimsy lace handkerchief was worse than
useless. There was no help for it: the purple silken
sword-sash, of which I was mightily proud, whose long
fringed ends, tied in a graceful knot, fell almost to
my knees, must be sacrificed. I hastily unknotted it,
and tenderly as possible, that I might not hurt the
poor fellow more than needs must (for his flesh quivered under my touch), I bound it round the shoulder
and with all my strength drew it tight. Quickly the
gushing fountain stayed, and then taking from my

pocket a flask that my mother herself had always bid me carry, I forced a few drops into his fast-setting jaws. I knew I had done the right thing when, by the time they had all come up, Leon had lifted his head and was feebly licking my hand.

Their first exclamations of horror were followed by a hail of questions:

"Who has done this?" "Where is he?" "Did you see him?" "How did it happen?"

To all their questions I made but one answer:

"I heard the shot, and ran up to find Leon lying on the ground, dying as I believed, and I have done what I could to help him."

"And you have saved his life, or, at least, if he lives, he will have only you to thank," said Dr. Saugrain, who had been on his knees beside Leon, examining him.

"You and your silken sash," he added, with the old twinkle of his eye. "'T was a noble sacrifice, and we all appreciate how great a one."

The good doctor was ever twitting me on what he was pleased to call my love of dress; but I made him no answer this time, for I was watching Black Hawk, who, with an Indian's cunning, had at once discovered the footprints in the snow and that there was but one pair of them, and was stealing off after them. That would never do.

"Great Chief," I cried, "'t is no use following the Red Dog; he has had too long a start. Will you help us to carry the dog of La Petite to the house, where we can put him in a warm bed? 'T will never do to let him lie in the snow, and 't will take us all to carry him comfortably.''

Black Hawk hesitated, and then grunted out an unwilling consent. I think it seemed to him somewhat beneath the dignity of a great chief to carry a dog, and only because of his love for La Petite did he bring his mind to it. Nor did my little fiction about the Red Dog deceive him.

"No Red Dog," he grunted. "White Wolf! Trail fresh. Black Hawk bring his scalp to La Petite."

But the doctor saved me the necessity of arguing further with him.

"Red Dog or White Wolf, Black Hawk," he said, " n'importe! 'T is the mastiff we must look to now. A sad day 't would be for all of us should he die; so lend a hand, vite, vite! "

And this from the doctor, who had told me when I first met him he would not have cared had I killed Leon, for he loved him not. The truth was that the doctor's devotion to Leon and Leon's to him were second only to the devotion of the dog and his mistress to each other, though, owing to the fact that Leon often stalked into his laboratory at inopportune moments, sometimes spoiling the most delicate experiment by poking his great inquisitive muzzle where it did not belong, the doctor's patience was sometimes tried almost beyond the limit of endurance.

The doctor's exhortation, uttered in a sharp and clipping way peculiar to him when excited, was effectual. Very tenderly between us all we managed to

lift the mastiff, and bore him to the negroes' quarters, where, in Narcisse's cabin, we made him a warm
bed and washed and dressed his wound, and left him
in a fair way to recovery.

I was a little behind the others in reaching the
house, for I had delayed about some last arrangements for Leon's comfort, and then it had been necessary that I should make a hasty toilet. Hands and
face were soiled with blood and grime (my purple
velvets I feared were ruined forever, but I would
not take the time to change them), and my hair was
in much disorder. A hasty scrubbing of hands and
face and a retying of my hair-ribbon to try to con-
fine the rebellious yellow curls that were tumbling all
over my head, and that I so much despised, were all
I permitted myself time for. Yet the few minutes I
had lingered had been long enough for the launching
of a thunderbolt, and I arrived just at the moment to
see the havoc it had made.

Mademoiselle in her ball-dress had thrown herself
on her knees beside madame, her white arms flung
around madame's neck, her face buried in her motherly bosom, sobbing piteously. Madame gently
stroked the dark curls, saying over and over only the
same words, "My child, my child, my poor child!"
while the tears flowed down her own cheeks all un-
noticed.

The doctor stood beside her, patting as he could
her white arm or dark curls or tender cheek, and saying helplessly:

"Voilà, voilà! Quoi donc! N'importe, n'importe!'' and many other as senseless words, and growing every moment more hopeless and helpless as mademoiselle but wept the more bitterly.

On the other side of the room stood young Papin, pale and rigid as if carved in stone, his eyes fixed on mademoiselle. I feared that for him too it had been a bitter blow, for I could not doubt that it was the announcement of mademoiselle's departure on the morrow that had created such consternation.

The captain had discreetly turned his back and was looking out of the window. At the sound of my entrance he turned and beckoned me to him.

'' I fear 't will never do,'' he whispered; '' the maiden is breaking her heart.''

As if she had heard his words, mademoiselle lifted her head, and though her face was tear-stained and her hair hanging in disheveled locks about it, it was still the most beautiful face I had ever seen.

At sight of me she flung her head back, and her eyes flashed. She extended one round white arm toward me, and in tones of bitter scorn she exclaimed:

"It is you, you, Monsieur, who have done this! I will not leave my guardians and my home and go away with you! You would not hear of my going with the chevalier, yet he was a French gentleman, and not merely a pretty boy!''

Madame and the doctor tried in vain to stop her tirade. She was in a fury; such blazing eyes, such crimson cheeks, and voice quivering with scorn. For a moment I was abashed and would have liked to slink out of sight. But when she was so ungenerous as to call me "a pretty boy," the fire returned to my heart, and I too drew myself up proudly.

"Mademoiselle, listen to me!" I said sternly. "I have but a few minutes ago spared the chevalier's life when I had him at my mercy, and shown him the way to escape from your friends here, who were running at the sound of his shot, and who, had they found him in Dr. Saugrain's grounds, would have made short work with him, I fear." (I could not but note out of the corner of my eye while I was speaking the quick start of young Papin at this announcement, the eager interest of my captain, and the doctor's look of dismay.)

" I spared him, and I told him that I spared him, only because you had begged me to do my utmost to save him if he should ever fall into my power. I cannot believe that he would have treated me or any one of your friends with the like courtesy. He is now well on his way to Cape Girardeau, but I think he is not gone so far but that he can be easily overtaken. Black Hawk is ready to set out at once; indeed, it is with much difficulty that I have restrained him from so doing. Then, if you desire it, and Dr. Saugrain and madame approve, you can return to France under the chevalier's protection."

I lifted my hand as the doctor and his wife both started to speak.

" Nay, my friends, permit that mademoiselle first tells me her pleasure."

Then, as mademoiselle (whose eyes were no longer flashing with scorn, but regarding me with the same

12

wonder I had seen in them before) did not speak, I
said, if possible with greater sternness:

" Speak at once, mademoiselle: shall we send for the
chevalier and bring him back? There is no time to
be lost; every minute is carrying him away from
you as fast as a very good pair of legs for running
can take him."

I hope I did not exceed the limits of courtesy in so
speaking of the chevalier, but it was hard to resist a
little fling at the " French gentleman " to whom the
" pretty boy " had been so disparagingly compared.
I caught a twinkle in the doctor's eye and a fleeting
smile on young Papin's face and on my captain's, but
I looked only at mademoiselle. She was meek enough
now, but she no longer looked at me; her dark lashes
were sweeping her cheek.

" You need not send for him," she said.

" Then, mademoiselle," I went on, a little more
gently, " it seems to me and to your friends that the
only other way to return to France is the way we have
planned. You will be as safe under Captain Clarke's
care as you would be under Dr. Saugrain's. He will
take you to his sister, Mrs. O'Fallon, who will be as
a mother to you, until a suitable escort can be found
for you to New York to place you under Mr. Livingston's care. As for me, I shall not in any way annoy
you: you need not know I am on the boat; and as
soon as you are placed in Mrs. O'Fallon's care I shall
say good-by to you forever, and continue my journey
east, since it is indeed time I should be starting homeward. Dr. and Madame Saugrain will assure you that

this is the most feasible plan, and I hope once more that you will not be deterred from accepting it by any fear of annoyance from me. There will be none. If you decide to go with us, we must make an early start, and there will be many things for me to attend to. Captain Clarke will inform me of your decision, and I will see Dr. Saugrain and madame in the morning. Till then, I wish you all a very good night.''

I made my grand bow, turned quickly, and left the room, though Dr. Saugrain and his wife both tried to stay me, and young Papin sprang forward with an eager hand to prevent me.

I was bitterly angry, and more hurt and disappointed than angry. Outside I strode furiously up and down in the snow, calling myself a fool that I should care. Mademoiselle might be a great lady in France, I said to myself, but to me she had shown herself only a fickle, capricious, silly maiden. But even as I so spoke to myself my heart revolted. I saw her once more weeping in madame's arms, and I began to think it was only natural and commendable in her that she should be so stirred at the thought of leaving friends who had been so good to her, and that I had been much harder with her than was well.

And at last, as I began to walk myself into a calmer frame of mind, I could have wished that I had not made that rash promise to keep myself out of her sight on the boat. My word was given and I would have to stick to it, but in my own room, as I listened to the murmur of voices still going on in the room below me,

I thought no longer with anger, but sadly enough, of the long delightful tête-à-têtes with mademoiselle I had dreamed of when I had first planned this trip on the Great River.

A bright drop suddenly fell on my hand. I brushed my eyes angrily.

" Domtiferation! " I whispered furiously to myself. " Mademoiselle was right! A pretty boy indeed! "

CHAPTER XIV

A CREOLE LOVE-SONG

"So sweetly she bade me adieu,
    I thought that she bade me return."

FOR three days we had been floating down the
Great River, and for three days I had kept my
word. Mademoiselle had not been annoyed by me;
she had hardly seen me. Much to my captain's vexation, I had refused to take my meals with him and
mademoiselle, though our cozy table of three had been
one of the brightest parts of my dream when I was
planning this trip.

It was nearing the supper-hour on the evening of
this third day. The men were making ready to tie
up for the night (for navigation on the river at night
was a dangerous matter), and for the hundredth time
I was wishing with all my heart that I had not been
so rash as to make that promise to keep out of mademoiselle's way. The vision of a hot supper comfortably served in her warm and cozy cabin was of itself
sufficiently enticing, as all my meals since coming
aboard had been brought to me in any out-of-the-way
corner of the deck, and I had found them but cold
comfort. Not that my resolution was weakening,

181

though my captain let no meal-hour pass without
doing his best to weaken it, and more than once had
brought me a message from mademoiselle herself begging me to join them at table. No; I was as fixed as
ever, and, in a way, enjoying my own discomfort, since
to pose as a martyr ever brings with it a certain
satisfaction which is its own reward.

The weather had been clear and mild up to this
time; but this evening an icy sleet was beginning to
fall, and I glanced at mademoiselle's cabin window,
brightly lighted and eloquent of warmth and dryness,
and fetched a great sigh as I looked. A voice at my
elbow said:

" Monsieur is sad?—or lonely, perhaps? "

I started, for I had supposed myself entirely alone
on that end of the boat—the men all busy with their
tying-up preparations forward, and mademoiselle and
the captain in the cabin. I lifted my hat and bowed
ceremoniously.

" Neither, Mademoiselle."

Mademoiselle hesitated. I saw she felt repulsed,
and I secretly gloried in her embarrassment. Neither
would I help her out by adding another word; I waited
for what she might say further.

" Monsieur," she said presently, " you have shown
me much kindness in the past, and done me great
service. I would like to have you know that I am not
ungrateful."

" I do not desire your gratitude, Mademoiselle,"
I said coldly (though it hurt me to speak so when she
was so evidently trying to be friendly with me).

"No gentleman could have done less, even if he were not a French gentleman."

The light from her cabin window fell full upon her. I could see that she colored quickly at my retort, and half started to go away, but turned back again.

"Monsieur," she said earnestly, "I have a very humble apology to make to you. I hope you will forgive me for my rude and wicked speech. I was beside myself with sorrow at the thought of being so suddenly torn from my friends, and for the time nothing else weighed with me, not even that you had just saved my life at the peril of your own. Ah, how could I have been so base! I wonder not that you will not even look at so mean a creature, and you do well to shun her as if she were vile."

No man could have resisted her sweet humility. For a moment all my anger melted.

"Mademoiselle, do not apologize to me!" I cried. "If there are any apologies to be made, it is I who should make them for not knowing how to understand and appreciate what you felt."

A quick radiance sprang into her eyes, and with a childlike abandon she extended both her hands to me.

"Then you forgive me?" she cried.

I took one hand and held it in both mine, and as I bent my knee I lifted it to my lips.

"If I am forgiven, my Queen," I answered softly.

Her dark eyes, tender and glorious, looked down into mine. For a moment I forgot she was a great lady in France; to me she was only the most bewitching and adorable maiden in the wide world. She was wearing a heavy capote to shield her from the weather, but the hood had fallen slightly back, and the falling sleet had spangled the little fringe of curls about her face with diamonds that sparkled in the candle-shine, but were not half so bright as her starry eyes. I could have knelt forever on the icy deck if I might have gazed forever into their heavenly depths. But in a minute she let the white lids fall over them.

"Rise, Monsieur," she said gently. "You are forgiven, but on one condition."

"Name it, my Queen!" And I rose to my feet, but still held her hand. "No condition can be too hard."

"That you come to supper with us to-night, and to every meal while I am on your boat."

The condition fetched me back to earth with a shock. I remembered all the cause, and I answered moodily:

"My word has been given, Mademoiselle; I cannot go back on my word."

"Your word was given to me, and I absolve you from it," she said.

"But in the presence of others," I objected. "I am bound by it, unless I be shamed before them."

"Only your captain is here," she said, still gently; "and he, too, urges it."

But still I was obdurate. Then at last she drew away her hand and lifted her head proudly.

"Your Queen commands you!" she said haughtily, and turned and walked away. Yet she walked but slowly. Perhaps she thought I would overtake her, or call her back and tell her I had yielded. But I was still fighting with my stubborn pride, and let her go. I watched her close her cabin door, then for five minutes I strode rapidly up and down the slippery deck.

"Your Queen commands you!" I thrilled at her words. My Queen! Yes, but only if I were her king. Now that I was away from her, and her glowing eyes were not melting my heart to softest wax, I was resolved never again to submit to her tyranny and caprice. I would go to supper, because she commanded it; but I would never for a moment forget that she was a great lady of France, and I a proud citizen of America—too proud to woo where I could only meet with scorn.

So I went to my cabin and made a careful toilet, and when Yorke came to call me to supper, I presented myself in mademoiselle's cabin. I had not been in it since she had come aboard, and, though I had carefully planned and arranged every detail of it for her comfort, I would not have known it for the same place. What she had done to it I know not; a touch here, a touch there, such as women's fingers know how to give, and the bare and rough boat's cabin had become a dainty little boudoir. The round table, draped in snowy linen, with places set for three; the silver and glass shining in the rays from two tall candles; Yorke and mademoiselle's maid Clotilde bringing in each a smoking dish to set upon it; and mademoiselle standing beside it like the glowing heart of a ruby, her dark beauty well set off by a gown of crimson paduasoy, with rich lace through which the graceful neck and rounded arms gleamed white and soft: it all looked to me like a picture from one of Master Titian's canvases, and I could hardly believe that if I should look through the closely drawn curtains I would see the rough and dirty decks of our barge, and, beyond, the dark forest of the Illinois shore, where even now hostile savages might be lurking, ready to spring upon us with blood-curdling yells.

The captain was already there, chatting gaily with mademoiselle as I came in, and he had the delicacy to make his greeting of me as natural and unsurprised as if I had never been absent from the little board, while mademoiselle added a touch of gracious cordiality to hers.

I was on my mettle. Determined that never again, even to herself, should she call me a boy, I summoned to my aid all the *savoir-faire* I could command. I was (at least, in my own estimation, and I hoped also in hers) the elegant man of the world, discoursing at ease on every fashionable topic, and, to my own amazement, parrying every thrust of her keen repartee, and sometimes sending her as keen in return. I think the situation had gone to my head. Certainly I had never before thought myself a brilliant fellow, but when I rose to make my bow to mademoiselle (and it was indeed a very grand one), I hoped that even in her mind I would not suffer by comparison with any French gentleman, no, though it were the chevalier himself.

I did not see mademoiselle again until the midday meal next day; for all the morning I was busy with the men, making the difficult and dangerous turn from the Great River into the Ohio, past Fort Massac. Once in the Ohio, there was no surcease from hard work—poling, paddling, or cordelling, sometimes all three together, to climb the rushing stream.

Punctually at the noon-hour I presented myself at table, and again at supper, and my good star did not desert me. Quip and repartee and merry tale and polished phrase were all at my tongue's end, and no one could have been more amazed than I at my own brilliancy.

But I lingered not a moment after the meal was over, and I never saw mademoiselle between times. If she came out to take the air on deck, I was hard at work with the men, sometimes taking my turn at paddling, sometimes, though not often, at poling; but our crew of French Canadians were better at that than I. Indeed, there are no such fellows in the world for navigating these dangerous Western waters.

The weather had grown mild, and often in the evening I envied Yorke (who had straightway, of course, made desperate love to Clotilde, who was old enough to be his mother), sitting in the bow of the boat and thrumming his banjo lightly as he sang her some creole love-song he had picked up in St. Louis.

Our trip was fast drawing to a close. The last evening on the river had arrived. We would tie up one more night; all hands at the cordelle and the poles, we would reach Mrs. O'Fallon's by noon, in time for dinner. I had determined not to linger there at all. I should go on, the same afternoon, to my uncle's plantation, not many miles away, and the next day start for the East. I had told mademoiselle I would say good-by to her forever when we reached Mrs. O'Fallon's, but in my own mind I was saying good-by to her now. It had been for several days that I had felt the weight of this approaching hour, and my brilliance had gradually departed. I had grown duller and quieter at each succeeding meal, and mademoiselle, too, had grown quieter (she could never be dull). Sometimes I fancied she looked sad, and once I was sure I recognized the trace of tears in her beautiful eyes. There was nothing strange in that; it would have been strange indeed if she could have left home and friends, and started on a long and dangerous journey (with no companion but the faithful negro woman who had been nurse and lady's-maid and trusted friend for ten long years, but who was still but servant and slave), and had not often been overcome with sadness. Indeed, there were times, when she was merriest at the table, when I had mentally accused her of heartlessness as I thought of the two fond old people mourning for her in Émigré's Retreat. So, though I would have liked to attribute some of mademoiselle's sadness to an approaching separation, I had no grounds for so doing, and I scoffed at myself for the attempt.

That last night at supper I made a desperate effort to be my gayest, but it was uphill work, and the more so because neither the captain nor mademoiselle seconded my efforts with any heartiness; so when supper was ended, feeling that the hour had at last come, I stood as mademoiselle rose from her seat, and instead of excusing myself at once, as had been my custom, I lingered.

"Mademoiselle," I said, "we have had our last meal aboard together (God prospering our voyage), and I desire to thank you for your courtesy, and to say to you that whatever there may have been in our intercourse during our brief acquaintance not pleasant to either of us to hold in remembrance, I hope you will banish it from your memory, as I shall from mine. I shall think of these weeks always as among the brightest of my life, and perhaps, had I been a chevalier of France instead of an American boy, I should not so easily have said good-by to the Rose of St. Louis; it would have been au revoir instead!"

I was standing as I said it all formally, with the air of one making pretty compliments: for I did not wish mademoiselle to know how every word was from the depths of my heart; nor would I have lightly betrayed myself before my captain, who was not apparently listening, but had turned to give some instructions to Yorke.

Mademoiselle's color came and went as I spoke. She did not answer me for a moment, and when she did it was in a low tone, and she seemed to speak with effort:

"Monsieur, you are ungenerous! You will never forgive my unhappy speech. Permit me to say you have taught me that a chevalier of France may be outshone by an American gentleman in bravery, manliness, truth, and honor—in every virtue except the doubtful one of knowing how to utter pleasant insincerities to us maidens. And I will not say good-by. Am I not to see you again?''

''I will certainly see you in the morning, Mademoiselle, but there may be no time for more than a word, and so I take this opportunity to say good-by.''

''I will not say good-by, Monsieur''—with the old wilful toss of the head. ''I will tell your captain he is not to let you go back to Philadelphia so soon. But no matter where you go, I will never say good-by; it shall always be au revoir.''

She smiled up at me with such bewitching grace that perforce I smiled back at her, and if she had but asked me this evening, as she had on many others, to linger in her cozy cabin for a game of piquet, I would not have had the courage to say no. But she did not ask me, and, much as I longed to stay, there was nothing for me to do but to pick up my hat and say, with the best grace I could:

''I thank you with all my heart, Mademoiselle, and, for to-night at least, au revoir!''

An hour later my captain and I were leaning on the rail in the stern of the boat, looking up at the tree-crowned bluffs standing dark against the moonlight and listening to the soft lapping of the water against the boat's sides. We did not realize that we were hidden by a great pile of peltries, as high as our heads, which Captain Clarke was taking back to Kentucky with him to sell on commission for Pierre Chouteau, until we heard voices. Mademoiselle and Clotilde had evidently found a seat on the other side of the pile of

pelts, and mademoiselle was speaking in plaintive
tone:

"And they would not let me bring Leon with me!
He at least would have loved me and been a companion
and protector when all the world forsake me."

Then Clotilde's rich negro voice:

"Mademoiselle, I find out why they not let you
bring Leon. Mr. Yorke tell me last night. Leon shot,
the night before we come away."

There was a heartrending cry, and then a torrent of
swift French:

"Leon shot! My Leon! Why have they not told
me? Oh, the villains! Who shot him, Clotilde? My
poor angel! My Leon! No one left to love your poor
mistress!" And much more that I cannot recall, I
was so excited and angry that that rascal Yorke should
have caused her such needless pain. But every word
of Clotilde's next speech was graven on my heart as
with a knife of fire.

"Mr. Yorke say they all hear the shot, and they all
run out to see what the matter, and there stood the
lieutenant with pistol in his hand, and Yorke say he
don' *think* he shoot him, but—"

Clotilde had no chance to say another word.

"Shoot my Leon! He! Ah, I could not have believed such baseness! He never forgave him for
throwing him down-stairs! His last act before leaving Émigré's Retreat! Oh, mon Dieu, what perfidy!
What a monster!"

And every word was so interrupted with sighs and
moans and sobs as would have melted a heart of stone.

As for me, I was nearly turned to stone, such horror did I feel that she should think me guilty of so base a deed. I had no thought of acting in my self-defense, but my captain started up at once with a quick exclamation, and, seizing my arm, dragged me around the pile of pelts. There was mademoiselle, seated on a low bundle of them, weeping as if her heart would break, and Clotilde trying in vain to stay the torrent she had set loose.

"Mademoiselle," said the captain, quickly, "there has been some terrible mistake. It was the chevalier who shot Leon; it was this lad" (laying his arm affectionately across my shoulders) "who saved his life."

Now half the joy of this speech to me was taken out of it by the captain's way of treating me as a boy—I think the captain never thought of me in any other light; and I made up my mind on the instant that I should seize the very first opportunity to beg him, at least in mademoiselle's presence, to treat me as a man.

But mademoiselle was so concerned with the matter of the captain's speech, she paid no heed to its manner; and it chagrined me not a little that her first thought was for Leon, and not that I was innocent.

"Saved his life!" she cried. "Is my Leon alive?"

"He is, Mademoiselle," I said coldly, "and I have every reason to believe he is doing well. My 'last act' before leaving Émigré's Retreat was to visit him in Narcisse's cabin. I renewed his dressing, and left minute instructions as to his care. We had thought to spare you this anxiety, Mademoiselle, but two blundering servants have undone our plans."

"Ah, Monsieur," cried mademoiselle, impetuously, springing to her feet and extending both her hands to me in her pretty French fashion, "how unjust I have been to you! How can I ever thank you enough for your care of my poor Leon? Your last act in the cold and dark of the early morning, and the hurry of departure, to see that my Leon was taken care of, and I have accused you of making it one of base revenge! Ah, Monsieur, can you ever forgive me?" half whispering.

I had taken her hands and was holding them as I looked down into her radiant eyes. I bent low and kissed them both, first one and then the other, as I said (very low, so that the captain and Clotilde should not hear):

"Mademoiselle, I can forgive you everything."

But I needed not to speak so low, for when I lifted my head the captain and Clotilde had both disappeared. And whither they had gone, or why, I neither knew nor cared. For now a mad intoxication seized me. This was the last evening I should ever spend with mademoiselle in this world; why should I not enjoy it to the full? For the hundredth time we had had our misunderstanding and it had cleared away; now there should be no more misunderstandings, no more coldness, nothing but joy in the warm sunshine of her smiles.

So I begged her once more to be seated and to atone for all that was unkind in the past by letting me talk to her. There could have been no better place, outside of her cozy cabin, for this long-dreamed-of tête-à-tête,

13

which now at last was to have a realization, than this
she had herself chosen. The pile of pelts at her back
kept off the east wind, the young moon in the west
shone full upon her face, so that I could feast my eyes
upon its glorious beauty (for the last time, I said to
myself) and interpret every changing expression.

And yet, just at first, I was afraid I was going to
be disappointed, after all. Mademoiselle was embarrassed and constrained, and it was I—I, the gauche
and unsophisticated "boy"—who had to gently dis-
arm her fears and lead her back to her bright and
natural way. And this is how I did it. Mademoiselle
had seated herself at my request, almost awkwardly,
if awkwardness were possible to her, so much afraid
was she she was not doing quite the proper thing.

"I cannot imagine what has become of Clotilde,"
she said nervously. "I did not send her away."

"I think she has gone to find Yorke and set him
right about Leon," I answered, smiling.

She smiled slightly in return, but still with some
embarrassment.

"Mademoiselle," I said, "have you observed that
Yorke has been making himself very agreeable to Clotilde?"

"What folly!" she exclaimed. "Clotilde is an old
woman. I spoke to her about it quite seriously to-
day."

"And what did she say, Mademoiselle?"

"She said that she found Yorke most entertaining.
'One must be amused,' were her words, and she made
me feel very young with her worldly wisdom.   'We

do not contemplate matrimony, Mam'selle, but Mr. Yorke and I both think there may be an affinity of spirit, regardless of difference in age'! I was amazed at her philosophical attitude.''

"How did you reply to her, Mademoiselle?''

"She quite took my breath away, but I only said, 'Clotilde, you will oblige me by seeing as little as possible of Yorke on the remainder of the trip.' I had fully intended to keep her with me this evening, and now she has slipped away. I think I ought to go and find her,'' half rising as she spoke.

"By no means,'' I answered quickly. "Indeed, I am quite on Clotilde's side.''

"On Clotilde's side! Impossible, Monsieur! Such arrant nonsense!''

All this time I had been standing, for from a maidenly shyness (rather new in her, and which I liked) she would not ask me to sit beside her, and there was no other seat. Now I said:

"Mademoiselle, if you will permit me to share your bundle of pelts, I believe I can prove to you that it is not such arrant nonsense, after all.''

"Certainly, Monsieur,'' a little stiffly; "I am sorry to have kept you standing so long.''

She drew her skirts a little aside, and I sat down, quite at the other end of the bundle of pelts, but nearer to her than I had been in many long days. Then, in a purposely didactic and argumentative way, I cited to her all the instances in history I could think of, winding up with Cleopatra and Ninon de l'Enclos, until by entering into the argument she had entirely forgotten herself and her embarrassment. Then suddenly into a little break in our conversation there came the clear whinny of Fatima. She was on the other boat, tied close to ours, and as we were in the stern and she in the bow, she had no doubt heard her master's voice and was calling him. I was greatly tempted to call her by the whistle she knew, but I did not quite dare. She would have broken all possible bounds to come to me in answer to that whistle, and I would not have been surprised to see her clear the space between the two boats.

"That was Fatima," mademoiselle said, and sighed a little.

"Yes," I said, "and I think I could tell what your sigh meant."

"Did I sigh?"

"Yes, and it meant, 'I wish it were Leon.'"

"Yes," she said; "I was thinking how much Fatima loves you, and Leon, too, as soon as he was able to forgive your disgracing him so. I think all dogs and horses love you, Monsieur."

"That is because I love them, Mademoiselle."

"Does love always beget love?"

"Not always, Mademoiselle; sometimes it begets scorn."

"Then I suppose the love dies?"

"No, Mademoiselle; unhappily, it but grows the stronger."

"That is folly, is it not?"

"Mademoiselle, if you will allow me to be a philosopher like Clotilde—love has no regard for sense or wisdom, else would Yorke love one of his own age, and I would love one of my own country and my own rank."

She said not a word for a long time, but sat with downcast eyes. Suddenly she lifted them, and they shone with a softer radiance than I had ever seen in them before.

"Of what were you thinking, Mademoiselle?" I said gently.

She hesitated a moment, and then like the soft sigh of a zephyr came her words:

"I was wishing you were a chevalier of France."

"And I, Mademoiselle, was wishing you were a maiden of St. Louis, as I supposed you were when I first saw you."

"I would not have been of your country, even then," she said, with delicious shyness, half looking at me, half looking away in pretty confusion.

"Not now, but you soon would be. St. Louis will belong to us some day."

"Never!" She spoke in hot haste, all the patriot firing within her, and looking full at me with flashing eyes. "St. Louis will be French some day, as it used to be, I believe with all my heart; but American, *never!*"

"Mademoiselle, we had a wager once. Shall we have one more?"

"Is it that St. Louis will one day be American?"

"Yes."

"I am very willing to wager on that, for it is a certainty for me. What shall be the stakes?"

"Mademoiselle, they would be very high."

"I am not afraid."

I thought for a moment, and then I shook my head.

"Mademoiselle, I dare not. I am sure St. Louis will one day be ours, but the time may be long, and by that day the worst may have happened. You may have found your chevalier of France."

She looked up at me in a quick, startled way, which changed gradually to her old proud look.

"Monsieur, I know not what stakes you had in mind, but this I know: if 't were a lady's hand it were unworthy you and her. A lady's hand is for the winning by deeds of prowess or by proof of worth, not by betting for it as though 't were a horse or a pile of louis d'or."

"Mademoiselle," I cried in an agony of shame, "forgive me, I beg. Forgive a poor wretch who saw no chance of winning by prowess or worth, and who was so desperate that he would clutch at any straw to help him win his heart's desire."

Her look softened at once, and when she spoke again 't was in her gentlest tones.

"Monsieur," she said, "to-morrow we part, and it would seem there is but little chance that we shall see each other again in this world. Fate has placed our lots on different continents, with wide seas between. But for to-night let us forget that. Let us think we are to meet every day, as we have met in these weeks, and let us have a happy memory of this last evening to cherish always."

I could not speak for a moment. Her voice, its sweet tones breaking a little at the last, unmanned me.

I turned away my head, for I would not let her see the workings of my face, nor my wet eyes, lest she think me boyish again. It was the sealing of my doom, but I had known it always. And there was a drop of sweet amid the bitter that I had never dared hope for. She, too, was sad—then she must care a little. In a minute I was able to turn toward her again and speak in a firm, low voice.

"You are right, Mademoiselle; we will be happy to-night. Come," I said, rising and extending my hand to her, "let us go watch the revelers on the other boat; they, at least, are troubled by no useless regrets."

She put her hand in mine, and we went back by the stern rail and stood watching the scene below us.

A plank had been thrown from one boat to the other to make easy communication, and the crew of our boat, with the exception of the two left always on guard, had crossed over. They had cleared a space for dancing, and lighted it by great pine-knots cut from the forest close by. Yorke, set high on a pile of forage with his beloved banjo, was playing such music as put springs into their heels. Canadians and negroes were all dancing together—the Frenchmen with graceful agility, the negroes more clumsily, even grotesquely, but with a rhythm that proved their musical ear. Clotilde and a negress cook were the only women, and greatly in demand by both Frenchmen and negroes. Clotilde rather scorned partners of her own color, and was choosing only the best-looking and the best dancers of the white men, with a caprice worthy of her mistress, I thought, and probably in imitation of her. Yorke did not seem to mind, but with the gayest good humor called out the figures as he played. Suddenly, as he wound up the last figure with a grand flourish, he beckoned to a little Canadian who had been specially agile in the dance, and they held a whispered consultation. Then Yorke resigned his banjo to him, and, leaping down into the middle of the floor, seized Clotilde about the waist without so much as saying "By your leave," and shouted:

"Choose partners for a waltz!"

Consternation followed, for not more than half a dozen had ever seen the new French dance. But when the little Canadian started up with his witching *trois-temps*, Yorke and Clotilde glided off rhythmically to its strains, the half-dozen followed, more or less skilfully, and the rest stood round gazing in respectful admiration.

Now I had learned the waltz at home in Philadelphia, but it had never been danced at the St. Louis parties, and I knew not whether mademoiselle knew the step or not. Yet was I seized with a great desire to follow Yorke's example.

"Mademoiselle," I said timidly, "why cannot we have a dance here? See, there is a clear space on the deck, and the music is good."

"I waltz but poorly, Monsieur," she answered, looking up at me with a bright blush. "Madame Saugrain taught me the step, but I have practised it but little."

"Then we will be the better matched," I answered gaily. But when I had put my arm around her waist, and one of her beautiful hands rested on my shoulder, and I held the other in my firm clasp, I was seized with such trembling at my boldness in daring to hold her so near that almost my feet refused to move. Yet as soon as we were both gliding to the Canadian's music there was no longer any fear in my heart, only a great longing that the music might never cease and that we could go on forever circling to its strains. Wild thoughts whirled in my brain. Why need mademoiselle go back to Paris? I believed, as I bent my head and looked into her dark eyes uplifted to mine, that only a little persuasion would be needed to make her give it all up. And I said to myself, "I will try."

But the music stopped. Mademoiselle gently withdrew herself from my encircling arm, and suddenly cold reason returned. How could I dream of betraying Dr. Saugrain's trust! How could I think of persuading her to relinquish the glories awaiting her for me! And, most of all, how could I dare to think she could be persuaded!

Mademoiselle had thrown off her capote before beginning to dance; I picked it up and put it around her, and led her back to her seat on the pelts. But she would not sit down.

"No, Monsieur," she said; "our evening is over. I am going to my cabin. Will you send for Clotilde and tell her that I want her?"

"Mademoiselle! Mademoiselle!" I cried, my heart in my mouth to beg her not to leave me without one word of hope. But then I stopped. It was all over; the world had come to an end.

"It is good-by, then, Mademoiselle?" I said steadily, and holding out my hand to her.

"No, Monsieur," she said, with that voice that from the first time I heard it had ever seemed to me the sweetest in the world. " 'T is *au revoir—toujours, toujours au revoir!*"

I watched her close her cabin door and turned back to my place by the rail, black despair in my heart, but just one little ray of hope brightening it—her courageous *au revoir.* Over the plank came Yorke and Clotilde, and strolled slowly up the deck together, Yorke thrumming his banjo and singing a creole love-song he had learned in St. Louis:

> " Tous les printemps
> Tan' de nouvelles,
> Tous les amants
> Changent de maîtresses.
> Qu'ils changent qui voudront,
> Pour moi, je garde la mienne."

Insensibly my heart lightened. "Pour moi, je garde la mienne," I said aloud, and added in a whisper:

"Yes—though I must first win her, and win I will!"

CHAPTER XV

"AU REVOIR"

"While memory watches o'er the sad review
Of joys that faded like the morning dew."

IT was a busy morning that followed—no time for idle thoughts or vain regrets. If we were to dine with Mrs. O'Fallon at Mulberry Hill, all hands must work hard.

A line of ten men with the cordelle was attached to each boat to pull it up the stream, and at the same time ten more on each boat planted the great pole at the bow, and then, pushing on it, walked back to the stern, lifted it out of the soft mud, carried it forward to the bow, planted it again in the mud, and, pushing mightily, again walked back to the stern. In this way we made great progress. We moved as fast as the ten men on shore carrying the cordelle could walk, and the men at the pole lightened their load so greatly, they were able to walk at a good round pace.

So it was not yet quite noon when the white walls of Mulberry House came in view, the blue smoke curling from its chimneys giving promise of good cheer awaiting us. The men at the cordelle walked faster, the men at the pole pushed harder, and, there being here a chance to use them, two great sweep-oars were fastened in the rowlocks, and, four men at each oar, we went forward at such a gait that the water curled back from our prow in two foaming streams, and before many minutes we were running our nose into the bank at the foot of Mulberry Hill.

Down the bank came a long line of men and boys, chiefly negroes, shouting in every key, and running to catch the ropes our crew were throwing them, and tying us fast to big stumps left standing on the bank for that purpose.

Foremost to step foot on board was young John O'Fallon, running first to greet his uncle William, whom next to his uncle General Clarke he thought the greatest man on earth, and then coming to greet me, whom he called "cousin" in his kindly Southern fashion, for I could not claim to be kin. He was a bright, engaging lad of twelve or thirteen, "with the manners of a chevalier of France," I said laughingly to mademoiselle, when my captain was bringing him up to present to her. She was greatly taken with him at once, and as for him, 't was a case of love at first sight, and he took full possession of her, giving me small chance to help her off the boat or up the hill.

At the top of the hill, Aunt Fanny, as his mother always insisted I should call her, was waiting for us. She kissed me on each cheek and called me "my boy" in a manner that made me feel very young indeed. Much as I loved her, I could have wished that in mademoiselle's presence she had treated me as one too old for such gracious liberties. But mademoiselle seemed not to notice her greeting to me; she had eyes only for the beautiful and charming woman and her manly little son. Indeed, I felt so much left out in the cold (for, after the manner of women, the two instantly made violent love to each other) that I was not sorry to find letters awaiting me from my uncle, inclosing letters from home that required my instant attention. When I had read them I knew not whether to be sorry or glad. I had fully intended to make no stay at all at Mulberry Hill, but go on at once to my uncle's; but now that there was no chance left me,—that marching orders I dared not disobey ordered me East at once,— I realized that lurking in the depths of my heart had been a secret hope that something would happen to delay me longer in mademoiselle's society.

I was at once busy with preparations for a more hasty departure than I had expected, so that I saw neither Mrs. O'Fallon nor mademoiselle again until we were seated at the long table in the great dining-room overlooking the river, which here makes a wide and graceful sweep to the south. The warm winter sun was flooding the room through its many windows, lighting up the table with its brave show of silver and glass and snowy linen, and by its cheery glow warming all hearts and setting all tongues free, so that there was a pleasant confusion of talk, such as a hostess dearly loves. It was a bright and happy scene, and every face was smiling and every heart was gay save one; for I could not hope that mademoiselle's bright smile and beaming glance disguised another aching heart.

I was seated at Mrs. O'Fallon's left hand; a Mr. Thruston, whom I had never met, but who was evidently paying earnest court to the charming widow, was on her right; and mademoiselle was almost at the other end of the long table, between Captain Clarke and young John—about as far from me as possible, which, since it was to be our last meal together, I felt to be a distinct grievance. But as no one was to blame but Aunt Fanny, and she had set me beside her to do me honor, I could not well find fault.

It was in response to her asking me to show some little courtesy to Mr. Thruston after dinner (I do not now recall what) that I told her I must set out on my journey as soon after dinner as I could start. Her short, sharp exclamation of surprise and displeasure caught the attention of all the table.

"Brother William, do you hear that?" she called to my captain. "Our kinsman leaves us immediately."

Aunt Fanny spoke with her knife poised in air. A noble great bird, a wild turkey, was on the platter before her, oozing a rich brown gravy from every pore. With a deftness I have never seen equaled, she had been separating joints and carving great slices of the rich dark meat, sending savory odors steaming up into my nostrils. Now, as she paused in her work to make her announcement, there arose instantly a chorus of remonstrances, loudest from young John and his younger brother Ben. I answered them modestly, I hoped, looking at everybody except mademoiselle, who yet, I saw distinctly, turned very pale, then red, then pale again.

I addressed myself directly to Captain Clarke:

"My uncle has forwarded me letters from home, requiring my presence there as shortly as possible. The letters do not enlighten me as to the reasons for haste, and I am naturally beset with some misgivings, but I hope all is well with my family."

My captain smiled inscrutably.

"Set your anxieties at rest, my lad. I also found a letter awaiting me from your father. It explains the reasons for haste, but wishes them kept from you for the present; but they are of the most agreeable nature, and all is well at home."

I was greatly relieved, and so expressed myself.

"But why start immediately?" my captain continued. "You will have to wait for a boat, and the waiting had best be done here."

"I have found one, sir," I answered. "It is expected up the river this afternoon, and goes as far as Clarksville. My instructions are to go by way of Washington, and call on Mr. Jefferson, so nothing could suit me better, for I find the road from Clarksville to Washington is comparatively short, and the boat is a small keel-boat and likely to make good time.".

"Well, well!" said my captain, pleasantly, "you must have been hard at work to find out all this between landing and dinner; but I know the reasons for haste are imperative, and you are quite right to set off at once."

Then suddenly mademoiselle spoke up:

"Mon Capitaine, if monsieur is going just where I must go, why do not I and Clotilde go with him?"

There was a moment's embarrassing silence, and

then I, feeling the silence unbearable and a great discourtesy to mademoiselle, answered her.

"Mademoiselle, nothing could give me greater pleasure if my captain and Aunt Fanny think it could be arranged. But I fear the route would be a hard one for a lady's traveling, since the boat goes only to Clarksville, and from there to Washington there is but a bridle-path, and a very rough one."

Then everybody broke forth at once, volubly:

"Oh, no, no, no! We cannot think of letting you go!"

"Indeed, miss," said Aunt Fanny, in her pretty imperious way, "you may think yourself fortunate if you get away from here any time in the next two months. We do not get hold of a lovely young lady visitor very often, and when we do we mean to keep her as long as we can. And here is my son John over head and ears in love." (Young John blushed like a peony.) "Would you break his heart, madam? And Ben is no better" (for Ben had been slyly laughing at his brother's discomfiture, but now looked very silly indeed as he took his share of his mother's tongue-lash). "You will be having my family at loggerheads if you stay, no doubt, but stay you must, for now that we have once seen you, there is no living without you."

Mademoiselle took the speech adorably (as I knew she would, though I doubt whether she understood half of it), smiling and blushing, and saying in her pretty baby-English that they were very good to her, and she would not break "Meester Jean's" heart, no, nor "Meester Ben's"; she would stay with "dear madame."

If I did not thereupon fetch a long and deep sigh from the very bottom of my boots, it was not because it was not there to fetch, as I thought of all I was missing in not spending a happy two months with mademoiselle under Aunt Fanny's delightful roof.

But I had short time to indulge vain regrets. We were in the midst of dessert, a huge bowl of steaming punch brewed by Aunt Fanny before our eyes, and a great Christmas cake, which she said she had saved for our home-coming, when a small negro burst open the door in great excitement.

"Hi, Miss Fanny, she 's comin'!"

"Who 's coming, Scipio? And where are your manners? Go tell your mother if she does n't teach you how to come into a room properly, I will have to take you in hand."

It was a terrible threat, and had been many times employed—always successfully, for "Miss Fanny" never did "take in hand" the small darkies, and so, having no notion of what taking in hand might mean, all the terrors of mystery were added to their fears. Young Scipio was greatly abashed, and pulled his forelock respectfully as he answered Mrs. O'Fallon's question.

"It 's de boat, missus; she 's comin' roun' de ben'."

In a moment all was confusion. There was no time to be lost. Yorke was despatched to get together my belongings, see that they were carried to the landing,

14

and himself lead Fatima down the bank and on to the boat; for to no other would I trust my beauty. The boat by this time had nearly reached the landing, and there was a hurry of good-bys, Aunt Fanny shedding tears of vexation that my visit should be so short, and calling me her "dear boy," and kissing me and scolding me in one breath.

She and mademoiselle walked as far as the top of the bluff with me (I would not let them come farther, for the bank was steep and muddy), and then I said my good-by to mademoiselle. I raised her hand to my lips as I said it, and she looked straight into my eyes with eyes that shone with something brighter than smiles as she answered:

"Au revoir, monsieur!"

The captain of the keel-boat was shouting to us to make haste, and there was no time for another word; and I was glad to have it so, for another word might have made me indeed the boy Aunt Fanny was always calling me.

The two boys, Mr. Thruston, and my captain went down to the boat with me (which proved to be a more comfortable one than I had dared to hope for), and Fatima having been coaxed aboard and quarters found for her in a warm shed, and my captain pressing my hand with an affectionate "Good-by, dear lad," that was once more near to my undoing, we were untied, and the men at the poles pushed hard and walked rapidly back to the stern, and the men at the cordelle pulled all together, with a long-drawn "Heave, ho, heave!" and we were off.

I stood in the stern watching the two figures on the bluff until one of them went away and there was only one, slender and of but little stature, with soft dark curls, and eyes whose tender glow I could feel long after the figure was but one indistinct blur, with a white hand waving farewell.

Then came another bend in the river and shut her from my sight. And there was naught left to me of Mademoiselle Pelagie but a memory of tears and smiles; of hard words and gentle ones; of cold looks and kind ones; of alternate hopes and fears on my side; of scorning and—yes, I believed it with all my heart—of scorning and loving on hers.

CHAPTER XVI

A VIRGINIA FARMER

"Statesman, yet friend to truth! of soul sincere,
In action faithful, and in honour clear."

"WHAT, Fatima! You refuse?"

I dismounted and led her carefully down the steep bank and on to the ferry-boat. She followed me very willingly, but I stood with my arm over her glossy neck, for I saw she eyed the water distrustfully, and while I had no fear of her being disobedient to my word of command, I knew it would comfort her to feel my arm about her neck. She neighed her appreciation, and gently rubbed her nostrils against my side, ever a token of affection with her. When the boat began to move, the two stalwart negroes pulling at their great oars and chanting dismally in time to their pulling, Fatima again showed signs of excitement, but I easily quieted her, and then I had leisure to use my eyes.

This crossing the Potomac to Washington reminded me vividly of crossing the Mississippi to St. Louis more than three months before. Nor did the capital look more impressive at this distance than the village of St. Louis. Both were embowered in trees, and but for the two imposing white buildings,—the President's Palace and the Capitol,—Washington was much the less prepossessing village of the two, and I thought how much more worthy was our own city of Philadelphia to be the capital of the nation.

Indeed, when I had led Fatima off the ferry, she sank over her fetlocks in mud, and I had to lead her some distance before I found ground firm enough to warrant my mounting her, lest my weight should make the poor creature flounder hopelessly in the mire.

I bore in my pocket a letter from Captain Clarke introducing me to Mr. Meriwether Lewis, which he had written at Mulberry Hill, after the boat that was to bear me away was in sight, and also an address he had given me of a respectable innkeeper where I might find lodging. The inn was my first quest, and that once found and a suitable toilet made, I was eager to present my letter of introduction, and, if chance favored me, meet the President also.

It was still early, and the road I found myself upon (for it could not be called a street, since there were no pavements and only at long intervals a house) was filled with a well-dressed throng all wending their way in one direction. It seemed to me too early an hour for gentlemen to be seeking a place of amusement, and too late and the throng too generally well dressed to be on their way to business. Some were in coaches, with coachmen in livery on the box and footmen standing up behind, and some were on horseback and some on foot, but all, or nearly all, were wearing silk stockings and fine ruffled shirts and carefully powdered queues and shining shoe-buckles.

A little stretch of brick sidewalk gave an air of distinction to a solidly built two-story house with sloping roof and dormer-windows, and in front of the house, on a stool planted on the curb, sat an old negro, bandy-legged, with snowy wool, industriously polishing a row of shoes neatly arranged in front of him, and crooning happily a plantation melody as he worked. I drew Fatima to the curb.

"Good morning, uncle," I said as the negro slowly lifted his head, bowed over his brush. "Can you tell me who all these people are and where they are going?"

"Mohnen, marsa," the negro returned politely, and then looked at me with round-eyed astonishment. "Yo' dunno whar they's gwine? Why, sah, dey's de Senatahs and Represenatahs, sah, and dey gwine to de Cap'tul, sah."

Of course! It was very stupid of me not to have thought of it. The negro evidently thought so, too, but a sudden excuse suggested itself to him.

"Mought yo' be a stranger in Washington, sah?" with a glance of such undisguised pity for any barbarian who did not know the capital that I felt myself coloring, and to recover my self-respect assured him that I had set foot in this "domtiferous" mud-hole for the first time just fifteen minutes before.

He was greatly impressed with my emphatic word, and addressed me with much-increased respect.

"Den, sah, if I might be so libertious, p'r'aps yo' like me to p'int out de 'stinguished gen'lemen."

Nothing could have pleased me better, and I drew

Fatima still closer to the curb while Bandy Jim—for that, he said, was his name—proceeded to point out the celebrities.

There was passing at that moment a very elegant coach, with mounted postilions in pink plush and gold lace, and an exceedingly handsome man with an aristocratic face leaning back among the cushions, his eyes half closed, as if mentally conning a speech for delivery in Congress. Bandy Jim did not wait for the eager question on the tip of my tongue.

"Dat, sah, is de welfiest and most 'stocratic gen'leman in Washington. Dat am Mistah Gubernoor Morris of de gre't city of New York. I 'low he studying dis minnit on a speech 'bout de Mississippi Riber and dem Spanish men."

I looked at him again, more eagerly than before. I knew Gouverneur Morris well by reputation, though I had never seen him, as one of the most polished and scholarly men of the country, and the devoted friend of Hamilton, whom I idolized as all that was brilliant, great, and noble. But my eagerness was largely due to Bandy Jim's suggestion that they were discussing the Mississippi question in Congress, and as I looked more keenly I hoped he was on the right side, for I thought that broad white brow could think great thoughts and those clear-cut lips could utter them with force.

"Why do you think it will be on the Mississippi this morning, uncle?" I inquired, amused that the old darky should seem to know the doings in Congress. "Do you go up to the Capitol to listen to the debates?"

"Sometimes, sah, but mos'ly I reads dem in de 'Post,' sah!" And the proud air with which he let me know of his unusual accomplishment beggars description.

"And so you can read, Uncle? And who taught you?"

"Ole Miss, sah. I's a free nigger, sah. Ole Miss gib me my papers so I mought stay wid my fambly when she follow de gin'ral and his father to Mulberry Hill in Kaintuck'."

I confess Bandy Jim seemed like an old friend at once when I found he had belonged to the Clarkes, and in my delight at seeing "one of the family" in a strange land, I slipped from Fatima's back and grasped him by the hand.

When he found I was just from Kentucky and Mulberry Hill, he was more excited than I, and especially was he eager for news of "Marse William."

"He mah baby, sah!" he repeated over and over, his old eyes shining with visions of other days.

"An' Yorke, sah,—you know Yorke?—he mah son!" with great dignity and much evident pride in a son of such distinction.

I had many things to tell him of Yorke's prowess and address that pleased the old fellow greatly. I might also have recounted the many times when I had had all the will in the world to horsewhip the rascal, but I did not distress his old father with any of his shortcomings.

The morning was fast slipping away when I bethought me it was time to be looking up my lodging and making myself ready for my call at the President's Palace. I flung Bandy Jim a piece of gold and told him I would see him again. And then as I was in the act of mounting Fatima it occurred to me he could no doubt direct me.

"Can you tell me how to find the Mansion House, Uncle?"

"Right here, sah," grinning with delight; and sure enough, what had seemed to me the home of some respectable citizen proved to be mine inn. And a very good one indeed; for when Bandy Jim had called a boy to lead Fatima around the house to the stables in the rear, and another to take me in to the landlord, I found myself in as clean and comfortable a hostelry as one could hope to find. My chamber was a large square one, on the second landing, and from its windows I could catch glimpses through the bare trees of the white building on the hill that I knew was the Capitol.

And when a boy had brought my saddle-bags, Bandy Jim himself hobbled in to help me dress. He had been body-servant to both General Clarke and his father, and, old as he was, bent nearly double and dim of sight, his fingers were skilled for lacers and laces, for buckles and ribbons.

I thought I looked quite as a gentleman should for a morning call at the "White House," for that, I understand, is what Mr. Jefferson prefers to have the President's Palace called. Indeed, I have heard he very vehemently objects to having it called a palace at all. I was wearing a plain cloth habit of dark green with no lace at wrist or knee and only a small lace tie at the neck. My shoe-buckles were of the plainest silver, but Bandy Jim had polished them till they shone like new. I had some thoughts of deferring my visit until later in the day, when I might with a good grace have worn satin and velvet and fine lace ruffles, for I am afraid I was something of a beau in those days in my liking for dress. But bethinking me that the plainness of my costume would only be an additional recommendation in the eyes of the President, should I have the good fortune to meet him, I set off on Fatima's back, following the straight road, as Bandy Jim had directed.

A more forlorn village it has rarely been my lot to see: stretches of mud road with neither houses nor fields to outline it, and then for a block or more bare and ugly houses, hideous in their newness, not having even the grace of age to soften their ill proportions. I was glad mademoiselle was not there to gaze upon the capital of America with eyes that knew so well how to be scornful, and that would so soon find her own gay French capital so beautiful.

I was in the very act of saying to myself for the twentieth time, "Idiots and dolts, not to have selected beautiful Philadelphia for a nation's capital!" when there rode up beside me a farmer in plain, almost rough, clothes, but riding a magnificent horse. He was about to pass me (for I was riding slowly, out of respect to the mud, which might easily have bespattered me so that I would be in no condition for a call), but I hailed him:

"Are you going my way, my friend?"

"If you are going mine."

"I am going straight ahead to the President's Palace."

"And I to the White House, sir."

"Then our ways lie together. Are you acquainted in Washington?"

"Somewhat, sir."

I began to think this rather a surly farmer, he was so chary of words, so I looked at him more narrowly. But I saw nothing surly in his face. Indeed, at a second glance, I decided it was as fine a face, its features as clearly chiseled, as one often sees, and the eyes, beneath the broad white brow, were full, open, and benignant.

"He is no ordinary farmer," I said to myself, "but most like a wealthy Virginia planter of education and social standing, but careless in matters of dress." Therefore I addressed him with a shade more of respect than I had hitherto used:

"I am a stranger in Washington, sir," I said, "and if you are better acquainted here, I thought perhaps you would be so good as to tell me something of the city."

He unbent immediately, and not only pointed out every object of interest on the road, but in a very delicate and gentlemanly manner proceeded also to pump me as to my name and errand in Washington. I was not more amused at his curiosity than at the skilful method he employed in trying to satisfy it, but, as I flattered myself, I gave him but little satisfaction.

In reply to some question of mine about the debate in Congress on the Mississippi question, he gave me such a masterly exposition of the whole subject, so clearly and concisely put into a nutshell, I began to think my eccentric planter was a political genius, possibly a member of Congress, though if so I thought his horse was headed the wrong way.

But evidently I had lighted unwittingly upon a rich mine of information. It was never my way to neglect my opportunities, and I began at once to ply him with questions about men and things in Washington. Last of all, I asked him about Mr. Jefferson.

Now my family was not of Mr. Jefferson's party: we were ardent admirers and strong partizans of Mr. Hamilton. Not that we had any fault to find with Mr. Jefferson, except for his quarrel with Hamilton. But bethinking me that it was quite possible my planter might be a "Democrat," as Mr. Jefferson calls his party, I spoke guardedly, I thought.

"Can you tell me something of the President, sir? Do you admire him? And is it true he is such a sloven in dress as they say he is?"

I could not tell from his face whether he were Democrat or Whig, for it changed not a whit. He answered readily:

"I know Mr. Jefferson quite well. I can hardly say whether I admire him or not, but I like him. In fact, he is quite a friend of mine. As to his being a sloven in dress, is that what they say about him? He dresses as well as I do: would you call that being a sloven?"

"Not at all, sir, not at all!" I answered quickly;

but to myself I said, "If he dresses no better, God help us!" I added aloud:

"I hope, sir, what I have said about the President has not offended you, since he is a friend of yours. I have never seen him, and was only repeating the general report."

The stream of people that had been setting eastward earlier in the morning had ceased entirely. We had ridden on some distance without meeting any one, but at this moment we met two gentlemen on horseback, and both took off their hats and kept them off until we had passed. I thought it probable that from my fine clothes (which, though plain, were of undeniable elegance) they took me for a stranger of distinction, and I bowed most graciously in return. My farmer friend but touched his hat with his riding-whip, and then pointed off through the woods to where we could see the chimneys of a large house, on the banks of the river.

"That," he said, "is Mr. Law's mansion. You may have heard of him?"

"Oh, yes," I answered; "he married Miss Custis, and I used to know her quite well, when we were both children."

We mounted a little elevation in the road, not enough to be called a hill, but enough to give a more extended view over the wide acres of brick-kilns and huts of laborers and dismal waste land unfenced and uncultivated. To the east, in the direction of the Capitol, he pointed out the towers of Doddington Manor, the house of Daniel Carroll. We had passed so many houses that seemed to me but little more than hovels or barracks that it was a relief to me to see from Mr. Law's and Mr. Carroll's places that there were some gentlemen's residences in the capital. When I said something of the kind to my guide, he replied, with some asperity, that there were many gentlemen's residences at Alexandria and Arlington and George-town, only a short gallop away, and that it would not be many years until Washington itself could claim as many as New York or Philadelphia.

I saw he was one of those violent partizans of the "ten-mile square" (probably because his farm lay somewhere near), so discreetly turned the discourse, since I did not want to bring up the vexed question of the superior merits of New York, Philadelphia, and the ten-mile square as a seat for the capital.

By this time the President's Palace was in full view, and a beautiful building it was, looking very large and very white, and, it must be confessed, very bare, since there were no gardens surrounding it, nothing but mud in front and marsh behind, between it and the Potomac.

Fatima picked her way daintily through the mud, often half stopping for better footing (as if she knew she must not bespatter me when I was going to call at the President's house), and by that means the farmer's powerful horse (who seemed not to mind the mud, knowing there was no finery to be hurt by it) got well ahead. I was myself so much engaged with the badness of the road that I did not, for a few min-utes, look up. When I did, I observed that two order-

" 'Welcome to the White House !' "

lies were holding the farmer's horse, from which he had just dismounted, while the farmer himself stood on the steps awaiting my approach. One orderly led his horse away as I rode up, but the exclamation of disgust for the mud that rose to my lips never passed them. As I glanced up at this "farmer" in corduroy small-clothes, red plush waistcoat, rough riding-boots splashed with mud, he had suddenly grown tall and majestic.

"Orderly, take this gentleman's horse to the stable!" he said, with an air of command, and then turned to me with stately dignity.

"Welcome to the White House, my young Philadelphia friend," he said, and smiled.

For my confusion knew no bounds. I was never quick where a puzzle or trick was concerned, but now it slowly dawned upon me that my farmer friend was the President of the United States! and I had been criticizing him to his face, and talking flippantly to him, and even superciliously. My consternation grew; I knew not what was the proper thing to do, but I stammered out the most abject apology I could think of.

Mr. Jefferson only laughed at my confusion.

"Come, come, sir," he said genially, "there is no great harm done. Don't you suppose I know what people say of me? You were only repeating the 'general report,' you know." And then he added seriously, as he saw my confusion was but increased by his raillery:

"Where no offense is intended, sir, none is taken.

I beg you will enter the White House, and I will send my secretary to you, Mr. Meriwether Lewis."

As he spoke he led the way into the house and into a very large and beautiful room, with a full-length portrait of General Washington on the walls.

"I shall hope to see you later," he said pleasantly as he left me; "if I mistake not, I have some communications of interest for you." Then he turned and went up the grand staircase and left me alone to my miserable pastime of recalling every word and every incident of that wretched ride to the White House, and from not one of them could I extract an atom of comfort to soothe my wounded self-esteem.

CHAPTER XVII

A GREAT DEBATE

They "of the western dome, whose weighty sense
Flows in fit words and heavenly eloquence."

I HAD been so abashed by my wretched mistake that I had not so much as told the President who I was (though, truth to tell, he had not asked me, and it would have been only another impertinence on my part to have volunteered the information). Yet as I sat waiting for young Mr. Lewis, and reviewing in my mind the miserable events through which I had just passed, it suddenly occurred to me as very remarkable that Mr. Jefferson should have known I was from Philadelphia, when I thought I had been so particularly skilful in betraying no fact concerning myself. Moreover, he had not only guessed I was from Philadelphia; he must have guessed my identity also, for he had "communications of interest" for me.

My curiosity was now so thoroughly aroused, both as to how the President knew me and what his communications might be, that it began to efface the keenness of my mortification. In the midst of my wondering surmises, Mr. Lewis appeared and greeted me most affably; and when I had presented Captain Clarke's letter of introduction, he was, if possible, more affable still. He was an older-looking man than I had expected to see, and with so much of seriousness in his countenance, and yet of such frankness and earnestness in his manner, that it drew my interest and liking at once.

He was the bearer of a very polite message from the President, inviting me to dinner at the White House at four o'clock that afternoon; and then he proposed that we should set out at once for the Capitol, where, as he said, a debate of special interest was on the calendar.

I was much touched at the generosity of Mr. Jefferson in returning my discourtesy to himself by so courteously placing his secretary at my disposal for my entertainment, and nothing could have pleased me better than Mr. Lewis's proposal. It had been my intention to visit the Capitol as soon as this visit of ceremony should be performed, but to visit it with a guide so much at home as the President's secretary was good luck indeed.

I thought it still better luck when I found that, by Mr. Jefferson's special invitation, we were to sit in a small gallery set aside for the President and his friends, and to which a guard in uniform admitted us with a key. I was much impressed by the exterior of the Capitol (though in such an unfinished state), but when I found myself seated in the seclusion of the President's own private gallery, looking down upon the horseshoe of grave and distinguished senators, I could have wished that one of the ladies (of whom there were a number in the gallery opposite, and who cast many inquisitive glances at the two young men in the President's box) might have been Mademoiselle Pelagie, for I felt sure she would never again think of me as a boy, could she but see me in my present dignified surroundings.

But it was only for a moment that my attention was distracted by the ladies and by thoughts of mademoiselle. A gentleman was speaking (Mr. Lewis told me it was Mr. Ross of Pennsylvania) in a most impassioned manner, and the magic word "Mississippi" caught my ear and charmed my attention. Mr. Ross was saying:

"To the free navigation of the Mississippi we have undoubted right, from nature and also from the position of our Western country. This right and the right of deposit in the Island of New Orleans were solemnly acknowledged and fixed by treaty in 1795. That treaty has been in actual operation and execution for many years, and now, without any pretense of abuse or violation on our part, the officers of the Spanish government deny that right, refuse the place of deposit, and add the most offensive of all insults by forbidding us from landing on any part of their territory and shutting us out as a common nuisance. I declare it, therefore, to be my firm and mature opinion that so important a right will never be secure while the mouth of the Mississippi is exclusively in the hands of the Spanish. From the very position of our country, from its geographical shape, from motives of complete independence, the command of the navigation of the river ought to be in our hands.

"We are now wantonly provoked to take it. Hostility in its most offensive shape has been offered us, and hostility fatal to the happiness of the Western World. Why not seize, then, what is so essential to us as a nation? Why not expel the wrong-doers? Paper treaties have proved too feeble. Plant yourselves on the river; fortify the banks; invite those who have an interest at stake to defend it. Do justice to yourselves when your adversaries deny it, and leave the event to Him who controls the fate of nations!"

Ah, how his words burnt my brain! I was for leaving Mr. Lewis in the President's gallery, running down to the great entrance where I had left Fatima in charge of a negro boy, mounting her, and riding straight back to Kentucky. Once there, I was sure it would be an easy matter to raise a company of eager patriots and march at their head down the Great River to the hostile city. But Mr. Ross had not finished, and I could not lose a word of his impassioned speech:

"Why submit to a tardy and uncertain negotiation —a negotiation with those who have wronged you? When in possession you will negotiate with more advantage. You will then be in the position to keep others out. The present possessors have no pretense to complain, for they have no right to the country, by their own confession.

"The Western people will discover that you are making every effort they could desire for their protection. They will ardently support you in the contest, if a contest becomes necessary. Their all will be at stake, and neither their zeal nor their courage need be doubted.

"But after negotiations shall have failed; after a powerful, ambitious nation shall have taken possession of the key of their Western country and fortified it; after the garrisons are filled by the veterans who have conquered the East: will you have it in your power to waken the generous spirit of the West and dispossess them? No, no; their confidence in you as their rulers will be gone; they will be disheartened, divided, and will place no further dependence upon you."

At this moment two officers in uniform entered the Senate, preceding a gentleman who carried on a cushion a document. Immediately the President of the Senate, Mr. Burr (a man whom I had been reared to dislike and distrust above all men, and whose enmity for Mr. Hamilton was sufficient cause to make me his foe, yet whose attractive personality, seeing him for the first time, I could not deny), called the house to order, and requested Mr. Ross to defer the completion of his speech until a message from the House of Representatives should have been read.

I was all curiosity, for it seemed to me an imposing ceremony and one that must be of great moment. But I was doomed to disappointment. The gentleman bearing the document said something in a low tone to the clerk, who repeated it to Mr. Burr. Whereupon Mr. Burr rose in his seat.

"Gentlemen of the Senate," he said, "the House of

Representatives sends you a confidential message. Sergeant-at-arms, clear the house!''

Mr. Lewis rose at once, and signaled to me to follow, which I did, very unwillingly. Outside in the corridors he said:

''I think this will be but a brief secret conference —most like we can return in a few minutes; and I will employ the interim in showing you the building.''

From his manner I thought he must know the subject of the secret conference, as, indeed, being the President's private secretary, he would have every means of knowing. But he gave me no hint of it, and it was not until long afterward that I learned that in the half-hour we were shut out the Senate had confirmed the House bill to place two million dollars at the President's disposal to commence with more effect a negotiation with France and Spain for the purchase of the Isle of New Orleans and the East and West Floridas.

When the doors were opened again, and we were back in our seats in the President's gallery, we found Mr. Ross already on his feet, continuing his interrupted speech, and evidently the sentences I first heard were in reference to the bill just passed.

''I know,'' he said, ''that some gentlemen think there is a mode of accomplishing our object, of which, by a most extraordinary procedure, I am forbidden to speak on this occasion. I will not, therefore, touch it. But I will ask honorable gentlemen, especially those from the Western country, what they will say, on their return home, to a people pressed by the heavy hand of this calamity, when they inquire: What has been done? What are our hopes? How long will this obstruction continue? You answer: We have provided a remedy, but it is a secret! We are not allowed to speak of it there, much less here. It was only communicated to us confidentially, in whispers, with closed doors. But by and by you will see it operate like enchantment. It is a sovereign balsam which will heal your wounded honor; it is a potent spell, or a kind of patent medicine, which will extinguish and forever put at rest the devouring spirit which has desolated so many nations of Europe. You never can know exactly what it is; nor can we tell you precisely the time it will begin to operate: but operate it certainly will, and effectually, too! You will see strange things by and by; wait patiently, and place full faith in us, for we cannot be mistaken!

"This idle tale may amuse children, but the men of the West will not be satisfied. They will tell you that they expected better things of you, that their confidence has been misplaced, and that they will not wait the operation of your newly invented drug; they will go and redress themselves!"

Then Mr. Ross proceeded to read a series of resolutions he had drawn up, the most important part of them being to authorize the President to take immediate possession of the Isle of New Orleans, and to raise a militia army not exceeding fifty thousand men in the Western States, to coöperate with the army and navy of the Union; and that the sum of five millions of dollars should be appropriated to carry out these resolutions.

They took my breath away. "What would I not

give to be back in Kentucky!'' I whispered to Mr. Lewis, in irrepressible excitement.

''Calm yourself, my young friend,'' he whispered back. ''War is not declared yet. Listen to this next speech; it is Mr. White from Delaware. See whether he supports or opposes the resolutions.''

His opening sentence answered the question:

''As to the closing of the port of New Orleans against our citizens, the man who can now doubt that it was a deliberate act of the Spanish or French government must have locked up his mind against truth and conviction, and be determined to discredit even the evidence of his own senses. But, sir, it is not only the depriving us of our right of deposit by which we have been grieved: it is by a system of measures pursued antecedent and subsequent to that event, equally hostile and even more insulting. I have in my hand a paper signed by a Spanish officer, which, with the indulgence of the chair, I will read to the Senate.''

Then he read a paper signed by Carlos de Grandpré, warning the subjects of his Majesty of Spain that they were to have no communications with America, and couched in the most insulting terms. My blood boiled as I listened!

''These,'' said Mr. White, ''are the measures that have been adopted by the Spaniard, excluding us from their shores for a distance of two hundred and seventy miles, treating us like a nation of pirates and banditti. Would the great Washington have permitted such an insult had he still been with us? Spain has dared us to the trial, and now bids us defiance. She is yet in possession of that country; it is at this moment within your reach and within your power. It offers a sure and easy conquest. We should have to encounter there only a weak, inactive, and unenterprising people. But how may a few months vary the scene and darken our prospects! Though not officially informed, we know that the Spanish provinces on the Mississippi have been ceded to the French, and that they will, as soon as possible, take possession of them. What may we then expect? When, in the last extremity, we shall be drawn to arms in defense of our indisputable rights, where now slumbers on his post the sluggish Spaniard we shall be hailed by the vigilant and alert French grenadier; and in the defenseless garrison that would now surrender at our approach we shall see unfurled the standards that have waved triumphant in Italy, surrounded by impregnable ramparts and defended by the disciplined veterans of Europe. I am willing to attribute to honorable gentlemen the best of motives; I am sure they do not wish to involve this country in a war—and, God knows, I deprecate its horrors as much as any man. But this business can never be adjusted abroad; it will ultimately have to be settled upon the banks of the Mississippi; the war is inevitable unless honorable gentlemen opposed to us are prepared to yield up the best interest and honor of the nation. I believe the only question now in our power to decide is, whether it shall be the bloodless war of a few months or the carnage of years.

"These observations are urged upon the supposition that it is in the power of the government to restrain the impetuosity of the Western people and to prevent their doing justice to themselves, which, by the by, I beg to be understood as not believing. They know their own strength; they know the feebleness of the enemy; they know the infinite importance of the stake, and they feel—permit me to say, sir, with more than mere sensibility—the insults and injuries they have received. You had as well pretend to dam up the mouth of the Mississippi, and say to its restless waves, 'Ye shall cease here and never mingle with the ocean,' as to expect they will be prevented from descending it.

"Without the free use of the river and the necessary advantage of deposit below our line, their fertile country is not worth possession; their produce must be wasted in the field or rot in the granary. These are rights not only guaranteed to them by treaty, but also given to them by the God of nature, and they will enforce them, with or without the authority of government!"

This long speech (and I have not remembered half of it) was interrupted by frequent bursts of applause, and when Mr. White sat down, it was amid such enthusiasm of cheering as quite carried me off my feet.

"Was there ever such a speech?" I shouted into Mr. Lewis's ear, for the noise was deafening. "That will surely win the day."

"Wait," he shouted back, "until you hear the other side. That is Mr. Jackson of Georgia trying to get the floor, and, if I mistake not, he will be in opposition, and he is a strong speaker, with plenty of caustic wit."

Mr. Jackson began to speak with so slow a drawl and in such low tones that at first I hardly thought him an adversary to be dreaded. But as he warmed to his work I changed my mind.

"What is the course," he began, "which we have to pursue? Is it to go immediately to war without asking for redress? By the law of nations and the doctrines of all writers on such law, you are not justified until you have tried every possible method of obtaining redress in a peaceable manner. It is only in the last extremity, when you have no other expedient left, that a recourse to arms is lawful and just, and I hope the United States will never forfeit their character for justice by any hasty or rash steps which they may, too late, have to repent of.

"Sir, we have been told much, by the gentleman from Delaware, of Bonaparte: that he is the hero of France, the conqueror of Italy, the tyrant of Germany, and that his legions are invincible. We have been told that we must hasten to take possession of New Orleans whilst in the hands of the sluggish Spaniards, and not wait until it is in the iron grip of the Cæsar of modern times. But much as I respect the fame and exploits of that extraordinary man, I believe we should have little more to fear from him, should it be necessary in the end to contend with him for the possession of New Orleans, than from the sluggish Spaniards. Bonaparte, sir, in our Southern country would be lost with all his martial talents. His hollow squares and horse artillery would be of little service to him in the midst of our morasses and woods, where he would meet, not with the champaign country of Italy,—with the little rivulets commanded by his cannon which he could pass at leisure,—not with the fortified cities which command surrounding districts, but with rivers miles wide, and swamps mortal or impenetrable to Europeans. With a body of only ten thousand of our expert riflemen around him, his laurels would be torn from his brow, and he would heartily wish himself once more on the plains of Italy.

"The sacred name of Washington has been unnecessarily appealed to on this as on many other occasions, and we have been boastingly told that in his time no nation dared insult us. Much, sir, as I revere his memory, acknowledging him among the fathers of his country, was this the fact? Was he not insulted?—was not the nation insulted under his administration? How came the posts to be detained after the definitive treaty with Great Britain? What dictated that inhuman deed to stir up horror and destruction among us—Lord Dorchester's insolent and savage speech to the hordes of Indians on our frontiers to massacre our inhabitants without distinction? Were those not insults? Or have we tamely forgotten them? Yet, sir, did Washington go to war? He did not; he preferred negotiation, and sent an envoy to Great Britain. Peace was obtained by a treaty with that nation. Shall we, then, not negotiate? Shall we not follow the leading feature of our nation's policy? We are all actuated, I hope, by one view, but we differ in the means. Let us show the nations of the earth we are not anxious for war, that scourge of mankind; that we bear patiently our injuries, in hope of redress.

"But, sir, if forced to war, contrary to our policy and wish, let us unsheathe the sword and fling away the scabbard until our enemies be brought to a sense of justice and our wrongs be redressed."

Now to every word of this speech I had listened breathlessly. There was a ring in Mr. Jackson's voice as he warmed to his theme, and his long body swayed in the power of his own eloquence, that moved me mightily, though I wished not to be moved.

I scarcely listened to the gentleman that followed (a Mr. Cocke from Tennessee), so intently was I reviewing Mr. Jackson's ringing sentences, and wondering if, after all, he was right, and all the brave Kentuckians who had been so loud in their demands for war were wrong. But one or two sentences of Mr. Cocke caught my ear; I heard him say:

"We were told by Mr. Ross that we were bound to go to war for this right which God and nature had given to the Western people. What are we to understand by this right given by God and nature? Surely not the right of deposit, for that was given by treaty, and as to the right of navigation, that has been neither suspended nor brought into question. But we are told by the same gentleman that the possession of New Orleans is necessary to our complete security. Leaving to the gentleman's own conscience to settle the question as to the morality of taking that place because it would be convenient, I beg to inform him that

the possession of it would not give us complete security.''

What further Mr. Cocke said I do not know, for at
that moment Mr. Lewis whispered to me:

''Do you know the lady in the gallery opposite?
She has been for some time covertly regarding one of
us, and I think it must be you. Do not look at her just
now; look at the right-hand gallery, and then gradually let your glance come around to the lady wearing
a black lace veil beside the pillar in the front row
opposite.''

I did as Mr. Lewis instructed—letting my glance
finally fall in the most casual manner where he indicated. But as I did so my heart gave a great bound.
Could that be Mademoiselle Pelagie? The pose of the
head, the dark eyes seen dimly through the lace veil,
the little ringlets in the neck, were hers; but after a
moment I convinced myself that it was only a chance
resemblance. I had left Mademoiselle Pelagie in Kentucky not three weeks before, with no intention of
coming to Washington, but of going direct to New
York as soon as suitable escort could be found. It
would hardly be within the bounds of possibility that
she should be in Washington as soon as I. It was
true I had been detained somewhat on the route, once
by losing my way, and once by Fatima laming her
foot and causing me to spend two days with a Virginia
planter while she recovered sufficiently to permit our
resuming our journey. But still I could not believe
mademoiselle could have accomplished such a journey
so quickly, and when I had left her there had been a

small prospect of an escort to New York, but none at all to Washington.

So I told Mr. Meriwether Lewis that the lady did indeed remind me of one I knew, but as she was at that moment (I had every reason to believe) safe with Mrs. O'Fallon at Mulberry Hill, it was impossible that it could be she. Then, though much disturbed by this chance resemblance and the thronging memories it awakened, I addressed myself once more to the debate.

I was just in time to see rising to his feet the handsomest man in the Senate, as I had long before decided. Mr. Gouverneur Morris, with his clean-cut, aristocratic features, his carefully curled peruke, his fine lace ruffles falling over his long white hands, and his immaculate stockings and pumps with their glittering buckles, was, to my mind, every inch the gentleman, and quite worthy to have called himself a blue-blooded Philadelphian, but that an unkind fate had given him New York for a birthplace. I was more than curious to know on which side he would be, and his opening sentence filled me with the assurance he was on the right side and every word was weighted. Clear-cut, each sentence dropped from his lips like a string of burnished jewels.

"Had Spain the right to make this cession to France without our consent? Gentlemen have taken it for granted that she had. But I deny the position. No nation has a right to give to another a dangerous neighbor without her consent. He who renders me insecure, he who hazards my peace and exposes me to imminent danger, commits an act of hostility against me and gives me the rights consequent on that act. Suppose Great Britain should give to Algiers one of the Bahamas, and contribute thereby to establish a nest of pirates near your coast. Would you not consider it as an aggression? It is among the first limitations to the exercise of the rights of property that we must so use our own as not to injure another, and it is under the immediate sense of this restriction that nations are bound to act toward each other.

"The possession of Louisiana by the ambitious ruler of France would give him in the New World the preponderance he has already obtained in the Old. It becomes the United States to show that they do not fear him who is the ruler of all; and it specially behooves the young and growing republic to interpose, in order to revive the energy and resistance of the half-conquered nations of Europe, and to save the expiring liberties of mankind!"

No one can imagine the fire, the grace, the inspiring tones and gestures, with which this last sentence was uttered. In my enthusiasm I looked across to my fair neighbor in the opposite gallery for sympathy. Through the veil I thought I caught her eye; but by the slightest turn of her head and an almost imperceptible movement of her hand she conveyed to me (whether intentionally or not, I was not sure) that she was not at all in sympathy with the speaker—indeed, that she disagreed with him wholly.

I looked down again into the arena below me. Slowly rising from his seat was a figure as ungainly as the other had been elegant. Red of face, with features almost coarse, and unwieldy from too great a burden of flesh, I recognized at once Mr. Morris's colleague, the famous Mr. Clinton of New York. What he said pleased me no more than his appearance, yet I could but own that no speaker had spoken with more force, more caustic satire, or more fluent eloquence. I had to admit, also, that there was a flavor of good sense and practicability about much that he said, though I was loath to admit it. He began ponderously, with pompous tones; but as he went on his voice changed until it became at times high and even rasping.

"Sublime, sir, as these speculations may appear to the eyes of some, and high-sounding as they may strike the ears of many, they do not affect me with any force. In the first place, I do not perceive how they bear upon the question before me; it merely refers to the seizure of New Orleans, not to the maintenance of the balance of power. Again, of all characters, I think that of a conquering nation least becomes the American people. What, sir! Shall America go forth, like another Don Quixote, to relieve distressed nations and to rescue from the fangs of tyranny the powerful states of Britain, Spain, Austria, Italy, the Netherlands? Shall she, like another Phaë- thon, madly ascend the chariot of Empire, and spread desolation and horror over the world? Shall she attempt to restrain the career of a nation, which my honorable colleague represents to have been ir- resistible, and which he declares has appalled the British lion and the imperial eagle of the house of Austria? Shall we wantonly court destruction and

16

violate all the maxims of policy which ought to govern infant and free republics? Let us, sir, never carry our arms into the territory of other nations, unless we are compelled to take them up in self-defense. A pacific character is of all others most important for us to maintain. With a sea-coast of two thousand miles, indented with harbors and lined with cities, with an extended commerce, and with a population of only six millions, how are we to set up for the avenger of nations? Can gravity itself refrain itself from laughter at the figure which my honorable colleague would wish us to make on the theater of the world? He would put a fool's cap on our head and dress us up in the parti-colored robes of a harlequin for the nations of the world to laugh at. And after all the puissant knights of the times have been worsted in the tournament by the Orlando Furioso of France, we must then, forsooth, come forward and console them for their defeat by an exhibition of our follies!

"I look, sir, upon all the dangers we heard about the French possession of Louisiana as visionary and idle. Twenty years must roll over our heads before France can establish in that country a population of two hundred thousand souls. What, in the meantime, will become of your Southern and Western States? Are they not advancing to greatness with a giant's stride? The Western States will then contain on their borders millions of free and hardy republicans, able to crush every daring invader of their rights!"

There was a slight stir in the gallery opposite. I looked up to see the figure in black rising from her seat. But even as I looked I thought I caught a direct glance from the dark eyes, and I could almost have sworn there was a slight wave of the hand as if in parting salute to me. Her companion, an older lady, rose with her, and together they turned and left the gallery. Once more I was struck by the startling resemblance to Mademoiselle Pelagie in every movement, and in the outlines of the graceful figure. I heard nothing more Mr. Clinton had to say; I was lost in an abstracted reverie as to the possibility of its being mademoiselle in the flesh. I would have liked to propose to Mr. Lewis that we go out and follow the mysterious figure, but cold reason assured me that mademoiselle was many miles away, and it was but a fond fancy that pictured her image in every dark-eyed maiden, and so shamed me from such a foolish pursuit.

"Shall we go?" said Mr. Lewis. "There will be no vote—probably none for a week at least."

I started from my reverie to find the debate over, the Senate adjourned, floor and gallery rapidly clearing. I answered with alacrity, hoping he had not discovered my abstraction:

"By all means. It has been a grand occasion, and I am much indebted to you, sir, for giving me the opportunity of hearing so great a debate."

Through the long corridors I hurried Mr. Lewis, eagerly scanning the throng for a glimpse of that figure, which I hoped we might overtake; but it had utterly vanished. Outside we found our horses waiting, and together we picked a rough and broken path down Capitol Hill, and then a smoother road where we could put our horses to a canter up the avenue; a gay throng in coaches, in saddle, and on foot accompanying us, and Mr. Meriwether Lewis saluting to right and left as we passed the more leisurely ones, or were passed by those riding or driving in reckless haste. And so on to my inn, where Bandy Jim, still industriously polishing boots on the sidewalk, ducked his white head with a joyous "Howdy, marsa!" and I felt as if an old friend was welcoming me home.

CHAPTER XVIII

A MAGIC COACH

"And we meet with champagne and a chicken."

I HAD made my toilet with such despatch that
scarcely an hour after parting with Mr. Lewis
at my inn I found myself once more at the White
House. This time I was ushered up-stairs into an
oval room, very gorgeously furnished in crimson,
where the President was waiting, and a few of his
guests. Beside him stood Mistress Madison, helping
him to receive; for his daughters were both away at
their homes. I improved the moment when she was
speaking to some guests, who had arrived just before
me, to look at her well. I had heard much of her, and
I knew my sisters at home would want me to tell them
exactly how she looked and what she wore.

I think I have often seen more beautiful women
(a dark-eyed maiden from France was in my mind at
the moment as far more beautiful), but rarely have
I seen a face lighted up with more of animation and
good humor. On her head she wore an article of dress
which I had heard described as worn by the ladies of
London and Paris, but which I had never before
seen; for the head-dresses of the Frenchwomen in

245

St. Louis, while in some respects quite as remarkable, bore not the slightest resemblance to this of Mistress Madison's. It was a Turkish turban of white satin and velvet, with a jeweled crescent in front clasping a bunch of nodding white ostrich-plumes. Her gown, of pale pink satin, was heavily trimmed with ermine, and she wore gold chains about her waist and wrists, and carried a jeweled snuff-box in her hand. She was truly regal-looking, and I did not wonder that people sometimes laughingly spoke of her as "her Majesty." Her turban especially, I think, gave her an indescribable air of distinction; but I was not quite sure that I thought it as becoming as the dark curling locks of the very beautiful lady who stood beside her.

Mr. Lewis, at this moment descrying me, came forward to present me to the President and to Mistress Madison, who put me at my ease at once by inquiring for my mother and for many of my Philadelphia kin, who, she declared, were old and very dear friends. I would have liked to linger at her side, for she made me much at home, and I liked not to turn away and find myself among a roomful of strangers; but I knew there were others waiting to be received by her, and I must move on.

As I turned from her, a voice in my ear said imperiously:

"Well, sir, and have you no word for your old friend, Fanny Cadwalader?"

I turned quickly; it was the beautiful lady with the dark curls.

"Miss Fanny!" I cried in joyous recognition, and bent low over her extended hand.

I had been but a young boy when Frances Cadwalader married Mr. Erskine and went to London to live; but we had been great friends as children, and I did not understand how I had failed to recognize her. She bade me stand beside her and she would point out all the distinguished guests, and I was glad indeed of her protection. In reply to my eager question as to how she came to be in Washington, she told me that her husband had been appointed minister from Great Britain in Mr. Merry's place, and they were but newly arrived.

"But where have you been living, sir," she asked, with mock severity, "that you know nothing of what has been going on in the great world? Or are we personages of so small importance that our movements are not chronicled in America?"

I had to explain that I had been in the backwoods for months, and for the last two months in the foreign colony of Louisiana, in the village of St. Louis, where little of the doings of the outside world penetrated.

She forgave me my ignorance, and immediately pointed out to me her husband, a fine-looking Englishman, talking to the most gorgeously arrayed creature I had ever beheld: satin, laces, velvets, jewels, gold lace, and powder made up a dazzling ensemble.

"That," said she, "is the Marquis de Casa Yrujo, and the lady with him is his wife, Sally McKean. He is magnificent, is he not? I would not quite like it if

I were the marchioness, for people look at him instead
of her, and she is quite beautiful enough to be looked
at herself.''

"Ah, why begrudge the marquis his meed of admiration, if he likes it?" I said. "And since he likes
it, let us be grateful, for his sake, that it is not Mistress Erskine who is the marchioness, for who can see
the glitter of the stars when the lovely moon is in the
sky?"

She laughed good-naturedly at my gallantry, but
I think she also liked it. We were standing near a
window that looked out on the front approach to
the White House. Suddenly Mistress Erskine exclaimed:

"Look, look quick, my friend! Here is magnificence indeed!"

I looked as she bade me, and saw what I conceived
to be a rolling ball of burnished gold borne swiftly
through the air by two gilt wings. As it came nearer
we both grew more excited—I because I did not know
what it was (and it looked more like a fairy coach than
anything I had dreamed of), and she both because
she enjoyed my bewilderment and because she loved
magnificence. By this time as many of the other
guests as were near windows and could look out without seeming to be over-eager, or discourteous to their
host, were doing so. The rolling golden ball came to
the very foot of the White House steps and stopped.
What I had taken to be two gilt wings proved to be
nothing more than gorgeous footmen, with *chapeaux
bras,* gilt-braided skirts, and splendid swords. They
sprang to the ground, opened the door of the coach,

and from it alighted the French minister, weighted with gold lace and glittering with diamonds and jeweled orders. He turned with stately ceremony to offer his hand to a lady who was alighting from the coach. First a tiny foot in high-arched slippers and embroidered stocking; then a glimpse of a skirt, pale pink and silver brocade, that had a strangely familiar air. I looked quickly at the head just emerging—waving black curls, dark glowing eyes, a complexion of ivory tinted with rose.

It was Mademoiselle Pelagie!

My head swam. Was it indeed all a bit of enchantment? The golden coach, the gorgeous footmen, the dazzling minister of France, and—Pelagie! Mrs. Erskine noted my agitation.

"Qu'as-tu, m'ami?" she said softly. "You know her, then?"

"Know whom, madam?" I asked, trying to get myself under control and seem indifferent.

"Our new sensation, the Great Lady of France, whom all the town is talking of. She arrived two days ago at the house of the French minister, and is staying there, it is said, under his protection, until she shall find suitable escort to Paris, where she goes to take possession of her estates returned to her by Bonaparte. This is what rumor says, and it looks as if it were true that she is a great lady, since the minister has handed her from the carriage before his own wife. We will wait now to see where the President seats her at table; that will decide it."

I was trying hard to hold myself in hand and make suitable answer.

"Is the President such a stickler, then, for form and ceremony? We had heard otherwise."

Mistress Erskine laughed:

"True, I forgot. If he had been as particular as he should concerning precedence, I should not be here. You know, do you not, that my husband's predecessor quarreled with President Jefferson because he gave his arm to Dolly Madison, in going in to dinner, instead of to the wife of the British minister?"

"Yes; I have heard of the 'Merry War,'" I answered, and stopped. Not another word could I utter. Nor apparently could anybody else in the room; for every voice was hushed as all eyes were turned to the door where the French minister was entering with his wife on his left arm, and what I veritably believed to be the most beautiful creature in the world on his right.

It was a brilliant spectacle; for the French minister and his wife dazzled the sight by the glitter of gold lace and the flash of jewels, and Pelagie blinded the eyes as truly by a vision of radiant dark eyes, soft black tresses curling around a white throat, the gleam of snowy neck and rounded arms through rare lace, and the color of the rose slowly tinting the rich ivory of her cheeks, as they passed through a double lane of guests to speak to the President.

Now was I in two minds whether to be supremely happy in once more beholding Mademoiselle Pelagie, whose graceful figure I thought had forever faded from my sight when the boat rounded the bend of the Ohio, or to be most miserable lest here among courtiers, and taking her rightful place with the great of the earth, she should no longer condescend to show me the friendliness she had shown on our last evening on the river. Neither was I quite sure whether it was my place to go forward and speak to her or to await her pleasure in speaking to me.

But Mistress Erskine solved the problem.

"You do know her," she said—"I see it in your eyes; and you must present me at once. And do tell me," she added eagerly: "is she so great a lady? We have heard so many rumors about her; what is the truth?"

"I have only known her," I answered, "as Mademoiselle Pelagie de Villa Réal. I know that in France she is of high rank, but I do not know what."

"Ah," she said, with a little gesture of disappointment, "then you cannot introduce me properly, and I shall have to trust to that astute diplomat that he gives her her right title. Does she know it herself?"

"I think she did not when she left St. Louis," I answered, "but her new friends may have revealed it to her."

"On second thought," said she, "I believe I will ask you to present her to me instead of the minister, if you will; I would like to see how she takes the 'Mademoiselle de Villa Réal.'"

So there was nothing for it but to brace up my courage and go forward to speak to mademoiselle. Nothing could have been sweeter and more friendly than her greeting, and with no trace of embarrassment, though I thought the French minister regarded me with a

coldly critical eye. Beside his magnificence I did feel
rather shabby; for, though Yorke had done his best
to freshen and restore my purple velvets by steaming
and other appliances, they still were the worse for
much service (especially the encounter with the chevalier), and for many packings in saddle-bags. Of my
lace ruffles I was justly proud, for no courtier's in the
room were finer or richer, and my sword and scabbard
were not to be ashamed of, for though not so bejew-
eled as some, they were of the finest workmanship and
inlaid with gold and pearl.

Mademoiselle presented me to the French minister
very prettily, however; and though I thought his
greeting somewhat scant in courtesy, I attributed it to
the suspicions he would naturally have, as mademoiselle's guardian, of a young gentleman of whom
he knew nothing, and whom mademoiselle received so
kindly.

I at once preferred Mistress Erskine's request, but
the minister gave Pelagie no chance to reply.

"I will myself present the comtesse to the wife of
the British ambassador," he said with alacrity, and led
her away to Mistress Erskine.

I saw that he had availed himself of this opportunity to cut short my interview with mademoiselle;
but, not to be outdone in diplomacy, I followed leisurely, and was in time to hear the minister say:

"It gives me pleasure to present to Madame Erskine
the Comtesse de Baloit." And I saw by the profound
curtsy Mistress Erskine made (and which mademoiselle returned very prettily, but with a touch of con-

descension, I thought) that that name meant something more to her than it did to me.

After the fashion of women, the two began at once a lively chatter in French, and I saw myself like to be shut out in the cold, with no further opportunity for converse with mademoiselle. But I would not desert my post, hoping sooner or later to get my chance. And I was rewarded; for in a few minutes Mistress Erskine was called to receive another presentation. But as she turned away she whispered in my ear:

"Be careful how you behave, sir; she is of the blood royal!"

Blood royal or not, she would always be Mademoiselle Pelagie to me, and I was not going to lose my opportunity.

"Tell me, Comtesse," I said, "how you came here. When I saw you last you had no idea of coming to Washington."

She did not answer my question at once, but, glancing up at me from under her long lashes in the most adorable fashion, she said softly:

"You used to call me Comtesse when you were angry. Are you angry now?"

"No, not when I was angry," I answered, "but when you were—were—"

"Proud and naughty and altogether disagreeable," she interposed quickly; "and that was very often, was it not, Monsieur?"

"Yes, Comtesse."

"I am not either now, am I? Then why do you not call me Mademoiselle?"

"No, indeed! You are"—I was going to say "adorable," but I finished tamely—"neither. But you are really Comtesse, and it is proper I should call you so." And before I was aware of what I was doing, I fetched a great sigh from the bottom of my boots. She understood, and looked up at me with a pathetic little smile that was sadder than my sigh.

"I am sorry, too; I think I would rather be mademoiselle," she said.

"And of the blood royal!" I added severely, as if accusing her of a crime.

She dropped her eyes.

"I cannot help it. I never knew till yesterday," meekly.

"And your guardian," I indicated the French minister with a slight nod in his direction, "thinks it great presumption for a plain Yankee gentleman to be talking on such familiar terms with a princess of the blood, and is coming in a few minutes to put a stop to it."

She looked at the minister quickly with a haughty turn of the head and a flashing glance, but in a moment she turned back to me with a smile curling her scarlet lips and a humorous twinkle in her eye.

"He would never dare," she said. "He is a good Citizen of the Republic."

"Nevertheless he will dare," I insisted. "I see it in his eye; so first tell me quickly how you got here, and when and where you are going."

"Your boat was hardly out of sight, Monsieur," she answered, "when another came up the river direct

from St. Louis with Monsieur and Madame Cerré
aboard. They brought letters from my guardian di-
recting me to go on with them to Washington (where
they were going to see the Spanish minister about
some trouble they had had with Americans—concerning peltries, I think, and land, perhaps), and they
would place me in the French minister's care. I did
not expect to find you here, for we were a whole day
behind you; but we traveled rapidly."

"And I was delayed," I said. "But when and
how are you to get to Paris? With the Livingstons?"

"No; Citizen Pichon says they sailed this week.
But he tells me, what is not generally known, that
your government is about to send a special envoy to
France concerning New Orleans—a Monsieur Monroe; and Monsieur Pichon has arranged that I shall
go with him."

"Do you know when?" I asked hastily, for I saw
the President moving toward us with the Marquis de
Casa Yrujo, and I was quite sure that meant an end to
all conversation.

"Not for several weeks, I believe; but I am not
sure," she answered.

"Will the Comtesse de Baloit permit me to present
the Marquis de Casa Yrujo, who will take her out to
dinner?" And the President was adding a pretty little speech of compliment, in his gallant way, and the
marquis was bowing solemnly and profoundly, and the
comtesse was curtsying and smiling, and I was left entirely out in the cold. I was rescued by Mistress
Madison.

"I would like nothing better than to give you your old friend Mistress Erskine to take out to dinner," she said, smiling. "It is forlorn for a young man among so many grown-ups, and the only young maiden snatched away from him. But the President is not going to blunder twice in the same fashion, and will take Mistress Erskine himself. Now I will give you your choice among the rest. Whom would you like to take?"

"Ah, your Majesty," I answered quickly, hand on my heart and bowing low, but smiling up at her,— for she was a woman into whose amiable, cordial face no man could look without smiling,—"I suppose I dare not lift my eyes as high as my heart would dictate, and since you are out of the question, I care not whom you give me."

"Saucy boy!"—and she tapped me lightly with her snuff-box,—"I vow I think you would be vastly more fun than the British minister, but my country demands that I sacrifice myself. I will give you the Marchioness de Casa Yrujo. If you do not know Sally McKean, she certainly knew you when you were in petticoats."

So I found myself seated at table between the most brilliant woman there and the most beautiful; for the Marchioness de Casa Yrujo was universally conceded to be the one, and the Comtesse de Baloit was, in my esteem at least, as certainly the other.

It was a long table, and bounteously furnished— lacking, perhaps, some of the elegance of the Philadelphia tables I had been accustomed to, but with a lavish prodigality native to the South. Two new guests had arrived while I had been so engrossed in talking to the comtesse that I had not observed their entrance, a gentleman and his wife. The lady was amiable-looking, but of no great distinction of appearance. The gentleman I thought I had seen before; his long, rather lean visage, somber but dignified, looked familiar to me. When the marchioness told me it was Mr. Monroe, I wondered that I had not recognized him at once, for he was a familiar figure on our streets during the ten years when Philadelphia was the capital. Moreover, I could have vowed he was wearing the same sad-colored drab clothes he used to appear in then, so entirely unchanged were both cut and color. I looked at him now with great interest, for was he not to decide the fortunes of the West? —in which I could have taken no greater interest had I been Western-born. And, more than that, was he not appointed to what seemed to me a mission of far greater importance, the conveying of mademoiselle in safety to her home?

I could have wished Mistress Monroe was to accompany him, for she had an air of motherly kindliness that I felt would be both protection and comfort to Mademoiselle Pelagie; and aside from the fact that there was something cold and austere in Mr. Monroe's face, I was sufficiently imbued with Mr. Hamilton's ideas to feel no great confidence in the man. (Wherein I have since thought I did Mr. Monroe great injustice, since in every act of his life he has proved himself a high-minded gentleman. But Mr. Hamilton's personal

17

magnetism was so great that it was quite impossible,
for us younger men at least, not to feel that every one
who differed with him must be, if not wholly unprincipled, at least worthy of doubt and suspicion.)

It was a brilliant dinner-table, for the exciting debate at the Capitol furnished a theme that loosed every
tongue. Yet I could see that the President, while he
kept the ball rolling with a gaiety and good humor
that rather surprised me, was himself most guarded.
Indeed, many were restrained, no doubt, from saying
quite what they thought by the presence of the Spanish minister, who at that time was at the height of his
popularity—his course in the Louisiana affair, which
made him so many enemies, not having been taken
until later.

Yet most of those present were more in sympathy
with Clinton of New York and Jackson of Georgia
than with Ross of Pennsylvania and Gouverneur Morris. When Mr. Erskine spoke of Gouverneur Morris's
speech as a masterly effort, the President, whom he addressed, replied only by a smile so coldly polite that it
was like a dash of cold water, not only to the British
minister, but to the whole table.

I was ever a blundering idiot, and knew not when to
leave well enough alone; neither had I ever the heart
to see fellow-man discomfited (especially if he were on
my side of the question) without going at once to his
aid. So, forgetting that it was the powerful minister
of a great nation, who needed no help from a man entirely unknown in the great world and of extreme
youth, I plunged boldly in.

"I agree with you, sir, most heartily," I said. "In force and polish and weight of argument it was beyond compare. But I expected nothing less from Gouverneur Morris."

There was a dead silence around the table; even the British minister had not the temerity to do more than bow his thanks in the face of Jefferson's icy smile. I caught a glimpse of the marquis's profile; he was frowning heavily. The French minister's face was a blank, and so was Mr. Monroe's. Pelagie looked the picture of distress, and Mr. Lewis made me a slight gesture which I took to mean, "Keep still." Even Mistress Erskine looked embarrassed, and I could understand none of it. But as I caught Mistress Madison's eye there was a twinkle of humor in it, and she gave the slightest, very slightest nod in the world toward the President.

Then at once it flashed upon me: Gouverneur Morris was bosom friend to Mr. Hamilton, and this was no place to be lauding him to the skies. Then was I seized with a rage against the restraints of society, that would not permit me to fling defiance in the face of all these grandees,—aye, and of the President himself,—and declare my allegiance to Hamilton and his friends. And mingled with my rage was an intolerable sense of mortification that I had made such an arrant fool of myself before all these older men and lovely women. But, with a tact for which I can never be sufficiently grateful to her, Mistress Madison turned at once to Pelagie.

"Comtesse," she said, "you are fresh from the colony of Louisiana, in which we are all so deeply interested; tell us something about your life in St. Louis, and how you found your Spanish rulers.''

And mademoiselle, understanding, responded at once with glowing descriptions of her happy life there, and the courtesy and polish of the people, with many gay little touches of rude and funny experience. Everybody thawed at once; for most of those present had been much in Paris and could understand her French as easily as I. The President became as genial as he had been icy, and he insisted on drawing me also into the conversation (I think for the purpose of giving me an opportunity of retrieving myself), in which I hope I bore my part modestly; for I like not to seem either presumptuous or vainglorious, though, because I am a blunderer, I no doubt seem sometimes to be both.

The curtains had been drawn and the candles lighted when we sat down to dinner, though the sun was still shining; but the short winter afternoon had rapidly passed into evening, and then into dark night, and we still lingered at the table. Talk had grown more and more animated as the wine flowed more freely, and toasts were drunk and bright speeches made in response. I had, as in duty bound, devoted most of my attention to the marchioness, and the marquis had engrossed Pelagie. Yet there had been chance for an occasional word with her. It was when the marquis was rising to respond to a toast to his Most Catholic Majesty of Spain, amid the ringing of glasses, that I turned to mademoiselle.

''Would it be permitted an old friend to call at the

house of the French minister on the Comtesse de Baloit?"

"It would be unpardonable if he neglected to do so," she responded, with a bright smile.

"Then to-morrow at two I hope to find you at home," I said, and then added quickly—"unless you are going to the Senate again?"

She colored a little.

"Did you know me?"

But she would not let me answer her own question, for the marquis was beginning to speak, and it behooved us to listen. In the midst of the applause that followed his speech, I saw the President whisper something to the black man who stood behind his chair and send him to me. For a moment, when the messenger told me the President wished to see me in his office after the others were gone, I thought I was to be called to account for my malapropos speech, but I was relieved when he added:

"The President hab a message from yo' home, sah."

And had it not been that I liked much feeling myself so near mademoiselle, even if I had only an occasional word from her, I would have been very impatient for dinner to be over, for a message from home sent to the President, it seemed to me, must be of importance.

Dinner was over at last, and there was but little lingering afterward. I had the pleasure of helping mademoiselle into her coach, though Monsieur Pichon looked cold and the Marquis de Yrujo tried to forestall me. But when she was shut up inside the golden ball, and the great golden wings were once more perched on either side of it, and it rolled away glittering and flashing in the light of the torches as it had flashed and glittered in the rays of the sun five hours before, I had a sinking of the heart such as I might have felt had she been snatched away from my sight forever in the prophet's fiery chariot bearing her to the skies.

Mr. Meriwether Lewis was waiting to conduct me to the President's office, and he stayed and talked with me pleasantly until the President arrived; laughing with me at my *faux pas*, but telling me I had nothing to fear from the President's displeasure, as he was not the man to harbor a grudge on so slight a matter, and he (though, to be sure, he was a lifelong friend) had ever found him to be kind, considerate, and genial.

And such I found him in our brief interview. He went directly to the point with me, which always goes far toward winning my liking.

"I know your family," he said, "have ever been friends of Mr. Hamilton, and so not particularly friendly to me in a political way; but your father and I have been associated much in scientific pursuits, and we have ever been congenial friends in our love of botanical research. He has sent me many rare plants and seeds to Monticello, and now he shows me the further courtesy of reposing a confidence in me, and I hope you will express to him my appreciation, which I will prove by reposing a like confidence in you.

Your father writes me that a letter has just been received from your uncle, Monsieur Barbé Marbois, inviting you to spend some time with him in Paris. He says that both he and your mother think it much to be desired that you should improve this opportunity for completing your education. He says, further, that a ship sails from New York early next week, and requests me, if you should be in Washington when I receive this letter, as he suspects, that I will instruct you to lose no time in reaching home. Indeed, so urgent is he, and the time is so short, I think, without doubt, you should set off by daybreak to-morrow morning.

"Now, as I said before, I am going also to repose a confidence in you. It is not generally known, nor do I wish it known for the present (therefore I speak in confidence), that I have decided to send an envoy extraordinaire to Paris for the purpose of discussing with the French government the possibility of purchasing New Orleans. I communicated this to the Senate to-day in secret session, and I now communicate it to you, also in 'secret session'''—with a genial smile.

"I have asked Mr. Monroe to undertake this delicate mission, and he has to-day consented, and is here arranging his plans and discussing with me and with Mr. Madison the points involved. He will not be able to set out for some weeks, but we hope now that he can sail by the eighth of March, reaching Paris somewhere near the twelfth of April. Mr. Livingston naturally knows nothing of this, and the favor I have to ask of you is that, immediately upon your arrival in Paris, you call upon him and deliver to him a note which I shall give you, and also explain fully to him all that I have said to you, all that you have heard at dinner this evening, and particularly repeat to him as much as you can hold in memory of the debate you listened to in the Senate to-day.''

The President paused for a moment, and then, with a smile of rare sweetness, he added:

''Is the ardent young friend of Hamilton willing to put the President under such a load of obligations?''

For a moment I hardly knew what response to make. Not that I dreamed of denying his request: I was only too proud and happy that he should have made it. But that he should have reposed such a confidence in me, when he knew me scarcely at all, seemed incomprehensible. I made but a stammering reply.

''Your Excellency,'' I said, ''I fear I have given you but a poor idea of my discretion, but since you trust me in spite of my blunder, I am very proud to be of service to you.''

It took but a minute for the President to give me his note to Mr. Livingston, and a few further instructions, and then he bade me God-speed with a warmth and cordiality I had never expected and certainly never deserved at his hands.

There was but little sleep for me that night. As Fatima clattered into the stony courtyard of my inn, I called loudly for Bandy Jim; and when the poor old man came stumbling out of some inner retreat, half blinded with sleep, I begged him to look after Fatima himself, and see that she was well rubbed down and ready for an early morning start, and that I was called and breakfast ready by six.

In my own room I spent not much time in packing my saddle-bags, but it took me a good half-hour to write a brief note to mademoiselle, explaining why I was compelled to cancel my engagement with her for the next day, and bidding her good-by in such fashion that, without seeming presumptuous, she might read between the lines how much of my heart I had put into it.

I had said nothing in my note about going to Paris. I very much desired to keep that for a surprise when I might some day meet her there. And, lest she should hear it from others, I wrote also a note to Meriwether Lewis, asking him to say nothing about it to any one, and to request the President to keep my secret for me.

Then, putting a bright new gold piece with the two notes to be delivered by the trusty hands of Bandy Jim in the morning, I lay down to get a brief sleep, if possible—but, sleeping or waking, to dream of Paris and the Comtesse de Baloit.

CHAPTER XIX

CHECK TO THE ABBÉ!

"When Greeks joined Greeks, then was the tug of war."

I HAD been in Paris three weeks, and they had been weeks of unalloyed delight. The life and gaiety of the brilliant capital, the streets lined with handsome houses and thronged with gay equipages, richly dressed people, soldiers wearing the tricolored cockade, students, artists, workmen, blanchisseuses, and nursery-maids in picturesque costumes tending prettily dressed children, made a moving panorama I never tired of. Even the great palaces and the wonderful works of art scarcely interested me as did this shifting kaleidoscopic picture, and I looked back at life in my native town on the banks of the Delaware as belonging to another world, incomparably tame and dull by comparison.

Every morning I accompanied my uncle, Monsieur Barbé Marbois, to the Treasury office, and left him at the door, to roam around the streets and watch the life of the town. I was at home again in time for midday déjeuner, and then on Fatima's back (for I had brought Fatima with me; no persuasion of friends could induce me to leave her behind, since she had twice rescued mademoiselle and so become my most trusted friend) — on Fatima's back I dashed out the Avenue to the beautiful Wood of Boulogne, sometimes racing with the young bloods to whom my uncle had introduced me, sometimes checking my horse to a gentle canter beside a coachful of Faubourg St. Germain beauties, exchanging merry compliments with the brilliant and witty mothers while I looked at the pretty daughters, who, for aught I knew, were as stupid as their mothers were brilliant, since they never opened their mouths. And so back to my aunt's in time to make a careful toilet for the four-o'clock dinner, when there were sure to be guests, more or less distinguished, but always interesting.

I had delivered my message and my note from the President to Mr. Livingston on the day of my arrival, and it seemed to me that it did not please him overmuch that an envoy extraordinaire should be sent to attend to his affairs; but he said nothing, and received me most graciously, both as a messenger from the President and because I was the son of his old friend.

Several times since my arrival at my uncle's house, both Mr. Livingston and his son the colonel had been guests there, and always the talk had turned on what most interested me, the purchase of New Orleans and the Floridas. At one of these dinners, Monsieur Talleyrand, the Minister of Foreign Relations, was also guest, and while there was but little reference to Louisiana at table, I was, with no intention on my part, a listener later to a most interesting conversation be-

tween Monsieur Talleyrand and Mr. Livingston that
was no doubt intended to be strictly private.

Thinking that it was very likely the three gentlemen
—the Minister of Foreign Relations, my uncle the
Secretary of the Treasury, and the United States minister—might have matters of importance to discuss
where my absence would be more desirable than my
presence, I left the salon immediately after dinner,
and went out into the garden, taking with me a Philadelphia paper that had arrived by that morning's express and that I had not yet seen. I took my paper
into the little summer-house at the farther end of the
garden, and was soon engrossed reading the debates
in Congress. I found there had been another of great
interest on the same Louisiana subject, and so deeply
immersed was I in my paper that I did not notice that
any one had entered the garden until the sound of
voices quite close to me roused me. A small table with
several garden-chairs surrounding it stood under a
spreading horse-chestnut tree, and there we often took
our morning coffee, if the weather was fine, or smoked
our evening cigars. At this table Monsieur Talleyrand
and Mr. Livingston had seated themselves, and how
long they had been talking I did not know, so absorbed
was I in my paper, when Mr. Livingston's voice, a little raised above its usual even tenor, roused me.

I sprang to my feet, realizing that I must seem like
an eavesdropper, should any one discover me there,
even though I had not heard a word. Mr. Livingston
was facing the door of the summer-house, and as he
saw me he nodded pleasantly to me to come forward.

"Here, Citizen Minister," he said to Mr. Talleyrand, "is a young man whose father would like to
train him for the profession of diplomacy. Perhaps
he could not begin his apprenticeship better than by
being present at our interview, and, if you have no
objections, I will ask him to remain. He can act as
secretary and take notes for the future reference of us
both, if you like."

I rather thought Mr. Talleyrand did *not* quite like,
though he assented to Mr. Livingston's proposal, but
with such cold politeness as made me exceedingly uncomfortable, and I would have been very glad to make
my escape to the house. But, for some reason, Mr.
Livingston seemed to especially desire me to remain,
and I saw no help for it but to sit down at a respectful
distance, take my memorandum-book out of my pocket,
and prepare, ostensibly at least, to take notes.

I was much concerned, also, at what Mr. Livingston
had said about my father desiring to train me for
diplomacy. He had never said anything to me about
it, and I determined on the instant I would never be a
diplomat. "The life of a soldier for me!" I said to
myself, and then suddenly realized that Mr. Livingston was talking, and it behooved me to listen carefully if I was to play the secretary.

Mr. Livingston was saying:

"Be assured, sir, that even were it possible that the
government of the United States could be insensible
to the sufferings of the Western people, they would
find it as easy to prevent the Mississippi from rolling
its waters into the ocean as to control the impulse of

the people to do themselves justice. Sir, I will venture to say that were a fleet to shut up the mouths of the Chesapeake, the Delaware, and the Hudson, it would create less sensation in the United States than the denial of the right of deposit at New Orleans has done.''

I liked the ring in Mr. Livingston's voice, and his words sounded very stirring to me; but I could not see that they made any impression on the impassive countenance of Monsieur Talleyrand. He was reclining in his garden-chair, and I could see that as Mr. Livingston spoke he was regarding him intently through half-shut eyes. His tones were of the sweetest and blandest as he replied:

''The First Consul, Mr. Livingston, has asked me to say to you that he proposes to send General Bernadotte as envoy to the United States to acquire such information as he may deem necessary, previous to his taking any measure relative to the situation in which the acquisition of Louisiana will place France with respect to the United States. I hope, moreover, that this measure on the part of the First Consul will prove satisfactory both to you and to your government.''

Now I cannot but think that Mr. Talleyrand is too astute a man to have thought for an instant that this would prove satisfactory, and so, I have no doubt, he was quite prepared for Mr. Livingston's indignant outburst:

''Satisfactory, sir! If, sir, the question related to the forming of a new treaty, I should find no objection to this measure. On the contrary, I should readily acquiesce in it as that which would be best calculated to render the treaty mutually advantageous. But, sir, it is not a new treaty for which we now press, but the recognition of an old one, by which the United States have acquired rights that no change in the circumstances of the country obliges them to relinquish, and which they never will relinquish but with their political existence!''

It was hard for me to sit still under such ringing sentences. I wanted to clap my hands and cry ''Bravo!'' For a moment all the glories of Paris turned dull and insipid; I would have given them all to be in Kentucky on Fatima's back, marching down the river to capture New Orleans.

But Mr. Livingston had not finished. Mr. Talleyrand made a slight movement as if to speak, but, with uplifted hand to prevent him, Mr. Livingston hurried on:

''In what situation, sir, are we now placed? An armament is about sailing for New Orleans. That port has been shut by the order of Spain. The French commandant will find it shut. Will he think himself authorized to open it? If not, it must remain shut until the envoy of France shall have arrived in America, made the necessary inquiries, and transmitted the result of those inquiries to the First Consul. In the meantime all the produce of five States is left to rot upon their hands. There is only one season in which the navigation of the Mississippi is practicable. This season must necessarily pass before the envoy of France can arrive and make his report. Is it supposable, sir, that the people of the United States will tranquilly await the progress of negotiations, when the ruin of themselves and their families will be attendant on the delay? I can never bring myself to believe that the First Consul will, by deferring for a moment the recognition of a right that admits of no discussion, break all those ties which bind the United States to France, obliterate the sense of past obligations, change every political relation that it has been, and still is, the earnest wish of the United States to preserve, and force them to connect their interests with a rival power! And this, too, for an object of no real moment in itself. Louisiana is, and ever must be, from physical causes, a miserable country in the hands of an European power.''

Mr. Talleyrand's eyes had not moved from Mr. Livingston's face during this long speech, but at his last words I saw a sudden spark leap into them.

"You no doubt think, sir," he said in his low, even tones, "that Louisiana would be a much better country in the hands of the United States. Would your government like to buy it from us?''

"You know, sir, and have known for some time," replied Mr. Livingston, "that we are ready to make an offer for New Orleans and the Floridas as soon as you are ready to listen to it.''

"But would you not rather have the whole of Louisiana? The rest of it, without New Orleans, would be of little value to us. What would you give for the whole?''

Mr. Livingston looked bewildered for an instant; it

was almost more than he could take in at once. But after a moment's thought he replied:

"It is a subject, sir, I have not considered; but I suppose we shall not object to twenty million francs, provided our citizens are paid."

"That is much too low an offer, my dear sir," responded Talleyrand, "but I see the idea is new to you. I would be glad if you would reflect upon it, and tell me to-morrow the result of your reflections."

"Mr. Monroe will be in town in a day or two." (My heart gave so great a thump when Mr. Livingston said that, I feared they might hear it—for would not the Comtesse de Baloit be with him?) "And I would like to delay any further offer until I shall have the pleasure of introducing him."

Mr. Talleyrand shrugged his shoulders slightly.

"As you will, Monsieur; but do not give Mr. Monroe reason to think that I speak with authority. The idea struck me that you might like the whole of the colony quite as well as part of it."

I thought this would have put an end to the conversation; but I soon saw that Mr. Livingston had another card to play, and that he evidently did not believe the minister was speaking entirely on his own authority.

"Monsieur Talleyrand," he said, "I have this morning received a notice from my home government that Mr. Ross's resolution authorizing the President to seize New Orleans was lost by four votes. Another was offered by Mr. Breckinridge of Kentucky, which was unanimously adopted. Mr. Breckinridge's reso-

18

lution was to the effect that the President of the
United States be authorized to require of the execu-
tives of the several States, to arm and equip, and hold
in readiness to march at a moment's notice, eighty
thousand militia; that money be appropriated for paying and subsisting such troops; and also that money
be appropriated for erecting on the Western border
one or more arsenals, as the President may judge
proper. Monsieur Talleyrand, this means but one
thing: that the United States is ready to act at once
if France does not recognize our right of deposit; and
I beg you will use your influence with the First Consul, that he will not send General Bernadotte until
this question is determined.''

Mr. Talleyrand, with another shrug of his shoulders,
seemed to disclaim any influence with the First Consul, though he said:

''If you will make me an offer for the whole of
Louisiana that I can convey to him, I have no doubt
it will carry great weight.''

''I must decline to do so, Monsieur, as I am expecting Mr. Monroe in a day or two.''

Suddenly Mr. Livingston changed his tone. It was
no longer one of mild argument, but as of one who
called another to account. I was astonished that he
dared so address the powerful Minister of Foreign Relations.

''I have long been endeavoring to bring you to some
point, Monsieur, but, unfortunately, without effect.
I wish merely to have the negotiation opened by any
proposition on your part. It was with that view I

sent you a note a few days ago, to which, as yet, I have received no answer.''

The great man sounded to me surprisingly meek as he replied:

''I would have answered your note earlier, Mr. Livingston, but I have been waiting, hoping I could give you some more satisfactory reply. I will delay no longer. I will answer it; but it will have to be evasively, for Louisiana is not ours.''

I caught a glimpse of Mr. Livingston's countenance; a more sardonic smile I have never seen—a smile which said as plainly as words, ''You are lying.'' He spoke with frigid courtesy:

''It seems strange that I should be better informed than the Minister of Foreign Relations,'' he said, ''but I have seen the treaty. Moreover, I know that the Consul has appointed officers to govern the colony, and he has himself told me that General Victor was to take possession. And, what seems to me most convincing proof—why does the First Consul send General Bernadotte to the United States to treat in relation to Louisiana, if Louisiana does not belong to France?''

I thought that would have floored even Talleyrand; but not at all. With another shrug of his shoulders, and putting together his finger-tips in a manner that gave him a most indifferent air, he only persisted in saying that they had it in contemplation, but had not yet secured it. I wondered what Mr. Livingston would say next, but I need not have feared for him. Quick as thought, and all smiles and amiability, he responded to the minister:

"I am very well pleased to understand this from you, Monsieur, because, if so, we will not commit ourselves with you by taking it from Spain, to whom, by your account, it still belongs. And as we have just cause of complaint against Spain, if Mr. Monroe concurs in my opinion, we will negotiate no further on the subject with you, but advise our government to take possession."

For the first time Mr. Talleyrand seemed moved. He sprang to his feet and spoke quickly:

"I beg you will take no such measures at present, Mr. Livingston. I will answer your note, though I must still say, as I have said before, it will have to be evasively."

Mr. Livingston, who had also risen to his feet, bowed formally.

"I shall be glad to receive any communication from you, Citizen Minister, but we are not disposed to trifle. The times are critical, and though I do not know what instructions Mr. Monroe may bring, I am perfectly satisfied they will require a precise and prompt notice. I am very fearful, from the little progress I have made, my government will consider me as a very indolent negotiator."

Mr. Talleyrand laughed, a high, rasping laugh, but evidently intended to be of great good humor.

"I will give you a certificate, Mr. Livingston, and you can send it home to your government, that you are the most importunate negotiator I have ever met with."

Their conference seemed to be ended; they turned and walked toward the house, leaving me to ponder with wonder and amaze at what I had listened to, and with keen admiration for the part Mr. Livingston had taken in the matter. I had always been led to believe that no man could hold his own against the shrewd and unfathomable Abbé; but, if I mistook not, this time Mr. Livingston had not only held his own, but got much the better of him.

Suddenly a thought flashed into my mind. What did Talleyrand mean by repeating over and over, and in such significant phrase, that his answer must be "evasive"? Could it be possible that he was intimating that a consideration would be necessary to make it more decided? I believed that he had so intimated, and that Mr. Livingston had understood him, and had repelled the intimation with scorn.

Then again there flashed into my mind the two million dollars that had been voted the President to use "as he thought best" in adjusting this matter. Was it intended to use in buying up "such creatures," I said scornfully to myself, "as Talleyrand"? Vague insinuations in those speeches in Congress I had listened to now seemed to me as clear as day.

Hot with indignation and shame,—my indignation for Talleyrand, my shame that my country could stoop to such measures,—I rushed into the house to my uncle. He had been entertaining Colonel Livingston while the other two were holding their conference; but all three gentlemen were gone now, and I found him sitting quietly in his library, reading. I had flung the door wide as I entered, and I stopped on the threshold.

"Monsieur, what does it mean?" I cried. "Does

Monsieur Talleyrand want Mr. Livingston to offer him a bribe? And were the two millions of dollars given to Mr. Jefferson for such base purposes?"

My uncle looked up, startled and amazed beyond measure. He did not at all take in my meaning, but he was very sensible of my rudeness. My uncle was ever the most amiable of men and the most tolerant, but for correctness of deportment and elegance of manner he was a stickler, and so flagrant a breach of both was intolerable to him.

"I think you forget yourself, sir," he said coldly; and that was all he said, but his words cut like tempered steel in quivering flesh. A great wave of mortification rushed in a crimson flood to the very roots of my hair.

"I am most truly sorry, sir, to have been so rude," I stammered, "and I beg you will not think that we do not know good manners in America. I fear I am ever slow to think and headlong to act, and it has often brought me to grief."

My uncle, who, as I said, was all amiability, forgave me at once, and invited me most cordially to enter his library. I was loath to intrude after my great rudeness, but he would not let me off.

"Come in, come in," he said, "and I will answer your question by another. What has led you to think that Mr. Talleyrand desires a bribe from Mr. Livingston? Has any one been saying so to you?"

Then was I in greater confusion than before. I did not know whether Mr. Livingston would desire me to say anything about the interview to which I had been accidentally made a party, and I had intended to say nothing to any one until I had had a chance to find out his wishes; and now, in my indignation, I had entirely forgot my resolution and betrayed myself. There was no way out but to make a clean breast of my part in it.

So I told my uncle how I had been caught in the summer-house, and been invited to become a listener to secrets of state. My uncle threw back his head and laughed long and loud. But when he had calmed down a little, he looked at me keenly.

"So you think Mr. Talleyrand wanted a bribe from Mr. Livingston? Would you mind telling me what he said that led you to think so?"

Now was I greatly embarrassed, for I had fully resolved that not one iota of information of which I had become the possessor so innocently should pass my lips without Mr. Livingston's sanction. My uncle noticed my embarrassment, and spoke quickly:

"Never mind, my boy. It is no doubt just as well that you should not tell me what you feel you have no right to repeat; but it would make no real difference. I see that you are trustworthy, and I do not mind telling you that the First Consul is of somewhat the same opinion. He does not altogether trust the Minister of Foreign Relations, and it is more than likely the negotiations will be taken out of his hands and put into mine. It is more than likely also that it was because Mr. Livingston does not trust him that he desired to have you present as a witness. Now you see how I trust you. These are matters of grave im-port, my boy, and if you had been eager to tell me all you had heard I would have been loath indeed to confide in you, as I have just done."

I glowed with pleasure at my uncle's words, and thanked him most earnestly for his confidence, which I told him was not misplaced. And then, fearing I was intruding too long upon his hours of privacy (for they were few indeed, and greatly prized, I knew), I bowed myself out of his library, and dashed for a ride on Fatima down the crowded avenue. For it was upon Fatima's back I could ever think best, and I had much to think over: the amazing conversation I had listened to; my uncle's confidence to me; and last of all, and which set my pulses throbbing and the blood tingling to my finger-tips—Mr. Monroe would be in Paris in a day or two!

CHAPTER XX

BONAPARTE GIVES ENGLAND A RIVAL

"Great let me call him, for he conquered me."

THE next morning was Easter, and, dressed in a new suit of puce-colored ferrandine, with fresh ruffles of finest lace, and a new plume in my hat, I walked decorously beside my aunt through the thronged streets, every one dressed in his best and every one going the same way—to the Church of the Madeleine, to see the First Consul attend service. The sun was shining, birds were singing, the air was soft and warm and filled with the mingled perfume of flowers and incense, borne out through the open doors of all the churches.

The world was happy, and so was I. I was greatly excited, too, for I was to behold, for the first time, the man who held in his hand the destinies of nations, and before whose terrible word even our own proud republic trembled.

I had been three weeks in Paris and had not seen him. It seemed to be my ill fortune never to be on the streets when he made one of his dashing progresses through them, and though there had been several levees my wardrobe had not been in condition to attend them. At least, so my aunt thought. I think I would have been willing to don once more the old plum-colored velvets for the sake of seeing the great Bonaparte, but Madame Marbois thought otherwise.

"Nobody is such a stickler for forms and ceremonies, or such a lover of magnificence, as the First Consul," said she, "and if you want to make a good impression upon him, or do credit to your family at home and to your uncle and to me, you must wait for your new costumes."

So she had me to the tailor's, and more suits were ordered than I thought I could wear in a lifetime. When they came home and my man Cæsar (my own colored boy whom I had brought with me from home) had laid them all out for me in my room, I thought them well worth waiting for. There were suits for church and suits for dinner, suits for riding and for walking, and, most resplendent of all, two court costumes. One especially of white satin with much gold lace and bullion quite took my breath away. Now I have always had a weakness for fine clothes that I secretly deprecated, for I feared it was a womanish weakness quite unbefitting a soldier of fortune, which was the career I had laid out for myself and was quite determined upon. Yet I have never found that my liking for fine clothes has made me less ready to draw my sword to help the innocent or weak, and so I hope it may not be a sign in me of any lack of true manliness.

Be this as it may, I was walking joyously beside my aunt that beautiful Easter morning, and part of the joy in my heart was for the beautiful puce-colored ferrandine that sat so well and had an air of distinction I was sure no other clothes of mine had ever had, for these were made in Paris.

I have no very distinct recollection of the services; indeed, I hardly paid enough attention to them to follow them decorously, for I was consumed with an eager desire for but one event—the entrance of the First Consul.

A subdued murmur (almost, it seemed to me, like suppressed ''Vive le rois'') announced to me that he was just entering the door, and as I sat by the aisle down which he was coming, and far to the front, by turning in my seat and stretching my neck shamelessly I had time to see him well.

Could this little fellow, who might easily have stood under my arm stretched level with my shoulder, could he be the hero of Marengo! the Dictator of France who held all Europe trembling in his grasp! I think that I had heretofore had an unconscious feeling that greatness of stature meant greatness of heart and mind and courage, and I had gloried in my inches. Now I was almost ashamed of them, for this little man coming rapidly down the aisle with a firm, quick step seemed to breathe power from the chiseled curve of the nostril, from the haughty curl of the beautiful lips, but most of all from the imperial flash of the dark eyes under level brows. If his face had not been so full of power, yes, and of arrogance, it would have been almost too beautiful for a man's face, framed in silky brown hair thinning at the temples, but curling in one dark lock above the broad white brow.

But if it humbled me to see so much greatness in such small stature, it comforted me not a little to observe that the great man was no despiser of dress. He might have been molded into his small-clothes and waistcoat of white doeskin, so exactly did they fit every line and curve of his perfect figure. His dark-blue military coat of finest cloth was set off by heavy epaulets of gold and by a broad azure ribbon crossing his breast and bearing the jeweled insignia of the Legion of Honor. The crimson sword-sash which bore his sword sheathed in a scabbard of gold flashing with jewels, completed in his own dress the tricolor of France. He wore high military boots, I think to carry out the military effect of his epaulets and sword, for it was in the character of soldier, the hero of many battles, the winner of glory for France, that the people idolized him.

To the right and the left, his eagle glance took in the whole great congregation, and as he passed it fell on me. His glances were never idle ones; I knew he had seen me, and my pulses quivered and fluttered like a young maiden's. From that moment I was as much his slave as any soldier of La Vendée, and had he not himself disillusioned me most bitterly, I should still have been regarding him as the hero of my dreams, *sans peur et sans reproche,* the greatest man and greatest soldier of all time. I still believe the latter title belongs to him, but not the first, for a great man must be a good man too, like our Washington, and that Bonaparte was not.

It is no wonder, then, that I was quite beside myself with excitement when at déjeuner my uncle said to me:

"Would you like to ride out to St. Cloud with me this afternoon? The First Consul has summoned me to a conference with him, if I mistake not, on the subject you heard discussed yesterday."

"Oh, thank you, sir. And shall I be present at the conference?" I spoke quickly and foolishly, for I was greatly excited.

My uncle laughed.

"Well, hardly, my boy, unless you find a way, as you did yesterday, of compelling the First Consul to invite you to be present."

I liked not to be laughed at, but I knew it was but my uncle's teasing fashion, and all the way out through the beautiful Boulogne woods, the birds singing, the sun shining, the soft spring airs blowing, the alders and willows pale pink and yellow in the distance, the great buds of the horse-chestnuts just bursting into leaf and everywhere the vivid green of the fresh turf; my heart beating high with happy excitement to be in beautiful Paris and on my way to historic St. Cloud, where dwelt the most wonderful man of the world; and Fatima prancing and curveting under me, her dainty hoofs scarce touching the earth as she danced along the green allées of St. Cloud's beautiful park, sharing my happy excitement (though only, I suppose, for a horse's natural joy in trees and grass and sunshine)—all that swift and beautiful ride, galloping beside my uncle's coach, his words rang in my ears, and I longed with all my heart to be present at that conference: not so much to hear what was said as to see the great Bonaparte saying it.

I parted from my uncle at one of the great fountains, he riding up in his coach to the palace doors, and Fatima and I starting off on an exploring tour around the park. He would not hear to my waiting for him, for he said he might be detained for hours, and indeed it was possible the Consul would keep him all night at St. Cloud, as sometimes happened, to call upon at any hour of the night when some new suggestion occurred to him.

Riding fast, as was my custom when alone with Fatima, it did not take us long to exhaust the beauties of the park, and my eyes began to turn longingly toward the palace. Somewhere within its stately walls I supposed the conference was going on. Verily, there were some compensations in diplomacy when it gave a man like my uncle a chance to hold close converse with a man like the First Consul. (And in that I do not intend to speak slightingly of my Uncle François, for he was ever in my regard the most admirable of men. Only, it seemed to me then that to be able to talk familiarly with the great Bonaparte was a privilege above the deserts of ordinary mortals.)

I intended to remain at St. Cloud until toward evening, for if the conference should prove short I might still have the pleasure of my uncle's company on the homeward trip. But time began to hang heavily on my hands, and it occurred to me that I would ask the sentry, whom I had seen from a distance walking up and down in front of the main entrance, whether it were possible to gain admission to the palace. I thought it probable that it was not open to visitors, since the First Consul was occupying it, but it would do no harm to find out, and if by chance I should be admitted, I would at least have the pleasure of wandering through the rooms where he dwelt.

It was necessary first to dispose of Fatima, and a thicket of evergreen at one side of the palace caught my eye as affording a grateful shade from the warm afternoon sun (which so early in the season could be found only under evergreens) and a hiding-place from any prowling thief who might want to steal her, or from any troublesome guard who might come upon her and carry her off to the Consul's stables.

So into the thicket I rode, following a winding path that led toward the upper end near the palace, and at the very upper edge I found just what I wanted— a clump of bushes so thick set that they formed an almost impenetrable screen. They were lower than the other evergreens—not much higher than my horse's ears, but that was high enough. Into the midst of this clump I rode Fatima and dismounted.

"Stand here, Sweetheart," I said softly, "and budge not a step for any man but your master."

She rubbed her nose against my shoulder in token that she understood, and I whispered again in her ear:

"Not a whinny, not a sound, my Beauty," and left her, feeling sure no man could steal her and no guard could lead her away by guile or force, nor would she betray her presence there by any noise.

As I left the evergreens, intending to go around to the front of the building and speak to the sentry, I saw, coming down the path toward me, a young and pretty woman, who, I recognized by her dress, must be in service at the palace.

"I will inquire from her," I said to myself promptly, "for she will know as well as the sentry whether there is any admission, and she will no doubt have a much pleasanter way of saying either yes or no."

So, as she was about to pass me with a little curtsy and a pretty smile, I stopped her.

"Mademoiselle," I said, and doffed my hat, "is it permitted to see the palace to-day?"

"No, Monsieur," she answered, "unless one is invited or has business of importance with the First Consul."

Now I have ever had great faith in woman's wit, and especially a Frenchwoman's, and it suddenly struck me if this one should prove as quick-witted as most of her kind, she would know how to secure my admission into the palace; and if she should prove as kindly disposed as I believed the sight of gold and a pleasant word might make her, then was my success assured.

"Mademoiselle," I said, and my manner was as deferential as it might have been to her mistress. "I am not invited, and I have no business of importance with the First Consul; but I am from America, and it would please me greatly to see the rooms where the famous general lives. Cannot Mademoi-

selle think of a way?'' and I slipped into her hand a
louis d'or.

She curtsied again and smiled again, and then she
answered:

''It is difficult, Monsieur, but I have a friend on
guard in the upper corridor. If I can arrange with
him to let us pass, I can show Monsieur the grand
salon, the little salon, and the state dining-room.
Would that please Monsieur?''

''Vastly,'' I answered, for though it might not
be seeing all I would like to see, it would be doing
something to while away the tedium of waiting, and
there seemed a little of the spice of adventure about
it that pleased my restless spirit.

''I will go and consult Gaston,'' said Mademoiselle
Félice (for that, she told me, was her pretty name, and
I took it as a felicitous omen), ''and I will return in
five minutes. If Monsieur will await me by the pines,
he will not have to wait long.''

Yet it seemed long. I am sure many five minutes
had passed, and I had begun to think I would never
see again either my gold piece or my pretty Félice,
when she came tripping up in an entirely different
direction from the one in which she had left me.

She had had trouble. Gaston had scruples. Suppose harm were intended his general? Women were
easily deceived. Her ''American'' might be a British
assassin in disguise. She had had to make herself responsible—she, Félice!—for my innocence and honor.
She had also been obliged to show Gaston the piece
of gold I had given her and to assure him there would

19

be another for him if he were complaisant. I judged, also, that she had found it necessary to offer him a bribe quite as tangible as the gold piece but less mercenary, for her face was rosier and her eyes brighter and her hair a little more disheveled than when I had first seen her.

And now began a real adventure, for Félice assured me much caution would be necessary. How we both slipped out of the pine thicket, she some distance ahead, I strolling carelessly behind, how by almost insensible little signs she indicated to me when to advance and when to stay my steps; how she finally guided me through a narrow rear entrance and by dark corridors and winding staircases to the very corridor Gaston was guarding; and how I slipped another gold piece into Gaston's hand as we passed him, would be too long in the telling.

Gaston was doing sentry duty before two doors some twenty paces apart. One of them opened into a dark side corridor (where we had passed him and I had slipped the gold into his hand), and the other into the head of the main corridor. We had just entered the main corridor, and Félice was leading the way into the grand salon, when she turned quickly:

"Go back, Monsieur," she said in an excited whisper, "here comes an officer!"

I had caught sight of him, too, and I was the more ready to turn back quickly, because in my hasty glimpse the officer had looked to me very much like the Chevalier Le Moyne. I thought it was more than likely I was mistaken, but I did not wish to run any possible risk of being seen by him, and I hoped that in the semi-obscurity of that part of the corridor he had either not seen us at all or at least not recognized us.

We fled precipitately back through the dark side corridor, I with a keen feeling of elation (for a sense of risk or peril of any kind always sends my spirits to the highest point), but Félice, I believe, beginning to repent of her bargain.

"Monsieur," she whispered, "we will go back the way we came—" but what further she was about to say I know not, for at that moment a door opened at the farther end of the side corridor. It was a door we must pass in finding our way out, and through it now we heard much loud laughing and loud talking of men. Evidently a party at cards was breaking up, and through that open door some of the players were about to pass. Our retreat was cut off.

Félice clutched her hair in desperation.

"Ah, mon Dieu!" she moaned, "I will lose my place! I will lose my life!"

I had hardly time to think of my own plight, I was so sorry for her distress, and so remorseful to think I had brought her into such straits for the sake of a silly adventure.

But an idea struck Félice. We had come to a stand beside Gaston and the one of the two doors he was guarding which opened into the side corridor. He had himself stopped a moment in his pacing to and fro, perplexed by our dilemma.

"Quick, Gaston," Félice whispered eagerly, "let

Monsieur into the dressing-room closet; it is the only place!''

Gaston seemed to demur, but Félice overruled him imperiously.

"You must, Gaston! And be quick! Would you have Monsieur Fouché throw us both into prison? I will be back for him in a few minutes, as soon as all is quiet.''

Gaston hesitated no longer. He threw open the door before which we were standing, and together they hurried me into a room which I saw at once was a dressing-room belonging to a gentleman.

"You must be very still, Monsieur,'' whispered Félice; then she opened a door and thrust me into a dark closet, closing the door noiselessly behind me as she whispered, "I will return in a few minutes.''

I was but as wax in her hands, for having led her into such distress and peril, I felt that I must submit to any means that would save her from disastrous results. Yet I liked not being shut up in a dark closet in a gentleman's dressing-room. I began, too, to think of my own peril, and for a full minute after finding myself in my hiding-place my knees did so shake beneath me, and my heart did so pound within me, I was as one deaf and unconscious to all surroundings.

But as my excitement began to calm itself I became aware that I had for some time been hearing several voices: one, which did most of the talking, high, rasping, vehement, passionate; the other two, making brief or monosyllabic replies, low-toned and restrained. I began to perceive, too, that I was not entirely in the dark. A faint light was coming through between slightly parted curtains which seemed to separate my closet from some other apartment than the dressing-room. I looked through this aperture, barely wide enough for the line of vision, not wide enough to betray me to any one in the room beyond, especially since I was in the dark and the Easter sun was flooding the richly furnished apartment.

Standing in an attitude of respect on either side of a low marble mantel bearing a wonderful golden clock stood two gentlemen. One of them was my uncle, Monsieur Marbois, and the other, whom I did not know, I learned later was Minister Decrés. Gesticulating vehemently and speaking with great excitement, through the center of the room back and forth strode rapidly the First Consul!

I was overwhelmed at the sight. By what trick of fate had I been thrust into the very midst of this conference at which I had so longed to be present? My blood rushed through my veins at such tumultuous pace as carried my reason with it. No thought of listening to what was not intended for me to hear entered my mind, only a great joy that I was in the midst of some strange adventure such as I had read of in books, where wonderful things happen to the hero who hides behind an arras. And no more wonderful thing could happen to me than to be seeing and hearing the great Bonaparte!

And this is what he was saying:

"I know the full value of Louisiana, and I have been desirous of repairing the fault of the French negotiator who abandoned it in 1763. A few lines of a treaty have restored it to me, and I have scarcely recovered it when I must expect to lose it. But if it escapes from me," he stopped and turned suddenly to the two ministers, lifting a threatening hand, "it shall one day cost dearer to those who oblige me to strip myself of it than to those to whom I wish to deliver it."

I thought at first this threat was uttered against the United States, and so terrible did he look, so like an avenging fury, that I shuddered as I thought of my country the object of his vindictive wrath. But his next words enlightened me. He resumed his rapid stride and went on speaking with the same excitement:

"The English have successively taken from France Canada, Cape Breton, Newfoundland, Nova Scotia, and India. They are engaged in exciting troubles in San Domingo. *They shall not have the Mississippi, which they covet.*

"Louisiana is nothing in comparison with their conquests in all parts of the globe, and yet the jealousy they feel at the restoration of this colony to the sovereignty of France acquaints me with their wish to take possession of it, and it is thus they will begin the war.

"They have twenty ships of war in the Gulf of Mexico; they sail over those seas as sovereigns! The conquest of Louisiana would be easy, if they only took the trouble to make a descent there. I have not a moment to lose in putting it out of their reach! I know not whether they are not already there. It is their usual

"He stopped and turned suddenly to the two ministers"

course, and if I had been in their place, I would not have waited. I wish, if there is still time, to take away from them any idea that they may have of ever possessing that colony.''

Once more he stopped and faced the two ministers, and gazed at them steadily for a moment, first one, then the other, before he uttered his next words. I know not whether he paused because he hesitated to utter them, or because he wished to make them more forcible. Then he said slowly and impressively, with no trace of the excitement that had characterized his former words:

''I think of ceding it to the United States.''

If he had expected to create a sensation he was not disappointed; the irrepressible start of each, the glowing eyes, the eager desire to speak expressed in both countenances were abundant evidences of it, and I in my dark closet was far more excited than either: for here was more than my wildest dreams to be realized. But Bonaparte had not finished his speech; with a gesture restraining them from giving utterance to the words that were hurrying to their lips, he went on:

''You will say that I can scarcely cede it to them, for it is not yet in our possession. If, however, I leave the least time to our enemies, I shall transmit only an empty title to those republicans whose friendship I seek. They ask of me only one town in Louisiana; but I already consider the colony as entirely lost, and it appears to me that in the hands of this growing power it will be more useful to the policy of France, and even to its commerce, than if I should attempt to keep it. Citizen Minister,'' looking at my uncle, '' what is your opinion?''

My uncle, who had been all eagerness to speak at first, seemed to hesitate now that the opportunity was given him.

''I believe, Citizen First Consul,'' he said slowly, ''that we should not hesitate to make a sacrifice of that which is about slipping away from us. War with England is inevitable. Shall we be able with inferior naval forces to defend Louisiana against that power? At the time of the discovery of Louisiana the neighboring provinces were as feeble as herself. They are now powerful and Louisiana is still in her infancy. The country is scarcely at all inhabited; you have not fifty soldiers there. Where are your means of sending garrisons thither? Can we restore fortifications that are in ruins, and construct a long chain of forts upon a frontier of four hundred leagues? If England lets you undertake these things, it is because they will drain your resources, and she will feel a secret joy in seeing you exhaust yourself in efforts of which she alone will derive the profit. You will send out a squadron; but while it is crossing the oceans, the colony will fall, and the squadron will in its turn be in great danger. Louisiana is open to the English from the north by the Great Lakes, and if, to the south, they show themselves at the mouth of the Mississippi, New Orleans will immediately fall into their hands. This conquest would be still easier to the Americans: they can reach the Mississippi by several navigable rivers, and to be masters of the country it will be sufficient for them to enter it. The colony has existed for a century, and, in spite of efforts and sacrifices of every kind, the last account of its population and resources attests its weakness. If it becomes a French colony and acquires increased importance, there will be in its very prosperity a germ of independence which will not be long in developing itself. The more it flourishes the less chance shall we have of preserving it.

"The French have attempted to form colonies in several parts of the continent of North America. Their efforts have everywhere proved abortive. The English are patient and laborious; they do not fear the solitude and silence of newly settled countries. The Frenchman, lively and active, requires society; he is fond of conversing with neighbors. He willingly enters on the experiment of cultivating the soil, but at the first disappointment quits the spade and ax for the chase."

Bonaparte, as my uncle ceased talking, had thrown himself into a fauteuil and signed to the others to sit down. He had listened with keen attention to my uncle's long speech, but now he interrupted him abruptly and harshly.

"How does it happen that the French, who are incapable of succeeding in a continental colony, have always made great progress in the West Indies?"

"Because," replied Monsieur Marbois, "the slaves perform all the labors. The whites, who would soon be exhausted by the heat of the climate, have, however, the vigor of mind necessary to direct their operations.''

''By whom is the land cultivated in Louisiana?'' asked the First Consul.

''Slavery,'' answered my uncle, ''has given Louisiana half her population. An inexcusable imprudence was committed in suddenly granting to the slaves of San Domingo a liberty for which they had not been prepared. The blacks and whites both have been victims of this great fault.''

''I am undecided,'' said Bonaparte, ''whether it would be better to maintain or abolish slavery in Louisiana.''

''Of all the scourges that have afflicted the human race,'' responded my uncle, ''slavery is the most detestable! But even humanity requires great precautions in the application of the remedy, and you cannot apply it if Louisiana should again become French. Governments still half resist emancipation: they tolerate in secret what they ostensibly condemn, and they themselves are embarrassed by their false position. The general sentiment of the world is in favor of emancipation; it is in vain that the colonists and planters wish to arrest a movement which public opinion approves. The occupation of Louisiana—a colony with slaves—will occasion us more expense than it will afford us profit.''

As my uncle ceased speaking, Bonaparte turned to Minister Decrés and with a motion of his hand indicated that he was ready to hear his opinion. The minister began eagerly:

"We are still at peace with England," said he; "the colony has just been ceded to us; it depends on the First Consul to preserve it. It would not be wise in him to abandon, for fear of a doubtful danger, the most important establishment that we can form out of France, and despoil ourselves of it for no other reason than the possibility of a war; it would be as well, if not better, that it should be taken from us by force of arms.

"You will not acknowledge, by a resignation of Louisiana, that England is sovereign mistress of the seas, that she is there invulnerable, and that no one can possess colonies except at her good pleasure! It does not become you to fear the kings of England! If they should seize Louisiana, as some would have you fear, Hanover would be immediately in your hands, as a certain pledge of its restoration. France, deprived of her navy and her colonies, is stripped of half her splendor and of a great part of her strength. Louisiana can indemnify us for all our losses. There does not exist on the globe a single port, a single city, susceptible of becoming as important as New Orleans, and the neighborhood of the American States already makes it one of the most commercial in the world. The Mississippi does not reach there until it has received twenty other rivers, most of which surpass in size the finest rivers of Europe.

"The navigation to the Indies, by doubling the Cape of Good Hope, has changed the course of European trade and ruined Venice and Genoa. What will be its direction if, at the Isthmus of Panama, a simple canal should be opened to connect the one ocean with the other? The revolution which navigation will then experience will be still more considerable, and the circumnavigation of the globe will become easier than the long voyages that are now made in going to and returning from India. Louisiana will be on this new route, and it will then be acknowledged that this possession is of inestimable value.

"Finally, France, after her long troubles, requires such a colony for her internal pacification; it will be for our country what a century ago were for England the settlements which the emigrants from the three kingdoms have raised to so high a degree of prosperity. It will be the asylum of our religious and political dissenters; it will cure a part of the maladies which the Revolution has caused, and be the supreme conciliator of all the parties into which we are divided. You will there find the remedies for which you search with so much solicitude!"

I thought this a very bold speech, and it was uttered with much fire and enthusiasm. I could not be sure how the Consul took it, for he said not a word through it all. When the minister had finished speaking he dismissed them both with a few words, but telling them he should expect them to remain all night.

As the door closed behind the two ministers, Bonaparte threw himself back in his chair, his arms folded across his breast, his head drooping forward, in an attitude of deep thought. It seemed to me more than likely that Minister Decrés's words had touched his pride and his patriotism, and he was hesitating now at the thought of getting rid of France's last important colony.

He was interrupted in his reverie by an officer bringing in the despatches from London which had just arrived, and he sent word by the officer to have Minister Marbois sent to him immediately.

It was only a few moments until the return of my uncle, but in the interval I could see that Bonaparte was glancing through the despatches with such lightning rapidity that to me, for whom all reading is slow work, it seemed impossible he should have grasped their meaning. As Monsieur Marbois entered the apartment Bonaparte greeted him.

"Citizen Minister," he said, "the despatches from London have arrived. Have you seen them?"

"I was just reading them," replied my uncle, "when you sent for me."

"Did you see that England is preparing for war? That both naval and military preparations are going forward with extraordinary rapidity?"

"Yes," said the minister, "so I understand."

"Perhaps you saw, too, that in the American Congress Mr. Ross proposed that the President should raise fifty thousand troops and capture New Orleans?"

"Yes," repeated my uncle, "I saw it, and I regret greatly that any cause of difference should arise between our countries."

The Consul sprang to his feet and resumed his rapid striding up and down the room without uttering a word for full two minutes, but with a deep frown

between his eyes, as I could see whenever he faced
me in his hurried pacing to and fro.

Suddenly he stopped and turned to my uncle.

"Irresolution and deliberation are no longer in season," he said slowly, and then added with sudden fire:

"I renounce Louisiana! It is not only New Orleans I will cede, it is the whole colony without reserva-
tion. I renounce it with the greatest regret! To attempt obstinately to retain it would be the greatest
folly. I direct you to negotiate this affair with the
envoys of the United States. Do not even await the
arrival of Mr. Monroe; have an interview to-morrow
with Mr. Livingston. But I require a great deal of
money for this war with England, and I would not
like to commence it with new contributions. I will
be moderate, in consideration of the necessity in which
I am of making a sale; but keep this to yourself. I
want fifty millions, and for less than that sum I will
not treat; I would rather make a desperate attempt
to keep these fine countries. To-morrow you shall have
full power."

I think my uncle was somewhat aghast at the sud-
denness of the decision to sell the whole country,
though he had himself advised it, and still more at
the great responsibility thrust upon him of conducting the negotiations in place of the Minister of Foreign Relations. Perhaps, too, now that the sale was
fully determined upon, he was touched with regrets
and misgivings. At any rate, he said, somewhat hesitatingly:

"You feel sure, Citizen Consul, that we have a right

to cede the sovereignty of a people without consulting the people themselves? Have we a right to abandon what the Germans call the *souls?* Can they be the subject of a contract of sale or exchange?"

Now I really think from what I had seen of Bonaparte's reverie while the minister was out of the room, of his frowning cogitations in that rapid walk to and fro, and of the solemnity of his manner when he finally announced his determination to sell, that he had been troubled by the same misgivings. But none the less did his lip curl satirically as he listened to my uncle, and his eyes narrow and glow with a malevolent fire. He hardly waited for him to finish till he burst forth bitterly:

"You are giving me, in all its perfection, the ideology of the law of nature and nations! But I require money to make war on the richest nation of the world. Send your maxims to the London market! I am sure they will be greatly admired there; and yet no great attention is paid to them when the question is the occupation of the finest regions of Asia!"

I thought my uncle would have wilted under such bitter sarcasm, for never have I seen anything more malevolent than Bonaparte's whole aspect, and I trembled for him. But he seemed not greatly afraid of the great man's bluster, and persisted in his argument when it seemed to me the part of wisdom would have been to keep silence.

"But, Citizen Consul," he urged, "are you not afraid by ceding such great possessions to America you may make her in the course of two or three centuries too powerful for Europe—the mistress of the world?''

The Consul's lip curled again. He answered in a harsh voice:

"My foresight does not embrace such remote fears. I have no children; after me the deluge! Besides, we may hereafter expect rivalries among the members of the Union. The confederations that are called perpetual only last till one of the contracting parties finds it to his interest to break them."

The minister made no reply, though Bonaparte waited a moment as if expecting one. Then he went on:

"Mr. Monroe is on the point of arriving. To this minister, going a thousand leagues from his constituents, the President must have given secret instructions for the stipulation of the payments to be made, more extensive than the ostensible authorization of Congress. Neither this minister nor his colleague is prepared for a decision which goes infinitely beyond anything they are about to ask us. Begin by making the overture without any subterfuge. You will acquaint me, day by day, hour by hour, of your progress. The cabinet of London is informed of the measures adopted at Washington, but it can have no suspicion of those I am now taking. Observe the greatest secrecy, and recommend it to the American ministers: they have not a less interest than yourself in conforming to this counsel. You will correspond with Monsieur de Talleyrand, who alone knows my intentions. Keep him informed of the progress of this affair."

All this was uttered in a sharp clipping tone of voice, at times harsh and rasping, that carried with it an inconceivable effect of autocratic power. As he finished he made a gesture of dismissal, but as the minister was about to withdraw he called him back again.

"Monsieur Marbois," he said in a far gentler tone than he had used at all heretofore, "there will be a treaty drawn up between you and the American ministers, of course, and I would like to write one article of that treaty. If you will sit down a few moments I will not detain you long."

My uncle bowed and seated himself, and with marvelous rapidity Bonaparte's pen flew over the sheet before him. In scarcely more than a minute's time he looked up from his paper.

"This is the article, Monsieur Marbois, that I wish you to make it your business to see embodied somewhere in the treaty." And then he read slowly, in a firm, clear voice, with no longer any rasping tones:

"The inhabitants of the ceded territory shall be incorporated in the Union of the United States, and admitted as soon as possible, according to the principles of the Federal Constitution, to the enjoyment of all the rights, advantages, and immunities of citizens of the United States. And in the meantime they shall be maintained and protected in the free enjoyment of their liberty, property, and the religion which they profess."

The Consul rose to his feet as he finished reading and extended the paper toward my uncle.

"Citizen Minister," he said (and I almost thought

20

there was a ring of sadness in his tone, but that I could not believe such an emotion possible to the imperious conqueror), ''let the Louisianians know that we separate ourselves from them with regret; that we stipulate in their favor everything that they can desire; and let them hereafter, happy in their independence, recollect that they have been Frenchmen, and that France, in ceding them, has secured for them advantages which they could not have obtained from a European power, however paternal it might have been. Let them retain for us sentiments of affection; and may their common origin, descent, language, and customs perpetuate the friendship.''

He finished speaking, and turned his back abruptly upon my uncle, who bowed silently and withdrew. I could not see the face of either, but I believe both were too deeply moved to utter another word. As my uncle left the room, Bonaparte threw himself once more into his deep-armed chair in the same attitude of reverie he had before maintained in the interval of the minister's absence—arms folded, chin sunk deep on his breast.

It seemed to me a long time that he sat thus, for I was growing every moment more anxious for my own safe escape from my hiding-place. Félice had promised to return for me in a few moments if the way was open, and I was sure it must have been more nearly hours than moments that I had been watching the foremost man of all the world decide the fate of a people and the future of my own proud nation. I had been so intensely interested that I had not noted the flight of time, but now that the First Consul sat wrapped in thought, I, too, began to think, to wonder, and to grow every moment more anxious. What had become of my little guide? Had she forsaken me and left me to my fate? And should she come for me now, would I be able, with my clumsy movements, to escape unheard, when the room was no longer ringing with the rasping tones of Bonaparte?

There was a deep-drawn sigh from the chair of the First Consul. He unfolded his arms, flung back his head, and sprang to his feet, once more pacing rapidly back and forth. Suddenly he stopped, lifted one hand as if calling on Heaven to witness, and exclaimed aloud:

"This accession of territory strengthens forever the power of the United States! I have just given to England a maritime rival that will sooner or later humble her pride!"

His hand dropped upon a bell which he rang violently. Instantly there was a little sound of scratching on the panel of a door leading into an apartment beyond.

"Enter!" said Bonaparte, and there glided silently into the room Rustan, the famous Mameluke attendant of whom I had heard much.

"I will dress for dinner, Rustan," said the First Consul; "call my valet and tell him to prepare my bath."

CHAPTER XXI

A TEMPEST IN A BATH-TUB

"The mouse that always trusts to one poor hole
Can never be a mouse of any soul."

"PREPARE my bath!" Did ever such simple words have so dire a sound? Now was all hope of escape cut off; for was not the Consul's bath in the very room into which the closet where I was hiding opened, and through which I had expected to make my exit as I had made my entrance? Now did I curse the folly that had led me into such a trap for the sake of a mere adventure.

Whereas a moment ago I had been congratulating myself on the spirit of enterprise and daring that had led me to be the witness of such great and stirring events, I now despised it all as a silly boyishness which had brought me into what seemed like to prove something more than a foolish scrape. Nor could I help reflecting that whether death or disgrace (which seemed to me far worse than death) awaited me, it would not affect me alone. My uncle's reputation, and honor also, might easily be involved in his nephew's downfall. And, most intolerable of all, what would the Comtesse de Baloit think when she should come to hear (as it was inevitable that she would) that I had been caught spying like any common eaves-dropper?—found hid in the Consul's private closet, taken and done to death, as I had not the least doubt in the world I should be!

Yet it was not in me to wait idly for the worst to happen; I began at once to plan other means of escape than those I had been relying upon. If I could not make my exit through the dressing-room, why not through the other apartment, from which my closet was separated only by a curtain?

As far as I could judge, the apartment had three entrance-doors. One which was not within my range of vision was the one by which the ministers had with-drawn and through which my uncle had returned. This, no doubt, was the main entrance, and led into some public corridor, where detection by passers-by would be certain, to say nothing of the fact that the door was no doubt strongly guarded, and by a soldier who would not be so complacent as Gaston had been (having neither handled my gold nor tasted a maid-en's kisses as reward for his complacency).

The second door led into the dressing-room, where even now I could hear the splashing of water and the vigorous preparations of the valet for the Consul's bath. That, of course, was not to be considered. The third one was the one through which I had seen Rus-tan glide; and at the thought of entering that room, and falling into the tender mercies of the mysterious Mameluke, I shuddered. A stealthy stiletto with poi-soned point I had no doubt would make short work

with me. And even could it be possible to seize a moment when Rustan was out of the room in attendance
on his master, it was more than likely the room would
prove a *cul-de-sac* and I would be more securely
trapped than ever.

In the midst of these perplexing meditations I
heard a heavy splash, followed by a vigorous sputtering, that assured me the First Consul was already in
his bath. A moment later I heard a scratching at the
door through which my uncle had departed. ('T is the
fashion, I have heard, at the Tuileries and St. Cloud,
to scratch instead of knock.) Rustan answered it immediately, and led the gentleman who entered directly through the outer apartment to the dressing-
room. This seemed a novel procedure to me, but I remembered that the French often received callers at the
toilet, and perhaps it was nothing unusual for the
First Consul to receive his friends in the bath.

I could hear all that went on in the dressing-room;
even the slightest sound was as audible in my closet as
if no door intervened. I was surprised at this until I
discovered that just higher than my head a small
panel, not more than three inches square, had been removed from the door of the closet, admitting a little
light and a little air. It was through this opening that
sounds were conveyed, and it was through it that I
heard the Consul's voice a moment after the visitor
was conducted through the outer apartment.

"Ah, my dear Lucien! Where were you last night,
and where was my brother Joseph? Did you not intend to join me at the Théâtre Français? I expected

you, and Talma showed great power in 'Hamlet.' I
was surprised and disappointed not to see you both
there.''

I do not remember what answer his brother made,
but Bonaparte replied with the greatest good humor:

''You might have seen, too, that the Parisians always like to see me. In fact, I scarcely flattered myself they would ever become so sympathetic when I
had to shoot them down that October day in 1795.''

I could scarcely believe it was the First Consul
speaking, so unlike were his tones to any I had heard
from him before,—playful, affectionate, almost tender,—and I said to myself, ''Ah, this despot has a
heart! He loves his brother.''

I did not hear anything more that was said for a
while, for I was revolving in my mind all possible
modes of escape. I had just come to the conclusion
that the only safe way was to remain quietly where
I was until Bonaparte should have finished his bath
and left his dressing-room (which I felt sure could
not be long, since he had already been in the water
for more than a quarter of an hour), when I heard
again that peculiar little scratching sound on the
dressing-room door, and Rustan entered, announcing
to the Consul his brother Joseph.

''Let him come in,'' said the Consul; ''I shall stay
in the bath a quarter of an hour longer.''

Black despair seized me. A quarter of an hour
seemed to me interminable when I knew not at what
moment the valet would fling open the closet door in
his search for some article of dress, and discover me.

There was nothing to do, however, but to make the best of it, hoping against hope that the great Bonaparte, who seemed inordinately fond of his bath, would some time be through with it and leave his dressing-room free for me to traverse it in safety. For I had made up my mind that I would wait no longer for Félice; the first minute that I could be quite sure that the dressing-room was vacant, I would open my closet door and escape, trusting to find Gaston still on guard at the outer dressing-room door.

It occurred to me that if I were only a little taller, and could look through that open panel just above my head, it would be well, for then I could assure myself that the room was empty before attempting my escape, and not stumble upon some lurking valet or Mameluke. Then I remembered what I had noticed on entering the closet, but had not thought of since, a low three-legged taboret, not more than five inches high, but quite high enough, were I once upon it, to enable me to look through the open panel. I stooped carefully down and felt around the floor of the closet in the dark. My hand struck against it. I picked it up and set it noiselessly directly under the small opening, and slowly and carefully, and absolutely without making a sound, I mounted upon it.

Just below me was the most remarkable group I had ever looked upon, or, I have no doubt, ever shall look upon. Respectfully standing near the bath were the two brothers Lucien and Joseph, and it was easy for me to decide at a glance which was Joseph and which Lucien, for I had heard much of both and knew their characteristics, though I knew not their faces. Joseph was the handsomer of the two, and looked more like his august brother, with the same fiery eye and mobile mouth, showing the same excitable temperament. Lucien had the calmer face that belongs to a scholar, though in some respects I thought it a stronger one than his brother Joseph's. In the marble bath lay Bonaparte, only his head and a little of his shoulders visible, for the water was frothy and opaque from quantities of cologne, whose sweet, pungent odor rose to my nostrils refreshingly. Bonaparte was in the act of speaking to Joseph:

"Well, brother, have you spoken to Lucien?"

"What about?" said Joseph.

"Of our plan as to Louisiana—don't you know?"

"Of *your* plan, you mean, my dear brother; you cannot have forgotten that—far from being mine—"

Bonaparte interrupted him with good-natured scorn.

"Well, well, preacher, I don't need to discuss that with you; you are so obstinate. I like better to talk about serious things with Lucien; for, although he sometimes takes it into his head to go against me, he knows how to give up to my idea when I think fit to change his."

Joseph's color rose quickly, and he spoke with some spirit:

"You are unjust enough to attribute to obstinacy what is the effect of wise reflection."

Lucien was evidently afraid of an outbreak, and he interposed quickly and laughingly:

"Then that means, brother Joseph, that I hold my ideas so lightly I can easily be reasoned out of them."

"Ah, my dear boy," said Bonaparte, with affectionate raillery, "fear not that any one will accuse thee of lightness. Thou art more likely to be named 'Iron-head.' "

For a few minutes the two brothers playfully called each other nicknames, going back to the days of their boyhood in Corsica, while Joseph stood by, looking bored and every moment growing more impatient. Finally he broke in quite brusquely:

"Well, you say nothing more about your famous plan!"

Bonaparte turned at once to Lucien.

"Well, Lucien, I have made up my mind to sell Louisiana to the Americans."

"Indeed!" said Lucien, in a tone of curiosity, but with so much coolness I suspected he was not hearing the announcement for the first time.

Bonaparte turned to Joseph with an air of triumph.

"Well, Joseph, you see Lucien does not utter loud cries about this thing. Yet he almost has a right to, seeing that Louisiana is, so to speak, his own conquest."

I knew what the Consul meant by that, for it was Lucien who had negotiated the San Ildefonso treaty which gave Louisiana to France. This speech of his brother's seemed to irritate Joseph still more, and he replied quite sharply:

"I assure you, if Lucien says nothing, he thinks none the less."

"Indeed!" said Bonaparte, his eyes beginning to

flash and his lip to curl. "And why should he be diplomatic with me?"

It was evident that Lucien thought it time to come forward to support Joseph, but that he also wished to placate the rising wrath of the Consul. So he spoke very gently:

"I really think as my brother Joseph does on this matter, and I undertake to say that the Chambers will never assent."

Bonaparte's head shot up above the rim of the bath-tub, and he leveled a fiery glance at Lucien.

"*You* undertake to say! A pretty piece of business!" with an air and tone of withering contempt.

"Yes; and *I* undertake to say," cried Joseph, in a tone of triumph, "that it will be so. And that is what I told the First Consul before."

"And what did I say?" said the Consul, his tone rising with his wrath, and with his head still above the rim of the bath-tub, looking by turns quickly from one brother to the other, as if not to lose any change in the countenance of either.

"You declared," said Joseph, his voice also rising, "you would get along without the assent of the Chambers; did you not?"

"Exactly," said Bonaparte, concentrated irony in his tone. "That is what I took the liberty to say to Monsieur Joseph, and what I repeat here to Citizen Lucien, begging him to give me his opinion about it, derived from his paternal tenderness for that mighty diplomatic conquest of his, the treaty of San Ildefonso."

Now I thought this a very unkind thrust at Lucien,

for I had heard his part in the treaty had been most creditable and that the First Consul had been much pleased with it. I could see that Lucien found it hard to brook, but he struggled for mastery with himself, and spoke still gently:

"My brother, my devotion is deep enough to sacrifice everything for you, except my duty. If I believed, for example, this sale of Louisiana would be fatal to me alone, I would consent to it to prove to you my devotion. But it is too unconstitutional."

Bonaparte broke into his sentence with a fit of rasping, sarcastic laughter, sinking back into the bath-tub almost in a convulsion of demoniacal mirth.

"Ha, ha, ha! You are drawing it fine. 'For example'!" His words struggled out in the intervals of his spasms of laughter. "Ha, ha, ha! 'For example'!"—catching his breath. "'Unconstitutional'! That's droll from you; a good joke—ha, ha!" As his laughter ceased an expression of ironical and contemptuous rage passed over his face.

"How have I touched your constitution?" he cried. "Answer!"

"I know well," said Lucien, still trying to control himself, "you have not done so; but you know well that to alienate any possession of the republic without the consent of the Chambers is unconstitutional."

That last word seemed to drive the Consul beside himself. Once more his head shot above the top of the bath-tub, and with blazing eyes he shook his fist at Lucien.

"Clear out!" he shouted. "'Constitution'! 'Unconstitutional'! 'Republic'! Great words—fine phrases! Do you think you are still at the Club of St. Maximin? We are past that, you had better believe! Parbleu! You phrase it nobly. 'Unconstitutional'! It becomes you well, Sir Knight of the Constitution, to talk that way to me. You had n't the same respect for the Chambers on the eighteenth Brumaire.''

Lucien, roused at last, broke in, in a tone as high as Bonaparte's:

''You well know, my dear brother, that your entry into the Five Hundred had no warmer opponent than I. No! I was not your accomplice, but the repairer of the evil which you had done to yourself!—and that at my own peril, and with some generosity on my part, because we did not then agree. Not to boast, I may add that no one in Europe, more than I, has disapproved the sacrilege against the national representation.''

Bonaparte's eyes blazed like diamonds.

''Go on—go on!'' he thundered. ''That 's quite too fine a thing to cut short, Sir Orator of the Clubs! But at the same time take note of this: that I shall do just as I please; that I detest, without fearing, your friends the Jacobins!—not one of whom shall remain in France if, as I hope, things continue to remain in my hands; and that, in fine, I snap my fingers at you and your 'national representation.' ''

''On my side,'' shouted Lucien, ''I do not snap my fingers at you, Citizen Consul, but I well know what I think about you.''

"What do you think about me, Citizen Lucien?
Parbleu! I am curious to know. Out with it!"

"I think, Citizen Consul, that, having sworn to the
constitution of the eighteenth Brumaire, as President
of the Council of the Five Hundred, and seeing you
despise it thus, if I were not your brother I would be
your enemy!"

"My enemy!" screamed Bonaparte. "Try it once!
That's rather strong!" And, shaking his fist at Lucien, as he had done once before, "Thou my enemy!"
he screamed again, and then sank back in the water
up to his neck, as if exhausted. In a moment he spoke
again in a somewhat quieter tone:

"Cease this miserable caviling which you and
Joseph are at work on night and day—ridiculous for
him, and still less appropriate for you. It is not from
you that I expect lessons in government. Enough!
Forget all you have said about it! I shall contrive to
dispense with you. A precious, well-disposed pair of
brothers you are! Please call back the valet; I must
get out of the bath-tub at once."

The valet had come in; Joseph and Lucien, thinking
the matter was dropped, were turning toward the
door; the valet was spreading open the sheet to wrap
up his master, when the Consul suddenly returned to
the charge, and thundered in a tone that made Lucien
and Joseph start and turn back quickly, and the valet
drop the sheet from his trembling hands:

"Well, sirs, think what you please about the sale
of Louisiana! but you may both of you put on mourning over this thing—you, Lucien, over the sale of your

province; you, Joseph, because I propose to dispense with the consent of all persons whatsoever. Do you hear?"

I fairly shivered in my hiding-place at such an outbreak on such a topic in the presence of a servant. Lucien shrank farther toward the door, but Joseph, who had held his peace through the quarrel of the two brothers, stung by the scornful words and manner, and especially by the contemptuous "Do you hear?" which was like a cutting snapper to the Consul's lashing wrath, rushed back, exclaiming:

"You will do well, my dear brother, not to lay your plan before the Chambers, for I swear to you I will put myself, if necessary, at the head of the opposition which will certainly be made."

There was no reply from Bonaparte but an outburst of loud and sardonic laughter.

Joseph flushed dark red, and, almost beside himself with rage, stooping over the figure that lay immersed in the bath, screamed out:

"Laugh! laugh! laugh, then! All the same, I shall do what I say, and, though I do not like to mount the tribune, this time you'll see me there!"

At these words, Bonaparte rose in the bath-tub so as to show half his body out of the water, opaque and frothy with cologne, and pale as his brother was red, he cried sternly:

"You will not need to play the orator, for I repeat to you that this debate will not take place, because the plan so unlucky as to be disapproved by you, conceived by me, negotiated by me, will be ratified and

executed by me—by me alone; do you understand?
—by me!'' Then he sank back once more to his neck
in the water. Joseph, whose self-control was all gone,
his face aflame, roared:

"Well, general, on my side, I tell you that you and
I and all the family, if you do what you say you
will, may get ready to join shortly those poor innocent
devils whom you so legally, so humanely,—above all,
with so much justice,—have had transported to Cay-
enne!''

This was a terrible home thrust, and I could see
Lucien draw hastily still farther back toward the door,
and the valet literally cowered.

"You insolent fellow!'' thundered Bonaparte. "I
ought—'' But I did not hear the rest of the sentence, for as he spoke he rose quickly from the water
and plunged heavily back, so that the water dashed out
in a flood on the floor. Lucien, who was back by the
door, escaped a wetting; but Joseph received the
splash full in his face, and his clothes were drenched.
The valet ran to Joseph's assistance, but had no more
than begun to sponge him off than he fell to the floor
in a fainting fit. The quarrel was calmed at once,
and the Bonapartes good-heartedly ran to the rescue. Joseph hurried to pick him up from the wet
floor; Lucien rang the bell so hard that Rustan and
another servant came running in, frightened; and
the First Consul, his eyes and lips just visible above
the rim of the bath-tub, called out sympathetically:

"Carry off the poor fellow, and take good care of
him.''

As for me, the excitement was too much for me also. I did not faint, but my stool, which was none of the steadiest on its three legs, suddenly tipped from the excess of my emotion, and, though I caught myself from falling entirely, I yet made what sounded to my horrified ears a deafening racket. In reality I suppose it was only a slight scuffling noise, but it was enough to catch the quick ears of the First Consul and Rustan.

"What was that?" I heard the First Consul say in a startled tone.

"I think, sir, it was some noise in the closet," I heard Rustan reply. "If Monsieur Joseph will assist in supporting your valet, I will investigate."

Now was my last hour come. But I was not going to die like a rat in a trap. I would rush out the door into the public corridor, and, if necessary, slay the guard and make one bold dash for safety. I drew my sword from its scabbard to have it in readiness in my hand for whatever might befall, pulled back the curtain, and came near running through the body my pretty Félice! She was coming to keep her promise to me and show me the way out. She did not seem to see my sword, but the moment she saw me she spoke in great excitement:

"Make haste, Monsieur; there is not a moment to lose. You can escape through the main corridor. But you must be quick, for the Consul may finish his bath at any minute, and his brothers retire here to await him while he dresses."

We were hurrying toward the door as she spoke,

21

but I, feeling as if the Mameluke were close behind me, seized her hand and dragged her roughly into the corridor as I whispered:

"Yes, we must be quick, for Rustan is after us!"

With a half-suppressed scream she let go my hand, turned to Gaston, who was standing at the door motionless as a statue and, to all appearance, deaf and blind as one also, uttered the one word, "Rustan!" and fled swiftly down the dark side corridor, leaving me utterly bewildered. The western sun was flooding the cabinet of the First Consul when I went into my hiding-place, but the sun had set and twilight had fallen and the candles had been long lit when I stepped out into the corridor. The wax tapers set in sconces along the corridor lighted it but poorly, and I knew not which way to go.

"Run, Monsieur!" cried Gaston, in a terrified whisper, "straight down the corridor till you come to the grand staircase. And run as if the devil was after you, for he is!"

That was all I needed,—a word of direction,—and I was off. But scarcely had I gone a few feet when I heard a great noise and shouting behind me, and Gaston crying, "Stop thief!" I thought at first he was turning traitor, now that he had my gold piece with no chance of gaining another from me. But as I ran the faster, and the noise behind me did not seem to gain on me, as I feared it might, I concluded he was making a great outcry to cover his own part in my escape, and perhaps was hindering the pursuit more than helping it.

Yet when I came to the turn of the grand staircase I thought for a moment I had also come to the end of my days; for just as I felt sure I was distancing those behind me, there came running swiftly toward me from the other end of the dim corridor an officer with sword drawn, and I saw he would meet me exactly at the head of the grand staircase. The light from a tall taper fell on his face as he neared the staircase. It was the Chevalier Le Moyne!

I had but a moment to think. Should I stop to engage with him, I had no doubt I could unsword him as easily as he had unsworded me in the dance by Chouteau's Pond; but the delay would bring a score to his help, and I would be quickly overpowered, if not done to death at once. Neither did I like to turn my back on that drawn sword as I fled down the steps, feeling sure it would spit me through the shoulders, much as Narcisse spitted the wild fowl for roasting at Émigré's Retreat. But above all I did not wish the chevalier to see my face; for, even should I make good my escape, Paris would be no safe place for me should he recognize in the flying "thief" his hated St. Louis rival.

I pulled my hat low over my eyes, lifted my left arm before my face as if to shield it from his sword, rushed straight toward him, met him, as I thought I should, at the top of the staircase, and, with a quick twist of my foot (a school-boy's trick), sent him sprawling down the stairs. In three great bounds I had cleared the staircase and his prostrate body, and like a whirlwind I threw myself upon the sentry at its foot, who—half dazed by this sudden descent of the chevalier and myself, one rolling and bumping from step to step, the other leaping through the air like some great winged creature—was nevertheless in the act of raising his gun to fire at me. As I hurled my great weight full upon him, the gun flew from his hands, and his little dancing-master figure went pirouetting across the terrace into the darkness beyond, in a vain struggle to recover his balance. I sprang down the terrace after him, and disappeared in the friendly darkness.

It was time. Starting from the gloom in every direction, armed figures seemed to spring from the ground, while down the great staircase behind me clattered, shrieking and shouting in every key, a throng of officers and soldiers, led by a dark figure gliding swiftly and silently far in advance, and holding in his upraised hand something that glittered as it caught the rays from wax tapers. In the very act of springing down the first terrace, I saw the glittering dagger leave Rustan's hand, hurled straight at my head, and heard it fall far below me on the stone parapet of the last terrace.

It was but the work of a moment to run swiftly to the pines and find Fatima, and lead her out of the thicket. I had not found my seat upon her back when she bounded away into the dark, straight down the broad green allée that led toward the Bois de Boulogne and Paris. Then was there hurrying to horse, and the pounding of many hoofs behind me on the soft turf, and the wild clamor of confused orders shouted

"Rushed straight toward him"

back and forth, and a fusillade of bullets firing into the dark, if by chance one might find its mark.

But I no longer felt any fear. Fatima was stretching away beneath me with the swift and easy motion of a bird, and I did not believe there was a horse in all France could overtake her. The night was my friend, too, and a dark night it was; for the clouds had gathered and shut out even the faint light of stars, and I could not so much as see my hand before my face. But I could trust Fatima to find her way, and I felt nothing but a wild exhilaration as we went swinging along in great strides through the cool, damp night breeze, and I could tell, from the clamor of voices and pounding of hoofs growing more distant, that we were gaining on our pursuers.

Out from the soft turf of the park we clattered on to the stony streets of the little village. Here there were lights, and people passing to and fro, who stopped and stared at the wild flight of horse and rider. But none molested until the hallooes and the clatter of hoofs of those following reached their ears. Then men rushed out from low taverns, from hut and hovel and respectable houses, brandishing arms and shouting "Stop thief!" and adding much to the noise and excitement, but availing nothing to stop the fugitive. Only one young fellow, an officer by his dress, snatched a gun from a bystander, and fired with so true an aim that had I not ducked my head I would have had no head to duck.

But in a few moments we had left the village behind us and were once more on the unlighted country roads.

Faster and faster we flew, by hedge and stone wall and orchard, whence the night breeze wafted the scent of blossoming fruit-trees, with ever the sound of hallooes and hoofs growing fainter in the distance.

Yet not until I had long ceased to catch even the slightest sound of pursuit, and we were well on our way through the gloomy depths of the Bois,—night haunt of robbers, suicides, and assassins,—did I draw rein and give Fatima a chance to breathe. As we ambled along, my pulses growing quieter as Fatima's breath no longer came in deep-drawn sobs, but regularly in warm puffs from her wide nostrils, I fell to thinking over the events of the afternoon.

Now that it was all safely over, and no ill had befallen me, and I had brought no disgrace upon my uncle, I was elated beyond measure that my adventure had exceeded my wildest hopes of its success. I had seen the great Bonaparte, and would henceforth know him as no man outside the circle of his intimate friends could possibly know him. He would no longer be, in my eyes, the impossible hero of romance, faultless and beyond criticism, but a man with more than the ordinary man's meed of shortcomings as to temper, yet with also a thousand times more than any ordinary man's power to control men and mold circumstance. Dictatorial, harsh, intolerant of all opinions that did not coincide with his own, brooking no interference with his methods or suggestions as to his duty, he could yet be playful and affectionate with the brother he loved, sympathetic with a servant whom his own harsh temper had frightened into fainting, and touched with a soft feeling of regret for the colony he ruthlessly alienated from the fatherland.

My mind pictured him vividly in every aspect in which I had seen him, but strongest and most persistent of all was the vision of the figure in the deep-armed chair, bowed in mournful thought, or with arm outstretched to my uncle, and voice trembling with suppressed emotion, saying:

"Let the Louisianians know that we separate ourselves from them with regret. Let them retain for us sentiments of affection. And may our common origin, descent, language, and customs perpetuate the friendship!"

CHAPTER XXII

MR. MONROE ARRIVES!

"No sun upon an Easter day
Is half so fine a sight."

IT was ten o'clock when I reached Monsieur Marbois's house and found my aunt anxiously awaiting me. I had to explain the lateness of my return and the bespattered condition of my garments by telling her I had lost my way in the Boulogne woods (which was true, for in those winding roads Fatima did for a time go astray), and such was her horror at the thought of the perils to which I had been exposed in that forest of evil repute that she questioned me not at all about my visit to St. Cloud, for which I was devoutly thankful. She had expected that my uncle would be detained all night, so that I had no explanations to make in his behalf.

The dinner-hour was long past, but she insisted on having a hot supper prepared for me, and though my conscience assured me I deserved to go to bed hungry, the little fillet of beef with mushrooms, flanked by an omelet *au gratin*, which Jacques, my aunt's accomplished chef, sent up to my room piping hot, with a glass of fine old Burgundy, tasted a little better to me than I ever remembered anything to have tasted before. *Le petit souper* was served in my room, because my aunt had insisted that my wet clothes should be removed (it had begun to rain long before we reached the streets of Paris) and I should get into a hot bath at once to prevent, if possible, the cold she was sure I had contracted on my wet and perilous ride.

Safe in my own comfortable room, warm and refreshed from my bath, with a delicious supper smoking before me, the memory of my exciting adventures and the discomforts of the latter part of the ride, lost in the dismal woods and chilled to the bone by the cold rain, already began to grow dim and hazy.

The April rain driving against my windows added to my sense of comfort and security. It had been a good friend to me in at least two respects: it had washed out every trace of Fatima's hoof-prints, so that not even Monsieur Fouché's lynx-eyed police could track me when the morning light should start them on the trail; and it had ruined my new pucecolored costume. Remembering how I had rejoiced in the wearing of it that very morning, its destruction might not seem to be a cause for thankfulness. But I would never dare to wear it again, lest some one who had seen me at St. Cloud (most of all, the chevalier) should recognize it; and yet I might have found it difficult to frame excuses for not wearing it that would satisfy my aunt's minute and anxious care for me, which extended to seeing that I wore the proper suit for every occasion.

But I did not feel quite so secure the next morning,

when I saw posted all over the city flaming accounts of
an attack upon the First Consul's life when he was in
his bath, frustrated by the vigilance of his faithful
Mameluke. There followed descriptions of the assassin as given by various witnesses who had had deadly
hand-to-hand encounters with him, no two descriptions
agreeing in any particulars, except that he was of
great stature and rode a mysterious steed that bore
him away on the wings of the wind.

There was great excitement throughout all Paris,
and there were not wanting those who hinted at
supernatural agencies. Some of those who had stood
gaping at our swift flight through St. Cloud village
were ready to swear that the horse the assassin rode
had wings from his shoulders and his feet, and one
poor lout added a tail and a pair of horns for the
rider!

I might have been amused at all this if it had not
been for the Chevalier Le Moyne. It was almost inevitable that I should meet him some day in the city,
and when he should come to know of my presence in
Paris he would at once connect the assassin of great
size and his wonderful horse with the horse and rider
that had snatched Mademoiselle Pelagie from his grasp
at Rock Spring. And I was quite sure, also, that no
considerations of gratitude for his life spared when
he was in my power would deter him from handing
me over to the merciless police with the greatest delight, now that I was in his power.

So it was not with a perfect sense of security that
I went about Paris for the next day or two, and I

left Fatima to pine in her stable rather than to run the risk of suggesting a resemblance to some St. Cloud villager while yet the apparition of horse and rider was fresh in his mind.

I did not see my uncle until late on Tuesday afternoon. He had gone direct to the Treasury office on Monday morning, and had been summoned to St. Cloud again Monday afternoon to spend the night. I had fully made up my mind to make a clean breast of it to him when I should see him, though I dreaded much the just reprimands I knew I should receive. It was with a very trembling heart, but striving to keep as courageous a front as possible, that I obeyed a summons to his private library late Tuesday afternoon. My uncle was sternness itself.

"Sit down, sir," he said as I entered, scarcely returning my greeting.

"If you will permit me, I would prefer to stand until I have made an explanation and my most heartfelt apologies," I replied, determined to speak quickly and have it over before my courage should desert me.

"I desire no apologies," returned my uncle, a little less sternly, I thought, "and I particularly desire that you make me no explanations. If you had any connection with the mysterious assassin and his horse, I prefer to be able to say that I know nothing at all about it. I may have my suspicions that only a daredevil young American could accomplish such feats of prowess as were ascribed to this 'assassin,'—overpower single-handed all the guards of the palace, and make good his escape on a steed of supernatural swiftness,—but I prefer that they should remain suspicions; do you understand?"

I bowed silently, too mortified to make any reply.

"I may have my theories, also," continued my uncle, "as to this young daredevil's presence in the First Consul's closet, and they would certainly not be those entertained by the police. Yet it would be a difficult matter to convince any one, least of all the First Consul and Fouché, that he could be there for any other purpose than assassination; and should his identity be discovered, I fear no influence could be brought to bear strong enough to save his life. Permit me to add, also, that an insatiable curiosity to be present at councils of state, such as I have no doubt led this young man to contrive an entrance into the Consul's private apartments, seems to me only one degree less culpable than the dastardly designs of an assassin."

It is impossible to describe the scathing tone with which my uncle uttered this last sentence. Nor, had I been receiving condemnation from a just judge for the most dastardly crimes, could I have felt keener humiliation. I dared not lift my eyes, and every pulse in my body sent the blood in waves to my already scarlet countenance. I broke out into a great sweat all over my body as I realized that I had forever forfeited the respect and confidence of my uncle, whom I greatly honored and admired. I felt that I must make one desperate effort to regain a little of what I had lost. Not until that moment did I dream that I would be suspected of deliberately hiding in that closet for the purpose of eavesdropping, and not to be allowed to explain to my uncle that my presence there was by accident was almost more than I could bear.

"Sir," I began, still not lifting my eyes, "you will not permit me to tell you anything when I had desired to tell you all, but I beg that you will allow me to say that it was not a spirit of mean curiosity that moved that young man, but a spirit of foolish and reckless adventure, of which he bitterly repents—most of all, because he has forever forfeited the respect and esteem of him whose good opinion he most prizes. He will return at once to America, where he will be in no danger of disgracing those whom he honors so highly. That his visit to Paris, so kindly planned by you, looked forward to with such delight, and, until the present moment, enjoyed so keenly, should end in such failure, is a greater bitterness than you can comprehend; but he feels that he has richly deserved it for his foolish recklessness. He only prays that in condemning his actions you will not judge too harshly of his motives, and that if it is possible to retain affection where esteem is forfeited, he may still be permitted to retain a little of yours."

I stood with my head bowed for what seemed to me a very long time before my uncle spoke. Then he said in the kindest of tones:

"Sit down, my boy; 't is not quite so bad as that."

I looked up quickly. My uncle was actually smiling, and a great load rolled off my heart. For whereas a moment before I had thought I could never look any man in the face again, least of all my uncle, it now seemed to me that there was almost as much of kindly

affection in his glance as I had ever found there. Yet
I would not sit down, as my uncle so kindly insisted,
feeling that I deserved still to retain the attitude of
culprit; seeing which, my uncle softened still more.

"Perhaps I have been too hard on you," he said;
"it was a foolish trick, without doubt, and you deserve some punishment for your thoughtlessness and
recklessness. From what I know of you, I can charge
you with no mean motive, and I am not sure but that
at your age an adventure of such kind would have
tempted me greatly. I do not mind saying, also, that
I am rather proud of the way you got yourself out
of your scrape, and I am glad there were no more
serious results than a sprained ankle for the Chevalier
Le Moyne and a temporary aberration of mind for the
sentry. I am told you sent him spinning in such
fashion that his brains flew out of the top of his head,
and it was some hours before he got them back again.
I hear, too, that he insists it could have been no less
a personage than his Satanic Majesty himself who
with a touch of the hand sent his gun flying when
he was in the very act of firing, and then gave him
a twirl that sent him spinning down the terraces in
the dark."

I did not want to laugh, but I could not quite suppress a sheepish grin at this picture of the dazed sentry, seeing which my uncle threw back his head and
laughed in a way I am sure he learned in America, for
I have never heard the like from these ever-smiling
Parisians. I would have liked to laugh with him, so
jolly did it sound, and my heart growing lighter every

moment; but I did not quite dare. In a minute my uncle stopped as suddenly as he had begun, and was all seriousness again.

"Well, well, my boy, it's all over," he said, "and I am thankful there was no bloodshed, and not very sorry that the chevalier must go limping for a while. I like not that fellow, and I don't understand why he is hanging around the First Consul so much of late. As to your going back to America, it would be the worst possible thing to do. You might as well make a confession at once. No; you must go about exactly as you have always done, no more, no less—certainly no less. And you must ride Fatima, but always at a moderate pace, and be sure you make no exhibitions of her training."

I hardly knew how to thank my uncle, and I told him so. I was indeed glad not to be sent back to America, and I had no doubt that he was right about the wisdom of showing myself in public places with Fatima. I was glad, too, to hear him say that he did not like the Chevalier Le Moyne. I thought I could have enlightened him as to the chevalier's reasons for hanging around the First Consul, but my uncle did not know that I had ever seen Chevalier Le Moyne before, and I could not explain to him without telling him also about the Comtesse de Baloit; and—I knew not why, but I shrank greatly from mentioning her name to my uncle. So I held my peace about the chevalier, and instead made many promises as to my future conduct, and expressed many regrets for the past.

I was leaving the room, feeling myself partly at least restored to my self-respect, when my uncle called me back.

"I 've a piece of news that may interest you," he said. "The President's envoy, Mr. Monroe, has arrived, and I am going to call on him at Mr. Livingston's this evening. Would you like to go with me?"

I thanked him much, and assured him that I was greatly honored and pleased at his invitation (which did, indeed, seem to me like a sign that his confidence in me had returned), and then I hastily left the room with my head in a whirl. Mr. Monroe had arrived! Then so also had mademoiselle. I knew of no way to quiet the tumult of my heart and brain but to go for a ride on Fatima, though in my state of excitement it was hard work keeping her down to the moderate pace my uncle had recommended.

I sought the Champs-Élysées, for it was the fashionable hour for driving, and I hoped that she might be taking the air there with all the rest of the world, though I hardly thought it probable so soon after her arrival. I rode slowly up and down the avenue, bowing to many acquaintances, and looking eagerly at every beautiful woman, whether I knew her or not, for fear that, seeing her in a strange city with strange surroundings, I might pass her and not know her.

I was about to give up the quest and go home, when I saw coming toward me a carriage that had just turned into the avenue from a street leading to the Faubourg St. Germain. It was more magnificent than any I had seen, with outriders in gorgeous liveries, but I thought that hardly accounted for the way people were staring, stopping to look back when the carriage had passed, and the young men bowing to the ground. My heart began to beat tumultuously, as if it knew what my eyes were soon to look upon; yet I am not sure that I really believed it until it burst upon me, a vision of dazzling loveliness. Had I forgotten how beautiful she was? or was it that the fine Parisian hat and dress had added the transcendent touch? Unconsciously I drew Fatima to one side, so dazzled was I by her radiance; and so she did not see me, though she was looking eagerly from side to side, trying to take in at once all this wonderful Paris of which she had heard so much. She seemed to me like a happy child, eyes and lips smiling with delight, and I was happy just to be looking at her, though I liked not the face of the proud and haughty lady who sat beside her, and who, I feared, would never let her speak to her old St. Louis friend.

The carriage passed, and I, too, looked back, as did all the rest of the world. Alas! in one moment was my joy turned to bitterness; for, sitting with his back to the horses and facing Pelagie, a proud smile as of ownership on his evil but handsome face, sat the Chevalier Le Moyne!

CHAPTER XXIII

THE CONSUL'S SENTENCE

"'T is an old maxim in the schools,
That flattery's the food of fools;
Yet now and then your man of wit
Will condescend to take a bit."

"I WONDER what her cousin will say about it? He is her next of kin, and I suppose will have some authority."

"You mean the young Duc d'Enghien? He is in Baden, you know, and not in a position to say anything. He is still émigré, and likely to remain so; for the First Consul distrusts all Bourbon princes."

"Yes; but he might use his authority with his royal cousin, even at a distance. I had always thought he and the Comte d' Artois had other plans for the comtesse—that she was to strengthen their house by an alliance with one of the royal houses of Europe."

"Without doubt that was their plan, but the other side of the house got ahead of them. It is to prevent just such an alliance, I believe, that the wily old duchesse is planning this marriage with the chevalier. He is too far down in the royal ranks to be a dangerous *parti*."

"Have her estates been restored, do you know?"

338

"I am not sure, but I think not. I have heard that Bonaparte is making this marriage a condition. He, too, wants to prevent anything that will strengthen the power of the Bourbons."

"Oh, then the marriage is assured, and the duchesse has accomplished her purpose. I am sorry. I wish the comtesse had remained a little longer in America."

"I am not quite so sure about it. It seems the comtesse herself is making difficulties. Perhaps, now that she has discovered her true rank, she does not consider the chevalier sufficiently noble."

"It will make no difference what she thinks or feels, poor child; with the duchesse and the First Consul both against her, she is as helpless as a bird in the snares of the fowler."

I was one of the group where this conversation took place, and so, though I had no part in it, I could not be considered an eavesdropper (for I had sworn that, rather than listen again to what was not intended for my hearing, I would go about with my ears stuffed with wax and be deaf to the whole world). No name had been mentioned, yet I knew well it was of the Comtesse de Baloit they were speaking, and every word pierced my soul like a knife.

A stir at the upper end of the grand salon put a stop to the conversation. Every voice was hushed, and all eyes were turned to where Madame Bonaparte and the First Consul were making a grand entry. They were followed by a throng of ladies and gentlemen in attendance, and the scene could not have been more magnificent had they been king and queen holding royal court, with lords and ladies in waiting.

I had eyes at first for no one but Madame Bonaparte (since coming to live at the Tuileries she was no longer called Citizeness Bonaparte), whom I had not yet seen, this being my first levee, and of whom I had heard almost as much as of the First Consul. I had heard that she was not faultlessly beautiful, but of great charm, and I could see at once that this was true. I do not know why she was not perfectly beautiful—perhaps her features were a little heavy, her nose a little long, her cheek-bones a little high, which just prevented her face from being faultless; but her eyes were large and lustrous and beaming with kindness, and her hair was soft and dark and abundant and gathered under a Grecian *filet* in rich waves and curls, and her skin was of that creamy whiteness so often seen in creoles, and which sets off so well dark hair and eyes. I have never seen more beautiful neck and shoulders and arms; they looked to me more like some of those beautiful figures in marble in the Louvre Museum, that Bonaparte brought back with him from Italy, than like real flesh and blood.

She was dressed all in white, and my aunt whispered to me that the First Consul liked her best in white, and that it was said when Madame Bonaparte (who was herself fond of more gorgeous costumes) appeared in white, it was a sign either that she was jealous of her husband and was trying to win back his straying affections, or that she wanted some special favor granted. Very likely this was only idle court gossip, but it might easily be true, for I could hardly think her so nearly beautiful in any other dress as in that softly falling white, with high girdle of gold, richly jeweled, and her dark waves of hair caught in a golden net under the Grecian filet.

The First Consul was very magnificent also; I think he likes dress as well as his wife. When I had looked well at these two, I had leisure to look at their retinue; and I looked first at the gentlemen, many of whom were wearing the brilliant uniforms of army officers. To my chagrin, my eyes fell almost instantly upon the Chevalier Le Moyne, wearing the very gorgeous uniform of aide to General Bonaparte. As I looked at him his eye caught mine, and I saw him start, turn pale, and then color violently. In a moment he forced a quick smile to his lips (to his teeth, I had almost said, for there was always something wolfish to me in his smile), and then he bowed. I returned his bow very coldly, and his presence there suggesting to me that I might possibly find Pelagie among the court ladies (for so 't is the fashion to call them in jest), I turned to look for her. Yes, she was there, and, like Madame Bonaparte, all in white. Only Pelagie's white was filmy and lacy, and fuller and more flowing than madame's, with jewels shining in its folds and in her waving hair. And whereas Madame Bonaparte made me think of a Greek goddess, Pelagie reminded me of one of Mr. Shakspere's fairies, sparkling, graceful, exquisite.

She did not seem to see me, and I could gaze at her no longer, for the First Consul was already moving about from group to group of the assembled guests, saying a few words to each, and he was just approaching our party. He greeted my aunt and uncle and those standing with us, whom he knew, very affably; then he turned his quick glance on me, and my uncle presented me.

"Ah," he said, "I was not mistaken. I thought you were from America when I saw you in church on Easter morning"; and, turning to my uncle, he added:

"We do not grow such great fair men in France, Citizen Minister."

"No," said my uncle, quickly; "we have small dark great men in France, Citizen First Consul."

Bonaparte laughed, pleased both with the play on words and my uncle's compliment, and turned quickly to the next group before I had time to stammer out how flattered I felt at his remembering me.

The next group happened to be the English ambassador, Lord Whitworth, and his friends. The Consul had been very affable with us, and I had discovered that his smile was of rare sweetness and gave great beauty to his face. But as he turned to Lord Whitworth the smile vanished and his brows were drawn together in a dark frown. Without the slightest word of greeting, he spoke to him abruptly and harshly:

"I find your nation wants war again."

Lord Whitworth bowed low, and a dull red slowly spread over his face as he answered:

"No, sir; we are very desirous of peace."

"You have just finished a war of fifteen years," said Bonaparte again, in the most offensive of tones, almost a sneer.

The ambassador bit his lip in his effort at self-control, but he answered with great suavity:

"It is true, sir; and that was fifteen years too long."

"But you want another war of fifteen years," insisted Bonaparte, his tones every moment harsher and louder, so that every one in that part of the salon could not help but hear. All conversation ceased, and every one listened with strained and painful attention. Lord Whitworth quietly reiterated:

"Pardon me, sir; we are very desirous of peace."

Then, in a tone that rang out like the harsh clang of crossing swords, Bonaparte cried:

"I must either have Malta or war!"

A shock ran through the whole assembly. No man dared look at his neighbor. This was nothing less than a declaration of war, and in the most insulting manner. Whether the proud representative of the haughtiest nation on the globe would receive such a rude insult to himself and his country calmly was very doubtful, and we all awaited Lord Whitworth's reply in trembling silence. With compressed lips and eyes that flashed in spite of himself, but with a calmness in marked contrast to Bonaparte's petulance, he replied:

"I am not prepared, sir, to speak on that subject; and I can only assure you, Citizen First Consul, that we wish for peace."

Bonaparte's frown grew darker, but he said no more; and with a curt nod, and almost a sneer on his lips, he withdrew at once into a small cabinet opening into the salon, leaving the rest of his guests without addressing a word to them, which I was told afterward was very unusual with him, and showed that his irritation must be very great.

An embarrassed silence followed the First Consul's exit. I had been looking forward to this levee for weeks, but it promised to be a very uncomfortable occasion for me as well as for others. I had a great desire to speak to the British ambassador and assure him of my sympathy, for none of the Frenchmen so much as dared to look at him, now that he was in disgrace, lest it be reported to the Consul, and they themselves fall under suspicion. But I feared it would be presumption in one so young and unknown, and I dreaded meeting the haughty British stare with which an Englishman petrifies one he considers unduly forward. Much to my relief, and indeed to the relief of the whole company, my uncle turned to him and began at once to talk in a most animated manner of the doings in the American Congress. That the relief was general was evident, for conversation was at once resumed, and with a gaiety that was somewhat feverish, I thought.

It was our turn now to pay our respects to Madame Bonaparte. I had been eager to meet her until I discovered the presence of Pelagie; but now it had suddenly become a trying ordeal to walk forward and salute madame, and perhaps stand talking to her a few moments, conscious that Pelagie's eyes, if they cared to, might be watching every movement. Should I be awkward (as I feared I would under such a scrutiny), I was sure there would be the old mocking light in them I had so often seen, and dreaded to see, in St.

Louis. I resolved not to glance at her once while I was going through my ordeal, lest she should prove my undoing; and I tried to think only of the charming woman who smiled bewitchingly when I made gallant speeches, and who tapped me with her fan in much the same playful fashion as Mistress Madison had tapped me with her jeweled snuff-box. Indeed, she reminded me much of the lovely Washington lady. Both had the same kind way of putting an awkward lad at his ease, and seeming to like him and be pleased with his speeches, especially if they savored a little of audacity. But Madame Bonaparte had not the dash and sparkle of Mistress Madison; instead, she had a lazy Southern fashion of speech and a wonderfully winning gentleness that I am not sure was not more charming than the gay brilliancy of the other.

She kept me talking to her longer than I had expected (or hoped for), and I began to see significant glances exchanged, while my color was steadily rising; and I was sure mademoiselle (if she looked at me at all), noting my shining curls, as yellow as the gold lace on my white satin court-dress, and my cheeks flaming like any girl's, was saying to herself with infinite scorn, "Pretty boy!"

I think Madame Bonaparte saw the significant glances also, for she said presently:

"You must meet the Comtesse de Baloit. She has just returned from your America, and you will have much in common to talk about."

And so I found myself bowing low over Pelagie's hand, and a moment later looking straight down into her lovely dark eyes, which looked straight up at mine with no hint of scorn in their shadowy depths, but only a great wonder, and a little of something else that set my pulses to beating like trip-hammers.

"I cannot understand, Monsieur," she said. "I shall have to ask you, as you asked me in Washington —how did you get here?"

"It was a lodestar drew me," I murmured.

But the warm light in her eyes changed quickly to proud disdain.

"I like not idle gallantries between old friends. Keep those for Madame Bonaparte. I saw they pleased her greatly, and that you were much flattered by their reception."

Could the Comtesse de Baloit be jealous? or was it the haughty Faubourg St. Germain scorning the parvenue of the Tuileries? I hoped it was the first, but in either case it behooved me to make quick *amende*.

"Forgive me, Comtesse," I said, as coldly as she had spoken, but in English, and so low that I hoped no listener could understand even if he knew the tongue. "It was true, but you could not know how true, and I have no right to tell you. I know well how great a distance lies between the proud Lady of France and a simple American gentleman. Permit me to inform you, Comtesse, that I have been in Paris for more than a month with my uncle, Monsieur Barbé Marbois. And permit me to add, as a simple fact in which you may be interested or not, that this is the moment for which I have lived through that month—the moment when I should meet again the Comtesse de Baloit."

It had ever been the way with the little Pelagie in America to meet her hauteur with hauteur, but I was not sure it would work here, and I trembled inwardly while I spoke so calmly. But it did. Her lids dropped for a moment, and a soft color stole up to her temples. When she lifted her eyes again, there was a sweet, shy light in them.

"Monsieur," she said softly, in her pretty English, "why do you call me Comtesse? Have you forgotten?"

"Is it still to be Mademoiselle?" I cried eagerly, and had hard work not to pick her up in my arms and run away with her, so adorable was she in her sweet friendliness.

"Mademoiselle always, unless it is—" But then she broke off suddenly and turned a rosy red, and added quickly, with something of her old sauciness: "Never Comtesse, unless I am very, *very* naughty."

My heart told me what she had meant to say, and I whispered proudly:

"Unless it is some day—Pelagie"; and I know my eyes told her all the rest I did not dare to say, for she looked away from me quickly, and I, glancing up, met a black scowl on the face of the chevalier, who, I knew, must have been watching this little by-play, though he could not have heard a word, such was the buzz and clatter of conversation about us. His face cleared instantly, and he stepped quickly forward with a forced smile and an extended hand.

"Permit me to greet an old friend," he said gaily. "When did you arrive in Paris?"

It would have been well for me if I could have swallowed my pride sufficiently to take his proffered hand; but it seemed to me the hand of a scoundrel and a dastard, and I could not bring myself to touch it. I pretended not to see it, and I hoped the chevalier and those who were looking on might be deceived into thinking I did not, as I answered politely enough:

"The Chevalier Le Moyne is very kind to welcome me so cordially to Paris."

And then, with a sudden recollection of our last encounter, and hoping to throw him off the track, I added:

"I have been in Paris but a short time; this is my first visit to the Tuileries."

But I had not deceived him. The black scowl returned quickly at my rejection of his proffered hand, and stretching himself to his full height, so as to be as near my ear as possible, he said between his teeth:

"It may be your first visit to the Tuileries, Monsieur; but, if I mistake not, you have been at St. Cloud before. If I had known you were in Paris I would have been at no loss to account for the mysterious horse and his rider. I suppose you have brought that accursed mare with you?"

I may have turned pale, for I saw black ruin yawn before me, but I answered steadily:

"I do not understand you, Monsieur. I beg you will explain."

"Diable! You understand well enough, Monsieur,"

he sneered, and turned and walked away with an exaggerated limp—it had been scarcely perceptible when he came to greet me.

I had little time to worry over this new peril that threatened, for my uncle came up to present me to more of the "court ladies," and I did my best to talk and be merry, while in the background of my thoughts I was trying to plan some way of escape from the meshes of the net I saw closing around me. Paris was no longer any place for me. I must tell my uncle at the first opportunity, and ask his help in getting away as quietly as possible to America; and at that thought, and that I was cutting myself off from ever seeing again the Comtesse de Baloit, I groaned inwardly, and could have cursed the reckless folly that had brought me to such a pass.

In the midst of my troubled thoughts I saw an officer approach the Comtesse de Baloit (for, no matter to whom I might be talking, the Comtesse was ever in my sight), bow low, and apparently deliver some message to her. I saw her turn to the lady who stood near her (the one with whom I had seen her driving, whose bearing was so stern and haughty, and who, I did not doubt, was the duchesse I had heard spoken of as desiring to marry her to the chevalier), and then the officer offered an arm to each of them and bore them away to the cabinet to which the First Consul had withdrawn.

I did not know why this should be cause for anxiety on my part, but none the less I felt anxious. When, a few minutes later, the same officer approached the

Chevalier Le Moyne and delivered to him also a message, and the chevalier deliberately turned to me with a smile of triumph, and then followed the officer to the same cabinet, I felt doubly anxious. Indeed, so great had my anxiety become that it was almost impossible for me to keep up longer the semblance of gay converse with the witty beauties about me.

The chevalier's smile of triumph meant one of two things—either terrible for me, but one impossible to think of. It meant, "You see, now I have my chance to denounce you to the First Consul, and I shall use it"—which would mean nothing less than death for me; or, it meant, "You see, the First Consul is bringing his influence to bear upon my marriage with the Comtesse de Baloit; it is all arranged"—which would mean something far worse than death for me.

I was not surprised, therefore, and I was almost relieved when ten minutes later the officer touched me on the shoulder.

"The First Consul desires your presence in his cabinet, Monsieur," he said; and I turned and followed him, conscious that I was followed in turn by all eyes. There had been no surprise when first the comtesse and then the chevalier had been summoned, for every one thought he understood—the First Consul's powerful influence was to be brought to bear upon a recalcitrant maiden; and while some pitied, none doubted that the First Consul's influence would avail. But no one knew what connection I could have with the affair, and the first moment of startled surprise was followed by a murmur of curious surmises.

Amid that murmur I walked as one who goes to his execution; for from the moment the officer touched me upon the shoulder I had known what the chevalier's smile of triumph meant, and I knew that I was on my way to be accused and condemned, and, for aught I knew, marched off to instant execution under the eyes of the Comtesse de Baloit. As I passed Monsieur Marbois, his eyes, filled with a startled alarm, met mine. I tried to reassure him with a smile, but I fear it was sorry work, for a sudden rush of remembrance of all his goodness to me overwhelmed me and came near to unmanning me.

Just inside the door of the cabinet the officer stopped, and motioned to me also to stay my steps. On whatever errand I had been sent for, it was evident that neither the First Consul nor any one else was quite ready for me. The Consul was seated, while on one side of him stood the chevalier, and on the other the duchesse and the Comtesse de Baloit; and that any man should remain seated in the presence of the comtesse filled me at once with a blind rage that ill prepared me to play my part in what was about to follow. The attitude of the three struck me at once as significant: the duchesse complacent, with almost a smile upon her haughty features, and to the best of her ability beaming upon the First Consul; the chevalier eager, obsequious, fawning; the comtesse her head held proudly up, a little frown between her brows, her eyes flashing; impatience, annoyance, disdain expressed in every feature. The First Consul was speaking as we entered, and I thought his tones were meant to be persuasive; they were less rasping than I had often heard them.

"The estates are very great, Mademoiselle." (And again I was indignant that he should address her as Mademoiselle, a title which I felt belonged to no man to use but to me. I knew, of course, that it was but the common usage,—that titles were not permitted in republican France,—but none the less I was angry.) "Your father was almost the richest man in France," he was saying. "Should I restore these estates to you, I must have some guaranty that they will be used for the welfare of the republic, and not against it. Citizen Le Moyne is such a guaranty. His sword is already pledged to the service of the republic, and to the Citizeness Le Moyne I will restore all the estates of her father."

A bright red spot burned in each of Pelagie's cheeks. I know not what she might have said (though she looked not as if she would meekly yield assent to this powerful plea), for at that moment the First Consul discovered our entrance and turned to the chevalier.

"Citizen Le Moyne," he said, "you asked us to send for this young man. He is here. What has the nephew of Monsieur Marbois to do with this matter?"

A malicious smile played round the chevalier's lips.

"If you remember, Citizen First Consul," he said "I told you that at one time mademoiselle was not averse to my suit—that in all probability I would have won her hand in St. Louis, but that her mind was poisoned against me by malicious insinuations and fabrications, the work of a rival who desired to win her for himself?''

The chevalier waited for the Consul's reply, and he nodded curtly.

"Well?"

"Citizen First Consul, that rival is the nephew of Minister Marbois, and I have brought him here to ask him to renounce publicly all claims to the hand of the Citizeness de Baloit."

I saw a flash in the beautiful eyes, and a proud toss of the little head that I well knew meant, "He has no claim," and I hastened to speak.

"Sire," I said quickly, and then stopped in confusion. How could I have made such an egregious blunder as to address the first citizen of the republic by a royal title? Yet it was a natural enough mistake, for no Czar or Sultan or Grand Mogul was ever a more autocratic ruler than he, or made men tremble more at his nod. I thought I had no doubt ruined my cause in the very outset, for a dark frown gathered between the Consul's brows, but it quickly disappeared.

"I believe you spoke innocently, young man," he said, with a smile of rare sweetness. "Speak on!"

"Pardon, Citizen First Consul," I said—"it was indeed an innocent mistake"; and then I added with a sudden impulse of audacity, "but a very natural one."

The Consul answered me only with his flashing smile, that transfigured his face, and I hurried on:

"I wish to say, sir, that I have no claim to the hand of Mademoiselle la Comtesse." I saw from the tail of my eye her head take a prouder pose and her

23

lips curl scornfully as she perceived that I was tamely
renouncing my "claim" at the chevalier's bidding;
but I went calmly on: "I have always known that
there was a great gulf fixed between the proud Lady of
France of royal blood and a simple American gentleman.   Mademoiselle la Comtesse has never given me
any reason to hope that that gulf could be crossed,
but," and I turned and looked straight at the chevalier,—and if my head was flung back too proudly and
my eyes flashed too fiercely and my voice rang out too
defiantly, it was from no lack of respect to the great
Bonaparte, but because my soul was seething with
wrath and indignation against that cowardly villain
—"but should Mademoiselle la Comtesse give me the
faintest hope that the honest love of an honest American heart could weigh with her against lands and titles, that the devotion of a lifetime to her every
thought and desire could hope to win her love, then no
argument the Chevalier Le Moyne could bring to bear
would have a feather's weight with me.   I would renounce my 'claim to her hand' only with my life!"

The First Consul's eyes were smiling as I ceased
speaking; there was no frown on his brow.   The duchesse looked aghast, as if it were inconceivable blas-
phemy that I should think of aspiring to the comtesse,
and the chevalier's face was dark, with an ugly sneer
distorting his lips.   But I cared little how Consul or
duchesse or chevalier took my speech: I cared only for
what mademoiselle might think.   I glanced quickly at
her.   Her head was drooping, her long lashes were
sweeping her cheek, her face was rosy red, and a half-

smile was playing about her mouth. My heart beat high with exultant joy. I turned proudly to the chevalier and awaited the thunderbolt I knew was sure to fall. He, too, had seen mademoiselle's soft and drooping aspect, and the sight had lashed him to fury. But before he had a chance to speak, the First Consul himself spoke with good-natured raillery:

"I think, Citizen Le Moyne, your golden-haired giant makes a very good plea for himself. Suppose I offer him a position on my staff and make a Frenchman of him, and then let the Citizeness de Baloit choose between you? Perhaps her estates would be as safe in his hands as in yours."

Had the First Consul uttered his speech with the purpose of lashing the chevalier to fury and goading him to still greater venom against me, he could have taken no better course to accomplish it.

"Safe!" he hissed. "Safe in the hands of an assassin! You would give mademoiselle and her estates to the man who hid in your closet to attempt your life in your bath! Regardez! the coward—the sneak—the villain! When your Mameluke discovers him he flees. I run to your defense. Does he meet me with his sword like an honorable gentleman? No! he trips me with the foot like a school-boy, and throws me down the stair, to be the laughing-stock of my fellow-officers! Because he is a giant, he falls upon your sentry of small stature and hurls him down the terraces! He calls to his trick horse,—trained in the circus, I do not doubt,—and rides away in the dark, and thinks no one will ever know! But *I* know. I have seen his tricks in America. He is a clown—a mountebank! No gentleman would touch his hand!''

The chevalier's voice had grown shriller and higher with each word, till he ended in a scream, tearing his hair, rushing up and down the cabinet in his fury, and pointing every epithet with a long finger extended toward me. I could have smiled at such childish rage but that it was too serious a matter to me for smiling. Mademoiselle's eyes were wide with terror and amaze, and the Consul's brow grew darker with every word of the chevalier's.

"Officer, call the guard!" he said in his rasping voice, as soon as the chevalier gave him a chance to speak, and I knew my doom was sealed.

But mademoiselle sprang forward, one arm outstretched to stay the officer, and one extended toward the Consul in supplication.

"No, no, officer, not yet!" she cried, and then to Bonaparte:

"Oh, Citizen Consul, it is all a terrible mistake! I know him well. He could not be guilty of so dreadful a crime! He could not do anything mean or low or dishonorable. There is no gentleman in the world more generous and noble! And the man who denounces him owes his life to him!"

"Look at him, Mademoiselle," said the Consul, harshly, "and see if his looks do not confess him the culprit."

I knew that I must look the very picture of conscious guilt, for every word mademoiselle had uttered had pierced me like a two-edged sword. I might have braved the chevalier's accusations and the First Consul's suspicions (for, after all, neither had any evidence against me), but I could not bear her generous confidence in me, feeling that I had so miserably forfeited my right to it by indulging in a foolish boyish prank. I did not raise my head (where it had sunk in shame), but by reason of being so much taller I yet could see her turn toward me, see her look of implicit trust change slowly to doubt and fear. Then I heard her utter one low cry, "Oh, Monsieur, Monsieur!" and turn away. In a moment my resolve was taken. I would make a clean breast of it; she should not think me worse than I was. I lifted my head.

"Mademoiselle!" I cried, and she turned quickly toward me and looked straight into my eyes with a look that was hard to bear. "I am guilty Mademoiselle! I am the man who was in the First Consul's closet, and who escaped on Fatima's back."

The Consul made a motion toward the officer, but I turned to him quickly.

"I beg you, sire,"—and this time I did not know that I had said it, not until long afterward, when one of those who heard told me of it,—"that you will not send your officer for the guard until I have made my confession; then you can send for it, and I will go away quietly, without resistance."

"Very well, officer; you can wait," said Bonaparte, still harshly. The rest of my confession I addressed directly to him.

"I am no clown, mountebank, or circus rider in my own country, sir, as the Chevalier Le Moyne would have you believe; I am the son of a Philadelphia gentleman, and the nephew of Madame Marbois. Unfortunately, life in my native land has bred in me a spirit of adventure that has many times been near my undoing. It has also bred in me a great love for the life of a soldier, and a great admiration for the famous soldiers of history. When I accompanied my uncle to St. Cloud, and knew that he was summoned there to meet the First Consul, I was seized with a desire to enter the palace and roam through the rooms where the First Consul dwelt. When I found admission was not permitted I thought it would be a fine adventure to find my way in without permission. It was a boy's wild spirit of daring, and a boy's almost idolatrous hero-worship that led me into such a scrape."

The Consul interrupted me here, but I thought his tones a little less harsh than before:

"Did your uncle know of your intention to enter the palace?"

"Most certainly not, Citizen First Consul," I answered, "else had I never accomplished it."

"Then how did you find your way to my closet?"

"I followed a servant through some winding corridors, but an officer suddenly appeared. I fled, opened the first door I came to, saw myself in a dressing-room, opened another, and found myself in the closet connecting with your cabinet."

All of which was literally true, and implicated neither Gaston nor Félice, I hoped. The Consul signed to me to go on with my story.

"All would have been well, and I should have

slipped out the way I came, had not the First Consul decided to take a bath.''

I was watching my auditor narrowly as I talked, for I felt my life depended upon his change of mood, and I thought I saw here the least glimmer of a twinkle in his eye; but if it was there it was banished instantly, and his face was as set and stern as before.

''I have never heard any words, your''—I started to say ''your Majesty,'' caught myself, and stumbled miserably—''your—your—Excellency, that filled me with greater dismay than these: 'Tell my valet to prepare my bath'!''

Again I thought I caught that fleeting twinkle of the eye, but could not be sure.

''There was no hope for me,'' I went on, ''but to wait for the First Consul to finish his bath; but, unfortunately for me, he is fonder of his bath than most men, and I stood in that dark closet in an agony of suspense, and revolving in my mind every conceivable plan of escape, for what seemed to me many long hours. All might still have been well,—for in the nature of things even the First Consul's bath must come to an end sometime,—had I not made a slight noise which the quick ears of the Consul and the Mameluke heard. I was discovered, and there was nothing for me to do but to flee through the audience-chamber and the main corridor, surprising the guard at the door, who, in his turn, raised the whole palace in pursuit.

''I was distancing my pursuers, and should have

gotten out of the palace without difficulty, but that at the head of the grand staircase I met the Chevalier Le Moyne, running from the opposite end of the corridor. I would not under ordinary circumstances refuse a sword encounter with the chevalier (though I would prefer an opponent with a nicer sense of honor), but there was no time for such an encounter now if I would not have the whole palace upon me, and, besides, it was most important that the chevalier should not recognize me. There was nothing to do but to hide my face with my arm as if shielding it from his sword, and trip him up, as he says, schoolboy fashion. I am sorry that it should have hurt his self-esteem to be vanquished by such a youthful trick, and regret still more that he should have suffered in the estimation of his fellow-officers thereby.''

This time the twinkle in the Consul's eye was unmistakable, and I could hear the chevalier grinding his teeth with rage.

''As for your sentry,'' I continued, ''he was aiming his gun to fire at me. There was no time for ceremony. I could have spitted him upon my sword, which was in my hand, and it might have been more respectful; but I dislike bloodshed, unless it is absolutely unavoidable, and so I threw up his gun with my arm, and sent him spinning after it in the dark. I had left my mare Fatima—who is no trick horse, but a young Arabian trained by myself from colthood to do my bidding—in a pine thicket close by. I was on her back and away just in time to escape your mounted guards, who thundered out the gates of the park scarce twenty paces behind me. Had Fatima been less swift I had not been here to tell the tale. I hope the First Consul will believe me when I say I have suffered much from remorse for my rash and thoughtless act. It was a wild spirit of adventure that led me into it, but I see clearly now that does not in the least excuse it, and I am ready to atone for it in any way you decree.''

The eye of the First Consul, clear, piercing, heart-reading, had been upon me through the whole of this recital; but I, feeling that I was keeping nothing back (save only Gaston and Félice), and being nerved up to meet whatever fate should befall, bore its scrutiny well. He was silent for a moment after I had finished speaking, and my heart sank steadily down, for life looked very bright to me and I began to be very sure I had forfeited it by my foolishness. Suddenly the Consul spoke, but it was not to me nor to the chevalier; he turned to Pelagie.

''Mademoiselle, that was a boyish escapade, certainly, and it was a very pretty boy that contrived it. What do you think would be suitable punishment for such a crime? You shall be the arbiter of his fate.''

Mademoiselle gave me one fleeting glance, saucy merriment dancing in her eye; then she turned to Bonaparte, and, curtsying low, she said with pretty archness:

''Citizen First Consul, I know him well, and I know that only death could be a greater punishment to him than to be called a 'pretty boy'! Do you not think his crime is atoned for?''

Bonaparte's wonderful smile lighted his face and fell on mademoiselle with almost too great sweetness, I thought.

"It is as you say, Mademoiselle," he replied. "Officer, you need not call the guard."

But I, suddenly relieved from the fear of death, stood there scarlet with confusion, head drooping, and ready to sink through the floor with shame, while I mentally anathematized my yellow curls and rosy cheeks and blue eyes, and most of all my *domtiferous* vanity that had led me to array myself in shining white satin and glittering gold lace, that I was sure made me look fairer and rosier and more than ever like a big blond baby.

CHAPTER XXIV

A NEW CHEVALIER OF FRANCE

"Our hopes, like towering falcons, aim
At objects in an airy height."

"OFFICER," said Bonaparte, in his iciest tones, "conduct Citizeness Capet and Citizen Le Moyne back to the salon. I have something to say to the others that it will not be necessary for them to hear. You need not return yourself until I ring for you."

Madame la Duchesse glared at the little figure lazily and haughtily reclining at ease in the deep-armed chair while we all stood meekly before him. I think for a moment she was tempted to spring upon him and tear his eyes out. That the parvenu ruler of the republic should so address a member not only of the old nobility but the old royalty, was more than she could bear. A cool stare from the fathomless eyes of the Consul made her think better of it; she turned and accompanied the chevalier (who was nigh to foaming at the mouth with ill-suppressed rage) back to the salon.

As they left the cabinet, conducted in state by the officer, Bonaparte turned to Pelagie.

"Mademoiselle la Comtesse," he said in tones whose suavity were in marked contrast to the coldness of his last speech, "will you not be seated? I am sorry to have kept you standing so long. I have asked you to wait while I spoke to this young man, because I have something more to say to you on the subject we were discussing. I beg, therefore, you will make yourself perfectly comfortable while you wait."

I think Pelagie was of half a mind to decline the Consul's courtesy, for she hesitated a moment, and I saw a dangerous spark leap into his eyes. I do not know whether she saw it also, or whether she simply decided it was better to be as complaisant as possible in small matters, since she might have to be recalcitrant in great ones. She sat down, apparently cool and collected, but in the chair most distant from the First Consul. I had noted the change in the form of his address, and wondered at it; but I believe he liked titles, and was glad to use them when there were no jealous ears about to find fault with his lapse from republican simplicity. He did not ask me to sit down, but turned to me as soon as Pelagie had taken her seat, and began abruptly:

"I made a proposition a few moments ago in jest; I now make it in earnest: I offer you a position on my staff as military aide. The young man who has the skill to extricate himself from such an escapade as yours is of the stuff I would like to use in my service, and when he adds to his other qualities the ability to tell his story so discreetly that it is impossible to guess whether or not he has heard anything of state councils and family quarrels, he is of still greater value in such a capacity."

I was overwhelmed. Lifted from the depths of disgrace and fear of death to the pinnacle of my daydreams realized (for it had ever been my fondest dream to be a soldier of fortune, and to serve under the great Bonaparte—one that I had hardly dared to confess to myself) was almost more than brain could stand. More than that, to hear such words of commendation from the great soldier, when I had expected severest censure, set heart throbbing and head whirling. I could only stammer out:

"It would be the greatest joy and glory of my life to serve under the First Consul! I shall have to get my uncle's permission; may I defer my answer until I have an opportunity to consult him?"

The Consul frowned quickly; I have no doubt he was used to receiving only instant acceptances of his offers. But in a moment his countenance cleared, and he answered, pleasantly enough:

"Very well; I shall expect to hear from you the day after to-morrow"; and with a slight nod from him I understood myself dismissed.

Somehow I liked not leaving Pelagie there alone with him, but there was no alternative. I thought, too, as I made my low bow to her in leaving the room, that her eyes met mine with a look of appeal in their dark depths it was hard to withstand. I determined to take my station in the salon near the cabinet door, so that if she should need me I would be near at hand.

And thus it happened that a few minutes later I heard the Consul's bell ring violently, saw the officer on duty enter the cabinet hastily, and immediately return, conducting Pelagie. Her eyes were shining with a fierce light, a bright spot was burning in either cheek, and her head was held so high and she was looking so straight forward with an unseeing gaze that she did not see me as she passed. I saw her take her place among the court ladies and Madame Bonaparte look at her with cold displeasure. Being no longer on sentry duty, I joined my aunt, and she whispered to me:

"The pretty Comtesse is in trouble. Madame will not easily forgive her husband spending ten minutes alone with her in his cabinet."

My soul raged within me, for I could see that others also were whispering about her, and for a moment I was ready to challenge all the world, including the great Bonaparte himself, who (though, I believed, innocently) had given occasion for the whisperings. Of course I knew that his interview with Pelagie had been entirely in behalf of the chevalier, but others did not seem to be so certain of it, and especially did Madame Bonaparte's attitude toward her give rise to unpleasant comment. I longed eagerly for a word with Pelagie herself, but I saw no chance of obtaining it. Yet fortune favored me, for later in the evening, when they were preparing the piquet-tables, I found myself placed next to her; and once, when excitement over some disputed point in the game was running high, and the din of contending voices made a friendly cover for a low-toned speech, I managed to say to her:

"You look troubled, Mademoiselle; is there any way in which I can be of service to you?"

She smiled up at me with a look of trust that touched me greatly, and said hurriedly, mentioning no names (which might have been dangerous):

"I wanted this chance to tell you. He insisted on that marriage, and when I told him I would never marry a man who had denounced and betrayed in such cowardly fashion the man to whom he owed his life, he was very rude to me."

"Rude to you!" I whispered fiercely. "Then I cannot take service under him."

But she looked greatly alarmed when I said that, and whispered eagerly:

"No, no, Monsieur; do not say that! Take the place, if you can, for your own sake,"—and then she hesitated a moment,—"and for mine."

There was no chance for another word; the game was breaking up, and the old duchess came and carried her off with a glare of distrust and suspicion at me, and I had no doubt she had been watching our whispered consultation.

There was no chance, either, to tell my uncle of my interview with the Consul; for I could say nothing before my aunt without entering into explanations that I did not want to make to her, and I knew the fact of my returning to the salon instead of being hurried off to prison had quieted his alarms. The hour was late, and we said good night to each other in the corridors when we returned home, going at once to our rooms.

I hurried down-stairs the next morning, hoping to find my uncle taking his morning coffee in the garden, as he often did in this lovely spring weather; but I had overslept, and he was already gone. Late in the afternoon I sought him in his library, for I knew my answer to the First Consul must be decided upon at once, and I was anxious to tell him all about my interview. He answered my knock by a quick "Enter, enter!" and I found him brimming over with gay good humor and excitement.

"You are just in time, my boy," he cried. "I am expecting the American ambassadors every moment, and, if they offer no objection, you may stay and see how history is made. We are to sign the treaty that is to give the First Consul the munitions of war, and that will place America in the very front rank of nations."

My own affairs seemed of small moment beside such stupendous ones, and I saw that my uncle had entirely forgotten his alarm of the evening before. I was myself very greatly excited, for this was the moment to which I had been looking for nearly a year, though the realization about to be consummated was far exceeding my wildest fancies.

The two gentlemen were announced a moment later, and they both greeted me cordially, for they knew my family at home and I had called on them several times in Paris. Nor did my uncle have to prefer a request that I should be permitted to be a witness of the sign-ing of the treaty. Mr. Livingston himself suggested that I be invited to remain, and, the others assenting most cordially, I thanked them heartily for their courtesy, and retired to a seat in the background, where I might not intrude upon their deliberations.

The document seemed long, and in fact, as I understood it, there were three documents—one which they called the treaty, and two others they called "conventions." They read them all over carefully several times before signing, and I heard the article read that I had seen the First Consul write, and discovered that one convention was to determine in what manner the sixty million francs were to be paid to France, and the other convention was concerned with the twenty million francs to be paid by the United States to such of its citizens as held claims against France.

There seemed to be some little discussions on a few minor points which were easily settled, and then very solemnly they each signed the three documents, Mr. Livingston writing his name first, then Mr. Monroe, and then my uncle. When this was done, the three gentlemen, as by a common impulse, rose to their feet and shook hands, their faces shining with a solemn light which I believe had nothing to do with self-glory, but with an unselfish joy at having accomplished an act that would bring honor and benefit to two great nations and to future generations. I, in my corner, was almost as proud as they, and quite as happy (when I thought of the honor that was to come to my country, and especially the blessings to that great West I was so interested in), and for the first time in my life I felt it might be almost finer to accomplish such great things by statesmanship and a stroke of the

24

pen than to win fame and glory by the sword. Then I saw that Mr. Livingston was beginning to speak. He stood up straight and tall and fine-looking, and his manner was very impressive and full of dignity and a kind of solemn joy. I was very proud of him as a representative of my country, and each word that he spoke made me prouder and happier.

"We have lived long," he began, "but this is the noblest work of our whole lives. The treaty which we have just signed has not been obtained by art or dictated by force; equally advantageous to the two contracting parties, it will change vast solitudes into flourishing districts. From this day the United States take their place among the powers of the first rank. The English lose all exclusive influence in the affairs of America. Thus one of the principal causes of European rivalries and animosities is about to cease. The instruments we have just signed will cause no tears to be shed; they prepare ages of happiness for innumerable generations of human creatures. The Mississippi and Missouri will see them succeed one another, and multiply, truly worthy of the regard and care of Providence, in the bosom of equality, under just laws, freed from the errors of superstition and the scourge of bad government."

My uncle and Mr. Monroe seemed greatly impressed by his words (as, indeed, no one who heard them could help being); and then there was half an hour of pleasant talk, in which the three gentlemen kindly included me. As the American ambassadors took their leave, my uncle turned to me.

The Signing of the Louisiana Purchase Treaty by
Marbois, Livingston, and Monroe

"Well, my boy," he said, his kind face beaming, "we have settled the affairs of two great nations most satisfactorily; now we will settle yours. What did the First Consul want of you last evening?"

I had made up my mind to tell my uncle all about my acquaintance with the Comtesse de Baloit and the Chevalier Le Moyne, if he had time to listen,—for otherwise it would be difficult to explain my interview with the Consul, or how I happened to be summoned to his presence,—and I asked him if he had time to hear a long story. He replied that he considered he had accomplished enough for one day, and he should do nothing more, until dinner at least; he might possibly be summoned to an interview with the First Consul at the Tuileries later in the evening.

He scarcely interrupted me through my long recital, unless an occasional heavy scowl at some special perfidy of the chevalier's could be called an interruption. He chuckled with delight when I told how I tripped up the chevalier on the grand staircase of St. Cloud, and uttered a vigorous "Diable!" when he heard how I came to be summoned before the First Consul. He listened almost breathlessly to my account of my interview with the Consul, and drew a great sigh of relief as I finished.

"Why, my lad," he said, "you have been having great experiences! I wonder you could forget them sufficiently to be so deeply interested, as you seemed to be, in the doings of three old diplomats."

I assured him that what the three diplomats had just accomplished was of greater interest to me than any of my own affairs could possibly be. In all my story I had touched as lightly as I could on the Comtesse de Baloit, hoping that my uncle would not discover that I had any special interest in that direction; but he was too astute a reader of human nature to be easily misled.

"That is all very well," he said, in reply to my assurance of a deeper interest in affairs of state than in my own; "I do not doubt for a moment that you believe what you say, and I could easily believe it, too, if it were not for the Comtesse de Baloit. Such affairs are more engrossing than all others in the world, if I remember my own youthful days aright. But I had no idea the wind sat in that quarter, as your Mr. Shakspere would say. Have you any idea how high you are aspiring? I know you Americans stop at nothing; but, my dear boy, you might as well aspire to the hand of the Princess Charlotte of England!"

"I am aspiring to the hand of no one, sir," I answered rather hotly, for I knew so well how hopeless any dreams of mine might be that I liked not to have any one think I was cherishing false hopes. "Whatever my feeling toward the Comtesse may be, I have never had the slightest hope. If Citizeness Capet, as the First Consul calls her, does not succeed in marrying the comtesse to the Chevalier Le Moyne, then her cousins the Comte d'Arbois and the Duc d'Enghien will probably marry her into one of the reigning houses of Europe. Mademoiselle la Comtesse has shown me some kindness, but only such as any right-feeling young maiden would show to one who has been able to do her some little service, and I am not one to presume upon her grateful feeling.''

My uncle looked at me for a moment with a little frown between his brows, as if he were trying to solve some perplexing question, and then the frown cleared away and he spoke smilingly:

''Well, well, we will dismiss the Comtesse; that is too difficult a problem. And now for what is, after all, a question of more practical importance. Do you want to accept this offer of the First Consul's?''

''Very much, sir,'' I answered eagerly.

''I doubt whether I have any right to give you permission to do so,'' responded my uncle; ''but this much authority I will assume. If the First Consul is willing to take you subject to the commands of your father when we can hear from him, I will give my permission, and I will write to your father by the first packet. It will be ten or twelve weeks before we can possibly hear from him, and it may be much longer. But I am rather relieved that you desire to accept the First Consul's offer. He does not like his favors rejected, and he is quite capable of holding me responsible for having influenced you, should you decline.''

The First Consul was willing to take me on those conditions (I think he felt no doubt of my father's answer; such confidence had he in the magnetism of his own name that he believed any man would feel proud to have his son serve under him), and a very few days saw me arrayed in my glittering uniform and spending every spare moment, when I was off

duty, riding up and down the Champs-Élysées in the
hope not so much of seeing the Comtesse de Baloit as
of being seen by her. For I felt that half the joy I
had in my gorgeous trappings would be gone if she
could not see them and admire them too.

And as my sword clanked and my spurs jingled
while Fatima pranced and curveted under me in the
bright spring weather, my heart sang an accompani-
ment to them.

Could it be possible that the great Bonaparte might
turn the rest of his speech from jest to earnest?
Would he, perhaps, now that he had made me his
aide, trust her to me as willingly as to the chevalier?

And higher still sang my heart as Fatima, in answer
to my excited touch, leaped and bounded along the
avenue, and I remembered that night upon *La Belle
Rivière* when mademoiselle had wished that I was a
chevalier of France. Was I not one now in fact, if not
in name?

CHAPTER XXV

THE COMTESSE DE BALOIT SENDS FOR HER HUNTER

"Take a straw and throw it into the air; you may see by that
which way the wind is."

ALL my riding up and down the Champs-Élysées
was like to have been for naught. We had received orders to be in readiness to start on the morrow
for Belgium, where Bonaparte was to make his headquarters while preparing for war with England, and
still I had not seen the comtesse, and she had not seen
my beautiful regimentals.

My packing was done, my last arrangements made,
most of my good-bys said; there was nothing left to
do but to take my last ride down the avenue. And
this time not in vain! There she sat in her gorgeous
coach of scarlet and gold with the footmen and coachmen in dazzling liveries of gold lace and scarlet plush,
and beside her, not the stern duchesse this time, but a
younger woman who looked as if she might be a less
formidable guardian.

She saw me, though for a moment she did not recognize me in my new and gaudy plumage. When she
did, her eager look of welcome more than repaid me
for my fruitless rides up and down the avenue. She

375

signaled to her coachman to stop, and with a pretty
little peremptory gesture summoned me to her side.
She seemed to have no fear of the lady beside her, and
no doubt she was merely a paid companion, for she ignored her entirely, or noticed her presence only by
using English when she had anything of serious im-
port to say.

" 'T is Fatima I wish to see, sir," she said as I
drew up by her coach, my hat tucked under my arm.
She put out her little hand and gently stroked the
white star on Fatima's forehead, and the mare whinnied softly and rubbed her nose against the little
gloved hand as if to say, "I remember you well; those
were famous rides we had in old St. Louis."

"And 't is you I wish to see," I responded boldly.
"I have been looking for you for many days; why
have you deserted the Champs-Élysées?"

She looked up at me quickly, as if pleased with the
audacity of the first part of my speech, but as I finished with my question she dropped her eyes and
seemed embarrassed. In a moment she spoke in a low,
constrained voice, and in English:

"My aunt and I have had misunderstandings. She
wishes me to appear in public with a man I do not
like. In Paris that means fiancé. I will stay in my
hotel with headaches rather than ride on the avenue
beside him!" with sudden fire. Then she added with
an attempt at her old lightness:

"But I must drive on. Should it be reported to
madame that I stopped to talk to Monsieur, I might
have to suffer for it."

A sudden horror seized me.

"Mademoiselle, they do not use force?" I cried. "You are not held a prisoner?"

"No—not yet," she said slowly.

"Mademoiselle," I said, looking steadily into her eyes, "I have tried to see you to say good-by; I leave Paris to-morrow."

I saw her go suddenly white, but in a moment she spoke very calmly, and in French:

"Do you go back to America, Monsieur?"

"No, to Belgium with the First Consul: to Antwerp, I believe."

I spoke also in French, but added in English:

"Mademoiselle, if you need me, I will not go to Belgium; I will resign."

She shook her head.

"No; I am sorry you are going, but I would not have you resign. The First Consul is vindictive, they say; should you reject his favors, he may remember your St. Cloud offense."

"I care not for that!" And then I added moodily, "They will compel you to marry him."

She threw up her head in much the same fashion Fatima throws up hers when she scents conflict in the distance.

"They cannot coerce me!" she said proudly, and then she added, half playfully, half defiantly:

"They tell me I have royal blood; they shall see I know how to use my royal prerogative." She held out her hand to me and spoke again in French:

"Good-by, Monsieur, and bon voyage!"

I bent low over her hand.

"Let me stay, Mademoiselle," I whispered.

"What! and lose your beautiful uniform! 'T is too severe a test of friendship. No, no, Monsieur," with the old mocking laugh. But before I had time to resent her teasing speech, her mood had changed. She leaned far out of the carriage and threw her beautiful arm over Fatima's arching neck.

"Good-by, Fatima," she cried—"dear, dear Fatima!" And as Fatima, in answer to her caress, drew closer to her, she dropped a light kiss on her soft muzzle, leaned back in her carriage with a signal to the coachman, and rolled away.

The weeks that followed were in some respects the strangest weeks of my life, and often in memory they return to me as a confused dream. War had been declared with England, and in Antwerp, in Dunkirk, on the Loire, in every little bay and inlet that indented the coast from Brest, where a great squadron was gathered, to Boulogne, where another was getting together, ships were building of every kind: floating fortresses of wood, light pinnaces and yawls for carrying the swift van of an army, and heavy barges for the impedimenta of war. A mighty flotilla, gathering from the Scheldt to the Garonne, from Toulon and Rochefort to Calais and Antwerp, to bear a vast invading army to the shores of England.

In constant communication with the great captain, I yet saw little of him, for day and night I was kept riding over the green fields of France, through the

beautiful May and June, carrying orders, sometimes
to little inland streams where tiny yawls were building, sometimes to great city dockyards where mighty
ships were on the stays. And though these were not
the deeds of valor I had dreamed of, I began to realize what a wonderful mind was planning all these
wide-spread activities, and to understand that a great
captain must be something more than a good fighter,
and prowess on the field of battle was not all that
was required of a soldier.

Yet I began to long for the din and stir of conflict
and to see my hero, as in dreams I had often seen him,
calm and unmoved, 'midst smoke and carnage, direct-
ing with unerring genius masses of men, infantry,
cavalry, artillery, through the mazes of battle; or
himself leading a resistless charge, sword extended,
waving his men forward to victory and glory.

So when an old officer who had seen many wars told
me he had no doubt it would be two years before the
preparations for war were finished and war actually
begun, my heart sank within me. Two years of hard
work day and night and no glory! To be aide to the
First Consul was not what I had dreamed of, and my
thoughts turned longingly back to Paris and the Comtesse de Baloit. All the more did my thoughts turn
in that direction because the Chevalier Le Moyne, who
was also on the general's staff, had been for some
weeks absent from headquarters. I always studiously
avoided him if we happened to be in quarters at the
same time, and so I did not at first miss him; but
when day after day and even weeks passed without

his reporting at mess, I began to be greatly troubled. My imagination pictured him as back in Paris urging his suit to Pelagie, and I feared greatly, either that she would at last yield to his importunities, seeing no way of escape, or that some trouble would come to her if she persistently scorned him.

In the midst of my anxieties a letter was brought me from home. The ten weeks were up when I could begin to expect an answer to my uncle's letter asking my father's permission for me to take service under Bonaparte, and I tore it eagerly open, hardly knowing, since hostilities would be so long delayed, whether I most hoped that it would contain his permission or his refusal. In my haste I had not noticed that it was not my father's writing on the outside, and that made it the greater shock to find within, in my mother's dearly loved penmanship, only these few words:

"Your father is very ill; come home at once."

I had never known my father to be ill even for a day. I knew this must be no ordinary illness to cause so brief and so peremptory a summons home, and all my world seemed suddenly topsy-turvy.

I loved my father, but I had been much away from home, in school at Princeton, and in my short vacations I had found him somewhat cold and stern in manner; so that my love for him was more of reverence and honor than the tender affection I felt for my beautiful mother. None the less was my heart torn with anguish at the thought of what might befall in the long weeks before I could possibly reach his side, and how vainly I wished that I had been a better son, and shown him more of the love that was really in my heart for him.

There was no time to be lost, and my first duty was to seek the First Consul and show him my letter. He was more kind and considerate than I could have expected.

"You have my sincerest sympathy," he said. "There is no question as to your course. Your first duty is to your father. I am sorry to lose my officer whom I have found even more efficient than I had expected and for whom I predicted great glory as soon as actual war should commence. But it may be possible you will find your father entirely recovered on your arrival at home; in that case, and should you have his permission to return, your old position will be open to you."

I hardly knew how to thank him suitably and to express my regret at leaving his service, and I have no doubt I did it awkwardly enough. As I was leaving the room he called me back.

"Will you go to Paris before you sail?"

There was nothing in the question to make me blush and stammer, yet I did both.

"I must sail on the earliest packet, sir," I said; "but if one is not sailing immediately I would like your permission to return to Paris and settle my affairs there and say good-by to my aunt and uncle."

"It is no doubt the wiser course," replied Bonaparte. "In sailing from Antwerp you are liable to fall into the hands of the English in passing the Straits of Dover. From Paris you can find a ship sailing from Le Havre carrying the American flag. It will be safer, and you will save time in going by Paris. Should you decide to do so, I shall have a commission to intrust to you.''

Since the First Consul advised it, I decided on the moment, and an hour later, saddle-bags packed, my man Cæsar holding his own horse and Fatima at the door, I was ready to start, only awaiting the Consul's commission. An officer rode up and handed me a packet.

"From General Bonaparte, sir," he said; and as I opened my saddle-bags to put the packet away for safe keeping, my eye caught the directions on the wrapper.

"To be delivered to the Comtesse de Baloit, Faubourg St. Germain.''

The sight of the inscription gave me only pleasure, and I was tempted to think that the Consul had devised this commission especially to give me an opportunity of seeing the comtesse. It seemed to me an evidence of wonderful delicacy of feeling and thoughtfulness for others on the part of the great general, and I could not sufficiently admire him or be grateful to him. There was no question but that his commission would be faithfully executed the very first possible moment after my arrival in Paris.

It was early morning, the dew still on the hedges and the lark still singing his matins, as we entered the city with a stream of market-carts bringing in fresh fruits and vegetables and flowers for the early morning markets. Only working-people were in the streets:

men going to their day's labor, blanchisseuses with their clothes in bundles on their heads, cooks and maids of all work with their baskets on their arms going to the market for the day's supply of food for the family.

Crossing the Place de la Bastille, a man on horseback rode up beside us and gave us good day. He had evidently come in with the country folk and was himself without doubt a small market-gardener, for the loam of the garden was on his rough cowhide boots and his blue smock was such as a countryman wears. I thought at first there was something strangely familiar in his face, and then I remembered I had seen him the evening before at the little country inn, twenty miles out from the city, where we had spent the night. He, like us, must have started at early dawn to reach the city by seven o'clock, very like for the same reason—to take advantage of the cool of the day; and like us also, he must have had a very good horse to make that distance in that time. I glanced at his horse as the thought occurred to me, and saw that it was indeed a good horse. Coal-black, except for a white star on his forehead and one white stocking, he was powerfully built, and yet with such an easy stretch of limb as promised speed as well as endurance. I thought it a little strange that a country farmer should own a horse of such points and breeding as this one showed itself to be, and perhaps my thought appeared in my face, for the countryman answered it.

"'T is a fine horse, Monsieur, is it not?" he said.

I noticed that he spoke with a very slight lisp, but that otherwise both his language and his intonations were better than I could have expected.

"Yes," I said. "Did you breed him yourself?"

"Not exactly," he answered, "but he was bred on an estate belonging to the Comtesse de Baloit, where I work, and I have helped to train him."

He must have seen my irrepressible start when he mentioned Pelagie's name, for he looked at me curiously with something like either alarm or suspicion in his glance. I was tempted to tell him that I knew his mistress and expected to see her that very day, but I was saved from making such a foolish speech by the fellow himself.

"I am bringing him into the city for the comtesse to try," he said. "He is a very fine hunter."

"Then your mistress intends to follow the chase?" I asked, feeling a queer little pang that I did not stop to explain to myself at the thought.

"I suppose so, Monsieur, since she has sent for her hunter."

We were now well down the Rue de la St. Antoine, just where the narrow street of François-Miron comes in; and as if a sudden thought had struck him, the countryman said:

"I go this way, Monsieur; adieu," turned into the narrow street, and Cæsar and I rode on into the Rue de Rivoli, past the Hôtel de Ville, and so toward my uncle's house.

"Marsa," said Cæsar, as we turned off the Rue de Rivoli, "dat fellah had a gold belt and a little dagger

stuck in it under his smock. I seed it when I's ridin'
behind youse bof and de win' tuk and blew up his
smock-skirt.''

I believed the ''gold belt'' and the ''little dagger''
were inventions of Cæsar's, for he loved to tell wonderful tales; but none the less was I uneasy and troubled, for suppose it should be true! I liked not the
thought of a man wearing a concealed weapon going
on a plausible errand to the Comtesse de Baloit.

25

CHAPTER XXVI

THE CONSUL'S COMMISSION

" Hope tells a flattering tale,
   Delusive, vain, and hollow.
Ah! let not Hope prevail,
   Lest disappointment follow."

NOT many hours later saw me seeking admittance to the stately but dilapidated hôtel of the Comtesse de Baloit in the Faubourg St. Germain. I was determined to see Pelagie, and if possible alone, so I sent up word that a messenger from the First Consul desired to see Mademoiselle la Comtesse on business of importance. I feared, should I send up my own name, that the duchesse would not permit her to see me, but, had I known it, I could have sent no message less likely to win Pelagie's consent to an interview. It was only through a lurking suspicion of whom the messenger might be that she consented to see me.

I was ushered into a room very luxuriously furnished, but in which everything had an air of faded grandeur—as if belonging to another age. The tapestries were not only faded but rapidly growing threadbare, and the gold of the buhl furniture was peeling off in strips, and in tables inlaid with fine mosaics many of the stones were wanting. All this lack of care or evidence of poverty rather surprised me, remembering the magnificent coach and gorgeously liveried servants I had twice seen on the avenue. Then I recalled what I had often heard since coming to Paris, that the nobility of the old régime would starve and go cold at home to make the display in public they considered befitting their dignity. It seemed very sad to me, and I wondered if it could be because mademoiselle did not have enough to eat that she had seemed of late to be growing thin and pale. To me, who am both somewhat of an epicure and a valiant trencherman (and remembering the abundance she had been used to in America), nothing could seem more pitiful than to think of my little Pelagie as going hungry.

Yet when, in a few minutes, she came in, radiantly beautiful in some Frenchy flowing gown of pale rose-color and much soft lace and ribbons, no one could think of her as hungry or poverty-pinched in any way, but only as some wonderful fairy queen who dined on peacocks' tongues and supped on nectar and ambrosia.

She was greatly surprised to see me; I think she thought of me as a kind of Daniel venturing into the lion's den. But the old lioness, the duchesse, was not with her, only the same companion I had seen in the carriage on the Champs-Élysées, and I felt once more that fate smiled on me. It meant much to me, for I knew not whether I should ever see her again, and I longed greatly to have a few minutes' untrammeled conversation with her, such as I had often had in St. Louis in those days that seemed so far away.

Perhaps my eyes dwelt too eagerly upon her. I never could quite remember how beautiful she was when I was away from her, and so every time I saw her I was dazzled afresh. This time, too, I was trying to fasten every lovely curve of cheek and throat, and glowing scarlet of lips, and shadowy glory of dark eyes and waving hair, and witching little curls about white brow and neck, yes, and every knot of lace and ribbon, so firmly in my mind that I might always have the beautiful picture to look on when there was no longer any hope of seeing again the bright reality.

So absorbed was I in fixing fast in memory every little detail of the bright picture that I think I must have forgot my manners: it was only seeing the long lashes on the rose-tinted cheek that brought me to myself. I bent low over her hand and then put into it the packet the First Consul had intrusted me to give to her.

"For me? From the First Consul?" she said, in slow surprise.

"Yes," I said; "and when you have opened it, Mademoiselle, then I crave a few minutes' speech with you."

I turned and walked to one of the windows and stood looking down into the courtyard where Cæsar was holding our horses, that mademoiselle might examine its contents unobserved.

I knew not what was in the package nor the contents of the note that accompanied it, but somehow I had had a feeling (perhaps because the First Consul had seemed so kind in his manner at our last interview, or perhaps only because my hopes pointed that way) that the Consul's note was to use his influence with her in my behalf, as he had once used it for the chevalier. Therefore as I stood with my back to her, looking down into the courtyard, my eyes saw not what they were looking at, for they were filled with a vision of future happiness and I was trembling with the beauty of the vision.

"Monsieur!" I turned quickly, for the voice was cold and hard, and it fell on my heart like the sleet of early spring falling on opening buds to chill them to death. And when I turned, the Pelagie that met my gaze was the Pelagie I had first seen in Mr. Gratiot's house: eyes blazing with wrath, little teeth close set between scarlet lips, and little hands tightly clenched. My heart froze at the sight. Could the Consul's plea for me have been so distasteful to her?

"Monsieur," she repeated, every word a poniard, "how did you dare bring me such a message!"

I found no words to answer her, for if the message was what I had hoped, then I began to wonder how I had dared, though my spirit, as proud as hers, brooked not that she should take it as an insult. But she did not wait for any answer.

"You!" she said, with inexpressible bitterness. "Has wearing the First Consul's uniform so changed you from the American gentleman I once knew that you delight to humiliate a poor and helpless lady of France?"

"Mademoiselle la Comtesse," I said coldly, for still the foolish idea clung to my brain that the First Consul had wished to further my suit, and that mademoiselle had regarded it as humiliating that I should so presume, "I know not the contents of the First Consul's note, but I think la Comtesse knows I would never willingly humiliate her."

"You know not!" and she half extended the note toward me, as if to show it to me, and then drew it quickly back, a sudden change in her manner from proud anger to shrinking shame. She turned to her companion and said in a cool tone of command:

"You may wait for me, Henriette, in the blue salon; I have something to say to Monsieur."

Henriette seemed to hesitate. No doubt in France it was not permitted to see a young gentleman alone, or perhaps Henriette had instructions from the duchesse to be ever on guard when she herself could not be present. Mademoiselle saw her hesitation.

"Go!" she said haughtily, and I believe no being on earth would have dared disobey that ringing tone of command. Henriette shrank from it, and as she hastened to obey, mademoiselle added in a gentler tone:

"You may return in five minutes."

As she left the room, mademoiselle turned quickly to me, as if to lose no moment of the few she had given herself.

"Monsieur," she said, and her manner was the manner of the old Pelagie, "I hope you will forgive me for supposing for a moment that you knew the contents of the First Consul's note. I cannot show it to you, but I am going to place a great trust in you. Monsieur, I cannot stay longer in France. Between the duchesse, the chevalier, and the First Consul, I will be driven to marry the chevalier, or—worse. Ah, Monsieur, if I had never left St. Louis!''

She had spoken hurriedly, as if fearing to lose courage otherwise, but she looked not at me as she spoke, and her face was dyed with painful blushes. A horrible suspicion of the contents of that note almost froze my blood, but the next thought, that mademoiselle must fly from France, sent it rushing hotly through my veins.

"Mademoiselle," I cried impetuously, "go home with me to America."

I saw her turn pale and draw herself up proudly. I did not dream she could misunderstand me: I only thought she scorned so humble a suitor. And the thought set fire to a pride that was equal to her own.

"Mademoiselle," I said sternly, "I cannot set you upon a throne nor place a crown upon your head, but in America the wife of an honorable gentleman is a queen always, his heart is her throne, his home is her kingdom, his love is her crown."

To my amazement, she was all soft and drooping and rosy and smiling. I was ready to pick her up and fly with her that moment, so adorable was she in this mood, but she would not let me come near her.

"Monsieur," she said, looking up at me most sweetly, "to be the wife of an honorable American gentleman, it seems to me, would be great happiness;

but you have not your father's permission to marry: he would not thank you for bringing home an émigré bride.''

There came to me a sudden vision of my stern father. He would certainly think that was a matter on which he should be first consulted. He was capable of making it very unpleasant for my wife should I bring one home unannounced, and if he did not cut me off with a shilling, he might easily put me on so small an allowance as would make it impossible for me to maintain her in the luxury suited to her position. I would be glad to work for her, early and late, but I knew nothing about earning my own bread, and while I was learning to earn hers she might suffer for the comforts of life.

Mademoiselle was quick to see my embarrassment, and I suppose her pride was touched, for when she spoke it was with her old hauteur.

''It is very kind of Monsieur to think of offering me a refuge, but my plans are made.''

I hardly heard her, for I was busy with my own thoughts. I interrupted her eagerly:

''Mademoiselle, let me take you back to St. Louis and put you in Dr. Saugrain's care; then I will make all necessary arrangements with my father and come for you.''

''You did not understand me, Monsieur,'' she answered coldly; ''my plans are made: I am going to my cousin the Duc d'Enghien.''

''The Duc d'Enghien!'' I repeated, in a dazed fashion. Had I not heard that her cousin would marry her into one of the royal families of Europe? This, then, was the knell to all my hopes! This was the reason she answered me so coldly: there was something better in store for her than to be the wife of a simple American gentleman.

Well, I had never cherished any hopes; had I not told both my uncle François and the First Consul so? Ah, but had I not? Had not every moment since I had first known her been a fluctuation between hope and despair? I had told the First Consul she had not given me any reason to hope; but had she not? Did she not seem a few minutes ago almost willing to become the wife of an American gentleman? What had changed her mood?

While I was trying to collect my scattered thoughts, she spoke again, hurriedly:

"I am telling you this in great confidence, Monsieur, because I can trust you. No one must know— least of all, any one in this house."

For a moment I could not speak. I turned away to the window and looked down once more into the courtyard with unseeing eyes. But it was no beautiful vision of the future that dimmed their gaze this time: it was the black darkness of despair that blinded them like a pall.

Then I made a great resolve. The Comtesse de Baloit, the Bourbon princess, was not for such as I; but to mademoiselle, to my little Pelagie, I might still be loyal friend and offer devoted service. I turned toward her again.

"Mademoiselle," I said, "I will go with you to the

Duc d'Enghien. I will never leave you until I see you safe under the protection of your cousin."

"What! The young officer of the First Consul aiding and abetting an émigré who flees from the First Consul! It is rank treason, Monsieur!" and Pelagie smiled with something of her old merry raillery.

"I am no longer an aide, Mademoiselle," I said seriously. "I have been called home by the illness of my father, and General Bonaparte has relieved me from duty."

Her quick sympathy was sweet to see and to feel, but I did not dare linger in its warmth, for the five minutes, I knew, must be nearly up.

"Now, Mademoiselle," I said, "since I am no longer in service to the First Consul, there will be no treason in helping you in your flight—"

But she interrupted me: "No, Monsieur, it is not necessary; the Prince de Polignac has made every arrangement and will see me safe to my cousin."

"The Prince de Polignac!" I exclaimed, in surprise. "But he is in exile, and almost as much under the First Consul's ban as Cadoudal himself; how can he help you?"

In my astonishment that she should think of relying upon Polignac, whose life I believed would be forfeit if he dared to enter Paris, I had unconsciously spoken his name with raised voice. We had heretofore been speaking almost in whispers for fear of a possible listener. As I uttered his name Pelagie started and looked nervously toward the door of the blue salon.

"I beg you to be careful, Monsieur," she said anxiously. "As you say, his life would be forfeit if any one suspected his presence in Paris. I do not know that he is here, but I am hourly expecting to hear from him. There is no one in the world I would have trusted this secret to but you, and I am relying on your discretion as well as your honor."

I bowed my thanks, grateful for her confidence and ashamed of the indiscretion that might so easily have betrayed her secret. But I had not gained my point.

"You will let me help in this flight, too, Mademoiselle? It is a great peril you are undertaking, and one more sword, whose owner will lightly risk his life for you, cannot come amiss."

But she only shook her head and whispered, "It is impossible," and at that moment Henriette entered the room.

"Mademoiselle la Comtesse," she said timidly (I fear Pelagie must have been at times something of a little tyrant, to make her companion stand in such awe of her), "I have stayed away, not five minutes, but ten. I come to remind you that the hour has arrived at which Madame la Duchesse returns."

"Thanks, my good Henriette," said Pelagie, sweetly; "it is true, and I had forgotten it."

She turned quickly to me: "You must go at once, Monsieur! It is much better the duchesse should not find you here."

"And can I not see you again? Shall I never see you again?" I asked eagerly, in English.

"No, no! Do not try—I will send word," she an-

swered, also in English, and then put out her hand.
"Go, Monsieur," she said in French, "and farewell!"

I took her hand and bent low over it.

"Farewell, Mademoiselle," I said, for it cut me to
the quick that she had not said "Au revoir," as she
had said it on La Belle Rivière.

Down in the courtyard, in the act of throwing my
leg over Fatima's back, there rode under the arch of
the entrance the countryman who had overtaken us
in the morning, leading the magnificent horse he had
said was for Mademoiselle la Comtesse, and riding another. It was not strange that he should be bringing
mademoiselle her hunter, but it struck me as somewhat strange that the moment he caught sight of me
a quick scowl should darken his brow and as quickly
be cleared away : as if it had come unbidden and been
driven away from a sense of expediency. As I passed
him on the way out he touched his cap to me politely,
and the sleeve of his rough jerkin falling away a little
in the act, I thought I caught a glimpse of a lace wrist-
ruffle.

"Perhaps Cæsar was not mistaken, after all," I
said to myself; "if he wears lace ruffles at his wrist he
may well wear a gold belt and poniard at his waist.
A strange countryman, forsooth!" And a secret uneasiness that I could neither explain nor dismiss returned to me as often as he came into my thoughts.

CHAPTER XXVII

"GOOD-BY, SWEETHEART!"

"I have found out a gift for my fair."

THERE was nothing to keep me in Paris. I could not see mademoiselle; she would not let me help her in her flight. I was restless and impatient to be off. No boat would sail from Le Havre for nearly a week. It would not take a week either by horse, as Cæsar and I would go, or by the river, where my baggage was to be floated down in a small yawl in the charge of a trusty boatman. But if I stayed in Paris I would be eating my heart out; it was better to be on the way and taking the route by slow stages.

So I made the plea to my aunt and uncle that I feared some unforeseen delay might cause me to miss my ship, and with feverish haste I made all arrangements for departure that very night. To my aunt my impatience seemed only natural. She herself was greatly distressed at the news of my father's illness, and would have accompanied me to America if it had been possible.

My first act on reaching home after leaving mademoiselle had been to tear off my gorgeous uniform, with such a mingling of loathing and regret as rarely comes to a man. If my suspicions of the contents of mademoiselle's note were correct, then I could not quickly enough rid myself of every emblem of the allegiance I had once owed to the First Consul. And yet when I remembered his invariable kindness to me, the magnanimity he had shown for what must have seemed to him criminal eavesdropping, the tenderness of heart I had seen displayed more than once, the wonderful powers of the man, master alike of the arts of peace and war, the idolatry in which his soldiers held him and in which I had hitherto shared, my heart lamented bitterly that its idol should have been so shattered.

Since we had time to spare and it was now the meridian of summer, I had decided to use only the cool of evening and the early morning hours for travel, as much, I think, for the sake of sparing Fatima as Cæsar and myself. Our first stage was to be to the same little inn, twenty miles out, which we had left only that morning to come into the city. It was not, perhaps, on the most direct route to Le Havre, but a large part of the way would lead through the forests of Montmorency and Chantilly and would be pleasant riding, and the inn was almost the cleanest and most comfortable of its kind I had found in France. My weeks under Bonaparte bearing messages to every little river big enough to build a boat upon had taught me the roads well; all this northern France was like an open book to me and I would find no difficulty in cutting across from the forest of Chantilly to the banks of the Seine, if I preferred to follow its windings to Le Havre.

So the long shadows of the late afternoon saw us riding under the Porte St. Martin; at sunset we were passing the hoary Basilique of St. Denis, tomb of the kings; through the long twilight we skirted the forest of Montmorency; and by moonrise we were entering the forest of Chantilly. Not more beautiful by early dawn and dew had been this ride, than it was through lengthening shadows, and violet glow of sunset, and silvery light of moon, the peaches ripening on sunny walls, and the odors of mint and sweet-smelling herbs rising through the gathering damps of evening, the birds singing their vesper songs, and in the deep forest glades the lonely nightingale pouring out his soul to the moon.

Yet my heart was heavier. On my long ride from Antwerp, with the buoyancy of youth, I had passed through all the phases from anguished fear to the almost certitude of hope, and I had entered Paris feeling sure that I would find my father well again when I should reach America. I had entered Paris also joyous with the thought of seeing mademoiselle once more, and with the unconfessed hope that the budget I was bearing from the great Bonaparte might be the means of bringing me the crowning happiness of my life. I was leaving it now with one word ringing in my ears as the death-knell to all my hopes—Farewell!

The hour was still early and my inn but a little way off on the western borders of the forest; I would make a little detour and see the château and park and still be not too late for a good supper and a comfortable night's rest. I left the "old road" (which crossed the forest directly) at the Carrefour de la Table, where twelve roads met in an open circular space surrounding a great stone table. From there I took one leading straight to the Grille d'Honneur. We crossed a little bridge that spanned the moat, and looking down into its waters, we heard the splash of the ancient carp that filled it. Then through the Grille d'Honneur and between two stone dogs at the foot of the slope that led up to the ruins of the Grande Château. There I drew rein and looked over the beautiful domain.

At my right was the ruined château; in front of me the châtelet, in perfect preservation, apparently floating on the bosom of a silvery lake that entirely surrounded it. Beyond were the famous stables of the Great Condé, holding two hundred and sixty horses in his lifetime. Beside them was the chapel, and everywhere a network of basins and canals gleaming white under the flooding moonlight. At my back were the gloomy towers of the Château d'Enghien, built to house the guests of the Condés who overflowed the Grande Château and the châtelet; and beyond was a mass of rich foliage belonging to the Park of Sylvie.

As I gazed a thousand thoughts crowded into my mind. This was the home of mademoiselle's ancestors; it should now be the home of the Duc d'Enghien; perhaps when mademoiselle came into her own it would be hers. No doubt in these very parks she had played in infancy. Generations of grandeur, of princely splendor, were behind her. How had I dared to dream of her! How had I dared to think she would stoop to my lowly rank!

I gave Fatima's bridle to Cæsar and told him to wait for me while I walked down the green slope into the Park of Sylvie. Enchanting vistas opened before me, the moonlight filtering through arched canopies of foliage just enough to show me the way. Old tales of the Duchesse "Sylvie" and the poet-lover, condemned to death, whom she had hidden in this park and its little château floated through my mind strangely mingled with dreams of a later daughter of Montmorency.

And then suddenly I came upon something that for a moment I almost believed to be a continuation of my dreams. I had turned to my right and a new vista had opened before me, closed by the little "Château of Sylvie." On the wide lawn before it, half hidden by the shadow of the château, half in the broad moonlight, was a strange group: a carriage and what seemed to me many horses and many men. I thought for a moment I had landed upon a nest of bandits such as might easily infest a forest like this, and it would behoove me to steal silently back to the horses and make good my escape; but I caught a glimpse of petticoats: they were not bandits; they must be Gipsies.

Then as I gazed there stepped out into the full moonlight a man leading a powerful black horse with one white stocking and a white star in his forehead. I heard the man call some brief order to some one in the shadow, and there was a slight lisp in his voice. In

26

a moment I understood it all, although the man was no longer wearing a countryman's coat, but the livery of a gentleman's servant. It was Pelagie and her party fleeing to Baden and the Duc d'Enghien!

I knew not whether I would be a welcome guest or an intruder, but I knew I was not going to miss this opportunity of seeing Pelagie once more. I stepped out boldly from under the shadows of the trees into the moonlight, and in so doing came near losing my life. There was the click of a lock and the flash of a gun-barrel in the countryman's hands.

"Don't shoot, Monsieur," I cried; "it is a friend."

There was a short, sharp cry, half suppressed, and Pelagie came running out of the shadow, both hands extended and her face glowing in the moonlight.

"Is it you, Monsieur?" she cried. "How came you here?"

I suppose I answered her in some fashion. I know I took her hands in mine and looked down into her beautiful eyes, but I know not what I said. She was wearing the cap and apron and simple gown of a lady's waiting-maid, and as she saw me look curiously at it she said, with the shrug of her pretty little shoulders that I had learned to know so well in St. Louis:

"It is a fright, is it not, Monsieur? But I am no longer the Comtesse de Baloit: I am Susanne, the maid of Madame du Bois, with whom I am traveling."

Her voice had the happy ring of a child's, as if she were glad to be free, even if only for a time, from the cares of rank and position; or, perhaps more truly, glad to be away from the surveillance of the duchesse,

"Pelagie came running out of the shadow,
both hands extended"

happy that she need no longer fear the chevalier and
the First Consul. I longed to think that a part of the
gladness was in seeing me once more so unexpectedly;
but I knew this was only my foolish vanity, and I
steadied my brain by saying over to myself, "She is a
princess of Condé in her ancestral home; you are only
the son of a plain American gentleman." So I made
her such a speech as I would have made to a princess
of Condé.

"If Mademoiselle were not the Comtesse de Baloit
I could wish she were always Susanne the maid of
Madame du Bois. 'T is a bewitching costume."

It was, and she knew it, as I could see by her dancing eyes and the smile (that she vainly tried to suppress) playing hide-and-seek with the roses in her
cheek as I spoke. Being a man, I could not name each
article of her costume; but what I saw was a vision of
little ringlets escaping from under a coquettish cap,
dainty ankles that the short blue skirt did not pretend
to hide, a snowy apron that almost covered the blue
skirt, and a handkerchief demurely crossed over the
beautiful shoulders.

She turned quickly, as if to escape my gaze, and
called to the countryman: "Monsieur le Prince, this is
the friend of whom I have spoken; I want him to meet
the Prince de Polignac."

The prince came forward at once; and as we
grasped each other's hands and looked into each
other's eyes, I think he knew that he need no longer
regard me with suspicion, and I knew that here was a
man to whom I could trust even Pelagie.

We laughed a little over our first meeting, and I told him how Cæsar had detected his weapon; and then out of the shadows came other figures: Henriette, to whom, as her mistress, Madame du Bois, Pelagie gaily presented me; a man in the costume of a well-to-do bourgeois, whom they called Monsieur du Bois, but who, Pelagie whispered to me, was the prince's trusted body-servant; and Clotilde, whom I had not seen since I had seen her on La Belle Rivière, and who wept at the sight of me, a tribute to the memory of other days. Last of all there came out of the shadows my burly host of last night's inn. He had brought over to the little château a relay of fresh horses and a hamper of supper. All arrangements had been made at his inn the night before by the Prince de Polignac in the guise of a countryman; for careless Boniface as my host had seemed to be, he was devotedly attached to his old masters, the Bourbon princes, and could be trusted to the death.

It amazed me greatly that they should have accomplished this journey in a shorter time than I, and still more that they should have succeeded in getting safely out of Paris with so large a party, and I so expressed myself to the prince.

"It had been all carefully planned, Monsieur," he told me. "My man, 'Monsieur du Bois,' had a traveling-carriage waiting at a little house near the Porte St. Denis, where an old servitor of the family lives. He had passports made out for Madame and Monsieur du Bois from New Orleans, traveling with their negro servant Clotilde, and with a maid Susanne, and a man

François. Mademoiselle la Comtesse arranged to try her hunter at three o'clock in the Bois, accompanied by her companion, Henriette (who in these few weeks has become devotedly attached to the comtesse), and by the countryman who had brought her the horse and understood him more thoroughly than a groom from the stables of the duchesse would have done. At the same hour the negro maid of the comtesse strolled out into a quiet street at the rear of the hôtel, where she was met by my man and conducted to the little house near the Porte St. Denis. At a little before four we had all gathered there; by half-past four the transformation had been made and we were leaving the house, Madame du Bois and her two maids in the carriage, Monsieur du Bois on the comtesse's hunter, I on my own horse and leading the one Henriette had ridden. We had arranged to meet Pierre here with fresh horses and provisions, and spend half an hour in changing horses, resting, and supper. Your unexpected appearance, Monsieur, has alarmed me. I had thought the Park of Sylvie sufficiently secluded to insure us secrecy, but if you have found it, others may whom we would be less glad to see, and I think I will form my little company into marching order at once. The comtesse is taking it all as a grand adventure; her spirits have risen with every step away from Paris: that is the princely blood of Condé that loves deeds of daring, and I would not say a word to dampen her ardor; but we know, Monsieur, it is a serious matter, and so, though our half-hour is not quite up, I think I will order the advance."

"You are quite right, Monsieur le Prince," I replied. "My man is waiting for me with our horses in the Court d'Honneur; will you permit me to ride a little way with you?"

The prince hesitated a moment, and then in his courtliest manner he replied to my request:

"I am sure Monsieur will not misunderstand me when I say nothing could give us greater pleasure if it seemed safe. But Monsieur's size and—appearance," with a bow and a smile flattering no doubt, but discouraging, "have made him well known in France. Moreover, Monsieur's friendship for the comtesse (which does him honor) is known also, and should a pursuing party make inquiries along the road, and should our party be described with you in attendance, I fear they will be able to identify us at once."

"I understand, Monsieur le Prince," I answered, much crestfallen. And then into my slow brain there popped another question.

"But will not the negro maid Clotilde betray you also?"

"Monsieur is very astute," answered the prince. "He has touched upon our weak point, and I am going to prove my friendly regard for Monsieur by asking of him a great service. We could not leave the negress behind in Paris: the comtesse would not stir one step without her, fearing that she would be very unhappy, if not come to want and suffering in a strange city. All the way from Paris I have been revolving plans in my mind as to how best to separate her from our party. I had thought of letting Pierre take charge of her, but that would not do; for should she be discovered, that would make Pierre 'suspect,' and he would be thrown into prison for aiding and abetting the flight of the comtesse, and it would be a clue to trace us. When I saw you, Monsieur, I said, 'There is a way out of our dilemma. If Monsieur will take Clotilde back with him to America, we are safe.' "

Joy filled my heart that I was at last to be allowed to do something for the comtesse.

"Gladly, Monsieur!" I exclaimed; "and it can be very easily arranged. We will strike across country to Pontoise and the forest of St. Germain, and head off my boatman. He was to tie up for the night at a little village near Marly-le-Roi. I will find him there and put Clotilde in his wife's care. His wife accompanies him, for the voyage and to cook his meals."

The prince's gratitude seemed to me incommensurate with so small a service, and so I told him. And then another difficulty suggested itself to me.

"Monsieur le Prince," I said, "I recognized you from the hunter of Mademoiselle la Comtesse; will not perhaps others also?"

"I have thought of this, Monsieur," he said; "but it seemed even more difficult to arrange than the other. It is necessary that the comtesse should have a swift and powerful horse, for if we are pursued, she and I will take to our horses and leave the others to shift for themselves. I had thought of asking Pierre to try to find another as good as this (though for speed and endurance I do not believe he has his equal in France), but even then I should not know what to do with this

one. I could not give him to Pierre: that again would
bring him under suspicion. I should have to shoot
and bury him. However, it is too late now to make
the change; we will even have to take the risk.''

''Monsieur,'' I said slowly, for willingly as I would
make any sacrifice for mademoiselle, even to my life,
I could not lightly do that which I was about to do—
''Monsieur, I have a horse who for speed and endurance has hardly her equal in the whole world. She
knows Mademoiselle la Comtesse well and will do her
bidding as she does mine. I will change horses with
you. The comtesse shall have my chestnut mare and
I will take her black beauty.''

The prince did not know that this was a far greater
sacrifice on my part than taking charge of Clotilde
had been, yet he knew a man loves his own mare well,
and in so far he appreciated the service and thanked
me for it.

But the matter of separating Clotilde from her mistress had to be broached to mademoiselle, and the
prince begged me to undertake the difficult task. All
the time while the prince and I had been holding our
conversation together aside from the others, she had
been exploring the purlieus of the little château with
frequent exclamations of delight, not one of which
fell unheeded on my ears, although I was deep in consultation. Now she came running up to me joyously.

''Monsieur, Monsieur,'' she exclaimed, ''I have
found the little arbor where I used to take my dolls
and play at housekeeping! Ah, how well I remember
it! How often I have thought of it! And how little

I ever expected to see it again!" and her eyes were as bright and as soft as the waters of the little lake stretching from our feet to the Grille d'Honneur and shining in the misty moonlight. I knew how quickly those eyes could change from dewy softness to lightning flashes, and it is not to be wondered at that I plunged into my subject with nervous haste.

"Mademoiselle," I said (and I thought the prince liked not the lack of formality in my address), "the Prince de Polignac has assigned to me an unpleasant duty; it is to tell you that we find it necessary for your safety to take away Clotilde."

Perhaps I was too abrupt; at any rate, much as I had expected a tempest I was not prepared for the tornado that ensued.

"Take away my Clotilde!" she interrupted. "Never! never! never!" And then there followed a torrent of tears mingled with reproaches as she threw herself upon Clotilde's breast—the breast she had wept upon since she was a babe of six. But Clotilde's cries were stormier than her mistress's: she literally lifted up her voice and wept. The prince was the picture of distress and dismay: there was danger that the sound of weeping might penetrate to unfriendly ears. Mademoiselle in tears was ever more formidable to me than an army with banners, but there was no help for it; I took my courage in my hand.

"Mademoiselle la Comtesse," I said sternly, "you are causing the Prince de Polignac great distress. You are in danger any moment of betraying his retreat to an enemy, and if he is captured, his life is forfeit, as you know.''

I spoke thus to arouse her from a contemplation of her own woes to his danger, for well I knew her generous soul would respond at once to such a plea, and I was not mistaken. Her sobs ceased instantly and she stilled Clotilde with a word; then she turned and looked at me quietly while I went on with what I had to say:

"It is to anticipate the danger of such discovery that we remove Clotilde, who, being almost the only negress in France, would betray your identity at once. I will take her with me to America, and from Philadelphia I will send her under safe escort to Dr. Saugrain in St. Louis, and when you are safely established in your own home you can send for her again.''

I think the thought of seeing St. Louis once more half consoled Clotilde for the parting, though she was a faithful creature and loved her mistress, and would have followed her to the ends of the earth. I know it helped to console Pelagie, for it was the thought of leaving Clotilde alone and unprotected in a foreign country that disturbed her most.

But all this had taken much time, and the half-hour the prince had allowed for rest was more than up. They had had their supper, the carriage-horses had been changed, the saddle-horses had been fed and watered, and the prince was in feverish haste to be off. I ran swiftly to the Court d'Honneur, where I had left Cæsar, and found him wondering anxiously what had kept me so long. He had fed and watered both horses and was now letting them crop a little of the luxuriant grass at their feet. I did not stop for explanations, but bidding him follow me with his horse, I led Fatima by a shorter and more direct route straight from the Grille d'Honneur to the little château. I found the carriage with "Monsieur and Madame du Bois"; the coachman and outriders had already started. Pierre had set out a luncheon on the little stone table for Cæsar and me (for since we were not to go to his inn there was no prospect for supper for us), and was getting the two carriage-horses ready to take them back with him. Clotilde was silently weeping and Pelagie was trying to comfort her. I led Fatima straight to Pelagie.

"Mademoiselle," I said, "the Prince de Polignac permits me to give you a farewell present. Will you take Fatima and keep her for me? She will bear you to your destination, I believe, more safely and more surely than any horse in the world."

"Oh, Monsieur, Monsieur!" she said, and then could say nothing more, her little chin quivering piteously. I could not bear to see it. I had motioned to Cæsar to put on Fatima the side-saddle lying on the grass, and now I said,

"Let me put you on her back," and bent to lift her; but she drew back.

"Oh, no, no, Monsieur!" she cried. "I know why you do it, and I know what a sacrifice it is to you. I cannot let you give up Fatima!"

"Then you are depriving me of a great happiness," I softly answered. "I had hoped you would take her

and keep her and love her. It would be a great comfort to me in distant America to think of you as being
kind to her sometimes for the sake of old St. Louis
memories.''

I looked steadily into her eyes.

"Mademoiselle, may I put you on her back?''

She bowed her head, and I lifted her to her seat, put
her foot in the stirrup and the bridle in her hand.
Then I threw my arm over Fatima's neck.

"Good-by, Sweetheart,'' I whispered, "take good
care of your mistress,'' and kissed her on the white
star on her forehead. Still with my arm over her neck
I reached up my hand to mademoiselle.

She put her hand in mine, and I kissed it as I had
kissed it when she chose me her king; then I lifted my
eyes and looked straight into hers.

"Good-by, Mademoiselle, and au revoir,'' I said,
and dropped her hand.

She could not answer for the same piteous quivering of the chin, but her lips formed "Au revoir''; and
then she turned Fatima and rode slowly under the
leafy arch that led through a long tunnel of foliage,
due east.

"Monsieur,'' said the prince, and I started; for a
moment I had forgotten his existence.

He had withdrawn courteously while I was making
my adieus with mademoiselle, busying himself with
little preparations for departure. Now he had
mounted and drawn his horse to my side.

"Monsieur, you have taught me to honor and admire all American gentlemen. If there is any service

I can ever do you, I hope you will give me the opportunity of showing you how much I appreciate the great service you have done us this night.''

''Monsieur le Prince,'' I answered quickly, too eager with my own thoughts to thank him for his kind words, ''there is one kindness you can show me that will more than repay me for anything I have ever done or ever could do. Write me of mademoiselle's safe arrival when you reach Baden. I will give you my address,'' and I tore a leaf from my memorandum-book, wrote my address upon it, and thrust it into his hand.

''It is a small commission, Monsieur,'' he answered, ''but I will be most happy to execute it.''

He grasped my hand, said ''Au revoir,'' and cantered quickly away after mademoiselle.

I watched them riding side by side under the leafy dome until their figures were lost in the darkness, mademoiselle still with bent head, and he with his face turned courteously away as if not to seem to see should she be softly crying. And if there was for a moment in my heart a jealous envy that he should ride by mademoiselle's side and I be left behind, I put it quickly away, for I knew him to be a noble and courteous gentleman, and one to whose honor I could trust the dearest thing in life.

CHAPTER XXVIII

EXIT LE CHEVALIER

> "The King of France with forty thousand men,
> Went up a hill, and so came down agen."

CLOTILDE, Cæsar, and I had ridden late into the night before we had reached the little village on the Seine where my boatman, Gustave, was to tie up. But it was moonlight and we rode through a beautiful country dotted with royal châteaus,—the birthplaces of illustrious kings,—and I had my thoughts, and Clotilde and Cæsar had each other: for Cæsar was the first of her kind Clotilde had seen since coming to France, and much as she might enjoy the attentions of footmen in gorgeous liveries, after all they were only "white trash," and she loved best her own color. Clotilde was rapidly becoming consoled; and though she only spoke creole French, and Cæsar only English, save for the few words he had picked up since coming to Paris, they seemed to make themselves very well understood.

So the ride had not been so tedious as it might have been. And when we had found Gustave's boat tied to the bank and had routed up him and his wife, and delivered Clotilde into their care (and their admiration

414

and awe of the black lady was wonderful to see), and
Cæsar and I had hunted up a fairly comfortable inn
and had two or three hours of sleep, we were all quite
ready to start on again.

Feeling that Clotilde was a sacred trust, I was anxious both for her safety and for her welfare, and thus
it was that the early morning found me following the
windings of the Seine by a little bridle-path on its
banks, hardly twenty feet from Gustave's boat drop-
ping down with the tide. Gustave's wife was in the
forward part of the boat, preparing breakfast for the
three, and the savory odor of her bacon and coffee was
borne by the breeze straight to my nostrils on the high
bank above her. Gustave himself was in the stern of
the boat, lazily managing the steering-oar and waiting for his breakfast, and incidentally grinning from
ear to ear at Cæsar, riding a pace behind me and casting longing glances at the thatched roof of the little
boat's cabin, whence issued in rich negro tones the creole love-song Yorke had sung to Clotilde on the Ohio
boat:

> "Every springtime
> All the lovers
> Change their sweethearts;
> Let change who will,
> I keep mine."

I had straitly charged Clotilde that she must keep
herself closely concealed within the cabin, but I had
said nothing to her about also keeping quiet. Now I
was idly thinking that perhaps I had better give her
instructions upon that point also, when down the

stony road some three feet higher than the bridle-path, and separated from it by a bank of turf, came the thunder of hoofs. I glanced up quickly. A little party of horsemen, five or six in number, were dashing down the road toward us, and in the lead was the Chevalier Le Moyne! At sight of us they drew rein, and the chevalier, looking down on me (for the first time in his life), brought his hat to his saddle-bow with a flourish.

"Good morning, Monsieur. I hear you are off for America."

"Good morning," I answered coolly, merely touching my own hat. "You have heard correctly"; and I wished with all my heart that I had had time to tell Clotilde to keep still, for up from the boat below, louder and clearer than ever, it seemed to me, came the refrain of her foolish song:

> "Tous les printemps,
> Tous les amants
> Changent de maîtresses;
> Qu'ils changent qui voudront,
> Pour moi, je garde la mienne."

The chevalier was listening pointedly.

"An old song, Monsieur, that I have often heard in St. Louis. And the voice, too, I think is familiar. It is the black maid of the Comtesse de Baloit, is it not? Perhaps her mistress is with her; if so, our quest is at an end."

"What do you mean, Monsieur le Chevalier!" I exclaimed, affecting virtuous indignation, and feeling a little of it, too, for I liked not the chevalier's manner.

"You have heard, I suppose," he answered, with a light sneer, "that the comtesse has disappeared from Paris. At almost the same moment it was announced that monsieur had started for America, and some of the comtesse's friends thought it not impossible that they had gone together. From the warbling of that nightingale yonder I judge they were not far wrong."

Not until this moment had it occurred to me that any one would connect the flight of the comtesse with my departure, and I hardly knew whether I was more ragingly angry at the thought or secretly glad. There was no question as to my state of mind toward the chevalier. That he should speak in such a light and sneering tone of any lady, but most of all that he should so speak of the loveliest lady on earth, was not to be borne. Yet I was glad, for some reasons, that such a mistaken surmise had arisen: it would throw pursuit off the track until Pelagie was well on her way to the German frontier, and the truth would come out later and my lady not suffer in her reputation (which indeed I could not have endured).

So instead of giving free vent to the anger that raged in my heart, as I longed to do, I thought it wise to dally with the chevalier and keep him as long as possible on the wrong scent, for every moment of delay to the chevalier was setting mademoiselle farther on her way.

"Your news, Monsieur," I said, "is most astonishing, but your insinuations also most insulting to a lady whose honor and reputation shall ever be my dearest care."

27

Now the chevalier was five to one (for I could not count upon Cæsar for fighting, as I might have counted upon Yorke). I do not say that that fact made the chevalier more bold or less careful in his manner, but I certainly think that had we been man to man he would not have answered as he did.

"Your virtuous indignation is pretty to see, Monsieur," he answered; "but I have the warrant of the republic to search whatever domains I may suspect of harboring the comtesse, and I think I will use my rights on yonder boat, where I see the face of her maid at the window."

I glanced quickly at the boat. Sure enough, in the little square of glass that formed the window of the cabin was framed Clotilde's black face. And her nose (already broad enough) being flattened against the glass, and her eyes rolling wildly with curiosity and fear as she gazed at the party of armed horsemen on the bank, she made a ludicrous picture indeed. I would have liked to laugh heartily but that it was my rôle to display chagrin and anxiety rather than a careless levity.

"Monsieur," I said seriously, "you are quite right: that is Clotilde, the maid of Mademoiselle la Comtesse. I was requested last evening to take her back to America and return her to her friends in St. Louis. It will always be my greatest pleasure to render the comtesse any service within my power, and I did not stop to question why she wished to get rid of her maid."

"Your explanation is most plausible, Monsieur,"—

the chevalier's tone was intentionally insulting, and, but that I had mademoiselle's interests more at heart than my own sensitive self-esteem, would have been hard to brook,—"but since I hold a warrant of search, if Monsieur permits, I will do myself the honor of visiting his boat."

Now I cared not at all whether the chevalier visited the boat or not, knowing well he would not find the comtesse there. My only anxiety was to temporize as long as possible and keep him still suspicious of my complicity with mademoiselle's flight, that she might profit by his delay in discovering the true scent. So I answered sternly:

"Monsieur, that boat is for the time being United States territory. You step upon its planks without my consent at your peril. I will at once report the matter to our minister at Paris, Mr. Livingston, and if a war between the United States and France is the result, you will have to give an account to the First Consul of your acts which caused that war."

I was not enough of a diplomat to know whether I was speaking within my rights or not, but I trusted to the chevalier being no better informed than I, and at the best I was but speaking against time. The effect of my speech was all that I could have desired. The chevalier looked immediately crestfallen, and turned to consult with his comrades. For full five minutes (I could have wished it ten times five) they carried on a conference that at times appeared to be heated, though always low-toned. Then the chevalier turned to me again, and his manner was no longer insulting, but of such respect as is due one gentleman from another.

"Monsieur," he said, "perhaps I have no right to *demand* that I be allowed to search a boat belonging to an American gentleman, but if Monsieur will permit me to do so he will oblige me greatly, and it will be the means of clearing him at once of suspicions that may have unjustly accrued to him."

There was no wisdom in delaying longer.

"Since Monsieur puts it in that way," I said, "I can have no object in refusing his request. I shall have to ask you, however, that you wait a few minutes until I step aboard and warn Gustave and his wife of the purpose of your visit, lest they be unnecessarily alarmed."

The chevalier showed that he liked not the last part of my speech. He no doubt thought that my purpose in going aboard first was to find a secure hiding-place for the comtesse. However, he had no alternative but to acquiesce. My real purpose was to warn Gustave and his wife that on no account were they to betray at what hour or where Clotilde had come aboard. She was to have come aboard at Paris at four o'clock the day before; and they, having no inkling of the true state of the case, but suspecting, I believe, some intrigue between the "dark lady" and her lovers, sympathetically promised implicit obedience. With Clotilde I was even more strenuous. Her story must agree with Gustave's: she had boarded the boat in Paris at four of the afternoon; but especially was she to know nothing of her mistress's plans—why or where she had gone. With her I appealed to her love for her mistress, and warned her that the comtesse's liberty, possibly her life, might depend upon her discretion. With the others a promise of liberal rewards if they proved true, and dire threats should they betray me, I believed secured their fidelity.

I had had Gustave tie the boat to the bank before boarding it myself; I now invited the chevalier and his friends to come aboard. Leaving two of their comrades to hold their horses, the three others climbed down the bank and hastened to comply with my invitation. As they did so I saw Cæsar dismount, tie his own horse and mine securely to two saplings, and clamber up the bank beside the horsemen. I thought his motive was probably to take advantage of this opportunity to stretch his legs, and perhaps also to indulge his curiosity with a nearer view of the French gentlemen, and I saw no reason to interfere—especially as the two gentlemen, young blades whom I knew by sight, not only offered no objections, but began at once to amuse themselves with his clownish manners and outlandish speech.

Of course the chevalier's quest was futile, as also was his examination of his three witnesses. They all stuck to their text,—the embarkation of Clotilde at four o'clock on the afternoon previous in Paris,—and Clotilde was as stupid as heart could desire, professing absolute ignorance of her mistress's plans, and knowing only that she herself was being sent home to America because she was homesick; and with a negress's love of gratuitous insult when she thinks she is safe in offering it, she added in her creole dialect:

"De Lord knows, I 's sick o' white trash anyhow. I 's mighty glad to be gittin' back to a country ob ladies and gen'lemen."

The chevalier's two companions laughed, but the chevalier looked perplexed.

"Monsieur," he said, with an air of exaggerated deference, "I have discovered nothing on your boat, either by search or by examination of the witnesses, that can implicate you in any way with the flight of the Comtesse de Baloit. But will you permit me to ask you one important question? How does it happen that you are not riding Fatima, and that you are riding the horse which answers exactly to the description of the one the comtesse was riding when she disappeared?" and the chevalier could not quite keep the tone of triumph out of his voice as he propounded his question. I had been expecting it, and I was prepared for it. I should have been much disappointed if he had not asked it.

"Monsieur," I answered, "Fatima met with a serious accident just after leaving Paris. I was obliged to leave her in the hands of a veterinary surgeon on the outskirts of St. Denis, who has also a small farm connected with his establishment for the care of sick horses. He promised me to take the best of care of her and to return her to me in America as soon as she was sufficiently recovered. I bought this horse from a dealer to whom the surgeon directed me. I cannot say whether it resembles the horse on which the Com-

tesse de Baloit left Paris; I did not see the comtesse
when she left Paris.''

Which was the only truth in my statement; but I
did not for a moment consider that I had told a lie,
but only that I had employed a ruse, perfectly per-
missible in war, to throw the enemy off the track. He
snatched at the bait.

''Will Monsieur give me the address of that horse-
dealer?''

''With pleasure, as nearly as I am able,'' and thereupon I described minutely a place in St. Denis that
never existed. But St. Denis was only four miles this
side of Paris, and should the chevalier go all the way
back to find out from the mythical horse-dealer where
he had procured my horse, much valuable time would
be lost and mademoiselle would, I hoped, be beyond
all risk of being overtaken.

By one little artifice and another we had already
managed to delay them for a good three quarters of
an hour, and now, by an apparently happy accident,
as long a delay again was promised. A great noise of
shouting and trampling of horses' hoofs arose on the
bank above us.

We looked up and saw the five horses plunging
frantically, with the two Frenchmen uttering excited
cries as they tried to hold them, and Cæsar doing
his share in trying to hold the horses and more than
his share in making a noise. As we looked, one of the
horses broke away and started up the road toward
Paris. The two Frenchmen dashed wildly in pursuit, each man leading a horse with him, and Cæsar

running on behind gesticulating madly, and bellowing at the top of his lungs.

I had taken advantage of the excitement of the fracas to slip from the post the rope that held us to the bank. We glided gently away down the river, with no one (unless it might have been Gustave, but he said nothing) noticing that we were moving until we were many yards below our mooring-place. The anger of the chevalier and his friends when they discovered it knew no bounds. Gustave was full of apologies for his carelessness, as he called it; I was dignified.

"Gustave," I said severely, "make a mooring as quickly as possible, that Monsieur le Chevalier and his friends may rejoin their horses."

Gustave made all haste apparently, but without doubt he fumbled, and we were some two or three hundred yards farther down the river before we were finally tied to the bank.

"Good-by, Messieurs," I said politely as the three hastened to leap ashore. "I trust you will have no difficulty in recovering your horses."

They stayed not upon the order of their going, as Mr. Shakspere says, but scrambled up the bank and on to the hot and stony road, and the sun, now well up in the sky, beating strongly on their backs, they started at a round pace toward Paris, their horses by this time out of sight around a distant bend in the road.

Cæsar had given up the pursuit and returned to where he had tied our horses. I signaled to him to bring them down the river, and mounting his and leading mine, he was soon at our mooring-place.

Riding down the soft turf of the shady bridle-path a few minutes later, I heard Cæsar chuckling behind me. I turned in my saddle:

"What is it, Cæsar?"

"I done it, Marsa!"

"Did what, Cæsar?"

"Done mek dat hoss run away. I put a burr un'er his girth. Den when he plunged I cotched de bridle and let him loose. He, he, he! Hi, hi, hi!" and Cæsar rolled in his saddle in convulsions of mirth, while the shore echoed to his guffaws.

I looked at him in astonishment for a moment. Then he had planned it all: tying the two horses, clambering up to the road, making himself the jest of the two Frenchmen, and all the time the burr concealed in his hand, no doubt, waiting his chance.

"Cæsar, you are a general!" I said. "Yorke could not have done better." And then, his mirth being contagious, I threw back my head and laughed as long and as loud as he.

I turned in my saddle once more and looked up the road. Through the hot sun plodded the three figures: the chevalier with bent head and, I doubted not, with gnashing teeth. I waved my hand toward him and called, though he could neither see nor hear:

"Good-by, Chevalier Le Moyne; this cancels a few debts!"

I have never seen him since.

CHAPTER XXIX

UNDER THE OLD FLAG

" And many an eye has danced to see
That banner in the sky."

IT was in the early days of March, some eight
months later, that the big barge in which I had
come down the Ohio, and thus far on the Mississippi,
put me ashore at New Madrid with my saddle-bags
and my horse Bourbon Prince; for so I had promptly
named the black beauty for whom I had exchanged
my chestnut mare. He could never quite take the
place of Fatima in my affections, but I had grown
very fond of him: partly for his virtues, for he was
a thoroughbred of famous lineage, and partly, I have
no doubt, because he had once belonged to mademoiselle.

Of mademoiselle I had not heard for many months.
I had arrived at home in the late summer, to find my
father a physical and almost a mental wreck from
the stroke of paralysis that had laid him low nearly
three months before. Yet I had never loved my
strong, stern father in the prime of manhood, managing great business enterprises, occupying places of
honor and responsibility in the State, as I loved this

feeble and broken old man with the face and the manner of a little child. As the weeks went on and he gradually grew able to move about, it was my pride and my joy to walk slowly down Chestnut Street, my father leaning heavily on my arm, and looking up into my face to comment with childish delight upon whatever pleased him in the streets.

I had had to assume, to the best of my ability, his heavy business responsibilities, and the charge of his great properties, and but that my mother was herself a fine business woman and thoroughly informed on my father's affairs I might have made shipwreck of it all. It was not the life I had chosen for myself, but it lay so directly in the path of duty there was no escaping it, and it kept every moment so fully occupied there was no time left for brooding over private troubles.

I had received a letter from the Prince de Polignac about two weeks after my return home, telling me of the safe arrival in Baden of the Comtesse de Baloit. It was a very courteous letter, thanking me once more for the great services I had rendered them on that eventful night in the Chantilly parks, and inclosing a pleasant message of acknowledgment from the Duc d'Enghien for the kindness shown his cousin the countess. Mademoiselle had added a line in her own writing:

"Fatima is well, and I love her for the sake of dear old St. Louis.

PELAGIE."

To most people that might seem a very common-place little message; to me those sixteen words were the most wonderful ever written. I twisted and turned them until each one became a volume of tender sentiments, and the little signature "Pelagie" almost too sacred to be looked at, and only to be kissed, shut up in my own room in the dark, or with none but the moon to see.

I had replied to the prince's letter immediately, sending a courteous message to the duke and a special one to Pelagie about Clotilde, whom I had sent under safe escort to St. Louis. But although I had intimated to the prince that it would give me very great pleasure to hear occasionally of the welfare of the countess, I never heard from any of them again.

This, of course, was an especial grief to me on Pelagie's account, but also it touched me a little that the prince should so soon have forgotten me and what he was pleased to term my "great services" to him, for I had been strongly attracted to him by his noble bearing and chivalrous protection of mademoiselle. Often, in thinking of them,—he a noble young prince of great manly beauty and endowed by nature with all charming and lovable qualities; she the most exquisite of womankind,—I thought it would be strange indeed if in the intimate companionship of that long ride together they had not become so deeply interested in each other as to forget the existence of a young American gentleman three thousand miles away.

When in the winter there came news of the Cadoudal plots against the life of Napoleon, in which the young Prince de Polignac and his older brother the duke were involved; that both brothers had been arrested, tried, and condemned to death; and, later, that Napoleon had granted them a free pardon, I could easily believe that other interests than love and marriage had so absorbed the prince as to make him forgetful of a distant acquaintance.

On the heels of this appalling news, which shook the world and which yet left me glad and grateful that the chivalrous young prince had been saved from the ignominious death of an assassin, there came a letter to me from Captain Clarke, written in St. Louis, inviting me to join the expedition of discovery and exploration which Mr. Meriwether Lewis and he were to conduct up the Missouri River and across the mountains.

Few duties have come to me in life more difficult to perform than the writing of that letter declining the invitation. It was the life I longed for, to be had for the taking, and an expedition of such kind under the leadership of two men like my captain, whom I still adored, and Mr. Meriwether Lewis, whom I greatly admired, was the strongest temptation that could be presented to me.

But I knew well it was not for me. It would, no doubt, be a year or two in the accomplishing, with many hazards to life and limb, and I was now the virtual head of the family, with mother and sisters and invalid father all looking to me for protection and guidance and comfort.   No, it was not to be thought of.

Without consulting any one I sent my answer, but I suppose my face was an open book to my dear mother, and in some moment of abstraction I had forgotten to be cheerful and so betrayed that something was troubling me.   At any rate, she came to my room one night, and there, in the way that mothers have, she beguiled my secret from me.   She agreed with me that it would never do in my father's state of health to join such an expedition, but she was greatly distressed for what she called my disappointment, though I tried to assure her it was not enough to think about.

Now mothers have a way of finding a salve for every hurt.   I suppose it is a talent God has given them, that this world may be a pleasanter place for living in, and that the rugged path we have to tread through it may be smoother and pleasanter to our feet. (Though I hope no one will think because I have said this that I am one of those long-faced people who think this world a vale of woes to be traversed as quickly as possible, looking neither to the right nor to the left, lest they see something to please their eyes. I have ever found it a pleasant world, and my path through it of exceeding interest, with some sorrows and many difficulties to test one's mettle and add to the zest of living; but also with many wonderful and beautiful things lying all along the path, that God has placed there that one may stop and enjoy them and rest by the wayside.)

Now the salve my mother found for this hurt was one to my especial liking.

"Though you could not be gone from home two or three years, my son," she said, "a matter of two or three months could make no great difference to any one; why not go out to St. Louis, see your friends there, and help the expedition get under way?"

My heart gave a great leap. "And get news of mademoiselle from Dr. Saugrain," I said to myself; but then I hesitated. Would my father miss me too sadly? for he had seemed to lean upon me much for comfort and companionship. When I expressed my fears to my mother, she hesitated also, but we both finally agreed we would leave it to her to broach the matter to my father, and if it seemed to distress him too greatly, we would say nothing more about it.

To my surprise, he was almost more eager for it than my mother. It need not have surprised me, for even in the old days my father, though stern, had never been selfish, and now all the unselfishness of his nature had seemed to grow strong with his feebleness.

Thus it was that I stood once more on the shores of the Great River. Had my impatience permitted me to wait a little longer at Pittsburg, I might have found a boat going all the way to St. Louis, but I had rather take the ride of nearly a hundred and fifty miles on Bourbon (for so I had shortened his name) than to spend a day in idle waiting. A barge going to New Orleans (New Orleans had been under our flag since the twentieth of December, and the river was teeming with craft bearing our merchandise to the once prohibited market) took me on board and put me ashore at New Madrid in the early morning, and I lost not a moment's time in getting started on my northward way.

The spring was early that year, and in the warm and sheltered valley, lying open to the south, where New Madrid nestles, the orchards were already a pink and white glory, and in the forest glades the wild azaleas and the dogwood were just ready to burst into bloom. Riding under leafy archways of tall trees garlanded with wild vines, or through natural meadows dotted with clumps of shrubbery, as if set out by the hand of man for a park, where the turf was like velvet under Bourbon's feet; crossing little streams that a sudden rush of headwater from the hills had swollen to dangerous torrents, or other streams that backwater from the Great River had converted into inland lakes; the air sweet with the fragrance of the wild crab and blossoming grape; woodthrush and oriole, meadow-lark and cardinal-bird, making the woods ring with their melodies—this ride through Upper Louisiana in the early springtime was one long joy to eye and ear and nostril. Farther north the spring was less advanced, only little leaves on the trees, and for flowers a carpet, sometimes extending for miles, of creamy-white spring-beauties, streaked with rosy pink, laid down for Bourbon's feet to tread upon; and for birds the modest song-sparrow and bluebird, earliest harbingers of spring.

I stayed the first night in Cape Girardeau (and

thought of the chevalier in hiding for weeks among the Osages near by) ; the second night I spent with the Vallés in Ste. Genevieve. I had known young François Vallé in St. Louis the winter before, and meeting me on the street as I rode into town, he carried me off at once to his father's house with true Louisiana hospitality—a hospitality that welcomed the coming but did not speed the parting guest. I found it hard work to get away the next morning, with such friendly insistence did they urge me to remain for a visit, seeming to feel also that I was putting a slight upon their quaint old town—the oldest in Upper Louisiana—by so short a stay.

But I was impatient to be on my way, and my impatience grew as I neared St. Louis. A long day's ride brought me toward evening to the banks of the Maramec, full to the brim of its high banks with backwater from the Mississippi. I thought, at first, I would have to swim it, but, fortunately, I spied a horn hanging from the limb of a sycamore above my head, and I knew enough of the ways of this frontier country to know that a horn by a river-bank meant a ferry. So I blew it lustily, and in five minutes there appeared from under the overhanging trees of the opposite bank a flatboat, paddled by an old man, who not only ferried Bourbon and me safely across dry-shod, but persuaded me to spend the night with him in his little cabin; for the night was coming on cloudy and dark, and there were still nearly twenty miles to ride, and swollen streams to cross that might mean trouble in the dark. He had not the great

28

house of the Vallés, with troops of slaves to wait on us and an abundance of frontier luxuries (for Mr. François Vallé, Sr., was the richest man in all that country) but his hospitality was as genuine. For the ferriage he took money, since that was his business; for the night's lodging and supper and breakfast he would have none of it. True, my bed was only a bearskin on the hard floor, and my supper and breakfast were the same,—a slice of bacon and a bowl of hominy,—but such as he had he gave me of his best.

In the early dawn I had a plunge in the Maramec for bath (and its waters had the icy tang of the melting snows on the distant mountains), and then I made a careful toilet, for in a few hours I would see my old friends in St. Louis, and, at thought of the merry glances from bright eyes I would soon be meeting, my heart sank within me that Pelagie's would not be among them.

As I neared St. Louis, every step of the way was full of reminders of her. Crossing La Petite Rivière, I thought of the day of the picnic on Chouteau's Pond, and involuntarily I listened for the call of the whippoorwill. But instead there was the happy song of the spring birds filling the woods that crested the banks, and my heart grew lighter in response to their joyous melodies.

I entered the town by the lower entrance, leading through the stockade on to the Rue Royale, for I was of a mind to ride through the streets of the town and see whom I should chance to meet before presenting myself at Dr. Saugrain's.

I had advanced no great distance when I saw coming to meet me a splendid procession: young men and maidens, parents and children, the whole population of the town, I should think, in gala array, and singing as they came.

I was overwhelmed at the prospect of such honor accorded me, and greatly touched, too, that my old friends should welcome me back so gladly, but I was in a quandary what to do: whether it would be more dignified to stay Bourbon in the middle of the road and await their approach, or whether to advance to meet them.

It puzzled me greatly, also, that they should have known the exact moment of my arrival, for although both Dr. Saugrain and Captain Clarke knew of my intended visit, they could hardly have calculated to such a nicety not only the day but the very hour of my entry into town. It must be that pickets had been stationed to descry my approach from a distance and give the signal.

Still puzzling my brains over the wonder of it all, and hardly knowing whether to feel more proud or more frightened at the honor intended me, and wishing with all my heart that I had known of it that I might have arrayed myself in a costume befitting the occasion, I slowly drew near the procession, and the procession drew near me.

Then suddenly I discovered what nothing but my domtiferous vanity had prevented me from discerning from the first: this was a religious procession bearing the banners of the church and singing Aves and Te Deums. I had known such processions before in St. Louis on saints' days, and always headed by the two most beautiful maidens in the town, bearing silver plates, who, as the procession drew up to the church, stood on either side of the door holding the plates to receive alms. I drew Bourbon to one side of the road and waited.

Yes, there were the two beautiful maidens with the silver plates, and I was not surprised to see that one was Mademoiselle Chouteau; and as she drew near she could not resist a saucy look of recognition in her dancing eyes, entirely out of character in the leader of a religious procession. I smiled back at her, my heart already growing warmer and lighter with her friendliness, and then I glanced at the other: a wavy mass of soft, dark hair, little ringlets about white neck and brow, lips like a scarlet pomegranate blossom, and long, black lashes lying on an ivory cheek, where the pale rose was fast turning to crimson under my gaze.

It was Pelagie! Her cheek told the tale that she knew I was looking at her, yet not once did she lift her eyes and look at me. I wonder that my heart did not break through my breast, so great a bound it made when I discovered her, and then all the blood in my body flowed back upon it, and I sat on Bourbon as one carved in marble, while friends and acquaintances passed by and smiled up at me in kindly welcome. Not until Josef Papin left the ranks and came up to me with outstretched hand could I recover myself and begin to feel alive again, with the blood slowly running back in its courses and tingling in my finger-tips.

"Come," he said, when the first greetings were over, "tie your horse to the tree, and we will fall in at the end of the line and go up to the church together. This is no saint's day, as you might think, but we are to have mass for the last time under the old rule. The United States troops come over to-day from Cahokia and take possession."

This was wonderful news to me, and I could not but feel a great sympathy with him, for he spoke with a voice that faltered. What would it not have meant to me if my own city of Philadelphia were being transferred to the rule of France or Spain!

On our way he told me what my soul most longed to hear: how mademoiselle came to be in St. Louis.

Her cousin, the Duc d'Enghien, had begun to feel that his home was no longer a safe place for her, for Bonaparte's spies were watching him, and he felt that though Baden was neutral territory he might at any moment be arrested and thrown into prison. That would leave Pelagie entirely unprotected, and he had begun to consider some other safer retreat for her. When mademoiselle found that she was to be sent away from Ettenheim, she begged that she might return to St. Louis, the only place she had known as home, and to the people she loved, who had been to her kindred and friends. It was only after much pleading that the duke had been persuaded to let her go so far from home again, but mademoiselle's heart was set on it.

"And," said Josef Papin, "as we both know, when she will, she will; I defy any man to gainsay her. She arrived two weeks ago by way of New Orleans, with a Monsieur and Madame Dubois, newly married, I believe, who were coming over to America to settle."

"Monsieur and Madame Dubois!" I said, in some excitement.

"Yes; do you know them?" asked Josef, curiously.

"I am not sure. I may have met them; I met a Monsieur and Madame Dubois once at Chantilly near Paris," I answered carelessly, "but very likely they are not the same."

"No, they could not be," answered Josef, "for they were married only just before leaving for America."

And then there was no chance to say anything more, for our end of the procession was nearing the church door, where on either side stood Mademoiselle Chouteau and Pelagie, holding out their silver plates already piled high with livres.

As I glanced at Pelagie I felt as if royalty radiated from her—from the proud pose of her dainty head to the high-bred arch of her little foot. "A princess of Condé!" I exclaimed to myself half angrily, "and meekly holding the church plate for negroes and Indians and humble habitans, and smiling up into the faces of her old friends with a royal sweetness."

I was on the side next her as we drew near the door. Will she look at me? I wondered. We were the last in the line; it would hinder no one if I stopped a moment beside her.

But I could not make her look up at me. One louis
d'or after another I piled upon her plate, but the
only effect it had was to make it tremble in her
hands and the color deepen steadily in her face. I
could not stand there gazing rudely at her, and I
went into the church beside Josef Papin as in a
dream, half doubting it was mademoiselle, yet watching her eagerly as she and Mademoiselle Chouteau
bore the plates up the aisle and held them aloft before the altar for the priest to bless.

The service that followed was indescribably solemn and touched me greatly; it was as though it were
a service for the dead, and the people (the whole village was there, every man, woman, and child I had
known the year before) chanted the responses with
the tears running down their cheeks. Josef Papin
had told me that the old priest who had baptized all
the younger generation and married their parents
was going away with the Spaniards, unwilling to be
subject to a foreign rule, and the mourning of the
people for their father was from the heart.

As they knelt upon the floor to receive the benediction (and the sound of their kneeling was like the
breeze among the dry leaves of autumn) they broke
out into a long, low wail that rose and swelled and
then died away in the sound of suppressed sobbing.
Nevermore under Latin rule would they kneel in
their dear old church, but under the rule of the
hated Anglo-Saxons, their hereditary foe. Nevermore
would the priest they had loved and reverenced for
years extend his hands over them in blessing. The
good father's voice broke again and again as he tried

in vain to utter the familiar words, until at length, his hands upraised to heaven, tears streaming from his eyes, he uttered the simple words, "Go in peace, my children."

I was near the door and I slipped quietly out. It was not a time to meet old friends, and I felt like one intruding upon a house of mourning. Heads were still bowed in the solemn hush that followed the benediction and no one saw me go. I hurried back to where I had left Bourbon, mounted him, and rode slowly up toward Government House.

Long before I reached it the streets were filled. With the quick change from grave to gay, natural to these volatile creoles, the same people that a few moments ago had been all tears and sorrow were now all excitement and curiosity. Down from the fort on the hill marched a troop of Spanish soldiers, stopping at Government House to salute the governor, and then forming in company order in front of the house to await the coming of the United States troops.

Beside Governor Delassus on the gallery of Government House stood my old friend Mr. Meriwether Lewis; for he seemed an old friend to me, though I had known him but that one memorable day in Washington. In response to a friendly wave of the hand from both I dismounted and ran up the steps to speak to them for a moment. They presented me to a third officer, Captain Stoddard, the officer in command of the United States troops who were to take possession, and also, as Governor Delassus informed me, empowered by the French prefect at New Orleans to receive the city for the French republic from the Spanish.

I stayed only a moment, for Captain Lewis told me I would find Captain Clarke and Dr. Saugrain at the landing at the foot of the Rue Bonhomme, so I followed in the wake of the motley crowd of habitans, negroes, and Indians trooping along the Rue Royale and filling La Place with a many-colored throng, as they had filled it on the day I first set foot in St. Louis.

Bourbon Prince picked his way carefully along the steep path that led down the bluff to the landing at the foot of the Rue Bonhomme, where the boats from Cahokia bearing the United States troops were already approaching the shore, and where I found awaiting them, as Captain Lewis had said I should, my old friend, the little doctor, and my captain (for so I shall always call Captain Clarke), and the warmth of their greeting set my heart to dancing merrily.

My spirits had been rising steadily every moment since I had recovered from my stupefaction at the sight of Pelagie. What though she would not look at me, I was nothing daunted; for now that she was safe on American soil,—yes, *American*, Spanish no longer,—nor chevaliers nor dukes nor First Consuls should deter me from boldly trying to win her. For the first time since I had known her I felt that I had a right to try. She was no longer a titled lady of France, and I was now my own master and could maintain her in greater luxury than she had ever known. I would take her home with me to Philadelphia! and my dear mother and my fond old father would love her as they loved my sisters. My spirit was exultant, and that she dared not meet my eyes lent more of hope than discouragement.

So it was with a happy heart that I met the little doctor's beaming glance, and felt the strong grasp of my captain's hand as he uttered his hearty "Welcome home, my lad." And little I cared that he called me lad; indeed, had he addressed me by any other title I should have missed some of the friendliness of his greeting.

"You are to stay at Émigré's Retreat, you know," said Dr. Saugrain; "Madame Saugrain is as happy in the thought of your home-coming as if you were her own boy."

But Josef Papin coming down the bluff at that moment and overhearing the doctor, interposed:

"No, Dr. Saugrain, he is my guest this time. You had him all last winter, and you have had Captain Clarke and Captain Lewis all this winter; you must share some of your honors with me."

It was not for me to decide a question of such kind, and though my heart turned longingly to the hospitable hearth that had first entertained me in St. Louis, feeling that in no other house would it seem so truly a home-coming, yet I was not sure but it was better that it was finally decided that I should stay with Josef Papin, for I was determined to put my fortune to the touch, and should Pelagie prove unkind (a contingency, however, that I refused to contemplate), it would be embarrassing indeed to be under the same roof with her.

But now there was no longer time for discussion of any kind, for the boats were running their keels into the bank, and Lieutenant Worrall, temporarily in command of the troops, was the first man to leap ashore. We all went down to meet him, and when he had formed his battalion in line, we accompanied him up the steep bluff and down the Rue Royale to Government House, a great throng following.

Then Lieutenant Worrall drew up his troops facing the Spanish troops. The open space where the Rue Royale crossed the Rue de la Tour was densely packed with people. Every man, woman, and child of the village, it seemed to me, must be there, yet I looked in vain for either Madame Saugrain or Pelagie. I fastened Bourbon farther up the street, and at the invitation of Governor Delassus sent us by an orderly I accompanied Dr. Saugrain, Josef Papin, and my captain to the gallery of Government House, where we found also both the Chouteaus and many of the leading citizens of the village.

As soon as the American troops were drawn up in line, Governor Delassus stepped to the front of the gallery, holding in his hand a document bearing the seals of the United States and of Spain, and at a sign from him, Captain Stoddard stepped to his side, a similar document in his hand. Then Governor Delassus held the paper up so that all the people might see, and, as every voice was hushed and all eyes turned on him, he read:

"Now be it known unto all men by these presents that I, Carlos D. Delassus, in quality of lieutenant-governor, at the requirement duly made to me by Amos Stoddard, agent and commissary of the French republic, have delivered to him the full possession, sovereignty, and government of Upper Louisiana, with all the military posts, quarters, and fortifications thereto belonging or dependent thereof."

Immediately Captain Stoddard took up the refrain, reading on from where the governor stopped:

"And I, Amos Stoddard, commissary as such, do acknowledge to have received the said possession on the same terms mentioned in these presents, of which I acknowledge myself satisfied and possessed on this day. In testimony whereof the lieutenant-governor and myself have respectively signed these presents, sealed with the seal of our arms, being assisted with the witnesses signed below. Of which proceedings six copies have been made out, to wit, three in the Spanish and three in the English languages.

"Given in the town of St. Louis of Illinois, 9th March, 1804.

"AMOS STODDARD   (seal)

"CARLOS DEHAULT DELASSUS   (seal)

"In presence of

Meriwether Lewis,

Captain First United States Regiment Infantry.

Antoine Soulard,

Surveyor-General, etc.

Charles Gratiot."

As Captain Stoddard finished reading, the governor turned to him and with formal courtesy placed him in possession of Government House. Captain Stoddard accepted it with a brief and appropriate speech, and then, the silence still unbroken, the stately don turned once more to the people and spoke to them directly:

"Inhabitants of Upper Louisiana:

"By the king's command I am about to deliver up this post and its dependencies!

"The flag under which you have been protected for a period of nearly thirty-six years is to be withdrawn. From this moment you are released from the oath of fidelity you took to support it."

There was a stir among the people. Tears were running down the weather-beaten faces of some of the older men, and many of the women were sobbing quietly. Visibly moved himself, the governor added another word:

"The fidelity and courage with which you have guarded and defended the flag will never be forgotten; and in my character of representative I entertain the most sincere wishes for your perfect prosperity."

The governor bowed and stepped back, and instantly there broke from the people a storm of *adios* and *benitos* with tears and waving of hands.

The governor motioned to a soldier standing by. The soldier stepped to a corner of the gallery which could be seen from the fort on the hill, and waved his hat. Instantly puffs of white smoke issued from the full battery of the fort, followed by the roar of the cannon rolling across the wide river to the distant bluffs of Cahokia. As the last echo died away the soldier waved his hat once more. Slowly the flag of Spain floating above the white tower sank. Once more the cannon roared, and slowly the banner of France rose, higher and higher, until its folds were flung proudly to the breeze, above the tower on the hill, above the Great River, above the old French town where it had floated thirty-six years before.

Almost every soul, save negroes and Indians, in that multitude watching in breathless silence the exchange of the flags, was French, and as the banner of the land they had never ceased to love and to call home floated out on the breeze, with one accord they fell on their knees, eyes streaming, arms outstretched toward the loved symbol of their fatherland.

It had been the intention that the flag should remain there but a few minutes—just long enough to show that Upper Louisiana was French, and that France ceded it to the United States. But now Pierre and Auguste Chouteau, the older Papin, Dr. Saugrain, all the leading citizens on the gallery of Government House, gathered around Captain Stoddard and begged him, with trembling voices and misty eyes, to let the old flag stay for another day.

"Let us be Frenchmen for twenty-four hours," they begged, "and after that we will try to be loyal citizens of the United States, as we have been loyal citizens of Spain."

When Captain Lewis and Captain Clarke added their plea for the Frenchmen, Captain Stoddard willingly granted it, and stepping to the front of the gallery, he announced that for twenty-four hours the flag of the French republic would float over St. Louis.

Then broke forth a delirium of joy. Men threw their arms around one another and embraced and kissed in a fashion strange, indeed, to us Anglo-Saxons; and women fell into one another's arms and sobbed. The roar of the cannon had not ceased to roll over the heads of the people at intervals of every two minutes, and now the United States troops took their line of march up the Rue de la Tour to the fort on the hill (for though the American flag did not float from it, they were to hold it in the name of France); and the Spanish troops marched away.

The ceremonies for the day were over; the cannon ceased to roar, and Captain Stoddard, who was now in possession of Government House, invited us all to stay to déjeuner. The meal was a long and ceremonious one, with the Spanish don on Captain Stoddard's right and one of the Chouteaus on his left, and I far down the table with some of the younger men; and through it all I was thinking of that first meal I had taken in St. Louis in this same Government House a year and a half before, and of the toast that roused such enthusiasm then; and every moment my impatience grew to get away and visit Emigré's Retreat and Madame Saugrain, and—the Rose of St. Louis.

CHAPTER XXX

THE ROSE OF ST. LOUIS

"What's in a name? that which we call a rose
By any other name would smell as sweet."

BUT my impatience was of little avail, for before
we left Government House Dr. Saugrain invited
me to dinner at Émigré's Retreat, and restless and
impatient as I might be, I did not dare show myself
there until the dinner-hour.

Five o'clock found me sitting in the dear old living-
room, awaiting with trembling the entrance of madame and Pelagie. It was the same dear old room I
had pictured to myself so often, and all the grand
salons of Paris that I had seen since last I saw it did
not make it look any the less cozy and homelike to my
eyes. It was a warm spring afternoon, and the western windows were open, and the white curtains were
stirring in the breeze, only there was no maiden in
white on the low seat by the window, and no guitar
and no Leon.

I had but a moment to wait. The door opened and
in came madame, both hands outstretched and running to meet me, and as I bent low before her, taking
my face in both her hands and putting a kiss on my

448

cheek and calling me "My son." And behind her came Pelagie, walking slowly but looking up at me, yes, looking at me at last, with starry eyes and a great pulse throbbing in her snowy throat, and little tongues of color coming and going in her cheeks. I was almost of a mind there, right before madame, to take her in my arms and call her mine, for mine I was determined she should be; and I looked at her with such a threatening glance I think she divined my half-purpose and shrank back a little.

So instead I merely bowed over her hand and said gaily:

"You condescend to look at me at last, mademoiselle; I feared to-day I was to be forever banished from your friendly glances."

And she, relieved from her first apprehension, answered saucily:

"If monsieur comes unannounced, how can he expect to be recognized after so many months of absence?"

And then in stalked majestically Leon, limping very slightly, and when he caught sight of me coming up to me and sniffing at me a moment, and then springing upon me with such wild bounds of delight that I had to call hold, lest his great paws play havoc with my fine Paris clothes that I had donned in mademoiselle's honor. And to quiet him I said in a high, small voice, in palpable burlesque of mademoiselle:

"Taise-toi, mon ange!" and we both laughed merrily.

I was so happy that I was ready to do everything

29

that was foolish, and I believe mademoiselle was happy, too, for nothing that I did was too foolish for her to laugh at.

Then in came the little doctor, running up to me and insisting on embracing me (because I was in his own house), pulling down my head and kissing me on each cheek, at which I blushed greatly, though I had not blushed when madame kissed me. And then came my captain and Captain Lewis, and every one talked at once, asking all manner of questions on all manner of subjects, and I had scarcely a chance to say another word to Pelagie.

And then came dinner. As usual, madame put me beside her, and Pelagie sat at the other end of the table. But there was no scorning this time, and I had better chance to look at her than if she sat beside me, and perhaps that was best, for my eyes could say to her much more than my lips would dare in such a company.

Narcisse waited on the table, and was all smiles of welcome; and half-way through dinner, on some pretext or other, in came Clotilde, and greeted me, half crying through her smiles at memory of our trials together. And last of all came Yorke, grinning from ear to ear, and "declarin' to gracious I'd growed a foot sence," whereupon I was of a mind to thrash him on the spot, and told him so, which made him grin the more, if that were possible.

It was a grand dinner, and I told Madame Saugrain I had never tasted in Paris anything half so good as her wild turkey and croquecignolles and gooseberry wine, which I meant with all my heart, and which greatly pleased her housewifely soul.

Back in the living-room, when dinner was over, I missed something, and looked around the room to discover what it was. It was the long French mirror in which I had once watched Pelagie—the pride of madame's heart.

"Why, madame," I said, "what have you done with your mirror?"

She shrugged her shoulders and looked ruefully at her husband.

"Antoine," she said, "needed some quicksilver for his experiments. Voilà! my mirror!"

I glanced at Dr. Saugrain; he blushed and looked guilty, and so, for some reason, I thought, did Captain Lewis.

"I will explain," said my captain. "You must know, my lad, that these two," indicating the doctor and Captain Lewis with a wave of his hand, "have been confederates all winter in black art. They have lived in the laboratory, and the instruments they have evolved for our trip up the Missouri and over the mountains are fearful and wonderful to behold. We are each of us provided with a box of little phosphorus sticks by which we are to do away entirely with all use of tinder. But much more wonderful than those, out of madame's mirror Dr. Saugrain has fashioned little glass tubes holding quicksilver, and with a measure laid off on the side by which we may be able to tell just how hot or how cold it may be. And more wonderful still, he has fashioned other little tubes by which we are to tell when it is going to storm and when it will be fair weather. And I cannot begin to tell you all the wonderful appliances this magician has fashioned for our comfort and safety this winter, aided and abetted by his willing slave, Captain Lewis.''

That unloosed the doctor's tongue, and there was no getting away the rest of the evening from the wonders of science; and so strange were the things he and Captain Lewis had to tell of what science could do that I could have greatly enjoyed their talk had I not been longing for a few words with Pelagie.

I determined that another day should not go by without my having them, and so, in the course of the evening, I managed to ask her if she would ride with me the next afternoon to Chouteau's Pond. A riding-party of two to Chouteau's Pond was of frequent occurrence in the village, and I would not have feared a refusal but that Pelagie had now been living so long where stricter social forms prevailed, so I awaited her answer with trembling. But she gave a shy assent, and for me the evening at Émigré's Retreat was a grand success.

Twelve o'clock the next day, March the tenth, saw us all once more at Government House; and once more the American troops were drawn up before it, and once more the people filled the streets.

The people were very quiet; there was no longer any rejoicing; but every eye was lifted to the flag that was so soon to sink from sight.

There were many Indians in the streets,—Delawares, Sacs, Shawnees, and others,—attracted to the town by the noise of firing the day before. Captain Stoddard had asked Governor Delassus to speak to them and explain to them the change of government, and the soldiers had been sent to gather them up close to the gallery of Government House, where Don Delassus might speak to them. A dark-faced throng, serious of countenance, they stood looking up at us, not a muscle of their countenances changing while the governor spoke to them in the formal and stately fashion they loved.

"Delawares, Sacs, Shawnees, and others, my red brothers:

"Your old fathers, the Spaniard and the Frenchman, grasp by the hand your new father, the head chief of the United States. By an act of their goodwill, and in virtue of their last treaty, I have delivered up to them all these lands. They will keep and defend them, and protect all the white and redskins who live thereon. You will live as happily as if the Spaniard were still here.

"I have informed your new father, who here takes my place, that the Delawares, Shawnees, and Sacs have always conducted themselves well; that the chiefs have always restrained their young men as much as possible.

"For several days we have fired off cannon to announce to all the nations that your father the Spaniard is going, his heart happy to know that you will be protected and sustained by your new father, and that the smoke of the powder may ascend to the

Maker of life, praying him to shower on you all a happy destiny and prosperity in always living in good union with the whites."

There were many guttural "Ughs!" as he finished, and I think, from the way the dark eyes scanned the faces of the new officers, they comprehended at least a part of what had been said to them.

Once more a soldier at the corner of the gallery waved his hat toward the white tower; once more the cannon boomed and slowly the tricolor of France descended, while the Stars and Stripes rose to meet it. Half-way up the flagstaff they stopped. For a moment they floated in the breeze, side by side, and an involuntary cheer sprang from the people at the friendly sight. Then slowly the tricolor sank, and slowly rose the starry banner, flinging out its broad bars of white and crimson, beautiful emblem of liberty and the sovereignty of a free people, over the little village, nestling among the trees on the bluffs, that may one day be a mighty city; over the Great River flowing to the Gulf that a not far future may see bearing the commerce of a world on its bosom; over the broad prairies stretching to the distant mountains which coming years will surely see peopled with happy millions.

My heart swelled within me. I swung my hat high in the air and lustily led the cheers of our troops and our little party on the gallery. But we were only a small band, and we made not much noise, and all the French and Spaniards stood and looked sadly on. And because our hearts were touched by their sorrow, we cheered no more, but looked up at our beautiful banner with pride and joy and love in our hearts.

Three hours later I was sitting on the gallery at Émigré's Retreat waiting for mademoiselle, as I had waited for her on the day of the picnic at Chouteau's Pond. Narcisse was holding Bourbon Prince by the driveway below, and I was struggling to preserve a calm exterior, for my heart was going like a trip-hammer while I listened for my lady's coming.

Out upon the gallery she stepped, riding-habit and hat and veil of latest Paris mode—not the little Pelagie of the picnic day, but Pelagie a princess of Condé, and my heart almost failed me.

I looked at her, and she was smiling at me with a smile I did not understand. Then she looked away, and my eyes followed hers. Around the corner of the house Yorke was leading a horse,—a white star on the forehead and one white foot like Bourbon Prince, but beautiful chestnut in color. For a moment I forgot my lady. Down the steps I sprang, and my arm was around the neck of the chestnut mare.

"Sweetheart!" I whispered in her ear. "Do you know me, sweetheart?"

She whinnied with joy and rubbed her soft muzzle up and down my arm, and whinnied again, while Yorke showed all his teeth in his delight, and my lady laughed and clapped her hands like a happy child.

I had not thought it possible she could bring Fatima with her and so had not asked for her, though, truth to tell, I had had but little chance to ask her about anything.

When I said so to her, "I would not have come without her," she said, looking shyly at me. "But I hope you do not want her back, for I love her dearly."

Yes, I wanted her back, I said to myself; but with her mistress, too; but my only answer to mademoiselle was a smile that I think she understood, for she looked quickly away from me.

Then I put her on Fatima's back, who bore a Parisian saddle now instead of a pillion, and out through the stockade we rode, and down the rough path to La Petite Rivière, and through the ford (deeper now, from spring freshets, than it had been when I listened to the whippoorwills), and along the wooded bank on the other side, where we had raced to get away from the redskin (though that she never knew), and still I had not said the words I meant to say.

Under the tree that had been the goal for our race I drew up a minute. Here, I thought, will be a place of happy omen, for here I won my first dance with her, and here I will win her. But suddenly I recalled that this was the spot where I had first seen the chevalier; no, it was of evil omen. "By hairbreadth escapes we always win," he had said. I feared the "luck of the Le Moynes" and their baleful motto.

Where we had stopped to look at the lake before, I stopped again. It was almost more beautiful in its setting of the soft pinks and greens of early spring than it had been under the golden sun of autumn, and here, I thought, I will say it. But the glimpse of the ivied mill tower among the trees, and the beautiful water and its wooded banks, reminded Pelagie of Ettenheim, and she began to tell me of a letter she had just received from the Duc d'Enghien, which made her very anxious.

"He writes," said Pelagie, "that he is being followed everywhere by an Englishman who, he feels sure, is a spy in the pay of Bonaparte—I will never call him emperor!" said Pelagie, with fiery eye. "And while he says he feels no alarm for himself, he is more and more glad to think that I am so safely away from all dangers."

But the thought of her letter had saddened Pelagie for a while, and I would not speak then. How little we dreamed that on that very day, perhaps at that very hour, the young duke was being seized by Napoleon's emissaries, in violation of all treaties of neutrality, and hurried to the gloomy fortress of Vincennes, where, ten days later, after a mock trial of two hours in the dead of night, with no chance of defense given him, he was taken out and shot and buried in the trench where he fell. When the dreadful news reached us, weeks later, it darkened for a while my sweet Pelagie's life, as it was the one crime not even the friends of Napoleon can excuse or forgive: the one dark blot on his fame time will never erase.

But that afternoon we were in happy ignorance of what was happening four thousand miles away, and Pelagie's sadness was but a passing shadow and in a little while we were both joyous again.

"Rock Spring," I thought, "beloved of lovers, will be the place." But at Rock Spring I could think of nothing but Yorke astride the chevalier's back, the grimy spectacle the chevalier presented when Yorke was dislodged, and then the fearful peril Pelagie had been in when I fled with her in my arms on Fatima's back. No, Rock Spring was not the place.

And so we were once more back at the ford, almost home, and the long shadows lying on the cool water, and a thrush singing his evening-song in the wooded crests behind us, and my tale had not been told. We had had much sweet converse, and many times the words were on my lips, but somehow—I know not how—Pelagie always managed to turn me aside. At least I think she did, for with the words on my lips I would find myself talking of something else.

Now, as our horses swashed their noses in the cool water, and sent the bright drops in showers about us, I looked down upon her, the dark green of her riding-habit making a rich foil to the soft glow of her cheek, and the drooping plume of her hat falling over her snowy neck and mingling with the dark ringlets, and one little hand from which she had drawn the glove playing with Fatima's tawny mane—and I took a sudden resolution.

"Mademoiselle," I said, "do you know that to-day you are no longer a proud lady of France, but a simple American maiden?"

She looked up at me, startled. I think she knew what was coming, but she answered bravely, though softly:

"Yes, monsieur," and then dropped her eyes and fell to playing with Fatima's mane again.

"Mademoiselle, do you remember on La Belle Rivière the wager you would not let me make?"

"Yes, monsieur," still more softly.

"Mademoiselle, if I had made that wager then I would have won it to-day. You taught me better, and I would not win you by a wager now if I could. But oh, mademoiselle, you said by worth and deeds of prowess a maiden's hand should be won; and there is no one in the world—least of all I—worthy of you, mademoiselle, and no deeds of prowess could be grand enough to deserve you, and I have nothing to win you with but my great love; will that avail me,—Pelagie?"

She did not answer for a moment; she was all rosy and drooping, and with a happy smile about her lips, as she had been in the cabinet of the First Consul.

I put my great hand on her little one, still playing with Fatima's mane, and clasped it tight, though it fluttered like a bird at first and then lay quiet.

"Pelagie, Pelagie, look up at me," I whispered. "I may call you Pelagie, may I not?"

Swiftly and shyly she looked up into my eyes, and I looked down into heaven.

"Yes, monsieur," she whispered.

Suddenly she broke into a low laugh, and tried to draw her hand away from mine.

"My name is not Pelagie," she said.

"Not Pelagie!" I exclaimed, thinking she was playing me some merry trick, and wishing she had chosen some other time to play it.

"No, monsieur," she said soberly. "They named me Pelagie when they brought me over sea, but my name is Louise Adelaide, for my aunt the Abbess of Remiremont."

I was silent for a moment, for I liked not to think of little Pelagie by any other name. Then I gently took her hand again and raised it to my lips:

"Louise Adelaide," I said, "may do for a princess of Condé, but you will always be my little Pelagie to me," and so great was the love in my heart that my voice trembled as I spoke, and we were both very still for a little, while her hand lay quietly in mine.

Suddenly a thought struck me:

"Pelagie," I said, "you have never spoken my name; I do not believe you know what it is."

"Yes, I do, monsieur." She looked up at me saucily. "Shall I tell you what it is?"

"Call me by it!" I implored her softly.

For answer she lifted her arms and drew my head down toward her and whispered it in my ear.

And I, what did I do?

What would any man have done whose heart was running over with love for the most adorable maiden in the world, and her sweet face so near?